CONTENTS

Quintus Propertius and the Affairs of Ventidius Silo 5

Quintus Propertius and the Case of the Counting-house Clerk 29

Quintus Propertius and the Estate of the Placid Praetorian 51

Quintus Propertius and the Demise of the Gullible Gaul 75

Quintus Propertius and the Misfortune of Marius the Glassmaker 101

Quintus Propertius and the School for Young Ladies at Ephesus 129

Quintus Propertius and the Treasure of the Dumnonii 151

Quintus Propertius and the Felgio Hypothesis 225

To my wife

for everything

Quintus Propertius and the Affairs of Ventidius Silo

I first met Quintus Propertius quite by chance. It was in one of those little taverns just off the Subura – one of the respectable ones, since you ask, owned by a veteran called Rufus. Rufus ran a very tight ship, and... But I'll return to Rufus's Place in due course. (I often do.)

I often do, and so do a group of us, settling down from time to time to chew the cud, put the empire to rights, and drink as much as is good for us – sometimes more than is good for us – of Rufus's remarkably acceptable, and by-no-means over-priced wine.

This promised to be a decently long and especially good session, except that we had come to an impasse. Some of us fancied ourselves as military historians, and we had been going over Caesar's campaigns in Gaul, making wise comments and pointing out expertly where the great man had, and had not, made the right decisions. But suddenly our collective memories gave out. We could not remember, any of us, the names of the two envoys sent to parley with Ambiorix, before that treacherous swine murdered Sabinus and Cotta and most of their command. We were pretty sure that one was a Roman knight, and thought the other could have been a Spaniard, but that's as far as we could go. Frustrating: enough to drive one to drink.

'Excuse me,' said a fellow at the next table, 'I couldn't help overhearing. You're thinking of Gaius Arpineius and Quintus Junius. Gaius Arpineius, you recall, was a friend of Sabinus himself.'

He was right, of course – *now* we remembered - and we thanked him. However, by this time our zeal for military history was on the wane, for we had reached that lovely warm stage in our proceedings when the world is a wonderful place and full of good fellows and 'Yes, Rufus, another cup all round, and one for our friend here; won't you join us, friend?'

He did so, and introduced himself: Quintus Propertius Mala. *Mala* – what sort of a name is that? 'My friends call me Djac,' he added: *Djac* – what sort of a name is *that*?

'I'm told,' he went on, 'that my family is descended from Sextus Propertius, the poet; but you know these family stories: more likely my ancestors were some yob from the Subura, and a young-lady from Britain with woad on her wobblies.'

We laughed as though he had said something witty, but in fact it was the Sextus Propertius connection that seemed to me eminently possible. The poet came of a very good family, as I'm sure you know, and there was something about his namesake's bearing, and indeed his diction, that signalled 'upper echelons' to anyone with a nose for these things – as who hasn't in to-day's Rome, especially those whose family, like mine, was equestrian – just: *just*.

And yet, at that, his speech wasn't spot-on. You've met these upper-class 'new citizens', from Gaul perhaps, or Mauretania, who cultivate the manners and the accent of the old patrician class, and whose background *ipso facto*, purports to be, like Caesar's wife, above suspicion. Mala was a bit like that – not so much in his mien, which though dignified was essentially friendly and approachable, as in his clipped vowels, his careful enunciation, his complete avoidance of slang, and the occasional word or phrase he came out with that was not – not *quite* – right.

He was aware of it himself, and on one occasion, perhaps like the rest of us somewhat under the affluence of incohol, he explained it – explained it away. 'I spent most of my childhood and youth in Britain,' he told us, 'down in the south-west of that benighted land, among a tribe known as the Dumnonii. I was allowed to mingle a lot with the sons of the local aristocracy – quite decent fellows some of them, for all their barbarous customs – and inevitably perhaps I picked up some of their habits and speech-patterns, which my tutors subsequently tried so hard to eliminate that I've probably over-compensated.'

We took that on board readily enough, and soon Mala (we could none of us feel comfortable with the outlandish 'Djac') was fully accepted as one of our circle. We were a very mixed bunch, ranging from, at one end, the son of a senator, to, at the other, a slave, the former tutor of the senator's son: Aspiades, a Greek, an aged and astonishingly learned philosopher. (He looked a dead ringer for those busts of Plato that used to be popular in some quarters, until it became more prudent to litter the landscape with effigies of the current emperor, be he tyrant, degenerate, madman, or self-appointed god.)

Aspiades and Mala got on like a house on fire, earnestly talking philosophy, Greek drama, you name it, Mala holding his own and more than holding his own, and displaying moreover a nimbleness and originality of thought that had the rest of us lost in admiration.

And yet in some respects he was remarkably ignorant. He knew nothing of the arena, and indeed tended to go very quiet when the subject came up; he was quite unaware that the Greens had been sweeping all before them for months; despite his love of drama, hardly any leading actor was as much as a name to him; and - perhaps most surprising of all - even in so basic a matter as food, he seemed unfamiliar with some dishes that any Roman of reasonable means would have had on his table scores of times a year.

Was he an imposter? Not a Roman at all? A rich barbarian, involved in some elaborate masquerade? At times it seemed possible; but at others, as he held us spellbound with his wit and scholarship, quoting verbatim Virgil or Cicero, Caesar or Livy, Ovid or Catullus, the very idea of his being other than an exceptionally learned Roman, of good and long-established family, seemed ludicrous. Indeed, if he had turned out to be the emperor's long-lost cousin, we should none of us have been surprised – except that surely he was far too decent a fellow to have any connection with that bastard Domitian.

But it was when Ventidius Silo disappeared that Mala showed his true mettle, and another side of his character altogether. Ventidius was something of the odd one out in our little group, older than all but Aspiades, richer than any other three of us put together (he was a highly successful businessman), and quite the least educated. I would have said that he was a mite slow-witted, but I was present once when he was concluding a business deal: then he was sharp as a razor, and had wrapped up the arrangements and made himself a tidy profit, when the rest of us would still have been dithering and wondering if we'd been had and debating whether we dared at last sign on the bottom line.

But he disappeared – apparently into thin air.

It was Ventidius's steward who brought the news – he knew we would be at Rufus's place – and he was as white as alabaster as he burst out: 'Ventidius Silo has disappeared!'

'Disappeared? What do you mean, 'disappeared'?' demanded Mala. I noticed that he, too, had gone pale, but whereas the steward Asinius was visibly trembling, and about as much in control of himself as a headless chicken, Mala was now alert, to the point, very much in control: no longer the eloquent scholar, but more like a military officer. ('Of course,' I said to myself, 'with his background he must have held command at some time.'}

'Where did this happen? When did you discover his absence? What makes you think he has not gone on a trip, perhaps to clinch some unexpected business deal? Why *disappeared*?'

Asinius looked frightened.

'Because, sir – please, please believe me sir – he disappeared almost before my eyes.'

'Mer..' Mala muttered something in a foreign language: perhaps some Britannic expletive he had picked up. 'Where was this? When?'

'At my master's house on the Aventine, only a short while ago. I was about to open the study door to take him the flask of wine and water he had asked for. I knew he was still in there because I heard him muttering to himself, as he often did when he was totting-up figures. But suddenly he went quiet, and when I opened the door – he was gone!'

'Windows?' asked Mala.

'Only very small ones, set very high, and unopenable.'

'Another door?'

'None'

'Does your mistress know of this?'

'Of course. She is very distraught, but she sent me here at once in case I had been mistaken and Ventidius Silo was here after all, as he usually is at this time.'

'I had better come back with you,' decided Mala. He had taken charge, and no-one gainsaid him. 'Marcus,' addressing me, 'would you care to come along with me?'

There was only one answer to that: I was intrigued, not merely by the alleged disappearance, but by Mala's reaction, and his sudden decisiveness and transformation into a man of action.

'Go back as swiftly as you can and tell your mistress we will be along directly,' he instructed Asinius; and then to the rest of the gathering: 'You must excuse us, gentlemen. This needs looking into without delay.'

'Do you think he's lying,' I asked, as Asinius hurried away.

'No,' said Mala; and then, with a little smile, 'he does want that glib and oily art, to speak and purpose not.'

It seemed a funny way to put it, but I took the point: Asinius was a trusted servant of long standing, and Ventidius treated him almost as a freedman, which he would undoubtedly become in the fulness of time.

'But a man can't simply disappear into thin air,' I said.

'No? That's what I used to think.'

Mala didn't elaborate on that unexpected remark, and after Rufus had found us a litter, we completed the journey to the Ventidius *domus* in silence.

It was a large house – though not so large and flashy as some in that location - and had clearly cost a pretty penny. The atrium was huge, and adorned with statuary that was not only clearly expensive – that could be expected - but, I was glad to note, in much better taste than one often found in the houses of rich merchants.

Asinius was waiting for us, and conducted us at once to his mistress's inner sanctum. Mala, I was surprised to learn, knew her, and he introduced me - she knew of me, of course, but we had never met – and then took her hands in his.

'Julia Drusilla,' he said, 'my condolences: this must have been a great shock. I do not know if we will manage to find your husband, but you may be sure we will try our very, very utmost.'

She gave her thanks. 'It is so unlike him,' she said; 'he knows I worry, and always lets me know where he will be when he goes out, even if it is only to join your regular discussion-group, as he does each month.'

('Discussion group': that's rich, I thought.)

Mala nodded in understanding, and then suddenly was all action again.

'We must start our investigation,' he said. 'First, I would like to examine the study.'

Asinius conducted us to the large and rather cluttered room from which Ventidius conducted his affairs.

I had thought about secret passages: some prominent people, it was rumoured, had had such passages built into their villas, years ago, when Sejanus's reign of terror was at its height. (They might be useful again, if Domitian continues on his present tack.) My theory would not do, though, for Ventidius's study projected from the main part of the villa, with three outside walls, and the fourth adjoining the atrium. Nor was there any hidden door in any of the outside walls: Mala looked, and he was very, very thorough.

The ceiling? Same story. No: the only way in and out was through the door Asinius had opened.

I again wondered if the slave lied. Maybe he had sipped a little, or a lot, of the wine he was taking to Ventidius – just to make sure it was fit for his master's consumption, you understand; such things have been known. Old and trusted servant he might have been, but even trusted servants are not *always* to be trusted. (Even wives are not, as C-c-c-claudius might have been prudent to realise; maybe Augustus too.)

Despite his earlier rejection, Mala was prepared to accept the possibility; then, however, he questioned Asinius, and the other household slaves, so thoroughly, so minutely, that when he had done, no-one of sound mind would have entertained the idea for a moment. Asinius was in the clear.

It was the muttering Asinius had heard that was the problem. If it had merely been that Ventidius had vanished between asking for the wine and Asinius bringing it, there would still have been a mystery, but, if I may so put it, by no means so mysterious a mystery.

Mala clearly thought so, too, but he persevered nonetheless, and it was an education to be with him as he searched and sifted, questioning all the slaves yet again, interviewing business associates, bankers, the slimy Egyptian in charge of the Ventidius warehouse at Ostia, even Julia Drusilla herself. His questions were probing, pertinent – and profitless.

I observed him closely as he worked, and noticed, first, that under the stress of the investigation, his diction began to slip a little. As often as not this involved his coming out with the odd remark in a foreign tongue, most of them, to judge from context, expletives. 'Mer-da,' was one, or some such word, and in what sounded like a quite different tongue, something like 'Helena Dalmatian.' (Who, I wondered, could Helena from Dalmatia have been?)

He was fond, too, of little aphorisms. Once, when we had been wandering around Rome for hours, and I complained, as was my wont, that I was hungry, he regarded me without sympathy.

'You must learn,' he said, 'that one has to eat to live, not live to eat.'

On another occasion, as we stood in the Forum shortly before dusk, our work done for the day, he looked up, rather dreamily, and said:

'The sky above the roof-tops, so blue, so calm; a tree above the roof-tops, its branches gently swaying...'

'You're quite a poet,' I congratulated him.

'No; not I.'

I did not pursue the matter: this was only one of the funny little things he came out with – as on another occasion, when I interrupted his train of thought: 'But…' I began. 'But me no buts,' he replied, pithily. I shut up.

Mala returned again and again to the household slaves. Was there anything unusual they had noticed? Any change in Ventidius's usual routine? Any change in his demeanour: did he seem worried, preoccupied, unusually short-tempered perhaps?

No. All was as it had been.

'Any unexpected or unusual visitors?' Mala asked the doorman, for the umpteenth time. Negative. Ventidius conducted his business partly from home, and some of his clients came to see him at more or less regular intervals. There was Eumenides, the Greek corn merchant, who had partnered Ventidius in a number of his ventures; there was his young slave, Ancus, who did a lot of leg-work for the two men, a pert and lively young retainer who was only to eager to tell us all he could: gossip, mostly. There was the woman who called from time to time, whom the doorman described in some detail.

'She came unaccompanied, strangely enough. Tall for a women, and on the heavy side. Indeterminate class – probably not very elevated. Ugly bint. She kept her face veiled most of the time, but I caught a glimpse once, and thought, no wonder: she had a nasty scar running the whole length of her left cheek, and I don't suppose it was a very pretty left cheek start with.'

Mala showed some interest in this woman, and we spent time trying to find her, but never did: another dead end, and another, and another. It grew ever more obvious that, despite Mala's Herculean efforts, we were getting nowhere. He knew it, and looked – and was – more dejected .than I had known him.

'He *must* still be there,' he said.

'Where?'

'In the study.'

'But he can't be.'

'He can't not be. When every other possibility has been exhausted, what remains, however unlikely, must be true.'

'But then he can only be…'

Mala looked grim.

'Tell me,' he said, 'where did we not look?'

'There's nowhere,' I replied. 'You yourself checked the outside walls, the windows, the ceiling, the…'

'The floor?' asked Mala.

'But the floor is as solid as the walls,' I protested; 'I noticed especially the mosaic, with that geometrical pattern, as elaborate as any I've seen, and it covered the entire area.'

'And did you notice the Parthian rug near the desk?'

'Of course; I was surprised – rugs on the floor are an affectation that smacks too much of the decadent East for my taste.'

'But rugs can hide things; I, of all people, should know that. Back to the Aventine!'

The doorman admitted us at once, and in moments we were again in that familiar study, and Mala was rolling back the thick rug – an impressive object, even I had to admit, beautifully woven in intricate and colourful detail.

Where the rug had been, the elaborate and repetitive pattern of the mosaic seemed just as elsewhere in the room, but Mala was soon down on his knees, examining it inch by inch. An age seemed to pass, and another; but then:

'Got it! Look,' and he traced out a line, almost circular, in the pattern, so cunningly hidden by the natural divisions of the mosaic as to be invisible except to the minutest scrutiny.

'What workmanship! But we didn't come here to admire the workmanship. How do we move this?'

He prodded here and there on the mosaic, and eventually seemed especially interested in one slightly indented pattern, a circle inside an ellipse inside a square, that was repeated seemingly at random throughout the room. He probed and pushed, working outwards from the area beneath where the rug had been, until at last, at the twentieth attempt or more, he hit the jackpot, and, with scarcely a sound, the circular area of mosaic lifted upwards and outwards on some ingenious mechanism, revealing steps which led down to what was obviously a sizeable chamber, perhaps almost as extensive as the study itself.

Mala called for torches, and soon Asinius and two of his fellows appeared with them. Mala took one, and signalling the rest of us to follow, he made his way down the steps.

It was indeed a large room, the walls lined with unlit torches. A desk, the double of the one in the study, laden with scrolls and tablets and styli, was prominent in one corner; there were couches, tables, a couple of huge amphorae - and Ventidius.

He was dead, of course, very, very dead: people usually are, when an eight-inch knife is buried to the hilt under their ribs.

He was not a pretty sight, nor, indeed, a pretty smell, for he must have been there ever since Asinius noticed his absence from the study, and that had been many days ago.

What followed was not easy, not straightforward, and not pleasant, but it had to be done.

Not easy or pleasant, either, was the job of informing Julia Drusilla, which fell naturally enough to Mala. Ever since Ventidius's disappearance, she had been hoping against hope, questioning us eagerly as we returned from our investigations, making suggestions as to whom we might contact next, almost embarrassingly anxious to help, to be involved. She even seemed ready, had she not been a woman, to join our excursions – as though by so doing she could keep alive some hope, could almost convince herself that her husband had not really 'disappeared' and any moment would turn up, large as life, perhaps triumphantly brandishing a new contract in one hand, and with the other proffering her an expensive piece of jewellery, as he had done more than once in the past.

But now…

We were glad to get away.

'Wine,' said Mala; 'if ever I needed a trip to Rufus's, it is now.' I concurred readily enough, as you might have guessed, but it was not to be, for as we were about to leave, Asinius came up to us. Naturally he was more worried, more agitated, than ever, as well he might be, for the murder of his master meant, for him and for the other slaves, at best torture, at worst execution: the Roman law is very specific, very unyielding on that.

'I thought you should know,' said Asinius, 'that Draco has not come back.'

'Draco? Who the hell is Draco?'

'He is a freedman who lives here on and off; he goes - went - on many errands for my master, sometimes here in Rome, sometimes to the farm, sometimes to Ostia; often he is away for several days at a time, perhaps a week: but I have never known him be as long as this before returning.'

'Was he on some errand when Ventidius disappeared?'

'I cannot say; it was not his habit to talk to us about his comings and goings; he ran a little business of his own, trading in a small way, I don't know what in, but my master always had first call on his time.'

'Why did you not tell me this before?'

'It did not seem important: as I said, he is often away for days on end, and I thought nothing of it until such a long time had passed.'

'You think there is some connection between this Draco's failure to return, and Ventidius's murder?' I asked Mala.

'How quick you are, friend Marcus,' said he with a smile. 'It is, don't you agree, at least a working hypothesis? And it means, I fear, more leg-work. Don't worry,' he added, seeing my frown, 'I'll see you get plenty to eat – and drink.'

And so, I thought, the whole rigmarole will have to begin again, questioning, probing, searching for information, for leads – except that this time, there was an urgency that even our desire to find Ventidius had lacked: Mala was worried sick about what would happen to the slaves if we did not come up with a solution to Ventidius's murder pretty damn quick, and finding the missing freedman seemed the most obvious thing to begin with.

I shared his concern about the slaves to some extent - and of course I did want to solve the murder - but this side obsession. I do not like cruelty to slaves, and Asinius and his fellows seemed decent enough people, insofar as you can regard slaves as 'people'. But, dammit, a Roman had been murdered; you can't have that sort of thing. Look what happened during the Spartacus revolt, when slaves and gladiators got too big for their boots, and hundreds of innocent citizens were slaughtered without remorse, and half of Italy shook in fear. Treat 'em decently, certainly; but there are limits.

Mala felt differently: another example of his rather outlandish attitudes and reactions; but there was no arguing with his feelings, and we went frantically about our task, our first task at least, of searching for Draco.

Curio Licinius – that's what he called himself, though it was no more the name he was born with than mine was Scipio Africanus – seemed the best bet. He was the Egyptian who looked after Ventidius's big warehouse in Ostia: looked after himself, more likely, with the interests of Ventidius Silo always taking second place to those of Curio Licinius; or so we surmised. He was shifty, nasty, as trustworthy as Nero after a bad night; and very frightened indeed when Mala came the heavy on him.

Yes, he did know Draco; yes, the freedman often came to Ostia, when Ventidius was otherwise busy, and, yes, he did have Ventidius's authority to do this, buy that, sell the other: a trusted envoy, no doubt about it, and one Ventidius relied on greatly. But, no, he had not been to Ostia for some time, and people had even begun to wonder where he was, and…

'You lie,' said Mala. 'What if I told you he was seen here, only days ago?'

It was a shot in the dark, but delivered so forcefully and with such conviction that the Egyptian swallowed very hard, and cracked.

'Well, yes, he was here, but he said he was on the most confidential business for Ventidius, and no-one should know of it. Naturally, with my employer's best interests at heart...'

'Spare the cant,' interrupted Mala. 'We need to find Draco, without delay, and anyone who hinders us will wish he'd never been born.'

One could almost see the wheels go round in Licnius's shaven skull. Did this Mala have enough clout, he was wondering, seriously to inconvenience him, or more than inconvenience him, if he did not co-operate? Could he be fobbed off with an excuse, a circumlocution, a lie?

He made up his mind: no, Mala did not look as though he could, at all. (Where, I wondered, was the genial stranger we had first met at Rufus's Place, quoting the poetry of Catullus, debating with Aspiades some moot point in the *Phaedo*? I had cause to wonder again, not long afterwards – but that in its place.)

Clearly Licinius did not think Mala looked very genial now, or that discussing the finer points of Plato would be a very fruitful gambit, and he gave us directions to a tavern on the waterfront where Draco was often to be found when he was in Ostia.

It was one of those places. I suspect Licinius was hoping we would get into a fight within minutes of entering the place, and emerge feet first with our skulls cracked in and our interest in Draco or anyone else finished for good.

It nearly happened like that. A fellow at the bar took an instant dislike to Mala as he was ordering the wine, and in no time was squaring up to him and reaching for an ugly knife that was tucked into his belt. What happened next was almost too quick for the eye to follow: one moment the bully-boy was confronting Mala, his hand on the hilt of the weapon, the next he was writhing on the floor, purple-faced, his breath coming in great gulping sobs, clutching his throat where the blade of Mala's hand had chopped into it like an axe.

'Carati,' explained Mala later, though what that meant I had no idea. The idea I did get was that Mala was a bad man to tangle with, and the others in the tavern, a tough bunch to a man, got the same message, mp misunderstanding, and were as nice as pie when he started questioning them, his erstwhile opponent meanwhile having become the one to be dragged out of the tavern feet first.

'Yes, citizen, Draco often came here. A bit uppity for a freedman, but a hard man too: he thumped a guy once almost as sweetly as you did Aulus just then; but he didn't look for trouble, and he was free with his money, and often found little jobs for one or the other of us, so...'

'And where is he now?' demanded Mala. 'When was he last here? Did he give any idea where he might be going when he left? This is heavy business, let me tell you; the Praetorians...'

I knew well enough that Mala had nothing to do with the Praetorians - but they didn't, and it worked; along with the summary way he had dealt with Aulus, the general air of command, the don't-give-me-any-nonsense look in his eyes as he asked his questions, it convinced them, as Licinius earlier had been convinced, that honesty was the best policy: tough they might be, but the idea that a bunch of Praetorians might pay them a social visit did not fit in with their plans at all.

'He was here seven or eight days ago,' said one unsavoury character, a sailor from the look of him, though from the look of him also probably a moonlighter: muggings on the side, reasonable rates; knife in the ribs for only a small extra charge. 'He had that scar-faced brother of his with him. They didn't take much notice of the rest of us, but I overheard them mention Veii several times.'

'Thank you,' said Mala. 'Proprietor, wine for the gentleman here.'

'Veii,' I said, 'is a ruddy long way, and I'm saddle-sore as it is.'

'We'll get back to Rome to-night, and set out for Veii early to-morrow morning.'

And so it was.

For all Augustus's efforts to revive the place, Veii is not nowadays a town to set the pulses racing. Its architecture is for the most part undistinguished, its arena unimpressive, a fair proportion of its houses slums as bad as any you will find in the Subura. Even its brothels looked like – well, like, one visit, and you'd probably swear to celibacy for life.

But it had taverns, and we visited several, though at that time in the morning most were fairly deserted. It was as we had just entered the fourth or fifth that Mala put out his arm and stopped me going further. With the very slightest inclination of his head he indicated two men sitting at a table in one corner, each with a hot pie and a glass of what looked like beer – beer: ugh! –

in front of him. One was a broad-shouldered, muscular man, ostentatiously well-dressed, the typical freedman-made-good; the other, smaller, scruffier, had a distinct facial resemblance to the big man, though his features were marred by a long scar running the length of his left cheek.

Mala hesitated a moment, and then decided to grasp the nettle. He walked up to the table and addressed the big man directly.

'Excuse me,' he said; always polite, was Mala. 'Are you not the trader named Draco who used to do work for Ventidius Silo?'

'What of it?'

'Some have been wondering why you had not returned to Ventidius's house before this.'

'Who might the some be, and what flaming business is it of theirs? What business is it of yours, for that matter?' And he stood up and glared menacingly. He was as tall as Mala, and heavier, but Mala did not flinch.

'It's my business,' he said, 'because Julia Drusilla asked me to make it my business.'

'----- Julia Drusilla: no ----- widow is going to interfere in my affairs. And ----- you too,' and his heavy fist crashed into the spot where Mala's face had been a moment before; but Mala had swayed backwards out of harm's way, and his counter-blow, square on Draco's temple, felled him like an ox.

It occurred to me then that it was time to make my own presence felt, since Scarface had produced a dagger that he clearly know how to use, and was advancing on Mala.

I knew nothing of the 'carati' Mala had demonstrated in Ostia, but I had done my stint in the army and you pick up some useful tricks on active service. I don't know if I actually broke Scarface's arm or not, but it made a satisfying crack as he dropped the knife with a yell, and his enthusiasm for further combat noticeably lessened.

'Thanks,' said Mala with a nod. 'Whatever that lout had in mind, you seem to have quite dissuaded him.'

The tavern-keeper had taken in the little fracas, and he objected; but not for long. To my surprise, Mala produced a parchment, and thrust it under the fellow's nose. There was no mistaking the seal.

'Do you want to argue with this?' he demanded.

The man didn't: the scroll must have been signed by an aedile at least, if it was genuine; if it was genuine…

We trussed up the Ugly Brothers, hired a cart and driver, and, with some difficulty, got them back to Rome.

'Forging official documents,' I mused; 'kidnapping Roman citizens: if this goes wrong, we'll be in the Cloaca Maxima without a paddle.'

Mala did not seem bothered, and by this time his air of confidence and competence was such that I ceased to worry also: this was all much more interesting, much more exciting, than sitting in Rufus's Place yakking about this or that, or attending to the minimal duties I was expected to carry out to justify my rank.

Neither Mala nor I doubted that Draco was the guilty party. His slip in referring to Julia Drusilla as 'widow' was almost a confession of guilt, for he could not possibly have known of Ventidius's death unless he had been involved, or, at the very least, had been informed of the fact by the person or persons involved: Scarface or whoever.

But how to prove it? That was the question; how even to *start* proving it?

There are those who would have opted for the direct method. Our local vigiles, when they dragged some unfortunate lout down to the station for 'questioning', favoured that approach: they believed in the two fundamental categories of mankind, the quick and the dead, and those who weren't quick with their answers.... (I exaggerate: but not much: and as for the urban cohorts proper...)

We did not think this would work with Draco. For a start, we were not vigiles: we had no official status at all. For a second, Draco was clearly a man who would not crack easily, and if we added G.B.H. to kidnapping and forging official documents, and turned out to be wrong, we might, just, just possibly, be made to feel rather sorry.

'What the hell,' I asked myself, my former optimism and joi-de-vivre beginning to evaporate, 'am I doing here?'

What I found myself doing, very soon, was bundling first Draco, and then Scarface, to the study, where Mala ostentatiously pulled back the rug, went straight to the raised pattern on the mosaic, and depressed it. Again the circular trap-door slid open noiselessly, and this time Mala did not send for torches: he cut through the ropes binding the prisoners' feet, and prodded them towards the opening.

Scarface aimed a vicious kick at Mala as soon as his feet were free, which was an ill-judged action, because by the time he came to he was in the underground room, somewhat bruised, with his feet again securely bound.

Mala picked up the ugly knife that had been in Ventidius's ribs, and held the point close to Draco's throat.

'Please,' he said, 'try something; have a go; I'm dying to shove this in your gut, but unlike you I don't knife people in cold blood. So give me an excuse, and I'll be only too happy to rid Rome of a murderer and a blackmailer. And his accomplice,' he added, turning on Scarface, 'unless, of course, he can tell me a little story.'

Scarface spat, and cursed Mala roundly, but even so I guessed the seed of doubt had been sown in his mind: might he, after all, get away with a whole skin, if he dished his brother and sang like a canary?

'What's this about blackmail?' I asked Mala as soon as we were along together.

'As you know, at Julia Drusilla's request I spent some time going over Ventidius's accounts: not the main set here in the study, but those that were on the desk underground. There were some very interesting entries: two sets in particular. Look them over: I've summarised them here.'

He showed me two columns of figures, one headed 'L.A.D.', the other 'L.J.'

'Aufidius Draco is the first, pretty surely,' said Mala. 'The other is almost certainly a woman: there are notes elsewhere with occasional references to 'Livia', and others to 'L. Justina'. Livia Justina it must be, and I think I can guess who she is. But that in its place: just look at the figures.'

I whistled. The records went back for the best part of a year, and they were staggering: a thousand sesterces here, two thousand there, three thousand…

'You'll notice the sums grow larger,' Mala observed. 'The last one, only days before Ventidius's 'disappearance', is for a whopping fifteen thousand sesterces. About a third of the payments are to 'Livia Justina', but the bulk go to Draco. And they are itemised simply as 'services'.'

We know that Draco performed 'services' for Ventidius, but not to the tune of almost a hundred thousand sesterces a year he didn't.

'There is little doubt it is blackmail,' said Mala. 'Draco and Scarface there discovered something Ventidius wanted kept quiet; and their silence cost him.'

We tried to speculate about what it might have been, with little success. Ostensibly Ventidius Silo had been a model citizen: prosperous, generous, a public benefactor in a modest way, a pillar of the community. He had built up his business empire and his considerable fortune by hard work and commercial acumen, and there had never been any breath of suspicion that his enterprises were anything but honest and above board. Though, wisely, keeping clear of politics, he had had the ear of Titus, and, before that, of Vespasian, joining the many who helped out a little when the emperor was short of the ready – as when wasn't he? Though not so close to Domitian himself – who is, to that suspicious swine? – he was still well regarded in imperial circles generally, and his eventual elevation to the equestrian ranks would have surprised no-one.

The breakthrough, when it came, was half-expected, and wholly welcome. Draco and Scarface had been taken from their prison, carefully watched over by me, by Asinius, and by Ventidius's former bodyguard, an ex-gladiator, all muscles and no conscience, who looked as though, like Mala, he would just love either or both of the prisoners to make a break for it, and suffer the consequences.

They didn't, and were taken to bathe and to do what they had to do, before being bundled back underground. But Scarface held back as we approached the study, and signalled to me that he wanted to say something. Draco was shoved down the steps before he know what was going on, leaving his so-loyal brother to face the questioning.

'Well?' Mala went straight to the point. 'What has Livia Justina to tell me?'

I confess I had been slow on the uptake: female visitor, tall for a woman, veiled, disfigured; woman blackmailer; as soon as Mala spoke, the penny dropped, and I listened with increased interest.

'Sir, I know who killed Ventidius Silo. It wasn't me, I beg you to believe me, I wasn't even there. Will I be spared if I tell all?'

'What is certain,' replied Mala curtly, 'is that you won't be spared if you don't tell all: *all;* so get on with it.'

We had rightly surmised that Scarface was no hero. Sing like a canary? He sang like a whole aviary of them. Yes, he and Draco had been blackmailing Ventidius; yes, when Draco was out of town, he had called, disguised as a woman as a safeguard against recognition, to collect the latest instalment; yes, Draco had murdered Ventidius: they had quarrelled, Ventidius had vowed he would pay no more and damn the consequences, Draco had threatened him, Ventidius had started to climb the steps that led out of the underground room, Draco had pulled him back and buried the knife in his ribs.

'Thereby,' said Mala, 'killing the goose that laid the golden egg.'

'How were you blackmailing Ventidius?' I demanded. 'What hold did you have over him?'

'Take me to Draco's room.'

Draco had had a small room, between the main living area and the slaves' quarters, less Spartan than the latter of course, but pretty plainly furnished except for a rather elaborately-carved three-legged table, and – here we go again, I thought – a Parthian rug, smaller than that in the study but no less elaborate.

Scarface rolled back the rug, but there was no underground chamber this time, merely a loose tile, revealing a cavity in which lay a sizeable casket. Mala at once took out the casket and tried to open it, but it was one of those cunning contraptions involving interlocking sliding panels and a concealed pressure point, which might have frustrated us for hours; but Scarface obliged.

Inside was a single scroll, obviously a letter. Mala read it out.

'Greetings, Lucius Ventidius Silo. I write to give you the good news that our little enterprise is very close to fruition.'

Innocuous enough, at first glance, don't you agree? But who it was from was all too clear: *Arrecinus Clemens*.

'Mair-da,' again that expletive from Mala. Like everyone, he knew of the sticky end of the ex-consul, whom Domitian had accused of treason the year before and summarily had executed. 'This letter is probably innocent enough: no-one who knew Ventidius would believe he was involved in any treasonable plot.. For that matter no-one believes Arrecinus Clemens himself was plotting anything. Nevertheless, in the eyes of our paranoid emperor, this could have been Ventidius's death-warrant.'

'We had better burn it,' I suggested. 'There's no telling what revenge Domitian would heap on Julia Drusilla if it fell into his hands.'

'It wouldn't help; Draco doubtless kept a copy somewhere.'

'Perhaps Draco will be in no position to use it,' I answered meaningfully, and saw Scarface blanch as I said it.

'And perhaps Draco has given instructions as to what to do with it in the event of his death,' rejoined Mala.

Scarface hastened to confirm that.

'But I don't know where he keeps the copy,' he added hastily; 'he never confides in me that much.'

We were inclined to believe him: he was a thoroughly frightened man, and once he had decided to co-operate he knew his best bet was to go the whole hog.

Mala was unimpressed.

'If you don't know where it is,' he said callously, 'you had better find out: and quick.'

'Don't put me back with Draco,' pleaded Scarface. 'If he knows I've been talking to you…'

'Tell him I held you back,' replied Mala, 'and questioned you about the payments you received. Say you told us nothing.'

Scarface seemed very doubtful, and very frightened, but had no choice; we bundled him down the steps, and left him to commune with his loving brother.

The commotion came only minutes after we had left him. We heard the scream, the thud, and when we opened the trap-door, saw Draco, sneering, standing over the body of his erstwhile partner-in-crime. Draco's feet had been tied, and his hands also, but not tightly: not tightly enough to prevent his taking food, or drink, or putting them round his miserable brother's throat, and strangling him to death.

'There goes our witness,' said Mala, bitterly. 'I should have listened to him: Draco was not one to take a chance on Scarface's not saying a word. Better safe than sorry was his approach, and there's the result; and I fear he *is* safe, unless we can come up with something pretty clever. How all occasions do inform against me!'

I do not know what he meant, but it was obvious he was blaming himself more than was called for, though I confess I felt, irrationally, a little guilty myself: if I had not dealt with Scarface's arm quite so effectively at Veii, he might have been able to defend himself just long enough for help to arrive. The guilt was short-lived when I thought back to the events in the tavern, and the knife in Scarface's hand and the look on his face as he advanced on Mala; but still…

Guilt or not, the fact remained that Scarface was dead, and the document in the casket, far from harming Draco, would serve only to exonerate him and incriminate Ventidius – and, by extension, us, which could be very greatly to our discomfiture.

'What would Sherlock have done,' Mala asked himself: outlandish names again – he knew more outlandish names than I'd had hot dinners. (Not, I found, that there was much point asking him whom the names were attached to.)

Mala threw himself on a couch, and remained there for what seemed like hours, silencing any interruption with a peremptory wave of the hand, thinking, thinking, thinking. Finally he rose.

'I believe I have it,' he said. 'It's a long shot, and it's certainly not honest; but desperate situations call for desperate measures. If it works we're home and dry. I'd better get moving.'

'Where are you going?'

'To visit the household of Arrecinus Clemens; you can come along if you wish.'

I did not. Events were moving just a little too quickly for my peace of mind, and I needed time to come to terms with them. I again went over what we had done: assaulted two citizens in Veii; kidnapped them, using forged documents; incarcerated them against their will; and now one of them had been killed. We had no way of proving that the killing had not been on our orders, and Draco, the real culprit, would doubtless allege as much if given the chance. Moreover, there was the letter from Arrecinus Clemens, which Draco would be only too pleased to use.

I was relieved when Mala returned, sooner than expected.

'They were only too ready to oblige,' he informed me, depositing several scrolls on the desk. 'And now for some creative writing: I have to out-Titus Titus.'

I had no idea what the reference to our late, great emperor implied, but let it pass. There was no point in hanging around: Mala was absorbed in his work, the scrolls spread out on the desk, stylus in hand, peering at the documents minutely, writing very, very slowly, carefully, painstakingly. He would obviously be at it for some time, and so I took myself off to the guest room Julia Drusilla had allocated to us, and soon was fast asleep. I have no idea what time Mala joined me, but have little doubt it was well into the night.

Next morning, Julia Drusilla joined us for a light breakfast, but little was said. I was still apprehensive about the hornet's nest we had stirred up, Julia Drusilla was still finding it difficult to come to terms with what had happened to her husband, and Mala was very preoccupied: one could almost sense his thoughts, as he contemplated first this course of action, then that, weighing up the pros and cons, raising objections and then knocking them down, thinking through the practicalities, the implications, the possible consequences; until, at last:

'It's got to be done,' he announced; 'we must grasp the nettle; beard the lion in his den. We must seek an audience with the emperor.'

I gulped a little at that. My feeling about Domitian was that if he never found out that I even existed, it would be too soon. I would as soon thrust my presence under his nose, as try to shake hands with a Nile crocodile.

'You do not have to come along, 'said Mala, 'if you don't want to; but I think you might be interested in what I'll be showing his high-and-mighty; and, incidentally, you might as well burn this while you're about it.'

He held out a scroll: the letter to Ventidius from Arrecinus Clemens. I raised my eyebrows as I took it.

'Go ahead,' he said. 'It's better out of the way now.'

I went out and summoned Asinius, and soon the scroll was reduced to ashes.

'Now look.' Mala handed me two further scrolls.

The one, at first glance, was a copy of the letter I had just burnt; the wording was identical – and yet I felt there were subtle differences, which I could not quite pin down.

I glanced at the other. Again the wording was the same, except for one rather significant difference: instead of being addressed to Ventidius Silo, this very clearly opened:

'Greetings, Lucius Aufidius Draco.'

And it was purportedly from, like the other, Arrecinus Clemens.

Mala explained his plans, and I was amazed alike by his daring and his ingenuity.

'And now to get that audience,' he announced. 'I know one or two people at the palace…'

It was easier and quicker than I had dared hope: Mala did indeed know 'one or two people at the palace', and clearly they had some clout. Too soon for my comfort or composure, therefore, we found ourselves ushered into the Presence, Draco bringing up behind in the grip of two tough-looking vigiles Mala had 'borrowed' from somewhere for the occasion.

Mala was not naturally a deferential man, but he was a wise one, and he was obsequiousness itself as he addressed the emperor; despite which, his exposition was crisp and clear.

'And so you see, great Caesar, that this parchment must be the later one; that this belongs to the same stock as the first, whereas the other is lighter and newer; that the way this letter here curls, and that, is subtly but clearly different: a good try, but a forgery once you know what to look for…' And then, almost as an afterthought, Mala added: 'There might be copies of the forged document around, but you will see…'

'I will see no copies,' said Domitian. He had been surprisingly patient, but when the explanation was finished, the look on the his face boded ill indeed for someone. 'Great Jupiter,' I pleaded silently, 'I pray that he accepts Mala's explanation.'

What followed showed he had, and caused me to shudder as I thought of what would have happened to us if he had not. He went up to Draco, and spoke to him very quietly – as a cat is very quiet, before it pounces on the hapless mouse.

'So,' he said; 'you would dare to plot against *me*; you would forge documents to try to deceive *me*; you would try to incriminate one of *my* loyal subjects. You are that most worthless piece of dung, a *lying* informer.'

'But, Caesar,' began Draco.

'Shut up.' The emperor struck him across the mouth. 'There is only one way to treat a lying informer, and that is to see his lying tongue lies no more. Guard!'

One of the huge Germans who had been standing passively observing the scene sprang forward.

'Cut out this man's tongue.'

It was done in a trice, but Draco's scream seemed to echo round the room for minutes, sending a chill through us all.

'I do not think his tongue will lie any more,' quipped Domitian, and his smile was evil itself. 'Come to think of it,' he added, 'I do not expect he will do anything very much, after to-morrow. I am told we have some new Nubian lions, big black-maned brutes, that haven't been fed for days. I am sure they would appreciate a little snack.' And he laughed his evil laugh again.

But then he was all business-like.

'You two have done well. Doubtless you would like to witness this scum pay his debt to society; I will ensure you have privileged seats. See my steward as you leave, and tell him to arrange the details. Dismissed.

I am not particularly squeamish about bloodshed: you do not get very far in the legions if you are. Nevertheless, I have never been an enthusiast for the organized and ritualised slaughter of the arena, and foul brute though Draco was, and thoroughly deserving of death, I would have preferred it to be some other way. Mala was even more appalled.

'I thought it would be the Tarpeian Rock,' he said; 'bad enough, even though he deserves it; but this...'

But the emperor had made us an offer we could not refuse, and so we watched Draco torn limb from limb, and scores of other criminals suffer the same fate, and others forced to fight fully armed and armoured gladiators, though themselves given no more than wooden swords, and scores of gladiators themselves breathe their last, even after they had acquitted themselves well.

But at last it was over, and we made our escape.

There remained only the task of explaining to Julia Drusilla just what had happened, and how Mala had put paid to Draco.

'The initial problem,' he told her, 'was Asinius's assertion that he had heard Ventidius in the study shortly before delivering the wine. He though it was Ventidius muttering as he worked through his accounts; in fact it must have been his talking to Draco, and he was not in the study, but in the underground chamber.

'Draco must have heard Asinius coming just as he killed Ventidius, and at once closed the trap-door. Asinius found the study empty, the fact that the rug had been moved did not register, and so we were led on our fruitless chase to find Ventidius. Draco must have stayed in the chamber until he judged it prudent to sneak out, perhaps in the middle of the night, and once he was away from the vicinity of the study he was safe, because he was semi-resident and would be known to anyone he might encounter.'

'But how did you find the evidence to convince the emperor that Draco was the guilty party?' asked the widow.

'It was not really evidence,' Mala replied. 'I framed him: I admit it. It was the only way, and I felt justified since there was no possible doubt of his guilt, and I could not otherwise save Ventidius's reputation and avoid the possibility of Domitian victimising you.'

'I obtained from Arrecinus Clemens' household some genuine documents that he had written, together with a blank sheet from his normal stock. On the blank sheet, I traced out the original letter, addressed to Ventidius, except that I deliberately mis-formed some of the letters. I then took a quite different sheet of parchment, and very carefully reproduced the original letter, but this time addressing it to Draco. Finally I took more of the newer parchment, and minutely copied some of the Clemens originals his people had let me have.

'After that, it was not too difficult to convince Domitian that the Draco letter was the original, and the Ventidius one the forgery. Once he had swallowed that, thank Jupiter, he was no longer interested in the documents, but if Draco's copy turns up, and he demands to compare it with those I showed him, he will find it displays the characteristics of the supposed forged document rather than the genuine one.'

Simplicity itself, you'll say; yes – if you have the wit to think up the idea in the first place, and the courage to carry it through. A real handwriting expert, and Domitian had several on his staff, might have seen through Mala's forgeries; Draco himself might have spun a yarn that convinced Domitian, or at least made him suspicious; the emperor himself might have been in one of his most paranoid moods, and not believed anyone about anything, in which case he could well have sent us to the lions along with Draco.

But it didn't happen that way, and Mala was the hero of the hour. Everyone at Rufus's Place congratulated him heartily.

'Ah,' he told us; 'it is ze little grey cells…'

We hadn't a clue what he was on about, and there was one incident that followed, weeks afterwards, that puzzled me further. We were again gathered at Rufus's Place, and had been joined by a newcomer, a rather eager and earnest young man. I had recalled something Mala had said, and – without, of course, mentioning that the remark came from him, still less the circumstances of his uttering it - I asked the assembled company if they had ever heard any rumour that the late emperor Titus was skilled at forgery. No-one had, except the young man, Tranquillus.

'I have,' he said; 'I collect scraps of information like that.'

I noticed that Mala smiled. Nothing more was said on the subject, and eventually the session broke up.

'That young man will go far,' remarked Mala.

'Tranquillus?'

'Yes; but that is his cognomen; he is also known as Gaius Suetonius.'

QUINTUS PROPERTIUS AND THE CASE OF THE COUNTING-HOUSE CLERK

Sextus Solvius Pansa – a big name for a little man – had been among the fortunate of the earth. At first sight, you would not have thought so. He lived with his wife and aged mother in a tiny apartment above a bakery, in, if not the least fashionable area of Rome, one that had certainly seen better days.

He was far from the poorest of the poor, and yet, like most freedmen and unlike those you hear so much about, he had not made his millions, or even many thousands: no Narcissus he, nor yet a Trimalchio.

As a government official he had a certain status, but it was no big deal, and nobody called him 'Sir'.

But he was lucky. He was lucky to be alive. He had first become a government servant during the reign of Nero, and had served five other emperors between that monster and the present one, outliving them all. (He might even have outlived Domitian, if someone brave and public-spirited enough had managed to put paid to that vicious swine before misfortune struck.)

The truth is that Solvius Pansa had survived, and even at his level flourished, precisely *because* he was a nobody, one of hundreds or thousands like him. Whether the emperor be a madman like Nero, a clod like Otho, a hero like Titus, or a worm like Domitian, the wheels of government must go round, the business of the empire be attended to, day after day, through revolution, fire, famine, assassination, pogrom or earthquake; and it is relative nonentities like Pansa who ensure that it happens, that the wheels do go round, the business does get done.

Who is it said 'the stylus is mightier than the sword'? (I think it might have been Mala.) It is not a sentiment it is prudent to utter in the confines of an army camp, or when having a friendly chat with a Praetorian (if that is not a contradiction in terms), and anyway 'stylus' is used metaphorically. Nevertheless, in a real and almost literal sense, it is true, and Pansa was as vital to the well-being of the empire as any squaddy stuck in a camp in Britain, or sweating it out on the Parthian border.

He was also a very pleasant man, modest (and aware that he had much to be modest about), self-effacing, completely lacking in side, or in malice.

That is why those of us who knew him were as surprised as we were shocked when we learned he had been murdered, and outraged at the brutal manner in which the murder had been carried out.

It looked, or was intended to look, like a mugging, a fairly ordinary event, except for the viciousness of the attack: both Pansa's arms were broken, his face was battered in, and there was a gash in his side that looked as though he had been hit by a pole-axe. His money was gone, of course, such little as he normally carried with him, though the cheap part-silver bracelet, a family heirloom, that was his only concession to personal display, was still on his wrist.

All this we learned from our friend Gaius Cornelius, an habitué of Rufus's Place, who knew the unfortunate man better than most of us, since they had worked together, though Cornelius in a more elevated post.

'I saw his body not long after the attack,' he told us. 'The vigiles who found him carried him to the station, and called on me to confirm the identification: neither easy nor pleasant, and I'm glad they had the nous not to ask his widow, Nysa. Afterwards, though, I did have to break the news to her, and that wasn't pleasant either.'

'Where was the body found,' asked Mala: Quintus Propertius Mala, our resident mystery man.

'That's the strange thing. It was just near the Theatre of Marcellus, and that is a fair distance from where he lived. He and I used to walk home together sometimes, until our paths split and he headed south: he had a little place beyond the cattle market, near the river.'

'So his detour was unusual?"

'Absolutely. Solvius Pansa was a creature of habit, and I would swear he took the same route home, same time, same brief stop for a small cup of wine and water, his only indulgence but for his occasional brief visits here, every day of his working life – or at least as long as I have known him. He worked for government for almost thirty years, and it might have been different in the old days, but I doubt it.'

'Could he have been lured to the Temple of Marcellus?' I asked. 'Or arranged to meet someone there? It hardly seems likely that he walked that far out of his way just for the exercise.'

'That much is obvious,' Mala observed. 'This was no ordinary mugging. Either the murder was premeditated, or Pansa was involved in something that went unexpectedly and tragically wrong.'

'But what?' I demanded. 'He wasn't the sort of person to be involved in shady deals, still less political skulduggery.'

'Nevertheless,' said Mala, 'I suspect his government work might be the connection we want. Just what did it involve?' He asked Cornelius.

'He was in accounts, as I am. He dealt with large sums of money, and he was a whiz-kid at figures, but he had no authority for the allocation or disposal of any of it, any more than I have, as his superior. He was a useful man, but no big wheel.'

'If he was that closely involved with money,' insisted Mala, 'then that is the first lead to follow up. Was he open to blackmail, do you think?'

'Pansa? My eye. He was looking forward to retiring before long, and he would have been quite comfortable: he had a little stashed away, and he actually owned his apartment outright – it was, believe it or not, a gift from Tigellinus, in one of that gentleman's better moods.'

'One of his few better moods,' I muttered: my family had no cause to love Nero's notorious enforcer, ever since my maternal uncle had fallen foul of him over some trifle, and been forced, like Petronius the Arbiter, to take his own life.

'I met Pansa a couple of times,' said Mala, 'and I admit my impression of him accords with what you say. But temptation can do strange things, even to the most upright-seeming of people. One cynic quipped that he could resist anything but temptation, and the evidence of life is that he wasn't alone in that. Still,' he went on, 'we'll continue giving Pansa the benefit of the doubt. We do, though, need to find out why he went to the Theatre of Marcellus.'

'Not exactly *to* the Theatre,' Cornelius pointed out. 'His body was found *nearby.*'

'True,' acknowledged Mala, 'and 'nearby' includes quite a number of buildings.'

'And perhaps he was simply passing by that way en route to somewhere else,' persisted Cornelius. 'We do not know where he was actually heading.'

'Then we'd better try to find out.'

'Here we go again,' I said to myself. 'If Mala gets his teeth into a mystery, there's work ahead.'

I could not quite understand why he was so interested. Ventidius Silo, whose supposed disappearance he had solved so spectacularly some months before, had been a personal acquaintance, and a citizen of substance to boot. Pansa, on the other hand, was a nobody, and known only slightly to most of us, and although we were all angry about what had happened to him, nobodies are mugged and murdered in Rome every day of the week: what was so special about his case, that it should so engage Mala's concern?

I put it to him as we trudged towards the Temple of Marcellus. He shrugged.

'I don't know. I was sickened by what happened to the poor fellow, I liked him, and, frankly, the anomalies in the case niggle me: I need to *find out*.' He smiled to himself. 'During my mis-spent youth,' he went on, 'for a time I was instructed along with a number of young ladies, if you can believe such a thing. On one occasion, our tutor announced that I had "an enquiring mind", and all the young ladies giggled. I wonder why that was?'

I could see that he was making some kind of joke, but what most struck me was that he had *shared a tutor with women*. Just what sort of an education *had* he had? He had told us previously that his youthful companions when he lived in south-west Britain had included some from the local tribe, the Dumnonii, and I do not know which surprised me the more, that, or this news about young women. A thoroughly unconventional upbringing, this Mala must have had.

Obviously, though, his education had been effective, since we knew him to be a most learned man ('But what about the women?' I wondered. The thought of female clones of Gaius Pliny let loose on the world made me shudder. There have been erudite, and very intelligent women, of course: one thinks of the notorious Clodia, and the empress Livia; but they are the exceptions, thank Jupiter. Now, don't think that I'm a reactionary: I do believe in women having a smattering of learning; it can make their conversation a little less boring, and that's a boon, for sure. But there must be limits...)

I was mulling over these matters as we made our way through the city, thick with unwashed humanity at this time of day, to our destination almost a mile away. Mala was still a mystery to me, often though I had been in his company since the Ventidius affair. Ostensibly a high-class Roman, a scholar and a gentleman, more and more he kept revealing little things that did not quite fit. His revelations about his education was one such: who ever heard of an upper-class Roman being tutored with *girls*? And then there were his little aphorisms: *one must eat to live, but not live to eat...* There were the expletives, too, in one outlandish tongue or another: *Merda*; *Helena Dalmatian*. There were the things he came out with, both prose and poetry, that sounded as though they might have been translated direct from such languages: *'The sky above the roof-tops, so blue, so calm...'*

What was one to make of it all? But I did not have much chance to think on it more, as we pushed and elbowed our way through the throngs who filled the narrow street adjoining the great vegetable market. They were slaves, mostly, though some of them as haughty and arrogant as though they had been old-style patricians who could trace their ancestry back to the first Brutus. These, as I'm sure you'll have recognised, were the cooks: slaves, minions, the lowest of the low, yet all arrogance, all hauteur, looking down their noses at the rest of humanity, even any broad-stripers who happened to come before their supercilious gaze. Perhaps they learn it in cookery school, for I've never known a single one who was not the same: 'We,' they proclaimed by their whole demeanour, 'we, masters of the kitchen, are the true aristocrats.'

Mala paused a moment to watch some of them haggling with the stall-holders.

'People nowadays,' he observed, 'know the price of everything and the value of nothing; and it was ever thus and ever will be.'

'Ever will be? You're a prophet now, are you?'

'In an amateur sort of way,' he answered, smiling; but then the smile vanished from his face, as we approached the place where Pansa's body had been found. Mala had been right to stress what was 'nearby'. It was said that Augustus had genuinely grieved when Marcellus, his nephew and heir-apparent, had died, and the theatre he had built in commemoration was not merely an empty gesture designed to impress the gullible. He spared no expense in its design and construction, and certainly did not want its imposing presence obscured by other buildings; consequently a number were pulled down. Over the years, however, others were built, not indeed obscuring the view of the magnificent colonnaded front of the theatre, but behind and to the side.

Mala looked around. There were numerous places where Pansa's assailants could have lain in wait, side roads, alleys, doorways, all ideal for concealment. It did not follow, then, that he must have known them and approached them without fear..

Nevertheless: 'Perhaps,' I said, 'we have been missing a trick. What if he was not killed here at all, but met his end elsewhere and his body was simply dragged here to put people off the scent?'

Mala nodded.

'You could, I suppose,' he agreed, 'drag a dead body here and not be noticed'

'Especially if it was dark…'

'It wasn't; it was not even dusk: Pansa was on his way home from his place of work as usual, and this is midsummer. They would have been taking a bit of a risk therefore, and I think it more likely that he was killed around here, out of sight; but we must bear the other possibility in mind.'

'It seems to me, then, that we are not much further forward, and coming here to the Theatre of Marcellus has not helped at all.'

'Not so. We now know that although Pansa *might* well have been coming here to meet someone he knew, it is not necessarily so. Moreover, it is always useful to have a picture of the scene of the crime in one's mind's eye.'

'I suppose so. Meanwhile, I'm hungry, and thirsty, and tired.'

'A real Roman stoic you are, friend Marcus: unyielding in the face of hardship, disdainful of your own comfort…'

I knew he was trying to needle me, in a friendly way of course, but I rose to the bait.

'I have demonstrated more than once,' I told him, 'that I can put up with hardship if I have to: or do you think it was all fun and games in Germany and Dacia? But I see no point in putting up with hardship if I don't actually *have* to, and I see no point in going hungry and thirsty when I am in Rome surrounded by food and wine shops.'

'As a matter of fact,' replied Mala unexpectedly, 'I agree with you. Let's go and attend to the inner man.'

'I fear, though,' he added, 'that afterwards we must go and interview Pansa's widow.'

Nysa was of Bithynian extraction, the daughter of a former slave who had achieved her freedom before her marriage - to a skilled glass-blower, of whom more anon. Nysa had been brought up as a Roman, though there was no hiding her origins. She must have been pretty, in an understated way, when she was younger, but rather self-effacing, and naturally enough still in shock at what had happened to her husband when we went to talk to her.

Mala, as one would expect, was tactful and considerate. It was hard work.

'So you have no idea whatever,' Mala persisted, 'why Pansa should have gone out of his way on this occasion?'

Nysa shook her head again miserably.

While Mala and Nysa had been talking, I had been observing the fourth person in the room. This was an ancient, frail figure, clearly, like the younger woman, a slave or descended from slaves, and yet strangely dignified, a woman of character, one would have thought, a presence. This, as we had learned at the outset, was Pansa's mother. Probably, I conjectured, she had been in her time body-servant to some great lady: from time to time one comes across these personal slaves to the great and the good, who, by some process of osmosis, acquire over time the same air of superiority, present the same *de haut en bas* front to the world, as the mighty ones whose minions was all they really were.

Aemilia Fausta had it in spades, and when she spoke, during a brief lull in Mala's questioning of Nysa, we listened.

'Tell them,' she instructed her daughter-in-law, 'of my son's worthless cousin.'

Nysa looked a little flustered.

'I did not really know him,' she said, 'and surely even he…'

'Tell him,' instructed the older woman.

'As I say, I hardly knew him. He only appeared a couple of months ago. Sextus Solvius had not seen him since they were children, when they were still in then household of Olfonius Tigellinus. The families had quite lost contact, and he was surprised when Lucius appeared and said he was back in Rome at last after his very many years in Spain.'

'My useless, delinquent nephew,' interrupted her mother-in-law, 'like his equally useless delinquent father, my half-brother, wanted nothing to do with the rest of us while he was prospering, but as soon as he fell on hard times, there he was, begging for help as though he had been in the bosom of the family for years, instead of out of sight since the emperor Nero's early days.

'I would have turned him away, but my son was a dutiful Roman: he did not like his cousin any more than I did, but he had been brought up to believe blood is thicker than water, and felt obliged to help.'

I suppressed a smile at this – it wasn't a funny business, after all – but it is amusing to observe how quickly these freed former slaves, hailing as they may from Jupiter knows what outlandish part of the world, hasten to adopt the customs and the characteristics of us *echt* Romans.

'Did Lucius come here,' asked Mala, 'or did Pansa usually see him elsewhere?'

'He came here only a couple of times, including the first, but Pansa could see I did not like him and took to seeing him near his place of work, during his meal-break. Lucius was always begging for money, but promising he would return it as soon as he was back in Spain, where he said some acquaintance was going to take him on as a business partner.'

Lovely term, 'business partner', I thought to myself: it could mean anything or nothing, respectable – or otherwise.

'But he never did hear from this acquaintance, as far as you know?'

'We thought perhaps he had: he did not appear for eight or nine days, but just as we had begun to hope we had seen the last of him, up he turned again out of the blue; and he said he needed two thousand sesterces, urgently.'

I raised my eye-brows at that. Two thousand sesterces is not big money in the overall scheme of things, but nor is it small change to a man in Pansa's position.

'Did your husband give it to him?'

'No; he said he would see if he could raise it, but would make no promises.'

'And did he tell you how Lucius took this refusal?'

'He said he was angry. He accused Sextus Solvius of being mean and tight-fisted and said he was typical of his filthy branch of the family – and all this after he had been given money time and again, money my husband could ill afford.'

Nysa broke down and began to sob. Mala tried to comfort her, but she was too wrapped up in her own misery. It was the older woman who took up the story.

`'A real chip off then old block, that Lucius,' she said bitterly. 'I know for a fact that my late husband gave his father hundreds and hundreds of sesterces when he gained his freedom, money he could not really afford either. It was a great relief when he took himself and his brood to Spain.

'He died there, some say of over-much wine and general debauchery; they say too that his son Lucius neglected him when he was most needing support, though Lucius at the time was doing quite well for himself in some shady business or other.'

'I don't think I like this Lucius,' said Mala. 'Nevertheless, I would very much like to meet him. Do you know where he might be found?'

'The Subura, somewhere,' was all they could come up with.

'This sounds like the breakthrough,' I said to Mala as we left. 'Obviously this Lucius character lured Pansa to the Theatre of Marcellus, murdered him there...'

'Why?' interrupted Mala. 'What could he gain by that, even if Pansa had had much money with him, which all the indications are that he hadn't? Don't forget that although his work involved his dealing with large sums, it was not real money: he didn't get the chance to paddle in a pool of gold pieces, like Caligula, and you can't purloin marks on a piece of parchment, even if you want to.'

'There's such a thing as creative accounting,' I replied. 'Cornelius says Pansa was a whiz-kid with figures: might he not have siphoned off more than was due to some crony or other, taking his cut when the hard cash actually arrived?'

'It would take some doing, from what Cornelius has told us of their checks and counter-checks: the emperor Vespasian, remember, kept a very sharp eye indeed on all monetary affairs, and it was he who instituted the accounting system Pansa and Cornelius had to work with; it's supposed to be fool-proof. And even if it's not, can you really see Pansa involved in fraud of that kind,? Even if he had the skill, and even if he wasn't as honest as he seems to have been, he was not the sort to risk the punishment that would have been his if he had tried and been found out; and especially to help such a creature as this Lucius.'

He had a point: Pansa had been one of the meek of the earth, and the thought of what had happened to Ventidius's killer* happening to him was as far-fetched as it was horrible.

'Nevertheless,' Mala continued, 'that does not mean that Lucius was *not* somehow involved in Pansa's murder, or in the events surrounding it. We still have to find this man.'

More easily said than done. For a start, you don't just go Subura-exploring as you would take an afternoon stroll in the park. Some parts are reasonably safe, though it pays to be very, very sure you've got your map co-ordinates right. For the rest, even the vigiles – *especially* the vigiles – tend to opt for safety in numbers when they venture into some areas.

'They go not as single spies, but in battalions,' as Mala remarked: he does have some funny ways of putting it, does that man.

We did our best, but we had so little to go on. 'A man called Lucius? You can't tell me anything more about him? Ha-ha!' As well go to the arena, and say the guy your were looking for had something to do with the games, or to an army camp saying you'd be bound to recognise the man you were looking for, because whenever you'd seen him he was carrying a spear.

There was the Spanish connection, but that did not help much: there are more Spaniards in Rome than Brits in Londinium, and more Gauls and Germans and Egyptians and Bithynians and Mauretanians too: it's a cosmopolitan city, right?

'He could be back in Spain,' I suggested. 'If he had anything to do with Pansa's death, it would make a lot of sense to make himself scarce; and if he is indeed in Spain, looking for him will be even more of a wild-goose chase than it is here.'

'Not necessarily. Looking in a Spanish town for a man who has just returned from Rome might be a lot easier than finding a Spaniard called Lucius in the Subura.'

'But which Spanish town?'

'On that, we would do well to ask the haughty Aemilia Fausta. She knows more of our friend than she's let on. Did you notice, that despite supposedly being out of touch with the Spanish branch of the family for decades, she knew of her half-brother's death, and its probable cause, and

---

* See *Sextus Propertius and the Affairs of Ventidius Silo*

of Lucius's unfilial behaviour, and that his employment had not been above-board?'

I had missed all that, which is why Mala is always the leader in our little expeditions, I the faithful poodle.

We tackled Aemilia Fausta forthwith. Luckily she came clean without too much need for cajoling.

'My half-brother divorced his second wife (not Lucius's mother: she died in childbirth) not long after they settled in Spain. Lucky woman – well rid of him. She married again, fine fellow, horse-breeder. Bore him two daughters, lovely girls from all accounts.'

'Whose accounts?'

'Hers: Vibia's, my former sister-in-law. We had been good friends. She writes long letters, at infrequent intervals, full of gossip. She occasionally mentions what my sometime family are up to: no good, usually.'

'And this delinquent nephew of yours, Lucius: where did he live in Spain? Cordoba?'

'Near Castalis: a little village just to the north.'

She gave us its name, but not surprisingly we had never heard of it. It was a lead, though, and Mala seemed delighted. I did not see why he should be delighted by the prospect of a trip to Spain: it's a miserable country at the best of times, and not that easy to get to. I did not fancy trudging around there, as we had been doing in Rome, probably with no more prospect of getting results.

Mala thought otherwise.

'*If* we go,' he said; 'and note I say "if", because this Lucius might still turn up in Rome; *if*, we have only a small village to home in on in the first instance, and even if our quarry is not there, Castalis itself is not a large town, and you know these small provincial places: no-one is anonymous, and everyone knows everyone else's business.'

I did know, having once lived in such a place. Very embarrassing, too: the girl's father… But that's another story.

'We seem,' said Mala, as we left the Pansa apartment, 'to have come to a natural break. Rufus calls.'

I'll say this: my reflexes are still good. I heard the magic name 'Rufus', and was about five paces ahead of Mala before he had finished his sentence. I've always boasted that I know the quickest way to Rufus's Place from any spot in Rome, and am ready to prove it at the drop of a hat. Mala had dropped the hat, and there we were in no time, gazing lovingly at the flask and two cups that Rufus produced the moment he saw us enter the door.

'Or perhaps you gentlemen want only a small cup each,' he grinned, and made as if to remove the flask.

'Of course,' I said; 'and plenty of water,' but just to make sure he hadn't misunderstood, I grabbed the flask and made for a table. Mala watched this little by-play with amusement.

'You'd think,' he remarked, 'it was Bojulae Nuvo.' (I think that's what he said, and I don't know if I've spelt it correctly. Don't ask me what it means – you know Mala and his little foreign phrases.)

I was all set for some serious drinking, but Mala was not quite in that sort of mood. He sipped his wine slowly, and looked pensive.

'We'd better take stock,' he decided. 'What do we know that we didn't know, what do we not know that we need to know, what do we need to do next?'

'I know that Rufus serves damn good wine,' I replied, but his frown told me that facetiousness would not be appreciated, and so I remained silent whilst he made a quick résumé of the situation. As he finished, I had a sudden thought.

'What if Lucius has been trying to get back to Spain, but hasn't enough money for the journey? It is possible he might have gone to the docks to try to fiddle something, maybe offering to work his passage. Perhaps we should investigate there.'

'Elementary, my dear Marcus, but a good point nonetheless. I had been thinking along the same lines, but since you have come up with the idea independently, perhaps you would like to take yourself off to Ostia and ask around; you'll enjoy the ride.'

He knew my lack of enthusiasm for horses, but would have his little joke; I let it pass, and reconciled myself to the trip.

First, though, there was the matter of Pansa's funeral. Mala was determined to attend, Gaius Cornelius would be there in his official capacity, and so, somewhat reluctantly, I went along.

I've never liked funerals – at such times, *timor mortis conturbat me* – and Pansa's was as bad as they go. It was, as you would expect, a modest affair, like the man himself, with only a very small group of family and friends attending, and no professional mourners. We were all in suitably solemn mood, only too conscious of the manner of his death; Nysa wept copiously, and Aemilia Fausta, though she retained her dignity, looked as though she had aged a dozen years. We were all more than glad when it was over

The next day, as it happens, was one of our get-togethers at Rufus's Place, and we were all there – except for Gaius Cornelius. It was unlike him to be late, and when he finally did turn up, he was looking unusually haggard. I passed him a cup of wine.

'You look dreadful; what is the matter?'

'Aemilia Fausta is dead.'

'I am sorry to hear that,' I said, 'but not altogether surprised. She was very old, very frail, and the shock of Pansa's death…'

'It's not that,' replied Cornelius. 'She has been murdered.'

'Tell us everything,' said Mala. 'What of Nysa?'

'She is hurt, but safe. Nigerius Veranius and I had gone to take her the little monies that were due to her after Pansa's death: not much, but as he was a member of the imperial staff, she was entitled to it, and we were delegated to deliver it. We tried again and again to make ourselves heard, but finally when no-one answered our knocking, we decided to force our way in.

'The apartment was in chaos. Furniture had been overturned, glassware smashed, there was blood on the floor – and Aemilia Fausta. One blow had been enough, she did not suffer, thank Jupiter; death must have been instantaneous.'

'And Nysa?'

'She was lying on the floor, with a wound to her head, but she must have tried to ward off the blow with her arm, which was badly shattered. I assume the assailant must have been disturbed before he could finish her off, and made his getaway.'

'Was anything taken?'

'Was there anything to take? You know the apartment: immaculate always, even though they had no slave – Nysa was one of those excessively house-proud women – but hardly full of luxury goods. I don't believe anything was worth much, except perhaps that little ivory-inlaid table, and it had been overturned and one leg smashed. Neither of the women had much in the way of jewellery; what little there was had not been touched.'

'And yet the place had been ransacked?'

'It looked like it, whether before or after the two women were attacked, I would not know.'

'Will Nysa be able to tell us, do you think?'

'Perhaps eventually, but not for a while. After we had called in the vigiles, we took her to my home, where my wife and daughter are looking after her. She was still unconscious when I left to come here. The physician says she should make a full recovery in time, but he could not say how long that time would be.'

'What of the neighbours? The bakery? Did you ask if anyone had been seen?'

'The bakery was closed; it is a lock-up place, and the owner lives on the other side of the river. The vigiles said they would question him, and the neighbours.'

'We had better see these vigiles,' said Mala, all thoughts of wine and talk now forgotten. 'Coming?'

Of course I was. I confess I was thoroughly sickened. It is one thing to kill even so inoffensive and mild-mannered a man as Pansa, but these things happen: Rome is a violent city. To attack two defenceless women in their own home, to batter to death a frail old lady, that's something else: it put whoever was responsible quite beyond the pale. If ever he – or they – were caught, it would not be a pretty death, and though as always I would be loath to watch it, I would hope that the lions had not been fed for weeks.

'Do you think it is the same person or persons who killed Pansa? Is the cousin involved?'

'The answer to both questions is that we do not know, but I'd bet my life it is 'Yes', and 'Yes'.'

'And so we are back to hunting the elusive Lucius?'

'Yes, with the advantage this time that the vigiles will be fully involved. They were not too interested in the Pansa case: just another mugging, happens every day, and they have far more important things to attend to. But this is different: a break-in, two women attacked, and this is not the Subura, it is a respectable neighbourhood, even if it is a bit run-down. My guess is that they will be dead keen to find the culprit.'

I nodded. 'And if they do, I would not be surprised if some little accident happened to him when he was helping with their enquiries.'

This was not cynicism on my part. Vigiles in general are not noted for their gentle natures: mostly veterans from the legions, they have seen active service all over the empire, they have killed men, and back in Rome had had to deal – and had dealt, summarily – with the scum of the earth. And yet, almost to a man they were transformed in the presence of little old ladies. Then it was 'Yes, ma'am,' this, and 'certainly, ma'am,' the other, 'let me help you with that heavy basket, ma'am' – they turned into big softies. It did not take much imagination to guess how they would feel about the brute who had battered Aemilia Fausta.

I knew how the local commander would feel, especially, for I was acquainted with the man. He had been a senior veteran during my military service: he had not quite made centurion, but at the next step down was one of the rocks on which the legion was built, strict, straight as a die, and once you got to know him, generous with his time and help: certainly this one junior officer had good reason to be grateful to him.

'A nasty business, Molo.' I said to him.

'Nasty? Foul. I've killed plenty of men, and even women too: but that was war. This...' He spat. No, I did not envy Lucius, or whoever it might be, if he fell into Molo's hands. The lions might not even be needed.

He was only too pleased that Mala and I were wanting to help in the investigation.

'Greatly appreciated, sirs; but if you do find the bastard, please leave him for me. I'd like a few words with the gentleman, I really would; the boys would be keen to make his acquaintance, too.'

He told us he had questioned Pansa's only neighbour. Pansa's apartment was the last in a small, three-story tenement, with access at the very end of the block. Only the neighbour above used the same stairs, and he was eliminated at once: a frail, semi-crippled ex-scribe, who scarcely had the strength to lift himself off his couch; indeed, he had been grateful to Pansa and Nysa for carrying his water up for him, doing a little shopping, and so on.

'And this man heard nothing?'

'As a matter of fact, he did, but he thought the noise was coming from the street, and he dragged himself to the top of the stairs to listen: there have been occasional break-ins at the bakery, though the owner has the sense now to take his till home with him at night. The old man slammed his door as he went back, and probably it was this the intruder or intruders heard, and decided to scarper – luckily for Nysa.'

'I would like, if I may, to examine the apartment,' said Mala.

'Go ahead, sir. We have looked it over, but have not had time yet to do a thorough search. Anything you might find I would be more than pleased to hear about.'

We were soon at the apartment, and it was as Gaius Cornelius had described: chaos and destruction, and yet whoever had perpetrated it had not done a very thorough job, presumably sufficiently alarmed by Pansa's neighbour to break off before the work was done. (If only he had known it was only a crippled old man, he would probably have murdered him as well, for he was undoubtedly ruthless enough.)

I keep saying 'he', but we did not take long to be convinced that there must have been more than one man involved.

'We do not know what the intruders were looking for,' Mala mused, 'nor whether they found it, but I suspect they did not. Let us look where they obviously didn't, and see what we can see.'

There was not much: Pansa's modest dwelling, as Gaius Cornelius had said, was devoid of anything likely to attract the attentions of a thief.

'My old grandfather used to quip,' said Mala, 'that in his impecunious youth, he decided that if ever he heard a burglar, he would go down and help the fellow look. Obviously Pansa could have echoed the sentiment.'

We continued searching nevertheless, finally coming to a tall, narrow wooden cupboard in one corner of the cooking area. It was not locked, and when we opened it, we could see why: it contained nothing but a mass of old glassware, vases, cups, a few bowls, one or two chipped or cracked, a few misshapen, all of them covered in dust.

'These do not look as though they have been touched in years, ' I remarked. 'I seem to remember that Nysa's mother was married to a glass-blower: these look like some of his trials, or cast-offs. I wonder why they have been kept.'

'Sentimental value, probably,' grunted Mala. 'They certainly do not look up to much.' Nevertheless, he examined each piece in turn, until at last his attention was caught by a very large bowl, thick with dust, on the top shelf. He took it out and wiped away some of the dust, and then a little more.

'This might be worth cleaning,' he said, and finding a pail of water and a cloth, he proceeded to rub the bowl vigorously. When it was done we could see that this was no cast-off, but a fine example of the glassmaker's art. Nuggets of glass of all shapes and sizes and colours were embedded in the circumference of the bowl, so that it shone almost like a thing on fire. Mala whistled.

'Whoever made this was certainly a very fine craftsman,' I said. 'I am no connoisseur, but I do not know that I have ever seen glass look so spectacular.'

'Glass?' said Mala. 'Don't you realise? These nuggets are not glass; they are all precious stones.'

I suppose I should have been impressed, but I was not. I have never seen why such stones were 'precious': they were still only bits of coloured glass to me, albeit of a superior kind. I suppose pearls are O.K. – Nero certainly thought so – but when all is said and done, even though pearls are pretty I prefer my oysters on a plate, preferably with a good Falernian to wash them down.

'So what is this thing worth?' I asked Mala.

'Whatever the market will bear,' he replied. 'There are some people who would give an arm and a leg to get hold of a bowl of this kind.'

'There are some people,' I responded, 'who would give someone else's arm and leg, and head too, to judge from past events.'

'Exactly, and it does knock the bottom out of my original theory.'

'Original theory?'

'You may remember that when we first heard of Pansa's murder, I hypothesised that it probably had something to do with his job in the imperial accounts office. It seems clear now that it is this that was the cause of all the trouble.

'It belongs to Nysa of course, and she presumably has no idea that she has had a thing of such value stored away all this time. We had better take it and put it somewhere safe until she recovers.'

I picked up the bowl, and we left by the rickety stairs that led down by the side of the bakery. By now it was late afternoon, the bakery was closed, and the street outside deserted – almost. There were two men there, just about to enter as we left. The first was a swarthy, evil-looking character who, I just knew instinctively, must be Lucius; the other was big, very big, just about the biggest specimen I had ever seen, about eight feet each way and apparently made of granite. Moreover, in direct violation of the law – not that they were the sort who would care, if they could get away with it – they were both carrying swords.

What happened next was like the little encounter in the tavern at Ostia*. Mala had summed up the situation in an instant, kicked the smaller man in the stomach before he had time to lift his sword, and then employed that vicious chop with the blade of his hand that he called 'carati', that cut the man down like a tree. Mala grabbed the man's sword as he fell, and turned to face the giant.

Unarmed as I was, there was nothing I could do to help, and so I placed my foot on the neck of the fallen man, making ready to run off with Nysa's bowl as fast as I could if Mala was killed – as I feared he must be, for I had recognised his opponent.

Oh ye of little faith. I reckon myself something of a connoisseur of swordsmanship, and know enough myself to hold a weapon by the blunt end; I practice regularly at the gym, and more than hold my own. Nevertheless, it is not false modesty for me to say that I knew immediately that I would not have lasted five minutes against either of the two who now squared up to each other.

For all his size, the giant was agility incarnate, and within seconds he had nearly decapitated Mala with a succession of wicked cuts that came apparently from nowhere. Somehow, though, Mala parried them, and each time produced a riposte that had his man leaping back out of harm's way just in time, cursing as he did so. He had thought, understandably, that he would get the affair over in no time; how wrong he was.

Mala had a most unusual way of fighting. Throughout, he kept sideways on to his opponent, right foot well forward, sword-arm outstretched, his free arm tucked into his hip out of harm's way. He kept his eyes fastened on the other's blade, and whatever attack came – and the giant knew some pretty good ones, as well he might – was able to parry it. When he in turn attacked, his lunge was a joy to behold, a couple of feet or more further than one would have thought possible, twice pinking the big man in the chest when he thought he was well out of range.

It would take more than pinking to stop this man-mountain, though, and Mala knew it. He kept on advancing and retreating more or less on a straight line, turning only sufficiently to keep his opponent's sword-arm in his sights, right foot thrust forward, blade extended, refusing to be drawn by the acrobatic antics of the other as he leapt around vainly seeking a way through Mala's guard.

---

* See *Quintus Propertius and the Affairs of Ventidius Silo*

On it went, and on: in the arena, it would have had them in ecstasy, men would have talked of it for years, would have told their sons proudly that they were there, when Quintus Propertius Mala crossed swords with the Iron Man Glabrus – for it was he, the incomparable.

I was transfixed; when Lucius stirred, I gave him not a glance, just a kick in the head to keep him quiet again. Back and forth they fought, cut, parry, lunge, riposte, every trick in the trade, and some I never suspected existed. Glabrus tried to get in close, where his superior weight would have told greatly, but Mala was too quick for him and too canny.

The end came very suddenly, almost as an anti-climax. The big man lunged mightily, Mala, with the tiniest circular movement of his blade, deflected the menacing point, and next second his own blade had gone straight through the other's sword-arm, to be followed immediately by an upward cut that almost took Glabrus's head from his shoulders.

Lucius stirred, and I kicked him in the head again with some pleasure; and then I looked at Mala with awe.

'You,' I said, 'have just disposed of one of the most efficient killing-machines the arena has ever seen. That was Glabrus, the Iron Man; he was awarded his wooden sword and his freedom less than a year ago; no-one could stand against him.'

'Really,' said Mala, strangely unimpressed. 'He must have been lucky. He knew some clever tricks, but he telegraphed his attack in sixte from a mile away; it was only a matter of time before I got him.'

So much for Rome's greatest gladiator; and I had no idea what Mala meant by 'attack in sixte'. I commented on his unusual style, which undoubtedly disconcerted Glabrus more than somewhat.

'Fencing is a sideways-on game,' he said; 'like cricket, as I remember one old-time player stressing ad infinitum.'

'Cricket?'

'A ball game the Brits play. It keeps them amused, though it's a bit of a mystery to most foreigners.

Lucius stirred again, and Mala dragged him to his feet.

'I think,' he said, 'we must observe the social graces, and introduce this gentleman politely to your friend Molo.'

I did not go to see Lucius's well-deserved end, but Gaius Cornelius did not share my dislike of the arena, and he gave a graphic description.

'Two lionesses went for him at once,' he said, 'and practically pulled him apart; but then a big black-maned specimen cuffed them out of the way and finished the job himself. I shouted out 'That's for Pansa,' but by then our friend Lucius was well past caring. A most satisfactory conclusion to the affair.'

The conclusion was satisfactory in a number of ways. Lucius had been 'persuaded' by Molo and his vigils to confess, and explain. He had indeed been looking for the precious stones, though he did not know Julius Varus, the glass-blower, had embedded them in the bowl: nobody did, for Pansa and his family did not even know they had existed.

That had been Pansa's downfall. Arranging to meet Lucius, and his gladiator side-kick, near the Theatre of Marcellus, supposedly to discuss the spurious two thousand sesterces (which, Nysa told us, he was to inform Lucius in no uncertain terms would not be forthcoming), he found himself being tortured to reveal the whereabouts of stones he know nothing about. Regarding Pansa's protestations as lies, and losing his temper, Glabrus had finally killed him out of hand.

Later, as we know, the two swine had forced their way into Pansa's apartment, and tried to get the two women to tell them where the stones were; again they were met with incomprehension, and again Glabrus killed for what he thought was obstinacy. Luckily for Nysa, it was Lucius who tried to bludgeon her to death, and he was less efficient than his companion; he was about to finish the job when, as we had already gleaned, he was disturbed, and the two decided to make themselves scarce.

'But how did Lucius know about the stones?' I asked Molo. 'And where did they come from in the first place?'

And now we come to the most amazing thing of all, because it involves a kind, caring, generous, good-natured man: one Gaius Olfonius Tigellinus.

'Poor Marcus: dementia has set in early,' I hear you say. 'Kind, caring, generous, good-natured: *Tigellinus*?'

I know; I know. He's been dead more than a quarter of a century, and still his name stinks in the nostrils. He was probably the foulest, most degenerate, vengeful, brutal, sadistic, commander of the Praetorians who has ever held the post: and the competition for that title is pretty fierce, as we all know. It is said that he had a private bet with himself, that he could wantonly destroy more totally innocent people even than the late unlamented Lucius Aelius Sejanus: and it must have been a damn close run thing.

Nor was he one of those men – and there have been a number – who was a devil in his public role, but an angel in private: good husband and father, loyal friend, that sort of thing. On the contrary: even among the debauchees who surrounded Nero at his worst, he stood out as the most perverted, the most degenerate, the most downright disgusting of them all. Caligula himself would have disowned him; indeed, that worthy did exile him, early in his career.

And yet, we are asked to believe, he was kind to his slaves. 'Pull the other one,' would have been my immediate reaction, if I had heard it from any other source. I would have expected Tigellinus rather to have them whipped twice a day, just for amusement, and when he tired of them, not free them and shower them with gifts, but send them to the quarries, or the arena.

And yet I would have been wrong. The older members of Pansa's family, and Nysa's too, had all been attached to the Tigellinus household; so had Pansa himself, and for that matter Lucius. Over the years, he had freed them all; we have seen that he paid for the little apartment Pansa lived in; and – why, under what impulse, we can only conjecture and wonder – he gave Varus, the glass man, the jewels that were to cause all the trouble and heartache.

`Somehow, somewhere, Lucius's father heard of the gift; so in turn did his son. But Varus had died, suddenly, before he could tell his wife, Nysa's mother, what he had acquired and what he had done with them. She kept the cupboard full of his work purely as a memento, a sentimental reminder of what he had been to her; in turn it passed to Nysa, and by extension to Pansa; and none of them knew it contained a small fortune.

When Lucius at last returned to Rome, he was determined to get the stones if he could; what followed, I have told you.

There was a final, fortunate happening to end it all. Nysa recovered, gradually, and she was now, if not rich, at least more comfortably off than she could ever have dreamed. Molo, commander of the local vigiles, took a special interest in her welfare, and saw her often. Though pushing forty, she was still a handsome woman in her way; Molo was a widower; Nature took its course; several of us attended the marriage ceremony, and, as

Mala put it, looked forward sincerely to the couple living happily ever after.

Quintus Propertius and the Estate of the Placid Praetorian

From time to time you come across so-called 'gentle giants', men of vast size and strength who could break most of us in two as soon as look at us, but who choose instead to be peaceful, friendly, obliging, above all non-violent. They have nothing to prove, and so they do not bother trying, and if anyone out of misplaced bravado does attempt to cause trouble, they put him in his place gently, firmly, ever so effectively; and most times the benighted fellow learns his lesson and does not do anything so silly again.

Publius Valgius was one such giant, and I had known him and liked him since I was a boy. He gave me my first lessons in swordsmanship, patiently parrying my childish swipes, gently replying with cuts that finished half an inch from my head. 'Get your blade up, little Marcus; you've a whopping great sword in your hand, use it, or you'll be dead as a dog's dinner.'

I lost contact with him as I grew older: military service called, and then my equestrian duties; my brief marriage; and by the time I took to wondering what might have happened to him and thinking I would like to look him up, I was told he had moved down to Rhegium, about as far away from Rome as you can get in Italy without falling off the edge and into the drink.

All the more surprising, then, one morning in early spring, as I sat in Rufus's Place chatting to Quintus Propertius Mala and trying yet again to fathom that fascinating man, that the doorway should suddenly darken and a huge bulk ease its way into the tavern and then ask Rufus politely for a pitcher of beer.

Beer! I'll never understand how civilised men can drink it. It's O.K. for German louts and other barbarians; the Brits are fond of it, Mala tells me, and that doesn't surprise me; but I'll take a lot of convincing that it's fit for human, let alone decent Roman, consumption.

I had often ribbed Publius Valgius on his taste for the stuff, and I did so again, calling out some ribaldry or other as he settled down with his vast pitcher – to his great surprise.

'Young Marcus!' His eyes lit up with pleasure, 'It must be years…'

'Come and join us,' I said, and introduced him to Mala.

'You two have something in common,' I told them. 'You both know which end to hold a sword, and what to do with it when you've managed.'

Valgius looked at Mala with interest.

'I've heard of you,' he said. 'You are the man who killed that brute Glabrus in single combat last summer. Sir, it is a privilege to meet you.'

Mala looked embarrassed, and I changed the subject.

'What are you doing in Rome?' I asked Valgius. 'The last I heard you were busy chasing the fair ladies of Rhegium.'

Valgius grinned. 'I caught one. She's a tyrant, my wife, keeps me on the straight and narrow something shocking. She even waits up for me when I've had a night with the boys…'

'Nursing her wrath to keep it warm,' put in Mala with a smile.

'Well put!' cried Valgius. 'But I'm very fond of her really, of course.

'It's because of her I'm in Rome,' he went on. 'Her sister here died some weeks ago; widow – died only shortly after her husband; we heard too late to get up for either funeral, and anyway my wife is in dodgy health and can't travel long distances. I'm here to wrap up the estate, and take odd bits and pieces my wife wants to keep back to Rhegium.'

'A rather melancholy task,' said Mala. 'Did the lady have no sons or daughters?'

'There was a son stationed in Britain: Eburacum - wild place; though he did say the beer was good.' He gave me a grin.

'Unfortunately he died of some outlandish disease a couple of years ago. Pity; promising lad.'

'Probably came of drinking the local beer,' I muttered; and then, realising that was in very bad taste: 'Sorry.'

'I'm not finding the job too easy,' went on Valgius. 'Livilla's husband had been a scholar of sorts – historian – and there are scores of scrolls to sift through that frankly mean nothing to me. I don't like simply ditching them in case they might be of some value.'

'Would you like me to look through them for you?' asked Mala. 'I know a little of such things.'

A little! Mala was one of the most erudite men I had ever come across.

'That's very good of you; it would certainly take a load off my mind.'

'I could help, too,' I put in: I am not in Mala's class as a scholar, but I'm not exactly ignorant or illiterate.

And so it was settled. Next morning we met up with Valgius in Rufus's Place – where else? – before going on to his late sister-in-law's dwelling. She had married well, and the *domus*, though not large, was quite exquisite, everything in impeccable taste, and some of the murals staggeringly good.

Mala looked around appreciatively.

'Not a bad little shack,' he remarked; 'and whoever painted these murals knew a thing or two: remind me a bit of Daveed.'

Daveed?

We were not there, though, to admire the murals, but to examine documents, and soon we were surrounded with scrolls, bits of loose parchment, scribbled notes, tablets, all the paraphernalia of the working scholar.

Most of it turned out to be of ephemeral or no interest, and soon Mala and I between us built up a little pile of discarded stuff that could be got rid of without fear. After a while Mala stopped work and reached for the wine Valgius had thoughtfully provided.

'This demonstrates what many of us have long known,' he said, 'that research for the most part is one percent inspiration and ninety-nine percent perspiration. Other workers in the field might find a little of this stuff interesting – we could perhaps pass some over to our friend Tranquillus – but for the most part it is as dry as dust and as dead as Dumnorix.'

'Except maybe this,' I said, and handed him a scroll I had read through two or three times with increasing amazement. It had been in a drawer under a pile of unused papyrus and a jar of gooey-looking paste, and was clearly far older than the rest.

Mala read it rapidly, and then like me went through it a second time and a third, and he too showed his amazement.

'If this truly is what it seems to be,' he said, 'we've got hold of a real hot potato.'

I made a note to ask about 'potato', but forgot: it did not seem important, compared with what was in the scroll.

'If this is genuine,' went on Mala, 'and I would bet my last aurus it is, it is very, very important indeed; and there are people who would kill for it.'

'Not least our dear emperor,' I said. 'After all, he would kill for most things, important or not; and as for *this*…'

'We had better tell Valgius, and see if he knows where it came from. Halvidienus might well have found it by accident – historians sometimes do – but just as possibly he was following a lead, and in that case I would be more than interested to know what it was.'

'I think I would be more worried than interested,' I said. 'I would be afraid of where it might take us. There is a lot to be said for letting sleeping dogs lie.'

'Agreed, but the dogs won't always stay sleeping,' replied Mala. 'If Halvidienus was on to something, you can bet that others will not be far behind. In the wrong hands, I shudder to think…'

True indeed: in the wrong hands, it could make more trouble than an augur at an orgy. I felt a strong desire to be elsewhere, and to forget the whole thing. Unfortunately, as Mala had said, the sleeping dogs probably would wake up, and we ourselves could not unlearn what we had just uncovered.

We questioned Valgius closely, but not surprisingly he had no idea where Halvidienus might have found the incriminating document.

'But what is it?' he asked. 'You seem to be a bit bothered about it.'

'It's nothing much,' I told him; 'nothing much at all. It is only an old letter, purporting to be written by Titus shortly before he became emperor, accusing his brother of treason, and giving chapter and verse: and apparently planning his assassination.'

·

Valgius is essentially a practical man, and like me he said something about letting sleeping dogs lie.

'After all, it is a very old letter, and Titus has been dead and gone these many years. Surely it would be better simply to destroy it. It is not as though we could do anything with it: even if we pinned it up where everyone could see it like an imperial edict, or sent a copy to every senator in Rome, nothing would happen. Domitian has the Praetorians to see to anyone who steps out of line – and the Praetorians are not nice people.'

He knew what he was talking about: he had been a Praetorian himself – he was a natural, with his size and skill at arms. The general ethos of braggadocio and brutality had not been at all to his taste, however, and when an unexpected glut of new recruits gave some the chance of opting out from the corps, he was only too ready to volunteer.

Mala explained patiently.

'If Domitian's opponents get hold of this,' he said, 'they would be foolish to try to use it, but that does not mean they wouldn't. Domitian would then simply deny the charges against himself, and go on to use the document as yet another weapon in his continuing campaign to denigrate Titus. Worse, it would give him the perfect excuse to lash out against anyone he wanted to get rid of.'

'He does not need an excuse,' I interrupted; 'but it would give him the incentive to launch a full-scale pogrom. If the document came into his hands first, he would suitably doctor it, and then the result would be the same.'

'Then burn the scroll,' said Valgius again.

'It's not as simple as that. In the first place, we do not know if there are copies; in the second, if it came from a cache of old papers, a mini-archive of Titus material, Jupiter knows what else might be there. We need to find that cache before anyone else does, not least Domitian himself or his agents. Somehow we must retrace Halvidienus's footsteps.'

'Did he have any co-workers?' I asked Valgius. 'Friends or fellow-historians he might have confided in?'

'There is Julius Silenus. In our absence he was chief mourner at the funeral; I met him just last week. Funny little cove. Said he was Halvidienus's closest friend, but did not seem to think much of him as an historian.'

'That's our man, then, to start with at least.'

'Had we better not look for more stuff here,' I suggested. 'There is still a lot we have not examined.'

'It does not seem likely there is anything else: this scroll was separate from the rest, and clearly is not part of the general collection. It is obviously older than anything else, too. Still, we must be thorough. At least we should be able to proceed more quickly now that we know just what sort of document we are looking for.'

We tackled the rest of the clutter in short order, but, as expected, did not turn up anything of note.

'That's it, then,' said Mala. 'Julius Silenus first thing to-morrow.'

He was a funny little man, just as Valgius had told us, somewhat bird-like in his movements, staccato in speech, clearly a denizen of the scholarly groves, and yet – I had my suspicions – very much of the real world also.

Mala had done a little homework the previous evening, and started by softening up Silenus a little.

'I read your monogram on Hieron of Syracuse,' he said. 'Most interesting, especially your suggestion of the Regulus influence.'

'Suggestion? Suggestion? I established the connection beyond reasonable doubt. Only a bunch of old fogies have questioned it. Cornelius Tacitus is convinced, and his opinion is worth all the rest put together. He would make a fine historian, that man, if he wasn't so wrapped up in public affairs.'

'I'm sure he'll come up with something substantial one day,' agreed Mala. 'So will his friend Pliny, no doubt.'

'Young Pliny? A lightweight. Not half the man his uncle was: I knew him, you know, when I was very young: a walking encyclopaedia. Great pity about the Vesuvius business.'

Mala agreed, and after a little chit-chat, steered the conversation around to Halvidienus.

'Halvidienus? Dilettante. Nice fella; liked him. No historian, though; rich amateur. Didn't publish much.'

We had already gleaned that Silenus was reluctant to acknowledge any merit in others: even his praise of Tacitus had been qualified. The documents we had examined certainly suggested that Halvidienus had been a conscientious and industrious scholar, with a genuine penchant for research and a talent for close scrutiny of evidence. We wondered just how much we would be able to rely on what this tetchy and self-opinionated historian might have to tell us.

In the event it was not much. No, he did not know what Halvidienus had been working on when he died. No, he had never collaborated with him on any research (it would have been beneath him, was the implication). No, Halvidienus had not seemed unduly excited or agitated in the weeks before his death. Yes, he believed the man had consulted the imperial archives once or twice – in an amateur sort of way, you understand. – but he had not heard that anything much had come of it.

'Insufferable oaf,' I said to Mala, as we thankfully made our escape. 'He is the sort of person who gives scholarship a bad name.'

'And there are more of them in the business than you might imagine,' observed Mala. 'It is a universal type. And yet his work is good, and he knows his stuff: they often do, these people, which makes them even more of a pain in the neck.'

'He is more than a pain in the neck: I don't trust him. Why was he so quick to dismiss Halvidienus's work in the imperial archives? Was it merely professional jealousy, or disdain, or did I detect something more? Perhaps I've a suspicious mind.'

'A very good thing to have in this wicked world. I, too, have my doubts about Silenus, but it's only a feeling, and feelings are not evidence. Until we actually find him with his hand in the till, we will have to put him on the back burner.'

I filed Mala's latest outré metaphors in my 'funny turn of phrase' notebook – mental notebook – that I had been keeping almost since I first knew him, and asked him what we did next.

'We could start hunting through the imperial archives.'

It seemed a reasonable idea, providing we had a plausible excuse. As citizens we were allowed to use any of the great public libraries first Augustus, and then in turn Tiberius and Vespasian, had set up, but to look in the imperial archives themselves required special permission: usually granted to bona fide scholars, but not readily to others.

'Time to put on my historian's hat,' Mala decided. 'I think I can remember most of that paper on the Iceni rebellion I perpetrated some years ago: suitably doctored, that should wow them.'

Next morning he appeared bright and early bearing a fresh-looking scroll, which he invited me to look at. Its title was eye-catching: *The Iceni Rebellion: a Trinovantean Perspective*.

I looked through it rapidly, It was a clever piece of work, with some interesting information on the relationship between the Iceni and the

Trinovantes in pre-Boudicca times, and a thought-provoking concluding passage on what might have happened had the two tribes not decided to make common cause: would Boudicca have gone it alone, would she have nursed her grievances and bided her time, perhaps to challenge Roman rule even more devastatingly at a later date, or would she have acknowledged the inevitability of our domination, and learned to live with it despite the way she had been treated?

It was a well-argued and well-reasoned paper, and when Mala asked me if it would convince the powers-that-be that he was a serious historical scholar, there was only one answer.

'I expect Silenus would find something to object to,' I said, 'but for my part I think it should more than pass muster.'

And so it proved, and, with me in tow as a supposed 'research assistant', Mala embarked on his ostensible latest project, which he submitted to the *Procurator Bibliothecarum*, or one of his half-backs, as 'an examination of the financing of the vigiles and the urban cohorts during the reigns of Vespasian and Titus'.

'That should get us into the right general archives,' Mala explained, 'although it will still be like looking for a needle in a haystack. The material will be scattered, too: more leg-work, Marcus, though looking for documents this time rather than bodies. We had better start at the Campus Martius. I suspect Augustus's library there is the very last place we are likely to find what we want, but we must be thorough.'

We were, but found nothing. Augustus's other library, which graced the Aventine, and which I had often admired from the outside, proved equally barren, at least for our purposes, though we did have the privilege of lingering there, admiring the wonderful murals, and the awe-inspiring statue of Apollo that dominated the entrance.

On to the next library, and the next. We came across one or two interesting nuggets in the Vespasian library, near the Temple of Peace, not strictly germane to our project but eyebrow-raising nevertheless (and quite unpublishable), but the Titus collection we were sure existed somewhere continued to elude us.

One advantage of the Vespasian library was that it was not too far from Rufus's Place, and so, when we were quite sure it had nothing more to offer, we repaired to that modest exemplar of the glory that is Rome, and sipped appreciatively at the nectar Rufus provided for us.

'A new one,' he explained. 'Not the greatest vintage in the world, but a lot better than most, I think you'll agree. You'll never guess where it came from.'

It was good: a firm bouquet, a touch of – how shall I call it? – *insouciance* that was very appealing, and an aftertaste that put me in mind of those vintages from the Perusia region, where they care more for getting the vintage *right* than seeing how many more amphorae they can fill this year than last.

'Excellent,' said Mala. 'And it is from…?'

'Gaul,' replied Rufus, and I thought I saw Mala nod appreciatively. 'I nearly turned it down, because you know my feelings – I'm not alone in doubting that anything fit to drink could come from that benighted land. This was a pleasant surprise.'

It was indeed, and we tackled it with increasing enthusiasm as the morning wore away and we took stock of our so-far-fruitless forays into the great libraries of the land.

Luckily we had almost had an elegant sufficiency when the Praetorians arrived, because they did not look as though they would be too keen on waiting around patiently while we tackled another jug or two.

'You are summoned to attend Lucinius Populus,' the centurion told us curtly, and we gained the impression that pleading a prior engagement would not be a totally acceptable reply.

'I'm surprised they haven't developed the goose-step,' Mala muttered, and though I did not know exactly what he meant, the general tenor of the remark was clear enough.

But since we were called, we went, soon to find ourselves in a small office in a corner of the Palace, where Licinius Populus was monarch of all he surveyed.

'Gentlemen, be seated,' he said, though there was about as much bonhomie in his tone as in Nero's saying 'Hi, guys!' to a bunch of manacled Christians.

Licinius Populus was at once a shadowy yet a well-known figure, shadowy in that few people came across him personally, and fewer still cared to, but well-known by reputation in his official capacity.

That capacity was in truth a bit nebulous, since his title was not officially recognised in the roster of government appointees, but 'Chief Investigator' was what he was called and investigator-in-chief was what he was, of anything Domitian might decide needed looking into – which was plenty: the emperor had never hidden his interest in opening windows on men's souls, and if he did not have time to look directly himself, Licinius Populus served as a very good proxy.

'Interested in history, then, are we?'

His question was direct and his tone was not affable: it could not have been more icy if he had been asking us if we still molested little girls and beat up their grandmothers for exercise.

'Recent history at that,' went on the Investigator, as though to imply that researching anything later than the first Samnite War ought to be a capital offence.

'Indeed, we are,' said Mala, deciding to meet him head on. 'We live in most interesting times, and the last twenty-five years have been among the most fascinating in Rome's history, wouldn't you agree?'

'Shut up. I am inclined to think you are not scholars at all. You have left acres of scrolls untouched that have a direct bearing on – what is it? - "the financing of the vigiles and the urban cohorts"; as though that's any damned business of yours.'

'But of course,' said Mala. 'We have only done the preliminary trawl. My colleague has a list of what we now propose to home in on, and quite a list it is. Show the gentleman, Marcus.'

I uttered a silent prayer of thanks to Mala for his foresight.

'We must guard our backs,' he had said. 'Ostensibly we are engaged in a specific piece of research, and that is what it must look like.'

In addition to searching for the Titus material, therefore, he had taken time to make notes of anything that looked as though it might be relevant to our putative project, and instructed me to make a list of what he had found. It was this that I made ready to hand to the Investigator, but he showed no interest.

'Forget it,' he said. 'I mean, quite literally, *forget it*. It does not meet the emperor's wishes that you, or anyone else, should pursue this kind of fatuous research. If you want to dabble in history, try something more suitable: the influence of Greek trade on the development of Egyptian manufacture, for example; or perhaps,' he smiled evilly, 'the interactions of the Iceni and the Trinovantes tribes before that bitch Boudicca got uppity.

'But your present mistaken enterprise is *quite out of order*. Don't think of it again - *ever*. You may go.'

We left the Palace, as we had entered, by a side door, and I saw that even Mala, normally so calm and composed, was looking more than a little frayed at the edges. For my part, I felt limp, disorientated even. Men like Licinius Populus, manifestly lacking normal human emotions, yet, equally, relishing the enormous power they wield, have that effect on those unfortunate enough to fall into their clutches, and indeed exploit it to their advantage.

Populus had not ranted, not threatened, had offered no physical violence, but for all that, we knew beyond doubt the danger we were in, and he knew we knew, and played on our knowledge, and revelled in it. This was what it must have been like to fall foul of Tigellinus, of Sejanus, of Macro, and a score of others, less elevated, but still men of frightening power who did their masters' dirty work with an efficiency, a ruthlessness, and an enthusiasm that went far beyond the call of duty.

'He knew what we were supposedly looking for,' said Mala; 'he knew that I had written about the Iceni and the Trinovantes; he knew which documents we had and hadn't consulted. Did he know, or guess, what we *really* were after?'

'Probably not,' I said,' or I doubt we would be here now; more likely we would be chained to a wall, while they sweated us to tell all we knew.'

'I think you're right, and for the time being at least we can hope Populus will lose interest in us. I would like to know why he was interested in the first place. At any one time there are scores of people innocently using the archives, and *prima facie* our little foray into economic history was as innocent as any. Why were we warned off?'

'Silenus?'

'Very possibly. He might do regular work for Populus: a name here, a hint there, betrayed confidences: I am sure he is capable of it. Alternatively, it might be that he has some little scheme of his own that our interest in Halvidienus is somehow thwarting, and he tipped off Populus anonymously to put a spoke in our wheels. I would like to learn a little more about friend Silenus, before tackling him again. 'Before that, though, there is the curious matter of Halvidienus's library.'

'But Halvidienus did not have a library.'

'That is what is curious. He was a man of more than average means; he was an amateur scholar; he was the sort of person to whom books are the very stuff of life; and yet he did not have his own library, only that rather cluttered and disorganised study where we found the miscellaneous scrolls.

'Where are his copies of the classics: Livy, Horace, Virgil, the Greeks? Where the contemporary plays and novels and satires? The scrolls we examined were only historical papers, or copies thereof, and Halvidienus's own scribblings. No educated Roman would have such a dearth of proper books in his house, even if he did not have a fully-fledged library. We must have a word with Valgius about it.'

We made our way to the Halvidienus dwelling, where Valgius was already waiting. He was, for him – normally so placid a man - in a state of some agitation.

'Halvidienus's scrolls,' he told us, 'have all been taken away.'

.

He had returned from his latest bout of trudging around Rome, meeting all the numerous people, bankers, lawyers, petty officials, and attending to all of the niggling tasks, inseparable from winding up an estate; he had been kept busy constantly with such matters while we were engaged in our abortive 'research' in the great libraries. This day had been an especially frustrating one, and he had been looking forward to relaxing with a jug of Halvidienus's best, and then putting the cook to work to provide all three of us with what he felt was a richly-deserved meal.

Instead he found the house in turmoil, and his late brother-in-law's chief slave badly shaken.

'I could not stop them, sir,' that worthy had told Valgius. 'There were six of them, they were armed, and they said they came with the authority of the Chief Investigator. They took every single one of my master's scrolls, both the pile you had put aside to destroy and those you had said were to be kept; they simply shovelled them up like litter, and then threw them in a sack and made off with them.

'They also stole things. They did not think I would notice, but I know riff-raff like that and I kept my eyes open. There was the little Etruscan vase my mistress used especially to treasure, and that gold statuette of Osiris my master had brought back from Egypt only last year: small things, but valuable.'

'Damn,' said Valgius. 'They were two of the pieces my wife particularly wanted me to look out for.'

'I fear you will not see them again,' I said. 'More serious still, though, are the scrolls. We know that most of the stuff is not worth the papyrus it is written on, but if they've got the Titus letter, all hell could break loose.'

'They haven't,' said Mala. 'It was too dangerous to leave lying around, and so with Valgius's agreement I removed it for safe keeping.'

'Thank Jupiter for that.' I spoke with feeling, for a further interview with the Chief Investigator was not something I would have looked forward to at the best of times, and if he had had the Titus letter in his hands, it would not have been the best of times.

Valgius had not yet heard of our encounter with the Investigator, and so Mala filled in the details.

'The removal of the scrolls might be a blessing in disguise,' he went on. 'As Marcus has said, we know they contain absolutely nothing of interest, nothing incriminating, and they may well convince Populus that we are indeed beyond suspicion: for which relief much thanks.'

'Nevertheless, I doubt that he will restore our right to work in the archives,' I had to say, 'and so we've hit a blank wall there.'

'What if Halvidienus had found more Titus scrolls, and simply destroyed them?' asked Valgius. 'Perhaps they did not add much to the letter we found, and he did not think they were worth keeping. Or perhaps they added all too much, and were too hot to handle.'

'I accept the first hypothesis,' said Mala, 'that Halvidienus might have stumbled on more documents than the one we've seen, but I don't buy the second. It goes against all a scholar's instincts to destroy original documents, and if they *were* innocuous, there would have been no need. If they were not, it is far more likely Halvidienus would have done his best to conceal them. After all, he did not destroy the letter we found, and that was not even thoroughly hidden. Anything else, if it exists, must surely be around somewhere.'

'But where? I went through this house very thoroughly even before you arrived, to make an inventory, and I assure you nothing was found.'

'We are back to the mystery of the non-existent library,' and Mala went on to repeat to Valgius what he had said to me about the strange absence of books.

'It had struck me, too,' replied Valgius. 'I had meant to question the slaves on the matter, but have been too tied up. Let's do it now.'

He summoned Camillus, Halvidienus's head slave and general factotum.

'Indeed, Halvidienus had a very extensive library, sir: he was very proud of it, said it was better than that of many a rich senator. It was housed in that large room next to the main bedroom, where there are now just a couple of couches and a solitary table. After my master's death, Livilla Plantina was persuaded to sell it in its entirety.'

'And who did the persuading?' asked Mala; and 'who bought it?' I added: our suspicious minds were very much on the same wavelength.

'But, naturally sir, the answer to both questions is Julius Silenus.'

'Surprise, surprise,' I said.

'Silenus also wanted to look through the papers in the study, but my mistress would not agree to this.'

'Did you have any idea what was in your master's library?' asked Mala. 'Did you have anything to do with it? Can you read?'

'Indeed I can, sir,' said Camillus proudly; 'I even helped my master once to re-catalogue his collection. The catalogue is with the household inventory, master,' he turned to Valgius, 'that you deposited with Mammius the banker the first day after you arrived from Rhegium.'

'I would greatly like to see that catalogue,' Mala said to Valgius. 'This is not idle curiosity: we need to try to fathom why Silenus bought the entire collection, when it must have included many standard works he almost certainly would already have possessed.'

'I'll have it collected from Mammius first thing in the morning,' promised Valgius. 'I must say, the plot certainly thickens.'

'More, perhaps, than you might think,' replied Mala. 'Now what I would like to know is how your sister-in-law and her husband died.'

'Surely you do not suspect foul play?'

'I suspect anything and nothing; at the moment I am merely gathering information. It does arouse my curiosity, though, when a man and his wife, still both in early middle age, die within a few weeks of each other.'

He turned to Camillus.

'Were your master and mistress in ill health? Were their deaths unexpected? What did they die of? The plague? Seizures? The falling sickness?'

'It was not my place to say anything, sir, but their deaths *were* unexpected. Decimus Halvidienus always prided himself on being fit for his age: he went to the gym regularly, and he was a great walker. But he did not die of illness. He slipped at the baths, and struck his head against the plinth of a statue. A most unfortunate accident.'

'Slipped? Was he given to slipping? Unsteady on his feet usually? It sounds unlikely, from what you say about his fitness.'

'No-one actually saw it happen, sir, but the floor was wet and slippery: everyone assumed it was an accident; there did not seem to be anything else it could be.'

'And who found the body?'

'Julius Silenus, as it happened.'

Mala and I exchanged glances.

'His slave had just helped him out of the pool; he says he heard Halvidienus cry out, and found him on the floor with a gash in his head, quite dead.'

'So much for Licinius Halvidienus,' said Mala. 'A fit man; no history of falling sickness; an habitué, like most Romans, of the baths, and as used to wet floors as he was to hot dinners; and yet he falls, and the fall is fatal. How many such fatal falls, pray, are recorded in Rome in an given year? And if they do happen, invariably it is to old, frail men, unsteady on their feet at the best of times.'

'But you can't suggest that Silenus was the murderer, if murder it was: *he* is the rather old man, and far from robust; Halvidienus was the middle-aged fitness fanatic.'

'Sirs,' said Camillus; 'if I may speak?'

'Go ahead.'

'Silenus was comparatively old, and comparatively frail, but his body slave who was there was a strapping young Greek, who at one time was thought maybe destined for the arena. I knew him: nasty character.'

There was silence as we digested this. Finally Mala addressed the slave again.

'And your mistress? Was she in good health normally? What did she die of?'

'She always seemed so, but after my master died, she just seemed to fade away. She grew listless, she took less and less food, it was almost as though she had lost the will to live. Some said she was simply pining for her husband.'

Valgius snorted.

'Livilla was very attached to her husband, there is no doubt, and she would have been sad when he died; but she was a mature woman, not some love-sick girl besotted by trashy Greek novels. Fade away? Piffle.'

'Did she have many visitors after Halvidienus died?' Mala asked the slave.

'Very few. Julius Silenus came regularly almost to the last.'

'I'll bet he did: anxious to grab Halvidienus's library, and then to get the widow safely out of the way in case she started wondering why. A slow poison, most likely.'

'Things are moving a bit fast for me,' I said. 'I share your dislike of Silenus: he's an arrogant, conceited, churlish popinjay, and deceitful to boot. It is a big jump, though, to imply he's a murderer: a double murderer.'

'I'm not implying,' replied Mala; 'I'm asserting ; and I intend to prove it. He had the means, he had the motive, he had the money to buy the Halvidienus library, which was central to his schemes, and, last but not least, he has the moral sensibility of an alley-cat.'

'Can you say that, after meeting him only once. I know he was unpleasant, but murder…'

'Villainy,' said Mala, 'is very often incremental: first a few sesterces, stolen from a blind man's bowl; then a handful, from a stall-keeper's till; next a mugging, mild to start with, a couple of thumps and away with the victim's purse; eventually serious bodily harm, and serious money; and at last, as sure as night follows day, murder, accidental perhaps to begin with, too much zeal, but at the end – murder most foul.'

'Are you suggesting Julius Silenus took money from blind men's bowls?'

'The equivalent: the scholarly equivalent. First, a few unkind comments about a rival's work; in time, the attempt to destroy a reputation; judicious 'borrowing' from what someone else has written; eventually downright plagiarism; first curtness and vagueness when questioned about a late acquaintance's research; shortly thereafter, an attempt to get the questioner into serious trouble with the Chief Investigator – or do you really believe our encounter with Lucinius Populus had nothing to do with Silenus? It all adds up, doesn't it? I've seen the same sort of thing, or its equivalent, all too often, perpetrated by so-called scholars: honest and humble seekers after truth and knowledge – *they* would have us believe. I tell you, I've seen it all before.'

'Where?' I wondered. From time to time Mala spoke as though he had had a whole career, a whole life, quite apart from his existence in Rome. I wondered, too, why he had spoken more heatedly than I had ever known before, when he came to the perfidy of scholars. His animosity towards Silenus seemed all-but visceral, and he confirmed it with his next remark.

'Until now I have only had my suspicions; after what I have heard this evening I am as sure of that man's guilt as it is possible to be.'

Valgius had been listening with growing agitation to what Mala had to say.

'If you are right, I will break every bone in his body.'

It was the first time I had ever heard him threaten violence to anyone. Always in the past, when confronted with villainy, he had shaken his head in disbelief at the wickedness of the world, and spoken more in sorrow than in anger. It was a measure of his outrage at what had happened to his sister-in-law and her husband that he should express himself as he had.

The next morning found Mala examining carefully the catalogue of Halvidienus's library Valgius had retrieved from the banker. He seemed especially interested in the Greek section.

'Why did Halvidienus have two identical copies of Aristotle's *Poetics*? Fetch Camillus.'

The slave provided the answer at once.

'My master bought the second only a little while before he died,' he told us. 'He dabbled in literary studies on the side, as a kind of relief from his historical labours, and he said he had some emendations to make and did not want to disfigure his present copy.'

'Emendations?'

'Something to do with *catharsis* sir, I think that's the word: whatever it means.'

'And those two copies of the *Poetics* both went to Silenus?'

'Yes, sir. He took the lot, though it was the history he was most interested in.'

'Good; let us hope that Silenus has been poring over Thucydides and Herodotus, rather than informing himself about the nature of tragedy: with luck, the tragedy will be his. But I need to see those two copies of Aristotle; just possibly one or the other will provide the clue we need. But how to get them?'

'I could offer to buy them back from Silenus,' said Valgius. 'If it is the history he is mainly interested in, he might agree. I could tell him they were of sentimental value.'

'*Two* copies? He would be suspicious at once. Trouble is, I don't know which one we are interested in.'

'How big a household does Silenus have?' he asked Camillus. 'I saw only the doorman, and a woman who seemed to be a housekeeper of some sort.'

'There are very few others, sir: Silenus is comfortably off, but not a rich man. There is a cook; a couple of young Egyptian girls, whose function I am not sure of.' He sniffed. 'And, of course, there is the Greek.'

'I think I must pay a visit to Silenus,' said Mala; 'but when he is not there.'

'You're not thinking of breaking in, sir?' asked Camillus, looking rather worried. 'At night Silenus has a huge mastiff patrolling the grounds – big as a Nubian lion, sir, and not half so friendly.'

'Nothing so dramatic,' smiled Mala. 'I will go in broad daylight, and talk my way past the doorman. I will choose a time when Silenus is visiting his patron – who, by chance, I happen to know. A word in his ear will keep Silenus away for long enough.'

I do not know how he managed it – I suspect he played on the doorman's assumed antipathy towards his master, reinforced with a silver coin or two – but he told the slave he had some books for the historian, and was allowed to wait in the library, well knowing that Silenus would not be likely to turn up for a long time.

'It did not take me long to find the scrolls,' he told us. 'Silenus had his own *Poetics*, but it was easy to distinguish it from the Halvidienus copies – which I liberated. I took some other scrolls with me to substitute, suitably tagged *Poetics* of course, and so he is not likely to notice they have gone, unless he suddenly takes an unwonted interest in Greek drama and criticism.

'But now to see what we have.'

He settled down on a couch, the scrolls spread out before him on a table. He did not attempt to read word for word, preferring only to unroll each scroll rapidly, his eyes glancing cursorily over the text as he did so. He soon discarded the first copy of Aristotle's masterpiece, and was half-way though the second before pausing, emitting a whistle of surprise, and then re-reading attentively what he had found.

'You are something of a Greek scholar, friend Marcus,' he said eventually. 'What do you make of this?'

I scanned the familiar words, and then stopped: no sooner had the topic of *catharsis* been introduced, than, suddenly, the Greek gave way to Latin; not only that, the very parchment the *Poetics* had been written on itself changed, to another of quite different texture, cleverly pasted onto the original. There were three separate documents, each pasted to the other, before the original parchment appeared again, and the argument of the *Poetics* continued where it had left off.

'That is as good a way of hiding documents as I can think of,' remarked Mala, 'providing you can be reasonably sure no-one is going to read the scroll all through.. And, by Jupiter, *what* documents.'

I nodded in agreement. If the original Titus letter was a – what was Mala's strange phrase: 'hot potato'? – then these were a positive oven-full.

'Everything falls into place,' said Mala. 'There still is not evidence to convict Silenus, I fear, but at least we now can see what the business was all about.'

'You had better tell me, then,' interjected Valgius, 'for I have not a clue what is going on.'

'Willingly; and call Camillus to hear this also: he deserved to know as much as anyone.'

Though, like me, Valgius appreciated a good slave, he was a little surprised at this, but agreed, and summoned the man. The three of us waited as Mala sat silent for a moment or two, and then launched into his explanation.

'The first clue that all was not as it might seem,' he told us, 'is in the status quo in Rome to-day: Domitian lives, he is emperor, and has been these many years – all too many. What, then, of the plot Titus supposedly uncovered, and his plan to have his errant brother removed? If the letter had been written immediately before Titus's death, the explanation would have been obvious: he would have had no chance to act on what he knew before Domitian succeeded to the purple. The letter, however, is dated almost a year before Titus died. What happened in the meantime?

'It seemed reasonable to assume there were more documents, a 'Titus archive', that might shed light on the matter, which is why Marcus and I spent the time we did in the libraries. We were pretty exhaustive in our searches, though, and I was ready to abandon that line of enquiry even before we had our friendly chat with Licinius Populus. There was, it is true, the possibility that what we were seeking had been deposited not in the great libraries but in one or other of the temple archives, but for a variety of reasons that seemed unlikely.

'The only other possibility, unless the missing documents simply did not exist, was that they were in private hands: Halvidienus's, or even Silenus's. Silenus I eliminated at once. Had he had any of the documents, even with Halvidienus possessing the first letter, he would not have needed to kill, nor to go to the lengths of buying the dead man's library.

'And so it had to be Halvidienus. But we must return to that original letter. It seemed a little strange to me, even at the time we found it, that it was not better hidden, but it dawned on me when I learned that Halvidienus had two copies of the *Poetics* that it very likely nearly was. Marcus, what was in the drawer where you found it, apart from Titus's letter itself?'

'Nothing, except for a pile of unused papyrus.'

'Nothing?'

'Only a little jar of some sticky substance, paste or something...' I gaped as the penny dropped.

'Paste,' agreed Mala. He then explained briefly to Valgius and Camillus how we had found the documents inserted into the second copy of the *Poetics*.

'Halvidienus had clearly been intending to hide the first letter in the same way the other documents, presumably the very evening he was killed. I suspect, however, that he dropped a hint, perhaps even a little more than a hint, to Silenus, that he had stumbled across something important.'

'Or possibly,' interrupted Valgius, and he looked black as pitch, 'Silenus and his bully-boy forced the information out of him before they murdered him: it was late and there were not many people in what after all are enormous baths: there might well have been no-one else in the tepidarium where Halvidienus supposedly had his fall; they could have had plenty of opportunity.'

'A distinct possibility,' agreed Mala. 'Silenus would not have been above torture to get what he wanted.'

'But, sir, what was in the remaining documents that made them so important?' asked Camillus.

'Money.'

'Money?'

'Not coin of the realm, but money nonetheless. Domitian survived because he paid to survive. Think back to Vespasian's reign. The emperor was forever short of money, yet obliged to spend it like water: the library, extending the Theatre of Marcellus, the Colosseum, the legions themselves. Even though on occasion, we know, he could be generosity itself, on the whole he squeezed every last sesterce from the rich, until the pips squeaked – sacrificing much popularity as a result. Money, from whatever source, was always welcome to him.

'Domitian was independently wealthy: most certainly he took bribes in his youth from Orientals, and some even suspected him of being involved in organised crime. It is true Vespasian had the power to simply strip him of his wealth, but he could hardly submit his younger son to such humiliation – especially as he had humiliated him often enough as it was, by his repeated refusal to appoint him to high office.

'Titus, ever the faithful lieutenant, knew all this. To oblige Domitian to liquidate a goodly part of his fortune, and pass it over to the Treasury, on pain of death for treason if he refused, must have seemed to him a very good idea. He might even have invented the treason plot, in order to raise the revenue: we know there was no love lost between him and his brother.'

I protested strongly at this.

'Get real, Marcus,' Mala told me curtly. 'I know you revere Titus, but try doing it this side idolatry. He was a fine emperor, but that does not mean his hands were wholly clean: what emperor's are? Ask Eprius, and Caecena, and their friends. Domitian being the kind of man he is, we are all disposed to believe him guilty as charged, but political reality is political reality.

'Whatever, it does not affect the present business: Domitian was accused of treason; he had to buy his way out of trouble; the documents pertaining to the affair exist; and somehow they fell into the hands of Halvidienus – and led to his death, and his wife's.'

'Which we still can't prove Silenus to be guilty of,' said Valgius bitterly.

'Perhaps not,' replied Mala, 'but that does not mean he will go unpunished. There are ways…'

How Mala managed to plant all the incriminating documents on Silenus, he never told us: probably the complaisant doorman had something to do with it. How he managed to hint to Licinius Publius that the Silenus residence would be worth investigating, without letting that worthy know where the tip-off came from, he also did not reveal. All we know for certain is that the historian disappeared, and was not seen for days, until, one dark night, his body was found dumped outside his own door. Not all his limbs had been broken, and several square inches of his aged body were not covered in bruises and lacerations.

There was one further development to the affair, and a coda. The development did not exactly please us, though Mala was confident he had covered his tracks: we were summoned again to wait on Licinius Populus. It is true that only two Praetorians came this time, and they were no more surly and unpleasant than could have been expected; but still…

The Investigator looked even more coldly menacing than on the previous occasion, though, surprisingly, he greeted us almost cordially – if a poisonous snake can greet one cordially.

'It seems, gentlemen, I owe you something of an apology. It transpired that one Julius Silenus had been dropping poison into my ear, and trying to incriminate two worthy Roman citizens. That was very wicked of him, wasn't it?

'He even tried it again when he was – er – helping us with our enquiries, libelling his late friend Licinius Halvidienus. What a thing to do, when he was the guilty party all along. N But all's well that ends well. I do not believe Julius Silenus will be spreading any more false accusations; none at all.'

He smiled his evil smile, as though to say: 'It is a wicked, wicked world, my friends, but, alas, we have to put up with it.'

He smile disfigured his face again for a moment, and then was gone.

'You are model citizens, gentlemen, I am sure of it. Do continue on that path, won't you? If you didn't I would be most upset; most upset indeed; very, very upset.

'Good-bye.'

But as we left he called out.

'Be very careful, won't you, what new research you undertake?'

We walked away from the Palace rather briskly; one does, after an interview with the Chief Investigator.

There was an item of news next day; Camillus told us as he opened the door of the Halvidienus residence.

'I've just heard, sirs: Silenus's Greek, Demetrius, is dead. He was found in an alley: his neck had been broken.'

We passed the news on to Valgius. He evinced no surprise; and did I notice on his face a strange look of satisfaction: a look of calm satisfaction on the face of that gentle, that oh-so-gentle giant?

Quintus Propertius and the Demise of the Gullible Gaul

Dabrix the Gaul was - or so we thought - a Gaul in name only. He was descended from some minor chieftain who had thrown in his lot with Rome from the start: I believe there is a kindly reference to him in the *Gallic Wars*, but can't put my finger on it. The chieftain, as they do, had become more Roman than the Romans, and indeed the entire family eventually had upped stakes and moved to the Imperial City itself. They had brought a small fortune with them, and were able to live in some comfort at five percent, augmented from the proceeds of a little import-export business they set up, trading chiefly with Britain and Belgica. Dabrix's father had been granted citizenship by Nero, had managed to keep his nose clean at the time of the four emperors, and flourished under Vespasian, but died rather unpleasantly, since he had unwisely chosen to take a trip to Pompeii in the August of 79.

Dabrix himself, when I first got to know him, was a tall, gangling middle-aged man-about-town, with widely-canvassed aspirations as an amateur sculptor and a decidedly effort-free lifestyle. He had a magnum opus, so he told us, almost ready to be shown, but somehow its appearance kept being put back and back, possibly because the amount of wine he drank made him incapable, most of the time, of holding a chisel steadily enough to find the marble he was supposed to be mutilating.

Withal, he was regarded as harmless, quite lacking in malice or mendacity, and by and large popular with the clientèle of the various wine-shops where he put in an appearance most days of his life. Young Servius Javolenius, it is true, tended to lose patience with him. Himself the younger son of a rich senatorial family, he too had had his stint as a young man-about-town, but he was scarcely half Dabrix's age, and he spent only a little time in riotous living, before the sense of duty and service that had been instilled in him since he was a boy asserted itself, and at the time I am referring to he was preparing diligently for his forthcoming tour of duty as a military tribune.

'That man,' he said of Dabrix, 'is a prime example of the dangers of riches without responsibility.'

'Seemingly, but some avoid the danger. Look at Septimus Dravidus: superficially he is the same type, though a literary man rather than a sculptor, and appreciative of the business end of a wine-cup, but he does actually write: I've seen some of his stuff, and it's not bad. A private income does not necessarily lead to a futile life – else where would you and I be?'

'We,' replied Javolenius, 'know our duty as Roman aristocrats. Besides, Dravidus is a literary man: have I not heard it alleged that the study of literature is essentially a civilising influence?'

'So some believe. Mala disagrees, and quotes in support some vituperative fellow called Fa Laevus: I think that's the name - I've never heard of him myself.'

Dabrix, emphatically not a literary man - probably he had not read half a dozen books in his life - continued on his rudderless round, perhaps chipping a bit now and then from his putative masterpiece, and doing his bit to keep the wine-merchants of Rome in the state to which they had happily become accustomed. Rufus once or twice had to ask him to leave the premises, but for the most part he sat in his corner and downed his Falernian – he could afford the best – and exerted himself only when nature called, or he could summon up the energy for a half-hearted game of dice.

One thing Dabrix was not, was street-wise. In one of the less reputable of the taverns he frequented, he was regularly overcharged for his wine, for he had a habit of never looking at his change, and it did not once occur to him that this might be happening. Hangers-on were prominent in this place, and they cheerfully downed the wine be bought them, without his ever cottoning-on to the fact that they were taking him for a ride.

His banker was Publius Lucius, who was widely known to be about as straightforward and trustworthy as Domitian was kind and considerate, but Dabrix was, in equal measure, hurt and uncomprehending, when some of us suggested he move his money to someone who at least paid lip-service to the banking code of conduct, and ipso facto was no more than about fifty percent devious and dishonest.

He was fond of the fair sex, was Dabrix, or had been in his younger days, when he was sober enough for long enough to manage what was required of him, and there were a few little lads and lasses running about Rome whose form and features were decidedly Gallic, but who did not know their daddy, and whose mummies were known to be hard-working girls. Even in these affairs he was exploited, and I know for a fact that he was paying maintenance to three pretty ladies, whose little curly-headed darlings had nothing whatever to do with him, but a great deal with their regular visits to the Praetorian camp, or, in one case, with an over-eager matelot who had made the most of his brief run ashore.

Dabrix lived in an apartment on the very edge of the Subura (conveniently close to Rufus's Place, as it happens), quite a respectable and well-appointed little pad. His brother, who was head of the family, had bought it for Dabrix outright, to get his sibling out of his hair and from under the feet of his wife, a prim and proper lady – *echt* Roman – who did not want her well-brought-up offspring to see more than was strictly necessary of their disreputable idle uncle.

I know what you're thinking. 'Just the type to get himself mugged on the way home from the wine-shop, or perhaps even murdered outside his own front door.'

Well, no. It was outside his own front door, as it happens, but the body was not his, it was that of Aulus Epirota; Dabrix was indeed right there, swaying in the wind as usual, with a very blood-stained dagger held in his trembling right hand.

It is typical of his worldly nous that he was standing there thus, in flagrente delicto as it were, just as the local vigiles appeared on the scene making their early-evening rounds.

"Allo,' said the perceptive vigil in charge. 'What's all this 'ere?'

It was all too obvious what it was, and so they bundled him off to the station, scraped the mortal remains of Aulus Epirota from the deck, and prepared to ask the uncomprehending Gaul a few decidedly leading questions.

Instead of answering, he mumbled my name, again and again, and he was so obviously under the affluence that the station commander, who happened to be Gaius Molo, sent a messenger to find me with a request that I hurry to the station.

'There's a fellow there,' said the messenger, 'drunk as a skunk, who keeps asking for you. It looks very much as though he has been sticking holes in an unfortunate gentleman: a very unfortunate gentleman, 'cos he was extremely dead when last I looked at him.'

It happened that Quintus Propertius Mala was with me, relaxing over a flask of my best, having dropped in unexpectedly to show me his latest acquisition. This was a beautifully-carved ebony stick, with silver bands at intervals down its length, which he told me he was going to carry regularly as a deterrent to the ungodly, and I agreed with him that was not a bad idea in these violent times. But of that more anon.

We hurried along with Molo's man to the rather forbidding red-brick building from where the vigiles plied their trade, and Gaius Molo met us at the door.

'It looks an open and shut case,' he told us. 'The fellow was caught literally red-handed; his tunic was splattered with blood too. The victim had been stabbed half a dozen times, and there was no doubt the dagger your friend was holding was the murder weapon. He is so manifestly drunk, though, that I wondered that he would be able to do damage to a ripe pumpkin.'

'He is not exactly my friend,' I told Molo, who was; 'more of a casual acquaintance. He drops into Rufus's pretty regularly, among other places: lots of people know Dabrix the Gaul, he's a bit of a local institution.'

'So that's who he is,' said Molo. 'I know of him, of course; it's more than once the lads have had to pick him up from the gutter and get his safely home, but I had never actually set eyes on him, and nor had any of the contingent who were actually on duty this evening. He's rather well-heeled, I understand?'

I nodded.

'There was certainly plenty in his purse, and his clothes are good quality, but he's not a narrow-striper or anything. One of the idle rich, then.'

'That's a reasonable description,' I agreed, 'though 'very well off' rather than rich. He does not have to work, and his allowance would make most honest toilers green with envy.'

'I would not be very envious of him at the moment,' said Molo. 'Unless something remarkable transpires, he has a date coming with the Tarpeian Rock – if he's lucky.'

'It seems so unlike him,' I told Molo. 'Until this evening, I would not have thought he would hurt a fly.'

'They are often the dark horses,' replied Molo, 'especially after they have had a few and the inhibitions are weakened. And do not forget, he is a Gaul: they can get very touchy sometimes if they feel they have been slighted. Whatever, when a man is found standing over a corpse full of holes, with a bloody dagger in his right hand, it takes a bit of doing to regard him as innocent.'

'But I think I might manage it,' put in Quintus Propertius Mala, who had been listening intently. 'You said his *right* hand? I know Dabrix only slightly, but I could swear he was left-handed.'

I had known Dabrix considerably longer than Mala had, yet I had not even noticed, but if he, with his powers of observation, said the man was left-handed, I was prepared to believe he was.

'Let's put it to the test,' said Mala. 'Is he in a fit state to talk to us?'

'He's just a little soberer now, but not exactly calm and collected. It can't do any harm for you to see him.'

Dabrix was indeed in a pitiful condition. He was pale as alabaster, trembling uncontrollably, and had obviously been weeping. ('No true Roman,' I thought to myself, 'would have lost control of himself like that whatever the circumstances; but after all, he *is* a Gaul.')

Mala came straight to the point.

'Dabrix, you must pull yourself together. It is important that you tell us in your own words just what happened this evening.'

It was not much. He had left Rufus's Place in a somewhat parlous state, and Aulus Epirota, a kindly man, had offered to help him home. (Rather a case of the blind leading the blind, I mused, for Epirota was far from a teetotaller, though in fairness I had never seen him in quite the state that for Dabrix was par for the course.) They had staggered back more or less successfully, Dabrix, as some wit had once put it, shopping on both sides of the road, until, right in front of his own apartment, his friend had removed his steadying hand in order to try to open the door. At that point Dabrix had gone out like a light, and collapsed in a heap. He knew no more until he found himself standing there, propped against the door, Epirota's body at his feet, and the vigiles grabbing hold of him and taking the knife from his hand.

Mala had been writing all this down on a piece of papyrus the duty-man at the desk had found him, and when he had finished he looked directly at Dabrix and handed the man what he had written.

'I would like you to read that, and confirm it is a true account of what you have told me.'

Dabrix scanned the papyrus, blinking back the tears as he read. Finally, he nodded.

'Please confirm that,' ordered Mala, and held out the stylus. Dabrix took it and scribbled at the bottom of the sheet.

Molo and I exchanged glances.

'We had better go to my office,' said the vigil. He turned to two of his men who had been standing by the door, looking bored. 'Keep your eye on the prisoner,' he ordered; 'not that he is likely to cause any trouble. *Treat him properly.* Got it?'

They had; Molo had a wonderfully persuasive manner. As we left I noticed one of them was even asking Dabrix if he wanted a cup of water.

'There's room for doubt, I think you'll agree,' said Mala, as soon as we were seated in the vigil's sanctum sanctorum. 'In the first place, violence of this kind is utterly out of character for the man; in the second, he was too drunk to pose a threat to anyone, let alone a big chap like Aulus Epirota; and in the third, you clearly saw him take the stylus and confirm the document with his *left* hand, though the dagger was found in his right.'

'It does look suspicious,' agreed Molo. 'I'll have to hold him, of course, but I'll report that there are serious doubts about his guilt and that he might have been the victim of a frame-up. If the true culprit is going it be found, though, it will have to be soon. You and I do not want to see a probably innocent man convicted, but the powers-that-be don't look at it quite like that. As far as they are concerned, a crime has been committed, a man has been caught apparently red-handed, and the District's crime statistics will get a much-needed boost. Justice, I'm afraid, will have very little to do with it.'

'Finding the perpetrator of a murder of this kind,' I said morosely, 'will be like finding a virgin in the Subura: not impossible, but the odds are against it. Dabrix's best chance is to get a good lawyer; his family is well-enough off to afford the best.'

'And justice even then will have little to do with it,' replied Mala with surprising vehemence. 'I find our much-vaunted Roman courts impress me less the more I see of them. The verdict more often than not goes not to the most water-tight case, but to the side whose lawyer is the best rhetorician – providing all the bribes have been properly paid.'

'You exaggerate, Mala,' I told him: some of my best friends are lawyers; 'though I admit there is an element of truth in what you say. All the more reason, then, to get the best lawyer, and for Dabrix's family to be prepared to splash their money around. We'd better get in touch with his brother right away.'

'Will you see to that, please? I want to tackle the Aulus Epirota angle. He is the real victim, Dabrix merely a convenient scapegoat. I want to know *why* Epirota was murdered. The answer to that might lead us to the killer, and if we find him, Dabrix is home and dry, lawyer or no lawyer.'

'And the best of luck, but nonetheless I'm going to see Dabrix's brother and help him organise a legal team.'

'Fair enough. Two strings to the bow are never a bad idea. Time is short, though, and so we had both better get moving.'

I took to Dabrix's brother at once. He, too, was taller than average, but elegant where Dabrix had been gangling, impeccably dressed, suave, svelte, and with a little amused smile in his eyes and playing around the corners of his mouth that showed he did not take himself, or the world, too seriously.

'This is such a bore,' he said. 'I knew my dear brother would get himself into something too big to handle, if I didn't lock him in his room and feed him bread and water for his sins. He really is most exasperating.'

But then his tone changed.

'What is to be done? Lawyers? Any chance of bail? If not, any little comforts he would be allowed? He will not take kindly to jail, I fear.'

'A good lawyer is the main priority,' I answered. 'Norbanus would be ideal, but he is tied up with that Lusitanian business and can't spare any time for anything else at present. His cousin, Hopridius the Younger, is almost as good, but his charges are exorbitant, and he is a lazy devil to boot. Fortunately that does not mater much in this case, because it is not the kind that needs much research or preparation.'

'I had thought Roman lawyers were not allowed to charge fees, but learned otherwise a couple of years ago,' said Aurelius Dabrix. 'They call it a 'donation to the charity', which sounds good, but we all know what it means.'

'It's for widow and orphans, especially orphans,' I said cynically. 'Hopridius's parents died ten years ago.'

'But the cost does not matter; the competence does. If this man Hopridius is the best available, I want him.'

'I'll introduce you: I knew him quite well when we were young: we used to go riding together, when horses and I got on better than we do these days.'

I had had a bad fall towards the end of my term in the army, which put me on my back for weeks, and I went from a lover to a hater of horses almost overnight; I still have to ride sometimes, but my instinct if I have to go any distance to get from A to B is to look for a litter, or wheels.

Hopridius was surprisingly cordial considering he had not set eyes on me for years, though I knew it was skin-deep. He was one of those you meet occasionally in public life, who have made good, risen above the common herd, but like to play at hail-fellow-well-met when they meet old acquaintances, to trumpet to the world that success has not gone to their heads, they are still regular guys who often think about the good old days and their friends from those times. All the while, of course, they are despising the oicks who have not 'got on' as they have, and as soon as said oicks' backs are turned, will make condescending or disparaging remarks that will leave all and sundry in no doubt that they have long outgrown such people, and are really being uncommonly generous in deigning to notice them at all.

Hopridius did not lay it on too strongly with me, neither the false bonhomie nor the bogus nostalgia, for as an equestrian, albeit a very lowly one, I might at some juncture be able to do him good, or harm; and right now it was good, in the shape of a potential 'donation' from Aurelius Dabrix.

I outlined the situation, and he tut-tutted a little.

'The dangers of drink,' he said, shaking his head. 'But I suppose,' turning to Aurelius Dabrix, 'your brother is a sociable chap, who likes good company and forgets to stop sometimes when in full flow. Salt of the earth, these fellows, usually, but occasionally they become a menace to themselves and others.'

Aurelius Dabrix said nothing, but I could see that he had already summed up this slightly nauseating pseud.

There was nothing pseudo, however, about Hopridius's legal mind, and he soon got down to business.

'A good witness,' he decided, 'is what we very much need, some chap who saw the fracas from a distance, and heard the footsteps of the real murderer running away.'

'There was no witness.'

He looked at me pityingly.

'As I said, a witness: standing a block or so away; perhaps heard rather then saw the commotion, but actually caught a glimpse of the assassin running off. I feel sure that we will be able to find such a person, if we look hard enough. Of course,' he added, 'they don't come cheap: expenses, you know, a litter to and from the court, meals and refreshments, compensation for lost earnings... I fear, gentlemen, we live in rapacious times. Of course, I myself can charge no fee, though a donation to charity is always appreciated.'

I nearly choked; Aurelius Dabrix, however, took it in his stride.

'Just let me have your bill for witnesses' 'expenses' and all when it is over,' he told the lawyer, 'and I will see it is paid immediately.'

'We will need an expert witness, too.'

'Expert witness?' I asked. 'Is not Dabrix's inebriation, and his left-handedness, and his previous good character, enough to convince – backed, of course, by the 'eye-witness', and by your eloquence in presenting the case?'

'My dear fellow: you say 'good character' – and yet you mention inebriation. You have no idea of the prejudice to be found in this city against those who like to drink their wine not wisely but too well. The mere fact that my client was in the state he apparently was, will condemn him in all too many eyes. However, there's medication.'

'Medication?'

'Was Dabrix suffering from some ailment, and taking any potion to try to control it? Some of these Greek doctors prescribe foul concoctions that are well known to have disastrous effects when mixed with even a small quantity of the cup that cheers. Now, if the gentleman had been taking something of the kind, his penchant for a glass or two – only a glass or two, mind – could have led to his otherwise unexplained inebriation. And the unfortunate events that followed.'

'Dabrix's inebriation,' I said, 'was the result of his trying to drink Rufus dry, as usual.'

'You are so literal. This is all about *perception*. If Dabrix is *perceived* to be the victim of unwisely-prescribed medication, then that is what he is. He will become an object of sympathy rather than censure. And so, as I said, we need to find a good doctor who will be willing to serve as our expert witness.'

'For a fee,' muttered Aurelius Dabrix, under his breath.

'He too, of course, will need expenses, which for a professional man will be rather steep,' Hopridius informed us, right on cue. 'I know one or two who will be willing to provide the court with their informed opinion. My clerk, doubtless, will be able to find our other witness. You may rest assured, Aurelius Dabrix, that we will do our utmost to ensure that your unfortunate brother is found innocent of any wrongdoing. And now, if you will excuse me....'

'Why does not that man call a bribe a bribe and have done with it: 'expenses' my eye. I'm convinced my brother is innocent and if takes a little bribery to get him off, so be it, I know that's the way the system works and I'll go along with it. But 'expenses'...'

And then he came up with a brilliant idea.

'You know, dear boy, I have a rather nasty taste in my mouth. Take me to this Rufus's Place I hear so much about.'

I told you I had taken to the fellow from the start.

Molo and the vigiles had been less successful in their quest. They asked around the most likely places, lined up the usual suspects, leant rather hard on a few, but still at the end of it drew a blank. Molo was not happy.

'Either the swine covered his tracks uncommonly well, which means he has not been boasting about his exploit as most of them tend to, or they are scared witless. I think it's most likely the former: some of the specimens we've spoken to don't scare easily, and they would sell their own grandmothers for a couple of sesterces, but it seems that they genuinely know nothing.'

'Surely it was a pretty hopeless business from the start? It was getting dark, there were no witnesses – unless Hopridius finds one – and the assailant could just have vanished into the mist and no-one any the wiser?'

'I know Hopridius's witnesses,' grunted Molo. 'Occasionally you find one who has been within a mile of what he claims to have seen, but it is unusual.'

'I do not really think it matters whether there was a genuine witness or not, unless he was actually close enough to recognise the thug we are looking for,' interrupted Mala. 'You are still assuming it was a casual attack; I am convinced it was not.

'In the first place, both men still had their purses, Dabrix's with a tidy sum in it, and what purpose would be served trying to frame him, if it was only a common mugging? Your average villain would more likely have skewered him too, and made off with his loot at a rate of knots.'

'Unless he was foiled by the arrival of the vigiles,' I pointed out.

'Dabrix was already propped up by the door with the knife in his hand when the vigiles arrived. Whoever committed this crime both wanted Aulus Epirota dead, *and* Dabrix to be found with the murder weapon, and he took some risk to see that that's what happened.

'We are back to the question of motive, and that's a tough one. Epirota was a popular man, not especially well off; his business was small and not very important in the scheme of things; he did not dabble in politics; he was the last person to attract the attention of the Chief Investigator; in all, like Dabrix himself, a most unlikely victim.'

'Mistaken identity?'

'Unlikely. Both characters are well known within their little circle, and very recognisable: you could spot Epirota's red hair a mile away.

'I am waiting for his two brothers to return. The three of them lived in that rambling old place near the Pons Sublicius, but the brothers are away on some business matter or other. I feel it is very likely they will hold the key to all this. They are due back later to-day, thank Jupiter, because time is getting short. Your friend Hopridius might be needed after all.'

'He has found a witness, he informs me.'

'No doubt,' said Mala dryly. 'It's a good job Aurelius Dabrix has deep pockets.'

'The funny thing is that the fellow claims he really did see something, but could only make out two figures and does not remember anything about a third man running away.'

'Clearly unreliable,' put in Molo, cynically.

'He is to be allowed to go to see Dabrix at the city jail to-morrow.'

'To be told what he *should* have seen,' replied the vigil. 'No doubt it will revive his memory no end.' He was fundamentally an honest man, and even though he shared our belief in Dabrix's innocence, he was not happy about the legal skulduggery that was so much a part of our system of 'justice'.

Next morning Mala and I set out to interview Aulus Epirota's brothers, having previously sent a message to let them know we would be coming. They were twins, a good deal younger than the murdered man, and were in some doubt as to which of them was now head of the family. They solved the problem on this occasion by acting wholly in concert, which I guessed they had done all their lives, as I knew one sometimes found with identicals.

They were very subdued, shocked by the news that had greeted them on their return the previous evening, and a little disoriented. Although they worked in the family leather-goods business, they were very much junior partners, and without Aurelius Epirota's guiding hand would be lucky to last in the often vicious competitive world in which they found themselves: the leather trade was well-known to be the most cut-throat of all.

'We offer our condolences on your brother's death,' began Mala. 'We knew him a little, as you may be aware, and are quite astonished that so popular and inoffensive a man could have come to such an end. Did he have enemies, do you know?'

'Obviously so: that layabout Gaul, may he rot in Hades. They quarrelled some months ago, something about a loan, but we thought they had made it up.'

That was certainly news to us.

'Tell us more,' said Mala. 'We have reason to believe that Dabrix did not commit the murder, despite appearances, and he does not seem like the type, especially over what was presumably a trivial sum.'

'It was not so trivial: something in the hundreds, though we cannot be more precise than that. Dabrix made the loan simply to save our brother a trip to his banker, and was paid back promptly, but then he accused Aulus of not returning the full amount. Probably Dabrix was drunk when he was paid back; maybe when he made the loan also. There was nothing in writing, unfortunately.'

'It still does not seem like a killing matter, and after all, they seemingly got back to good enough terms for your brother to help Dabrix get home.'

'That's what we would have thought. Our brother was not one to bear a grudge, and would have believed the whole matter was behind them. Any ill-feeling must have been wholly on the Gaul's part. Bloody barbarians.'

The usual prejudice, I noted. Dabrix had been born a Roman citizen and had never been near Gaul in his life, but some would never accept his kind as 'proper' Romans: certainly not this rather strait-laced pair. They obviously disapproved, too, of their easy-going late brother's relaxed lifestyle and catholic friendships.

'My brother and this Gaul even joked,' one of them said primly, 'about a lady friend they shared when they were younger: actress, and you know what that means.'

What it meant was that this young prig was prejudiced against a whole class of relatively innocent and talented young women, who brought great pleasure to Roman theatregoers, simply because a few of them were reputedly no better than they should be (including, I had to admit, the lady they were referring to).

I let it pass, not least because I thought I knew something of the young Thespian in question, and where to find her. She was the one who had not only been very close – *very* close – to Dabrix and Epirota; she had been fond of our nautical confrères also, and her household included a little ten-year-old matelot to prove it.

We left the brothers to their hand-wringing, and at Mala's suggestion made a courtesy call on Aurelius Dabrix, to let him know the state of play.

'I think it might be worth while having a word with this actress,' Mala told him. 'We are heading there as soon as we have had a quick meal.'

I suspect that Aurelius Dabrix knew that his brother had been making regular payments to the lady in question, and knew that we knew, but none of us mentioned the fact: tactful silence is sometimes best .

I half expected him to invite us to share a quick bite with him, but he didn't, and so Mala and I were soon tucking into our hot pies at the little eatery close – conveniently close – to Rufus's Place, and discussing our plans.

'Beard this lady in her den at once,' decided Mala. 'Eat up: we do not want her to get wind of our coming and concoct some cock-and-bull story.'

Yet that undoubtedly is what happened. She lived 'way, 'way out near the city wall, in a little shack among other shacks in an otherwise deserted and derelict area I would have thought no respectable woman would have gone within miles of; but perhaps Amelia had friends...

She was a seductive, come-up-and-see-me-some-time kind of creature, once no doubt pretty but far too blousy for my taste, and some way past her sell-by date – though that did not prevent her trying at first to vamp us for all she was worth. It was water off a duck's back, and Mala got down to business right away.

'I understand you know Dabrix the Gaul?'

'Which one, dearie, Aurelius or his little brother?'

'The younger one.'

'Oh, the sweetie who is said to have put paid to Aulus Epirota?' News travels fast in Rome. 'I would not have thought he was man enough.'

'He was man enough to present you with a little gift you were not planning on,' I retorted, 'or is that brat outside playing in the alley someone else's, and you have been taking maintenance from Dabrix under false pretences?'

'I would not know what you mean, I'm sure,' she said sniffily. 'The child is my late sister's boy; I've looked after him since he was a baby.'

I'll bet you have, I thought.

'And the maintenance?'

'How dare you call it that. If a gentleman wants to help a girl out a little,' – *girl* – ' when he knows she has fallen on hard times, that's his business; and it certainly is not yours. You be careful. I have friends: I'll have you know; I have even had priests among my admirers...'

'Now we'll hear what the bishop said to the actress,' muttered Mala, but I had no idea what he meant.

We tried a little further, but it was useless: she clammed up, was alternately sullen and hostile, until at last even Mala tired of the game.

'You, *lady*,' he said, and his emphasis was an insult in itself, 'know more than is good for you, and if you won't tell my friend and me, we will see how you would like a little chat with the vigiles.'

'Vigiles,' she replied scornfully; 'I eat vigiles for supper.' I could believe her: this was one hard-boiled cookie.

We left, and made our way across the ugly patch of waste-ground that adjoined the insalubrious estate where the actress's shack was situated.

It was Mala who saw them first.

'Marcus,' he said; 'we have a problem.'

There were four of them, and they were all carrying swords: illegal, certainly, but who is going to enforce the law in an area like this? The vigiles come only rarely, and then armed to the teeth and in sufficient numbers to quell a riot.

They came at us in pairs. I held my dagger at the ready, well knowing that against a swordsman it would be pretty useless, and quite useless when the odds were two to one. I supposed Mala might get in a blow or two with his ebony stick, but any half-competent swordsman would cut a wooden weapon in two in short order, and, again, there were two to Mala's one.

What happened next was an eye-opener indeed. Mala grasped the handle of his stick in one hand, twisted one of the silver bands with the other, and suddenly the bottom length dropped off to reveal a wicked-looking, three-foot long blade, slimmer than a normal gladius and longer, with an edge as sharp as a razor and a point that looked as though it could go through a man like a gimlet through an orange.

It did. The foremost of the attackers, unluckily for him a couple of yards or so in front of his companion, was skewered through the gut before he know what had hit him. Mala grabbed the man's sword as he fell and hurled it to me, and turned to face his other assailant.

I caught the sword Mala had thrown just in time to parry my first opponent's wild slash, and then received a pleasant surprise. He was a typical denizen of the underworld, one of the Subura rent-a-mob, and he know as much about swordsmanship as I about Egyptian hieroglyphics. He had managed to steer clear of the army all his life, and maybe had had a couple of lessons in some run-down gym from an 'instructor' as inept as himself. He, too, advanced a couple of yards in front of his comrade-in-arms, and by the time that worthy realised his mistake in not rushing to force me to defend myself from two sides, the other was prone on the ground, and it was one-to-one.

This other man without doubt *had* been in the army, and was a different proposition. He had been well-drilled, and his style was text-book, but it was a book I knew like the back of my hand: I was not in Mala's class, but I had twice reached the semi-finals of the legion games, and I knew at once that this hopeful was not going to cause me too much trouble. Even so, he held out for longer than I expected, until he tried a clever little move from page eight of the manual, and found to his dismay that I had read page nine. He gave a funny little gurgle as my blade disappeared into his stomach, and that was that.

Mala, meanwhile, was having a most interesting time. His opponent was a Thracian, and like all Thracians, he was good. He was not the size of Glabrus, the champion gladiator Mala had disposed of some time before, but he was even quicker, and fought in the characteristic Thracian crouch that many orthodox swordsmen find difficult to cope with. (I do, most certainly: both times in the games it was a Thracian who stopped me in the semis.)

Mala fought in his usual fashion, sword-arm well in front, knees slightly bent, front foot pointing directly at his opponent – 'It's a sideways-on game,' he had told me – and from time to time lunging a prodigious distance that had the Thracian jumping back only barely in time, and on occasions not in time at all, so that soon the front of his tunic was stained red where Mala had hit him, without quite managing to press home his thrust fatally.

As against Glabrus, he used his point far more than the edge, though from time to time essaying economical little cuts that had the Thracian parrying frantically, and once futilely as Mala's blade deftly removed his right ear. The Thracian was using the standard army-issue gladius, instead of the curved sword favoured by most of his compatriots, but I do not believe any weapon could have saved him. Mala wielded his slim blade with such dexterity that it almost seemed to have a life of its own, its needle-sharp point probing in and out like the tongue of some deadly snake.

I hovered, sword in hand, ready to attack the Thracian from behind if Mala seemed in any trouble, but it was his opponent who was having all the trouble, as Mala pressed his attack relentlessly, and soon drew blood almost at will with his graceful, deadly lunge.

He finished off the bout, though, not with such a lunge, but in a fashion that had me as amazed as the hapless Thracian. Suddenly, like a coiled spring, he launched himself forward, becoming completely airborne, his body almost horizontal with the ground, sword-arm raised and outstretched, that vicious point propelled so far forward that it tore its way into the Thracian's throat and out beyond, before the man had the slightest chance to parry or to react at all.

'Good,' said Mala. 'I have not forgotten how to manage the flèche.'

I made a mental note – there were so many mental notes I had to make, when Mala spoke spontaneously – of the word and of the attack it designated, and indeed of Mala's whole style of swordsmanship.

'You must give me some lessons, friend Mala,' I said feelingly. 'You have an unusual way of fighting, but, by Jupiter, it is effective.'

'You have not done too badly yourself,' he replied, looking at the bodies of the two louts I had despatched. 'I will give you lessons with pleasure, but in turn you must teach me more about the gladius: I find I am a little clumsy with so heavy a weapon.'

'I don't think Glabrus the Iron Man found you clumsy,' I observed.

'He was disconcerted by my style. I am glad I did not have to meet him in the arena, armoured: the lunges I kept pinking him with, as with this fellow too, would not have been much use if his chest had been protected by a plate of iron. What I would really like is to have a proper sabre made: with one of those I would back myself against anyone – except perhaps a samurai.'

He smiled.

'You do not know what I am talking about, do you, Marcus? No use telling you I once, using a practice sabre, took on a kendo expert - and won. But it might have been very different against an old-style samurai using real weapons. I will tell you about the samurai sword some day, Marcus: it is possibly the deadliest hand-to-hand weapon ever devised.

'But you must excuse my rambling on about swords: they are something a passion of mine. I nearly made the Olympics, in my youth.'

Olympics? Those were the ancient Greek games: what could he be talking about?

'Enough. These fellows have certainly given me something to think about.'

'We gave them something to think about,' I said, pointing to the four bodies.

'Indeed, but that is not what I meant. Where did these fellows come from? How did they happen to be there just as we left the actress's place? Who sent them?'

'You don't think they were just a chance bunch of thugs grabbing an opportunity when it presented itself?'

'No way. Even around here, they would not normally have been carrying swords, nor would they have appeared from nowhere the moment we started crossing the waste ground. They knew we would be there, they were waiting for us, and they meant to kill us.'

'And they would have succeeded, but for that little contraption of yours: an interesting "stick" indeed.'

'Yes, and I am glad we killed them all, because if it was known what is concealed here, I too could be in trouble for carrying a sword within the city limits.'

'I promise not to tell,' I replied, 'if you can find me a decent meal as soon as we get back to civilised parts: that pie was not enough to keep body and soul together.'

He tapped me on the stomach with his stick.

'Oh, that this too, too solid flesh would melt.'

'Not if I can help it,' I replied. 'Look, I keep fit, I'm not overweight – much; I hardly broke sweat in sorting out those two louts; but if the gods did not want us to eat all the delectable food we are blessed with, they would not allow our cooks to prepare it. I'm the last man to offend the gods, as you know.'

What he knew was that I was pretty sceptical of the whole pantheon of them, though of course I was not fool enough to say so out loud in the wrong company. (Once when we were discussing such matters, Mala observed that if he did not know it couldn't be, he would assume I had 'read too much Air and Rustle in my youth'.

Air and Rustle?

'Very well,' said Mala; 'we will go to my place, and get Diogenes to rustle up something.'

I was away like a greyhound from the traps. Diogenes was Mala's Greek "chef", as he called him, and as far as I was concerned the most valuable slave in Rome, a veritable genius. If he had ever read the *Satyricon*, and been given his head, he would have produced a meal, not so pretentious-looking indeed, but one that nevertheless would have made Trimalchio's feast taste like something from a fast-food outlet.

'Now you're talking,' I said to Mala as we walked briskly away. 'There's just one thing: do we have time to stop off at Rufus's for a quick pre-prandial?'

Replete, I reclined on my couch, and surveyed the assembled company. Gaius Molo and his wife Nysa, almost fully recovered now from her ordeal*, had been collected *en route*, and likewise young Servius Javolenius, now looking resplendent and every inch the military man in his new rig-out: in only a few days he would be joining his legion in Dacia.

Molo and I had been filling him in on the do's and don'ts of that fair land, like never turning one's back on anyone – *anyone* – and never going for a walk in the woods without a couple of cohorts for company. He listened wide-eyed, perhaps wondering at first if we were coming the old-sweat line a bit strong and having him on, but he was too intelligent not to realise very shortly that we were giving him good advice, and he duly took it aboard.

'He will make a good officer,' I said to Molo, when Javolenius was temporarily out of the room.

'Yes, and we'll need all we can get if that place ever goes ballistic again.'

'I suspect,' remarked Mala, somewhat to our surprise for we did not know he followed military matters that closely, 'that Marcus Ulpius Traianus might be a good general to have in charge there. He seems to me a man destined for great things.'

But this conversation was not pursued. After we had finished our meal it was Javolenius himself who brought up the burning subject.

'From what you say, there is a great deal more to this Dabrix business than meets the eye.'

'The understatement of the week,' smiled Mala. 'We know it was not a simple mugging; we know someone wanted Epirota very dead; and now we know that once that someone became convinced we had twigged the fact, he wanted us dead as well.'

'And that he wanted Dabrix blamed for the Epirota murder.'

'Do you know,' said Mala, unexpectedly, 'I am not at all as sure of that as I was.'

'But…'

'But me no buts,' I remembered his using the phrase once before. 'I must come clean: in point of fact, I believe I know who the culprit is.'

As we looked at him in astonishment, he corrected himself.

'Perhaps I should say 'culprits'. The problem now is to prove it.'

---

* See *Quintus Propertius and the case of the counting-house clerk*

The proof, or at least the final certainty, fell into his lap the very next morning, as he told us all after the arrest had been made. Molo had come to me first, and then we had gone to tell Mala the depressing news.

'Hopridius's witness has been found dead.'

Far from being downcast, Mala seemed almost cheered by the news.

'Damn; if I had been a bit quicker off the mark, I might have saved the poor fellow; but things do now fall into place. They have finally made a major mistake, and it will be their last.

'The man was in a safe house, presumably?'

'Of course.'

'And how did he die? Poison, I presume.'

'How on earth did you know? There was not a mark on his body, but when the slave went to rouse him this morning, he was lying there quite dead, and, according to the man, a sickly green in colour, and with a look of terror on his face.'

'Green? And a look of terror?' repeated Mala. 'If they used what I suspect, it would take him like that He would come to realise what was happening to him, but by that time it would be too late, for he would be quite paralysed. Let me be clear about this man's movements: Vatius, you say his name was?'

Molo nodded.

'And he was kept in Hopridius's safe house?'

'Yes.'

'But yesterday, he was escorted to the jail, to interview the younger Dabrix?'

'Yes.'

'And then straight back to the safe house?'

'No; Aurelius Dabrix had asked to see him first. My own men escorted him, and stayed while Aurelius Dabrix questioned him. Cordial man, that: offered my men wine – which they should not have accepted when on duty, but they said it would have discourteous to refuse – and took Vatius by the hand and thanked him profusely, and then they returned to the safe house.'

'Vatius took no wine?'

'No.'

'I would like to see this witness's body.'

Molo took us to the safe house, and we entered the little room where the corpse had been laid out. Mala very carefully examined each of his hands, and then with a little gesture of satisfaction pointed to the base of one of the fingers. There was a very, very tiny puncture, and the skin around it was slightly tinged with green.

'I believe we have a little call to make. Molo, may I suggest you collect some of your men?' He took him aside and whispered something. The vigil seemed at first surprised, but after a few more minutes slowly began to nod his head.

'That's good enough for me,' he said. 'Let's go.'

We arrived at the villa in a body, Molo and his vigiles, the slave who had found the witness's corpse, Mala, and me. The vigiles and the slave waited by the door, but we were shown at once into the inner sanctum.

'Gentlemen, how unexpected at this early hour; I was just about to call on my patron.'

Molo was the only one to answer.

'You need not bother your patron. Aurelius Dabrix, I arrest you for the murder of Junius Vatius, and as an accessory to the murder of Aulus Epirota.'

I have never seen a man so utterly transformed. In an instant, gone was the suave, well-to-do Roman; gone was the good companion I had yarned with at Rufus's Place after our visit to the lawyer; instead we were suddenly faced with a fearsome, snarling savage.

'So you've got me, have you, you filthy Romans. You think you're so superior, don't you, gods of the earth, destined to conquer and rule all you come into contact with, and then lie to them that it's for their own good. Well, here is one Gaul you won't be able to do with as you please.'

Molo leaped forward, but he was too late. Aurelius Dabrix, in one swift motion, had produced a dagger from his tunic, and plunged it into his heart with a cry almost of triumph.

We assembled, at Mala's request, at my small domus, Molo and his Bythinian wife Nysa, Servius Javolenius, the Epirota brothers, Hopridius, whom I had invited on impulse, and one distinctly less brazen actress, who, we were told, had looked quite flustered when my litter arrived to collect her, especially as it was escorted by a bunch of very tough vigiles, whom she somehow omitted to eat.

Mala launched into his explanation as soon as we were all seated.

'It was a matter, as it so often is, of little things gradually falling into place to make a coherent picture. Perhaps the first piece was the remark you made, Molo, about how touchy Gauls can be if they feel slighted. I know you are not a racist, and we are both aware that the generalisation can apply to more than Gauls, but nevertheless it was a characteristic based on your own observations over a long career.

'Ironically, I pushed the thought to the back of my mind, because you followed with the information that the dagger had been found in Dabrix's *right* hand, which I naturally seized on as a significant point.

'Next was Hopridius's eye-witness. By a remarkable coincidence,' – begging your pardon, Hopridius – 'he turned out to be genuine, and yet he disclaimed any knowledge of a third person at the fracas. Yet how could that be? Epirota, we were by then all convinced, could not have been killed by Dabrix, so how had he died? It could not have been suicide: a man does not stab himself half a dozen times, deeply at that, and then hand the dagger to a convenient onlooker. So that was something else to put at the back of my mind, to let my unconscious ponder.

'Next was the strange business of the loan Dabrix had made to Epirota. Epirota had a reputation for honesty second to none, and if he borrowed say two hundred sesterces from Dabrix, two hundred sesterces is what he paid back, and pretty damn quick at that. Dabrix, though, in his usual stupor – though I will qualify that in a moment – thinks otherwise, and resents what he thinks is Epirota playing him for a sucker. Ostensibly they make up their quarrel, but Dabrix does not forget, and what is more, he tells his brother. More of that anon.

'We come to the quest for the supposed real murderer. I talk to Epirota's surviving brothers, and learn not only of the loan, but also of the supposed infatuation, in their younger days, on the part of both Dabrix and Epirota, for a certain charming young lady.' He nodded pleasantly to the actress, who looked smug at the complement: she was a bit slow in spotting irony.

'Here was a further possible cause of friction between the two men, since she manifestly preferred Epirota, and yet Dabrix – it was a commonplace of tavern ribaldry – was still paying for the consequences of his earlier fling.'

The actress affected to look uncomprehendingly into the distance, but Mala took no notice.

'We decided we would call on our Thespian friend, but by the time we arrived, she had already been warned of our coming, and told to say nothing about anything.'

'He told me you were from the law,' she interrupted. 'He said there was some irregularity concerning Dabrix's payments – little gifts, I mean – that might cause them to dry up.'

'And so *you* dried up,' continued Mala, 'but not before you had let slip an interesting nugget of information: not only did you know the younger Dabrix, and not think much of him, but you were also acquainted with Aurelius Dabrix himself, the head of the family.

'Now tell me: when you were – acquainted – with Aurelius Dabrix, were you also still seeing Aulus Epirota?'

Her answer was almost a whisper, but it was 'Yes.'

'And when did Aurelius Dabrix discover that you were sharing your favours in this way?'

'Only recently: two or three weeks ago.'

'And his reaction?'

'He told me to stop seeing Epirota – or else.'

'Another piece of the jig-saw falls into place,' said Mala. (What is a 'jig-saw', I wondered.) Not only has Aulus Epirota insulted Dabrix over the money, and by extension the family and Aurelius Dabrix himself, he is now fishing in waters the elder Gaul considers strictly his own: and we all know how possessive the Gauls are about their womenfolk.

'Now we come to the attack on Marcus and me as we left Amelia's house.'

House? Shack; glorified shed.

'Who knew we were going to see this young lady?' Amelia preened herself again: she had totally forgotten how Mala had used the word 'lady' at the end of our interview with her. 'We did not mention it to the Epirota brothers; we did not make contact with Molo; the only person we informed, when we paid him a visit en route, was Aurelius Dabrix.

'By now the pieces were almost all in place, and as though to confirm it, there came the stupid murder of the eye-witness, Vatius. I need not go into detail there; it's an old trick. The vigiles told how Aurelius Dabrix took Vatius's hand and thanked him. A signet-ring and a very strong poison are all that is required. Presumably he had not been persuaded to 'remember' the hypothetical third party, and that sealed his fate.'

'It is true,' said Hopridius. 'He would not budge from his story, and could have ruined the case. I was going to dispense with his services forthwith.'

'Quite understandable,' said Mala drily. 'But now to the final piece of the puzzle, Dabrix's supposed inebriation, and the fact that he was holding the knife in his right hand. Both facts are easy to explain. The drunkenness first: he was faking it. Rufus has confirmed that he had not had an excessive amount, by his standards, and was a little surprised that he seemed to need helping home.

'As soon as we accept that he was not drunk and incapable, the left-hand-right-hand problem disappears: he simply stabbed Epirota with his left hand, transferred the dagger to his right, propped himself against the door, and waited for the vigiles to arrive, knowing they were due on their rounds shortly. The rest we know – and his performance took us all in.'

'He always fancied himself as an actor,' volunteered Amelia. 'He wasn't bad, either – for an amateur.' She spoke with all the condescension and disdain of the third-rate professional.

'He was taking a great risk, of course, but he calculated that the combination of his left-handedness, his ostensible incapacity, and the supposed third party whom a 'witness' would swear to, would be enough for a first-rate lawyer to get him off.

'I say "he" calculated, but more likely it was his brother; to some extent perhaps the younger Dabrix was manipulated. Aurelius Dabrix, beneath his oh-so-civilised and sophisticated exterior, must inside have harboured a seething hatred of Rome and all things Roman, despite all that had been done for his family from Julius Caesar's time onwards. Add that to his exaggerated sense of family honour, and the supposed insult meted out by Aulus Epirota, both with regard to the disputed loan and his daring to touch *his*, Aurelius Dabrix's girl, and you have a potent mix that has led to the death of seven men, and probably now an eighth.'

He was right about the eighth. Hopridius withdrew at once from the task of defending the now friendless Gaul, who in the event did not even stand trial: the original case against him was deemed sufficient for summary conviction, and summary execution. They put him in the arena, gave him a wooden sword, and pitted him against a big hairy German, armed to the teeth. I suspect someone – Mala perhaps? – got to the German and bribed him to make it quick, because, to the anger of the mob, it was all over in seconds, and the wine-merchants of Rome mourned as one man. Whether this was just, in view of the Gaul's ingrained befuddlement in the face of the world, or whether, in view of what he did to Aulus Epirota, he deserved worse, I leave you to judge.

There was a somewhat happier sequel, if 'happier' is not a loaded word in the circumstances. Towards the end of Mala's explanation, I had noticed Amelia, the actress, making eyes at the elder of the surviving Epirota brothers (they had sorted out which was which by then). He, poor sap, had there and then resigned his membership of the moral majority, and presumably fell headlong for her well-rehearsed, heart-rending performance as the girl who had too affectionate a nature for her own good and look where it had got her.

The next we knew, he had invited her under his roof, ten-year-old miniature-mariner and all. (We never did discover whether the twins continued to maintain their share-and-share-alike life-style.)

'He is learning,' said Mala, of the new head of the Epirota household, 'one of the great indisputable facts of life.'

'Which is?'

'It is a truth, universally acknowledged, that a single man in possession of a good fortune, must be in want of a woman to help him spend it.'

The spending did not last long: Amelia's new paramour put up with her for only two months – to complicate life, the matelot had come back to town - but she departed laden with jewellery and laughing all the way to the bank.

'Pity,' said Mala.; 'she must have looked quite interesting in leather.'

Quintus Propertius and the Misfortune of Marius the Glassmaker

The small village where I was born and spent my early childhood is not that far from Rome, but I will not name it: it makes me too sad to think of it. It has gone, of course, which is to say changed beyond recognition. It was too close to that accursed town (which also I will not name) that spread its tentacles over the surrounding countryside towards the end of Vespasian's reign and into that of Titus and the present incumbent, becoming a magnet for speculators, fortune-hunters, riff-raff of all kinds, until it finally succumbed to delusions of grandeur, and now has its own arena, no less.

The small villa my father owned, and the few acres he farmed, had gone long before that. The woods and fields where I played as a boy, along with my long-dead younger brother, are now built over; the open countryside I enthusiastically explored, where I learned to ride, to fish, to hunt, the very hills and valleys, now all gone, or hideously transformed.

I was telling Quintus Propertius Mala about it, and about the idyllic childhood I had enjoyed, and he was more than sympathetic.

'Your are very emotional for a Roman, friend Marcus; but how well do I understand what you mean.'

'It is called Progress,' I said bitterly, 'and we are supposed to welcome it with open arms. For my part I try to ignore it as best I can, and solace myself with Hesiod.

'And yet it is inevitable, I know. The empire is growing ever larger – though surely there must be a limit to expansion some day – and ever richer; tens of thousand of newcomers are flocking to Rome, and to other parts of Italy, every year. The process is inevitable. Progress! I hate it.'

'As for the empire,' replied Mala, 'I should not be at all surprised if some strong emperor does not put a halt to expansion, within the next thirty or forty years I would guess, though not until still more of our neighbours have been conquered and subjugated.

'But Progress is something else; do not condemn it all. It was Progress when the great aqueducts were built, and who would be without them now? It was Progress when our ancestors first started to build the fine roads that criss-cross Italy and the empire, and who does not rejoice that they did so? It was Progress when Augustus, in his own words, found Rome brick, and left it marble; look around you: can you say you are sorry? It was Progress, too, when the vigiles were first instituted, to try to control the fires Rome was plagued with, and then to make our streets safe to walk in. There is Progress, and "Pseudo Progress", friend Marcus, and we must learn to recognise what is the real thing, and what is simply change for its own sake, bringing benefit to few and misery to many.'

'You are right, I know. But, Mala, if only you could have ridden with me across those hills, have paddled in the little stream that formed the southern boundary of our farm…'

'And stolen a handful of grapes the moment they were ripe, and smelt the perfume of new-mown hay, and watched the sunset over the hills; and then the moors, the country lanes, the village greens; cricket… Mala, you fool, shut up; this sort of thing gets you nowhere, and you're old enough to know it.'

I had no idea of the places he had mentioned: *country lanes; village greens* – what in the empire were *they*? And this 'cricket': a ball game the British play, I remember his telling me once. How can one be nostalgic about a *game*, and one devised by savages at that? But my mood of nostalgia he had most certainly caught, until he finally snapped out of it so abruptly. His next remark, therefore, took me all the more by surprise.

'To revert to the notion of Progress, Marcus: I'm going into the Progress business myself, in a small way; I have procrastinated far too long. What do you think of this?'

He handed me a circular piece of glass, with a metal rim around its circumference and a wooden handle protruding. It was not a pretty piece, being quite plain and unadorned, though the glass was unusually clear and transparent.

'Put your left hand on the table,' instructed Mala. 'Hold this by its handle, about this far from your eyes.' He demonstrated. 'Now look at your hand, moving the glass backward and forwards a little until it is clearly in focus.'

It was amazing. With the glass at just the right distance, my left hand was clearly to be seen through it – but it had grown to three, four times its normal size!

'Look at this coin,' said Mala next, putting a silver denarius on the table. Like my hand, it appeared to grow: Domitian's head was enormous, the ugly sneer on his face even more prominent, the lettering around the outside thrown into sharper relief than I had ever seen.

'This is a clever toy indeed!' I exclaimed.

'Toy?' snorted Mala. 'This is one of the most earth-shaking objects you have ever set eyes on, friend Marcus; Rome will never be the same again. Gaius Pliny refers to a similar device, but that was primitive, and nothing came of it. This is as different again. It took Marius the Glassmaker months to get the glass that clear, and more months to grind the lens to just the right shape. It cost me, too: lucky my ex-wife is not here, she'd have had my guts for garters for spending that kind of money.'

Ex-wife? I did not know Mala had ever been married. I knew he had a keen eye for the ladies: he had been quite smitten by that young beauty from Campania, but she had been promised to Manus Cottius, and you don't mess with the women of generals of the army, not if you have any sense you don't. Mala had been tempted to try, but luckily I managed to dissuade him.

But back to the – 'lens', did he call it? I did not see how such a thing could be 'earth-shaking', and I told him so.

'Sheer ignorance, Marcus, and you've every excuse; but wait and see. Now Marius has mastered the technique, there will be much more to follow. Wait until we have telescopes, microscopes, perhaps even spectacles to perch on your nose. My lad, you can't imagine what's coming.'

So be it. I know Mala well enough, notwithstanding the aura of the exotic that surrounds him, to be sure that he was not trying to fool me. If he said this bit of glass was important, it was important.

He tried to explain.

'The science of optics is fundamentally quite simple,' he told me. 'Let me show you.'

He took out a tablet and stylus, and began drawing various shapes: first what he said was a sideways-on view of the 'lens', and then little arrows, lines representing, he said, 'rays of light'... Perhaps it was all simple to him, but I was soon quite lost. He did not give up, however, and gradually things began to fall into place: I will not say I understood fully, but I began to get the general idea.

I was especially taken by his schematic diagram of a thing he called a 'telescope', and his outline of its capabilities.

'And this really would, with two suitable pieces of glass, enlarge objects a great distance away, as your lens has just enlarged my hand, and the denarius?'

'Look south from here,' said Mala. 'You can just see the Colosseum, but it is far too far away to make out individual people standing in front of it. With even a small telescope, you could do so.'

'That is quite remarkable. However did you discover this?'

'I? Would that I had. Far cleverer men than I developed the science of optics, and other clever men applied that science to the making of instruments. I am, in effect, simply heir to their knowledge and skills.'

'And you intend to make these instruments? This 'telescope'?'

'With the aid of Marius the Glassmaker and his workshop, yes. Just wait, Marcus, until you see the craters on the moon, the rings of Saturn, the nebula in Orion; then you will indeed wonder.

'Nor is that all. I hope these optical instruments will kick-start the proper study of science in Rome, and then – who knows? There are many very clever men in Rome and the empire – and women, too, if you would give them the chance to show it - not least your wonderful engineers. When their eyes are opened by what I will be able to show them, I am utterly confident they will go on to achieve things that will surprise even me.'

'And you will take some surprising, Mala, for now I am quite sure of what I have always known in my heart: you are not, simply not, what you seem. You are not a magician: I do not believe in magic. You are not a god: I do not believe in gods, though it is as well the mob should do so. You say you were brought up in Britain, but Britain is a primitive place, and its inhabitants savages. To all outward appearances you are a Roman, and a fine one, but you are not. Nor are you a Greek, a Parthian, an

Egyptian. What are you, Quintus Propertius Mala? Where are you really from?'

'I am a Roman citizen, and proud of it, and my allegiance now is wholly to Rome, as I am sure you know. But you are right: I am not *only* a Roman citizen, and where I come from originally you could not in your wildest imaginings begin to guess.

'I have told you that, as a youth, I lived in south-western Britain*, the land of the Dumnonii, and that is true, though the people I knew there did not call themselves Dumnonii, nor was I educated with local aristocrats. That was a little fib I had to tell on the spur of the moment, to forestall embarrassing questions I could not possibly answer. It was what we call a "white lie", untrue in the strict sense, but not intended in essence to deceive: rather to avoid misunderstanding and hurt.

'For the rest: I will tell you all some day, friend Marcus - for you *are* my friend, and a man I would trust with my life. Trust me, then, in this, that as soon as I can reveal all, I will, even though you might not understand, might not believe. What I will relate to you will be unvarnished truth. Trust me.'

I was moved by his speech, as who would not be. In the year or so I had known him, I had come to recognise Quintus Propertius as one of the finest people I had ever met, and the mystery surrounding him was not going to change that. He might not be, as we had all at first surmised, scion of an old and noble Roman family, but what of it? He was an aristocrat in the true sense, a member of that finer aristocracy that does not depend on rank and outward status.

These are un-Roman thoughts, I know, especially coming from one of the equestrian order, and some will say they smack of treason. Wrong: I am no traitor to Rome and its ideals, but I have been around and learned much, even in my comparatively short life, not least from Mala himself, and I have come to recognise that, in the quaint way he himself put it, a man's a man for a' that. (I cannot go along with him in believing that slaves are 'as good as us' – that really is subversive. Almost as bad, he goes so far as to suggest that women also are our equal. That is a step too far, and I wish he would see reason; and yet, I confess, even on these matters he is beginning to wear me down.)

- See *Quintus Propertius and the Affairs of Ventidius Silo.*

I must stop philosophising and pontificating, and get back to my story, because it is indeed quite a story, especially the episode that comes next.

First, a word about Marius the Glassmaker. Memories are short, reputations fade, and I suppose that nowadays there are even benighted souls who have never heard of him. Not so in the time whereof I write: in those days he was a phenomenon, and an institution.

Marius the Glassmaker: *the* Glassmaker. Marius first, every other glassmaker nowhere. 'Marius' alone would identify him, though there are thousands of others named Marius in Rome. It is not merely that he was the best man at his craft in Rome, though he was, by far; it is not simply that the business he had built up dwarfed every other such establishment in the empire, though it did; it was not chiefly that he had made himself, by his own efforts, a millionaire, several times over, though he had. It was not even because, by his outstanding talent and phenomenal success, he wielded enormous influence, both within his chosen calling, and without. Rather is it that all these combined with a quite remarkably powerful personality, and a drive that would have done credit to Gaius Julius Caesar himself, to transform him into a Somebody: Somebody Big.

Senators deferred to him, as did other business millionaires: I have heard the late Ventidius Silo speak of him with awe. Great generals, after their victories, asked him – *asked*, not ordered – for commemorative bowls and vases, which they proudly displayed with the gold and silver and ivory they had acquired, or looted, in parts exotic. Even those of us – and we are numerous in Rome – who do not value glassware highly, recognised his stature, and acquiesced in it.

And yet he continued working at his craft, long after he needed. He employed a staff of the very best in Rome, who turned out work of the highest standard and could satisfy the most fastidious taste; with the mere imprimatur of his company on their products, they sold like hot-cakes to the rich and famous of the land. But still Marius went to his workshop each morning, overseeing their efforts, even taking a hand himself at the bench when he felt like doing so.

It was a measure of the interest he took in Mala's unusual commission, and a tribute, too, to Mala's own force of personality, that he had been prepared to devote so much of his own time and effort and skill to producing the lens that Mala had specified.

And so it was a shock to Romans great and small when they woke up one morning, and heard the news that Marius the Glassmaker had been found dead in his workshop, his head caved in, signs of a struggle all around, the murder weapon, an immensely heavy glass vase, lying by his body in a pool of blood.

'I suppose you will want to look into this business?' I asked Mala, 'though I confess it looks to me like a fairly standard break-in and robbery. The burglar probably did not expect to find anyone working at that hour, and killed on impulse. Robbery was obviously the motive: he took quite a few valuable items.'

'You're damn right I'll be looking into things,' replied Mala. 'And I have a double motive. In the first place, Marius was a remarkable man; I got to know him quite well during the time he was doing the work for me – though even if he had not been, that kind if cold-blooded thuggery needs rooting out, and the perpetrator punished.

'Secondly, though, my motive is more personal: among the things the swine stole was my magnifying lens. I had taken it back to Marius for a minor correction, and he said he would see to it at once; very possibly he was actually working on it when he was attacked. I need hardly tell you I am pretty devastated. I want to find Marius's murderer, most certainly, but just as much *I want that lens back.*

'There is – or was, or will be,' he went on 'a class of obnoxious parasites known as *fences*: receivers of stolen goods, middlemen who act as intermediaries between the thief and the eventual purchaser.'

'I don't know about 'was', or 'will be', Mala,' I interrupted, 'but 'is' I can tell you a little about. There are a number in Rome who are reputed to deal in dodgy merchandise, though nothing can be proved against them because their suppliers and their customers alike have a vested interested in keeping their mouths shut. Occasionally we hear that one or the other of them has come to a sticky end, presumably by pushing a supplier too hard, or even a powerful customer, who comes to think the man has outlived his usefulness. For the most part, though, they have a very comfortable existence, battening on the labours of the thieves who take the real risks, and catering to the wants of rich buyers – kleptomaniacs would be a better term – who care not about the origins of what they acquire so long as it is what they need for their precious collections.'

'Names?'

'Carilius Milo is one that springs to mind, though I would not advise tangling with him, Mala: he is very rich, very powerful, keeps a private army of ex-gladiators and other thugs, and they say he works hand-in-glove with Licinius Populus, the Chief Investigator. It is rumoured that when Populus wants someone worked over but for whatever reason does not want to use his official bully-boys, he whispers in Milo's ear, and a body is fished out of the Tiber shortly afterwards.'

'Milo? A name to conjure with, and it seems gang warfare runs in the family.'

'Yes, and this Milo is no more scrupulous than his famous namesake. Be careful.'

'I will. Any other names?'

'One or two come to mind, but you would do well to have a word with Gaius Molo: he keeps his ear pretty close to the ground and doubtless knows more villains than I have even guessed existed.'

'Milo, Molo, Mala' I though to myself; 'it sounds like a verb. Can ever three such different men have had such similar-sounding names?'

Gaius Molo was a watch commander, one of those vigiles – and there are rather more than you might think – who cannot be bought, cannot be intimidated, and has the quaint idea that since he is paid from the public purse (albeit a pittance) to detect and discourage the ungodly in our midst, that is what he ought to spend his time doing. He had helped us in our investigations before, most notably to the severe discomfort of a louse called Lucius the Spaniard*, and I knew would be only too happy to do so again.

We went to see him together.

'Fences? The place is crawling with them. We keep an eye on them as best we can, and lean on them sometimes if circumstances permit, but all too often they are like bad weather: an unfortunate phenomenon you can't do anything about and have to put up with. Frankly, I believe the real criminals are not so much the fences, odious lot though they are, nor even the thieves themselves, but their customers. If they were not prepared to pay over the odds for what they want and to blazes where it came from, the crime-rate in this city would be a lot lower than it is.'

---

* See *Quintus Propertius and the Case of the Counting-house Clerk*

'Do they specialise?' asked Mala. 'Some in silver, some in ivory, some precious stones? Or are they mostly generalists who will take anything that sells?'

'Generalists for the most part, like Carilius Milo: anything is grist to *his* mill. A few of the smaller people do specialise, catering to a niche market. There's an Egyptian we are hoping to nab before too long, who has a hot-line to a gang of tomb-robbers back home; there is a gentleman who poses as a corn merchant, but does a nice line in statuettes on the side – his days are numbered, too.'

'Glassware?'

'There's Macrobius Pulcher, bless his cotton socks. We've had him in for questioning a couple of time, but he has a very good lawyer in his pocket and always manages to wriggle out. I especially want him, and I'll get him if it's the last thing I do. I can't prove it, but I know for sure he was behind the death of young Balbus, one of my most promising men – nasty business of a collapsing staircase in a tenement he was investigating. I doubt, though, that Macrobius would touch the Marius stuff – I presume that's what you are interested in? – because it's too hot. Only the really big boys would risk it, if even they. More likely the thief will lie low for a while, and nothing will surface until the hullabaloo has died down. That would be the intelligent thing to do.'

'The thief is not necessarily intelligent,' I put in. 'It was a stupid thing to kill a man as prominent as Marius, and let loose a hue and cry of dangerous proportions. Knocking him senseless would have served his purpose just as well.'

'Unless he knew Marius would recognise him,' said Mala.

'Marius would hardly be likely to recognise a common burglar.'

'Precisely.'

Mala's keen mind had obviously been working overtime. I had assumed without further thought that the culprit was an ordinary burglar, working for someone bigger maybe, but one of that all-too-familiar fraternity who inhabitant Rome's murkier regions, and would do any job, any, if there was loot to be gained from it. Mala had thought beyond that.

'So you think it is an inside job?'

'It's a reasonable assumption. I'll get around to looking into that when I've had a little chat with these stolen-goods merchants.'

'Which?'

'Why, Macrobius Pulcher, and Carilius Milo.'

'I will come with you if I may,' I replied, 'and I will bring along that 'stick' you were good enough to have had made for me.'

'You will be welcome as always, Marcus, though I hope we won't have need of our little –"sticks".'

Macrobius Pulcher, we ascertained, had two strings to his bow: glassware, and property. Molo had made clear that the glassware business was both legitimate and not; the other was wholly legitimate, which says a good deal about the laxity of our property laws in Rome. The vigiles had told us the area where most of Microbus's tenements were situated, and we shuddered: trans-Tiberian rabbit-warrens that made the worst of the Subura look like luxury town-house developments.

Macrobius had an office only a stone's throw from the river, though on the 'wrong' side, and a shop nearer the centre of things where he peddled his glassware. We went to the latter first, but were told it was his day at the other venue, and so with rather less than enthusiasm, we went in search of him.

Whenever I cross the Tiber, I feel I am entering a different world. It is not just the subdued menace of the surroundings, though that is a factor: no less than in parts of the Subura, one feels one has constantly to guard one's back, and one's front also if one steps too far off the beaten track. Nor is it the general poverty and squalor: one can see that in all too many parts of Rome. Rather is it that it seems, indefinably, *alien*.

There are, as we all know, many foreigners in Rome nowadays: it has famously become a cosmopolitan city. But it is still Rome. However many Egyptians or Greeks or Bythinians or Numidians one might encounter, however strange their garb and outlandish their accents, one is still in familiar surroundings, the Forum is still the Forum, the Palatine is still the Palatine, the *atmosphere* is Roman.

Not so once you cross the Tiber. Some areas, true, are no different from what one has left; but others… As I have said, it is a different world.

Macrobius's office, though not far from the Tiber, was definitely in one of those areas where you would feel safer with a cohort or two at your back. In odd doorways, as we drew nearer, we could see disreputable-looking multi-coloured characters, some ostentatiously carving pieces of wood with ugly knives that manifestly had not been devised primarily for the hobby trade, others, with no weapon in sight, managing to look infinitely evil nevertheless.

We grasped our sticks tightly, hoping we would not have to reveal their hidden charms, and a few minutes' brisk walking brought us to the Macrobius headquarters, which looked less like a place of business than the entrance to an army camp. It was set back in a little compound of its own, with two hulking fellows at the gate, looking for all the world like nervous and suspicious guards at an isolated outpost in darkest Germany.

They stopped us and demanded to know who we were and what we wanted. If I had expected the fact that neither Mala nor I were, nor looked *hoi poloi*, would at all signify, I was kidding myself: their attitude was neither respectful, nor, indeed, remotely polite.

'You want to see Macrobius Pulcher? Do you have an appointment? Does he know you? What makes you think you can just barge in on an important man whenever you feel like it? Wait here, and don't be surprised if you are sent packing when I have had my instructions.'

He turned and walked towards the office, but not before summoning another surly lout, who had been lounging with three or four equally surly clones over a game of dice, to come and take his place.

He was back in no time, looking even more displeased.

'You're lucky,' he said – snarled, rather; 'The boss will see you. Follow me.'

The interior of the office was as sparse as the exterior was unprepossessing. A scowling man was seated behind a long table; two thugs stood near the door. We were not asked to sit: I guessed this was where Macrobius met any of his tenants who might have any requests or even – if they were especially daring – complaints, and clearly they could not expect V.I.P. treatment

'Well?'

'I am in search of good glassware, and I am told you are the man to see,' said Mala.

'And who told you that?'

'Your reputation, Macrobius Pulcher, is...'

'My reputation is none of your business. I've heard of you two: fancy yourselves as 'investigators', do you? And you,' he looked directly at Mala, 'are the louse who murdered that fine man Glabrus.'

'Yes – if it is murder to fight for one's life when one is attacked by a gladiator with a sword in his hand. I prefer to call it self-defence.'

'I don't care a ---- what you call it. I don't like you and I don't like your activities, and I let you in here to tell you so, and to warn you that if you ever cross my path again, you might finish up in the Tiber with your throats cut. You have been warned.'

Mala said nothing, but raised his eye-brows insolently. The effect was instantaneous.

'Throw them out,' Macrobius shouted to the two heavies.

It was the tavern at Ostia all over again*, and Mala's 'carati' was just as effective. The guard made a grab for his arm, and next moment was on the floor, choking and gasping.

'The next man who tries to lay a finger on me, or my friend,' said Mala very quietly, 'will be sorry; and so will anyone who orders him to.

I could see Macrobius Pulcher struggling with the impulse to call for the guards outside, but they were there, we were here, and the remaining bully-boy inside did not look at all keen to find out whether Mala was to be taken at his word; he could see, too, that I was ready to join in if he or his boss tried anything.

'We are going for a walk,' Mala informed Macrobius. 'If you had behaved in a half-civilised fashion, this need not have happened, but since you did not, let me remind you that it was you, not I, who broached the possibility of people finishing up in the Tiber.'

Macrobius did not know whether or not Mala and I had concealed daggers, and he was not in an inquisitive mood. When Mala instructed him, therefore, to order the guard in the office to stay where he was until further notice, to walk out with us talking amiably, and to instruct those outside not to leave the compound while he walked with his 'friends' as far as the bridge, he did exactly as he was told.

'You will pay for this,' he hissed, as we prepared to cross the bridge; 'you are history.'

'And you are an unspeakable louse,' replied Mala, 'but whereas your statement is idle speculation, mine is a matter of verifiable fact.'

Gaius Molo whistled when he heard what had happened.

'You've made a dangerous enemy there.'

---

* See *Quintus Propertius and the Affairs of Ventidius Silo.*

'Do you know,' said Mala, as though our friend had just advised him of some arcane and hitherto-unsuspected nugget of information, 'I do believe you might be right.'

I marvelled at his composure. I am as brave as the next man, but I was far from sanguine about our little encounter. Macrobius Pulcher might not have a private army to compare with that of Carilius Milo, but he did have a small gang of thugs who would do his bidding, and would not baulk at murder if that was required. I was more than ever pleased at the 'stick' Mala had had made for me.

I wondered if we might have been more conciliatory, but Mala scotched that suggestion immediately.

'He was obvious expecting, or half-expecting us, and must have known that we believed, or even were certain, that he traded in stolen goods. Maybe he does or maybe he doesn't have any involvement in the Marius business, but either way he does not want us or anyone else prying into his affairs. He had obviously decided to get his retaliation in first – hence our hostile reception.'

'We are keeping an eye on him as a matter of course,' interjected Molo. 'If he steps badly out of line, we'll have him, lawyer or no lawyer, but unless and until we do – be careful.'

'Of course,' replied Mala; and then, almost as an afterthought, 'I do hope Carilius Milo proves more accommodating,'

As we were to discover, Milo was not a big man, but he most certainly was a Big Man, with – choose your metaphor: a finger in every pie, a host of strings to his bow, a business as diversified as it was profitable.

He catered in bulk to the poor, and provided luxuries of all kinds to the rich. His chain of bakeries could have fed half Rome, and probably did; his exclusive, oh-so-tastefully-decorated little salons, dotted here and there throughout the city, were stocked with a vast variety of exquisite items, from all over the empire, sufficient in range and quality to make a Crassus green with envy.

We entered one of these exclusive mini-emporia, a couple of days after visiting Macrobius's rather different premises, and our reception too could not have been more different. An impeccably dressed and coiffure young lady – probably, despite her appearance, a slave, but a slave whose lot many a free woman would have envied – greeted us with that mixture of deference yet subtle hauteur one often finds in the very best of boutiques, the fruit of years of training.

'Gentlemen, welcome to Milo's; what can I do for you?'

Mala explained succinctly what he was after. 'A glass bowl,' he told the girl, 'as near as possible to the one I had on order from poor Marius. It was almost finished, but most unfortunately it was among the items stolen. I do not expect to find anything quite the same, but if there is a suitable substitute... It is for a special present,' he went on, 'and I am anxious to get just the right thing.'

We were shown some beautiful bowls, as well as vases, jugs, sets of wine-cups, but although Mala expressed a connoisseur's admiration for many of them, he shook his head each time.

'Beautiful; superb; but it isn't *quite* what I want. You know,' he confided to the young woman, 'I am tempted to take something just for myself, quite apart from the present: they are all so fine.

'But I mustn't,' he sighed. 'We who are impecunious must curb our desires, I fear.'

Impecunious? It was so obviously untrue as to be risible: Mala's toga would not have been out of place on the richest senator in the land, and his tunic made mine, which was a good one, look like something bought in a jumble sale. But the girl knew it was untrue, knew Mala knew she knew, and knew that each knew it was just one of the little games filthy-rich clients liked to play in such establishments.

'I am wondering,' went on Mala, 'whether Cornelius Milo himself might know of anything? Perhaps a recent purchase – it is well-known he takes a very hands-on approach to his business, despite having such a large and excellent staff.'

She acknowledged the implied compliment with a little bow of the head. Now they were playing another game, tacitly and tactfully ignoring the fact that she was but a slave, who could be whipped at her master's whim, stripped of her finery, and sent to the slave market to be sold to anyone who would pay for her, just like any common serving-girl or drudge. And to make the game more amusing still, both knew, and knew the other knew, that any master who thus simply threw away the education and training that had been invested in this woman, would have to be out of his mind.

I could see Mala was enjoying the little exchange greatly, as was the woman. Yet there was no sale, and Mala was almost apologetic.

'I will return,' he promised, 'and buy something for myself after I have found what I want for the present; meanwhile, thank you for being so helpful – and if you could let Carilius Milo know what I am looking for... Tell him price is no object – within reason, of course.'

She promised she would do so, and we left.

'We have seen some beautiful objects,' remarked Mala, 'but I am not sure the most beautiful was not the young lady who served us.'

'I could see you were quite smitten; perhaps you should make Carilius Milo an offer for her, though she would cost you more than the bowl, I am sure.'

'If I thought he would sell, I would do so. She is remarkable: every bit as good-looking as that girl from Campania I was once keen on, and twice as intelligent. And there is something else about her, almost as though...' He shook his head. 'But no: it couldn't be.'

As usual I did not know what he might be talking about, and as usual he did not enlighten me.

The responses that Mala's request that Carilius Milo be informed of what he was looking for came after only three days, but in the meantime Gaius Molo had brought us up-to-date on what the vigiles had been about.

'None of our usual sources will tell us a thing: it is the Aulus Epirota* mystery all over again, except that on that occasion, as we know now, we were hunting a chimera, whereas this time we know there is a murderer out there.

'You suggested it could be an inside job; I am not wholly convinced, but it is very possible. We questioned all of Marius's workmen, but none of them – they claimed – knew anything. Most of them have cast-iron alibis for the time of the murder. The chief foreman, though, a Greek called Heliodorus, is missing. I do not mean he has disappeared, but that he left Rome on some business or other the morning after Marius's death, and is not due back for several days.'

'Presumably no stolen goods have put in an appearance?'

'Not a thing.'

'This man, Heliodorus: what do you know about him?'

'Not a great deal. He is a highly-skilled workman, and had been Marius's right-hand man for years. Bit of a loner, but got on well enough with most of the workers.'

'Married?'

'No; lives by himself in a little place just off the Via Lata.'

---

* See *Quintus Propertius and the Demise of the Gullible Gaul*

'I would like to talk to this Greek when he returns. First, though, I am hoping we will hear something from Carilius Milo.'

Gaius Molo looked anxious.

'Be very, very careful, Quintus Propertius. Milo is in a different league from Macrobius, and far more dangerous. He is very, very clever, and makes sure not a breath of suspicion attaches to him personally: he portrays himself as just an ordinary well-to-do Roman citizen who keeps himself to himself. Everyone knows, though, even though it cannot be proved, that he deals in dodgy goods, and also that he is protected by the rich and powerful who are his customers. Everyone also knows that if he looks too closely into the Milo empire, he will soon wish he had found some other way to occupy his time.'

He spoke with the bitterness of the honest cop who knows he is powerless in the face of forces too big for him.

'And yet,' said Mala, 'I hear Carilius Milo is a charming man, a good host, kind to children and old ladies…'

'I've never met him, but I've heard the same thing; the trouble is that his charm is only skin-deep.'

'A man may smile, and smile and prove a villain: that observation was made many years ago, Gaius Molo – many years ago in a manner of speaking. I have never doubted its truth. So, yes, I will be careful of Carilius Milo, and most especially if he exercises his charm. So far, though, I have not heard from him.'

Nor did he: the letter from Carilius Milo was addressed to me. The reason for that was obvious enough: rank. Though Mala on a score of counts was a more substantial citizen, he did not belong to the equestrian order, and I did, however shakily. Milo was simply observing the proprieties.

'I am advised that you and your friend,' the letter began; he must have been told by the woman that it was Mala, and I was only along for the ride, 'are interested in fine quality glassware. I dabble in glass, among other things, and I have a few items that have not yet found their way into my little shops. If you and Quintus Propertius Mala would care to call on me at my villa in the next few days, I will be most pleased to show you what I have. Please let my messenger know what day would suit you best.'

It was a cordial enough note, and I sent a cordial reply, suggesting two days hence.

Carilius Milo owned a large town house in the best part of the Esquiline, and another as close to the Capitol as any private residence could get, but his main abode was a few miles beyond the city walls, just off the Appian Way. It was reputed to be of enormous size and opulence, looked after by no fewer than two hundred slaves.

I had assumed we would ride to the villa, but on the morning of the appointed day learned otherwise. Milo had sent two litters, which were to take us to the city limits, where wheeled transport would be waiting for us.

'We can still take our sticks,' said Mala when he learned of the arrangements that had been made, 'but if we had been riding I had something rather better lined up. I will show you on our return.'

He did, though, sling over his shoulder a small leather bag, which apparently contained something heavy: a large dagger, I wondered, or even a short-sword?

I have seen large villas before: some of my friends are aristocrats whose wealth exceeds many times the senatorial minimum of a million sesterces. They have built themselves villas in various delectable parts of Italy that are masterpieces of architecture, a wonderful tribute to the Roman art of gracious living. When you have seen my friend Septimus Servolus's little place overlooking the Bay of Baiae, for examine, or his richer-still cousin Lucinius Cottius's impressive pile on the Isle of Igilium, you are not likely to be impressed by any nouveau-riche merchant's ostentatious and vulgar heap, trumpeting its delusions of grandeur.

And yet I was impressed. Size is one thing, and big, Milo's villa was, not so much a building as a whole complex of buildings, all of substantial dimensions; aesthetic quality is something else, and whoever had designed these buildings had an eye for beauty that smacked of sheer genius. The landscape architect who had set out the immense grounds, too, must have been a man of enormous talent and sensitivity.

Even Mala, normally so undemonstrative, could not repress a whistle of astonishment.

We were met in the atrium by one of those mock-obsequious servants, a slave to his master but used to lording it over everyone else in the household, and probably regarded as a minor god by those under his command.

'You will want to bathe after your journey,' he informed us; (not 'would you like to…'). 'If you will follow me I will show you the bath-house.'

'Upstairs, downstairs,' I heard Mala mutter, though since we were still on the lower level of the villa – I had almost said 'palace' – his remark made no sense to me.

And so we entered the bath-house; and what a bath-house!

'I've no doubt the baths of Diocletian will be bigger,' remarked Mala, 'but not much; and not half so luxurious. This little complex is not here in the cause of cleanliness; it is meant to overawe visitors, and it does.'

It was efficient as well as awe-inspiring. The naked slave-girls who were obviously there to cater to our every need were almost painfully eager to please, but we asked them to confine themselves to wielding the strigil, and we emerged cleansed, refreshed, and smelling of roses. Another slave, who presumably had been waiting for us, then conducted us into the Presence.

There was nothing ostentatious, at first glance, about Carilius Milo, though it was obvious enough who was the big wheel. He was reclining, around a table, with a small group of people, and he greeted us profusely and indicated an empty couch.

'How pleasant, gentlemen! I trust your journey from Rome was not too onerous?'

It had been uncomfortable, necessarily: those wheeled vehicles always are, however many thickly padded cushions might be provided – and our conveyance certainly did not lack them. Mala said something about the 'need to invent the spring' – I think the word was 'spring' – but as usual did not explain. Nevertheless the journey had been relatively short, and the trip to the bath-house most welcome, and so I answered politely and thanked Milo for providing the carriage, as well as the litters that had carried us to it.

He dismissed my thanks with a wave of the hand.

'It is a pleasure,' he smiled. 'It is so rarely I see fresh faces here. Let me introduce you to my other guests.'

The first was a swarthy, evil-looking man, Spanish most likely, who, we afterwards learned, was Milo's chief of operations in Africa. (I wondered idly if he was aware of the competition from Molo's Egyptian suspect, he of the hot-line to the tomb-robbers.)

Next to the Spaniard was a tubby little fellow who looked inordinately pleased with himself, and kept rubbing his hands together, half nervously and half in satisfaction, who might have been anything, a banker, an accountant, or just someone to provide comic relief. He kept his eyes closely on Milo, as though ready to sit on his hind legs like a pet dog if that worthy ordered him to.

'A slight, insufferable man,' Mala said of him afterwards.

The other two were quite different. The first was a woman: none other than the charming person we had met in Milo's salon in Rome. She looked exquisite as before, but sat there quietly and rather stiffly on an outer couch, as befitted her lowly status. Milo did not introduce her.

The remaining man, far more thoroughly out of place in these surroundings, shouted 'artisan' in accent, in gesture, in every item of clothing, in the very look in his eyes. Yet the look was not one of discomfort only, I reckoned; there was more than a suspicion of cunning there. This is an underhand sort of character, I decided at once. I looked at him squarely when we were introduced, and was not surprised that almost immediately he averted his gaze.

'And finally,' beamed Milo, 'this is my Greek friend, now probably the most accomplished glassmaker in Rome; his name is Heliodorus.'

When we compared notes afterwards, Mala and I were agreed that Milo must have known we were aware of who Heliodorus was, and introducing him to us was no accident. During the whole visit, indeed, there was nothing accidental about anything Milo said or did: all had been thought through beforehand, to impress, to warn, to bribe, or to trap. It is a tribute to Mala's nous, and to his quick perception of what was what, that the trip turned out so well; indeed, for him, in two different respects, so very, very well indeed. It was an indication also, however, that Milo had decided – on balance, no doubt: everything was on balance – that it would serve his purpose better simply to warn us off than to have us summarily eliminated, which there is no doubt he could have done at the drop of a hat.

At the superficial level, however, an innocent observer would never have guessed that anything more was going on than a genial host entertaining his guests, or a businessman ingratiating himself with prospective clients. Milo liberally deployed his legendary charm.

'This wine is one you might find interesting, Marcus Vectorius. It comes from your esteemed late mother's home region, where you and I know they produce some of the best wine in Italy.'

He really had done his homework. My mother's family had indeed been prominent wine-growers in a noted wine-growing area, before selling out and moving down to Rome..

'Very fine, Carilius Milo, very fine indeed. It makes me proud to have an ancestral connection with a place that produces such nectar.'

'Quite so; quite so.

'And you, Quintus Propertius: I would have paid you a similar compliment, but your ancestors seem to have been – hard to locate.'

It was not a flat insult, but could have been construed as one. Mala preferred, wisely, to take it as simply a friendly interest in his background.

'My parents died when I was quite young,' he volunteered. 'I spent much of my youth in Britain, mostly in the south-west, but we moved about a good deal: my father was loosely attached to the staff of the governor.'

'Loosely attached?'

'He had a kind of roving commission, sounding out local chieftains, investigating trading possibilities, recommending sites for possible Roman settlements.'

'Most interesting sounding work; I am surprised I have never heard of him.'

'He was no big wheel,' smiled Mala. 'He had hoped for equestrian status some day, but did not survive to achieve it. My mother died shortly after he did. As for the rest of my family: I had no uncles or aunts. I was told we might be distantly related to the poet, Sextus Propertius.'

'Let us talk no longer of the past,' said Milo suddenly. 'In the here-and-now, I learn you are interested in good glassware. I have some that might suit your purpose. Come; and Heliodorus, would you come also, and give us the benefit of your expertise?'

We moved to an adjoining room, and there, on a long table, was a mass of the finest glassware, from all over the empire and beyond: from Bythinia, from Egypt, from Parthia, even from Germany, vases, jugs, bowls – everything.

A little group of items separate from the rest took Milo's attention.

'Here,' he indicated the collection, 'you might find what you want. You are in search of a bowl, I believe. A present, is it not?'

They were all of the highest quality, and the centrepiece, a huge bowl of strikingly elaborate design, was overwhelming.

For all its magnificence, however, it was not the bowl that took Mala's eye. Lying next to it, small and plain and quite insignificant, was Mala's magnifying lens.

'Will this, perhaps, suit your taste? ' asked Carilius Milo. 'I would have to ask a premium price, naturally, for a piece so fine; but to a true connoisseur, what does price matter?'

Mala kept his composure wonderfully.

'It is,' he said, 'a magnificent piece: worthy of Marius at his best.'

He looked the other man straight in the eye as he spoke; Milo did not blink.

'Perhaps it *is* Marius at his best; what do you think, Heliodorus?'

The artisan stammered.

'It is certainly not unlike my late employer's work; there are similarities in...'

'Spare the cant,' said Milo pleasantly. 'You were more forthright than that when you brought them to me.'

The man said no more, not quite knowing what was expected of him. Milo turned to me, and suddenly his charm had gone.

'Marcus Vectorius, you are an intelligent young man, as I am sure your friend is also. Let us see if we agree about one or two of the facts of life – for life itself could depend it.'

'First, I am an honest trader. I buy and sell merchandise: any merchandise, gold, silver, grain, wine; precious objects. I am good at it, which is why I live in this pleasant little place, instead of an attic in the Subura.

'Secondly, I buy and sell, but especially buy, where I like. It is neither my inclination nor my obligation to bother myself with the provenance of what I acquire: I assume that those who sell to me are honest men, as I am, and once I have bought what I believe my customers might want, I think no more about it.

'Others are very wise if they, too, think no more about it.'

There was no mistaking the cold menace in his eyes now, and I remembered, with a shudder, the old quip: the best way to survive an encounter with Carilius Milo, is to be somewhere else.

His next words were more conciliatory, though the coldness in his eyes was still there.

'But these are grave matters, not the kind of thing Roman gentlemen should concern themselves with. Quintus Propertius, you seek a bowl. This is a fine one. It is yours for ----.' He named a price that, though high, was by no means unreasonable for so fine an object. 'I am sure we do not need to trouble ourselves about provenance: it is obviously, shall we say, *in the style of* Marius?'

'It is, as you say, in the style of Marius, and every bit as good as the master's work. I am tempted to keep it for myself, and seek something else for my present. You price is a most fair one, Carilius Milo, more than fair; I accept with pleasure. As you say, provenance is such a dodgy business; why worry our heads about it, if the goods are acceptable?'

It was surrender, and Milo recognised it at once. His tone became even more conciliatory.

'I would hate to think,' he said, 'that any of these goods are by Marius, despite what the good Heliodorus has to say. No doubt it is a matter of artistic influence: a master craftsman has seen Marius's work, and felt bound to imitate it; with some success, we both agree.

'As for poor Marius himself,' he went on, 'I do not suppose his stuff will ever be recovered. I do hope, though, that they find the man who murdered him – or that *you* find him, Quintus Propertius, for I am told you are something of an amateur investigator. We cannot have our leading citizens killed out of hand like that, and I for one will rejoice if the culprit is found and sent to the arena.'

I thought I saw the Greek look most unhappy as he spoke, but perhaps I imagined it.

Milo, now that he had got what he wanted, was ever more expansive.

'Quintus Propertius,' he smiled, 'I have made a good sale, and you have made a good purchase – and I have taken a liking to you. Is there any little favour I can grant you, to seal our transaction and our friendship?'

This was a crunch question as Mala was well aware, and he paused a little before replying.

'As a matter of fact,' he said, 'there are two; but I will quite understand if I am asking too much.

'The little circular object, that was lying next to the bowl: it is an amusing toy, quite clever in its way. I had one once, long ago, and I had not expected to see anther. If you would suggest a price…'

'Price? For this gewgaw? My dear fellow, take it, with my compliments.' How Mala concealed his delight, I do not know, but he thanked Milo profusely, and the lens disappeared into his leather bag.

'And the next favour, Quintus Propertius?'

'I scarcely like asking this. Let me explain. A short time ago, I lost one of my most valued slaves – a young girl, of German ancestry, though born in captivity in Rome. So far I have found no replacement. I have a weakness, I must confess, for fair-headed pulchritudinous young women. I must tell you that I was instantly attracted to the young slave who looked after your salon in Rome, and who is here to-day. Name your price, Cornelius Milo: I would buy her from you.'

I wondered that Mala had dared make such a request. The woman was highly trained, and manifestly a great asset to Milo's trading empire. The reply was unexpected.

'No, Quintus Propertius. I have others who have been trained to do Julia's work, but what if they are taken from me? Sickness, the plague, an accident even? Yet I have said that I am anxious that there should be goodwill between us. I will not sell the slave, but you may have her, on indefinite loan. I reserve the right, however, to ask for her return if I need her. And so there is no need for payment, my dear fellow; enjoy her services.' He leered.

And that was that. More wine; idle banter; smug satisfaction on Milo's face, apprehension on Heliodorus's; Mala's inscrutable. Finally, the carriage arrived, the slave girl with her little bundle was summoned, and we were away.

'He has won,' said Mala, 'but the battle, not the war. He has bought me off, and is gloating about it. There will be no awkward enquiry, as there would have been had he simply had me killed – and you, a knight; there will be no further black mark against his name, which there would have been, even if nothing could be proved; there will be no more futile searches for Marius's missing artefacts, which he flaunted in front of our noses, and dared us to challenge him about; and he even issued an open invitation for us to try to find the murderer, and deal with him, knowing full well that no connection could be established between him and the guilty man.

'He held all the cards, and he played them one by one: the implied threats; the glassware; the bribery. I let him think they had worked, which in the short run they did: I don't go in for pointless suicide; but how surprised he is going to be, one day.'

'And the murderer?'

'We still go after him.'

'Do you think the Greek has anything to do with it?'

'I would be surprised if he didn't have everything to do with it. Whether he worked on his own initiative, or on Milo's instructions, who knows? When he returns to Rome, Molo will have him in for questioning, but before that, I would like to take a look at his apartment.'

'His apartment?'

'Specifically, his wardrobe.'

He did not elaborate, and we sat and suffered in silence as the carriage creaked and groaned and bounced its way along the road.

At last we arrived, and looking at the solitary driver, and our own apparently unarmed state, the guards looked a little perturbed.

'You shouldn't be out here without swords, sir, or better still guards, especially with a lady to look after. There are some nasty characters around these days.'

We thanked the man for his advice and promised we would take note, Mala and I smiling slightly as we looked at our sword-sticks.

The litter bearers, poor devils, were waiting for us, as they had been all day; fortunately there were little food shops not far from the gate; there was even a wine-shop, where one of them in particular must have passed a good deal of the time. They were up to the job, however, even with an extra body to carry, and eventually we were back at Mala's door. I saw him press coins into the hand of the leading litter-bearer, and we went in.

It was just as we had entered Mala's impressive but unusually furnished 'den', as he called it, that it happened. The slave looked in amazement at the chairs and couches, of such unorthodox design, that Mala had had specially constructed. She took in, too, the walls, plain instead of decorated with the murals one might have expected, but hung with little, individual paintings, done on separate boards with elaborate wooden frames, hanging individually at head height, and depicting, some of them, scenes and people like nothing I had ever seen before.

'Good heavens!' exclaimed the girl; I reproduce her words as best I can*, for they were unmistakably in one of the outlandish tongues Mala occasionally lapsed into. 'It can't be...'

The effect on Mala was immediate. He stared at her in disbelief, and then:

'Heaven be praised.'

A moment later she was in his arms, and this strong man was close to tears also as he comforted and consoled her. From their very first encounter it had been obvious that there was mutual attraction; now I saw that attraction blossom into something much, much more.

The slave girl – though I could never again think of her as a slave – was now alternately laughing and crying, Mala himself making little effort to hide his emotions, while I stood there, scarcely comprehending, frankly embarrassed by this oh-so-unRoman display of naked emotion, yet moved in spite of myself by its depth and intensity. This was Catullus and his Lesbia – a thousand fold.

After a time I tip-toed out, my thoughts in something of a turmoil.

Next day Mala and I again found ourselves with Gaius Molo, filling him in on our meeting with the ' honest trader'.

'And now, Gaius Molo, I have brought this for you.' Mala handed the vigil a large, heavy box. 'It is material evidence. You have a strong-room where it can be kept safely? Eventually I hope it will be needed, to convict a very wealthy villain. Meanwhile, however, let us see if we can convict a rather poorer but more hands-on one: the murderer of Marius the Glassmaker.'

Accompanied by Molo and two of his vigiles, and by one of Marius's workman we collected on the way, we were soon at the little apartment where Heliodorus had his being. It did not take Molo's men long to force entry.

It was an unprepossessing little pad, and we did not stop to admire it.

---

* In truth Mala helped me when I came to write up these accounts: 'You might as well get it right if you are to be my Watson,' he told me, and now, you see, I know what he meant by that; of which more anon.

'I am looking,' said Mala, 'for clothes, tunics especially. I presume Heliodorus owned more than the one he stood up in when we met him at Milo's villa. First, though, I want to be very sure of what you told me before, Gaius Molo. Heliodorus lived quite alone?'

'He did.'

'No aged mother in the background. No lady friends? – or others?'

'No; he was the quintessential loner.' The man from Marius's workshop hastened to confirm this.

'Excellent; that makes our task so much easier. I cannot be sure, mind, that we will find what I want, but we must keep our fingers crossed.'

We soon unearthed a little basket, with some of Heliodorus's discarded clothing in it.

'It is lucky he went away early the very next morning after Marius was killed. He did not have time to wash his garments, or send them to the laundry across the street.'

There were two tunics, of the kind one would expect: not of the very poorest quality, but modest enough. One of them, plain white and unadorned, had a smallish stain in the front, and this Mala selected.

'This could well be blood,' he said, 'but we have no way of proving it, and even if we had, Heliodorus could simply say he had cut himself: he does work with glass, after all.' He turned to the workman.

'Can you say whether this is the tunic Heliodorus was wearing the day Marius was murdered?'

'It was. We only ever saw him in three: this one, the one with the blue belt there, and another that had green edging.'

'He was wearing the green-edged one when we saw him at Milo's,' I reminded Mala.

He nodded, and taking the tunic, he spread it out on a table, front upwards; and then, to the surprise of the others, who had never seen it, he produced his magnifying lens. Painstakingly, through the glass, he examined every inch of Heliodorus's tunic.

'Look,' he said at last, pointing to a spot quite near the stain. We could see nothing.

'Now look.'

Through the lens, just visible, were five short hairs. Three of them were black; the other two, in strong contrast, were purest white. Mala spelled it out for us, though it was not necessary.

'Heliodorus was a Greek: swarthy, black haired. Marius, as we know, was of advanced years, and his hair was as white as snow.

'And now,' he said to me, smiling, 'do you still call this little thing a toy?'

'That is brilliant,' said Molo. 'This should be enough to send him to the arena.'

I doubted it. I could well imagine what a good lawyer would make of such a single piece of evidence, cleverly though it had been uncovered (assuming Heliodorus, who was only an artisan, could have found a good lawyer).

In the event it did not matter, for Heliodorus did not return. He had obviously got the wind up at Milo's, and whether that gentleman helped him to skip the country, or even helped him to explore the bed of the Tiber whilst tied to a bucket of stones, we never discovered. Mala demonstrated his little trick with the lens to the presiding magistrate, to that worthy's great astonishment, and the Greek was pronounced guilty *in absentia*..

'It was not a very tidy conclusion,' observed Mala, as we relaxed after one of those wonderful meals Diogenes, his genius of a cook, had produced, 'but in the circumstances, it could have been worse.'

There were just the three of us, Mala himself, me, and Julia Carolina now looking radiant, dressed in all the finery of an upper-class Roman lady.

'The time has come,' said Mala, 'when I was going at last to tell you my story. I fear it will have to wait a little longer, because now it will have to include Julia Carolina's. Please go on being patient – and trust me.

'But first, I must explain to you the functions of a best man.'

QUINTUS PROPERTIUS AND THE SCHOOL FOR YOUNG LADIES AT EPHESUS

The dislodgement of Licinius Populus, after his long period of predominance, was effected with remarkably little fuss. A large bunch of the emperor's German rottweilers paid him a social visit, and proceeded to demonstrate their devotion to the notion of freedom.

Freedom? They had heard it said that 'freedom is choice', and so they gave Populus the choice - of falling on his own sword, or of being cut down on the spot. He chose the former option, and Rome was temporarily without a Chief Investigator.

'He paid the penalty,' said Mala, 'of over-reaching himself. It is a common failing in those who do the dirty work of tyrants. They do their master's bidding, they terrorize the populace, they acquire more and more power, and then, inevitably, they are tempted to follow their own agenda rather than that of their boss. I call it the Beria syndrome.' (*Beria syndrome?* I think 'Beria' was a name but am not sure.) 'Once the boss gets wind of it, and realises they are getting too big for their boots, he quietly asks for their resignation - with immediate effect..

'For the moment, therefore, we have a power-vacuum. Eventually Domitian will appoint a new Chief Investigator, but until he does, and even for a little time afterwards while the new incumbent is finding his feet, ordinary people can sleep a little easier in their beds, and the villains who worked hand-in-glove with Licinius Publius will find things are not so rosy as they were.'

'Which brings us to Carilius Milo.'

'Indeed: the greatest villain of all. For a while, he will be at his most vulnerable. Like a wounded animal, however, he might also be at his most dangerous. He may well decide to lash out wildly at whoever happens to be in the way, simply to demonstrate that he still has the power to do so.'

How right Mala's prediction was, the very next day revealed. He looked grim as he entered Rufus's Place, and sat down at the table where several of us were already gathered.

'I will not be staying long,' he told us. 'I have some rather important matters to attend to. I have just received an invitation to visit Carilius Milo at his villa, and he especially adds that he expects Julia Carolina to accompany me.'

'Shall you go?'

'No. I will tender my profuse apologies for not being able to accept, and thank him for his kind thought, but as things are at present I have no intention of going within miles of his villa, and even if I had, I would not take Julia with me.'

Next day I called on him, and he looked even more sombre. He showed me a letter than had arrived only minutes before. It was from Milo, and it was brief: he demanded the return of his slave, Julia, whom he had 'lent' to Mala in the course of their previous encounter.*

'The litter is coming for her to-morrow morning, Milo's goon informed me; Milo expects her return without delay.'

'He is within his legal rights,' I said.

'Legal rights be ------.' He used one of the foreign expletives I had heard him come out with before, though never quite so vehemently.

'Life could get very difficult. If Milo invokes the law, as he doubtless will, Julia Carolina could be dragged back by force; and if he doesn't, he could send his own thugs, with much the same result.'

'Milo's thugs would come seriously unstuck, unless he sent an army: I have a little gadget, Marcus, which I will show you some day, that is very much more effective than my sword. I have taken to carrying it with me wherever I go.' He tapped the little leather bag that I had first seen when we visited Milo's villa on the former occasion. I wondered what could possibly be more effective than his sword, which in his hands was about the deadliest weapon one could hope never to engage with.

---

* See *Quintus Propertius and the Misfortune of Marius the Glassmaker*

'But that would only give temporary respite; I could not hold back an entire band of Milo's thugs. Fortunately I have seen this coming, and I took the precaution of making arrangements almost immediately after returning with Julia Carolina. Long before Milo's litter, and its escort, arrive, we will have left Rome.'

'They will have all exits guarded.'

'I would be disappointed if they did not. That means they will continue looking for us in Rome long after we have left the city, which will only aid our escape. I wish you could come with us, for you too might well be a target, but I know you have your duties here.'

Duties? Piddling little tasks as fatuous as they were futile, devised by some imperial bureaucrat to keep us junior equestrians out of mischief.

'As a matter of fact,' I told Mala, 'some cretin sitting safely behind a desk has just had the bright idea of re-allocating and re-scheduling a whole raft of duties for us younger knights, It doesn't signify – it's just something to keep him happy – but the good news is that I have no duties for the best part of two and a half months - more, if I use a proxy for some of the minor stuff, which I am entitled to do.'

'Excellent! I will feel much better with the redoubtable Marcus at my side. I fear, though, my friend, that your social status is about to be terribly transformed.'

The following morning, a motley band assembled outside the city walls, and began to pile themselves and their effects into the wheeled vehicles that had been awaiting them. All shapes and sizes and ages and nationalities they were, many of them dressed outlandishly, all in high spirits and chattering a hundred to the dozen.

Obviously in charge, a lean, middle-aged bundle of energy of indeterminate origin, was a man all addressed as 'gaffer', and any theatregoer in Rome would have recognised him as Pedius the Impresario, whose Sophocles cycle had only recently had such an outstanding success. Among the actors and actresses and attendants now milling around, no-one could fail to recognise the deep-voiced Creon, whom everyone had loved to hate, or the Greek, as refined as she was aloofly beautiful, whose Antigone had moved so many to tears.

All were contracted to Pedius, and had been temporarily 'resting' after their Theban labours, until it was unexpectedly announced that they were to travel to Ostia to give two unscheduled performances, of *Antigone* itself, and, by way of contrast, Aristophanes' *The Frogs*.

In charge of the props, fussing incessantly and impatiently as masks, garments, mock weapons, and the rest of the paraphernalia were piled into one of the vehicles, was an aged, grey-haired retainer who had obviously been a member of the troupe for aeons. Doing his bidding were two slaves, Africans, black as ebony, a sturdy young fellow who looked as though he was lucky to have escaped the arena, and a young woman of lovely figure who drew admiring glances, only for such glances to turn to embarrassment as they alighted on her hideously pock-marked face: a victim of the plague she had been, her beauty gone forever, and slave though she might be, no-one could but be sorry for her plight.

They broke up, this theatrical ménage, when they reached Ostia, some to tread the boards again and present Sophocles to the masses, some to head for the nearest tavern and do what actors do when nectar calls, and three to make their way to a big merchant ship, on which, the moment they were aboard, the hortator began pounding his drum, and the vessel ponderously made its way out of the harbour and started its voyage to distant Rhegium.

Any who had witnessed the exodus from Rome of the theatrical group would have looked in vain for the props manager and his black slaves; and just as surely they would not have recognised the three who boarded the merchantman. Instead they would have seen a dark-haired Spaniard, almost smelling of horse-flesh, his impatience to get off the ship and astride one of his thoroughbred stallions almost palpable, and his two companions, an equally swarthy younger man, ostensibly his brother, and a haughty dark-haired beauty who for the whole of the voyage kept her face well-veiled, and averted her eyes from the gaze of any lascivious male misguided enough to let it linger on her for more than the tiniest instant.

The ship reached Rhegium; they disembarked; and then they vanished, these three, as effectively as had the old man and his Africans.

'Thank goodness,' said Mala, 'to get that filthy greasepaint off, and thank goodness, Publius Valgius, to be safely in your hands, and for the time being at least away from the cares of Rome.

'We cannot, alas, linger. It will not take Milo long to realise we are not in Rome, and soon enough he will find out, if he does not already know, that you and we are friends, and will send his minions to search for us in Rhegium. You will not be molested if he discovers we are genuinely not with you, but the last thing I would want is to expose you to any danger.'

'Danger? Let them come.'

Valgius's four litter-slaves, we had noticed, were almost as big as he himself, and I would not fancy the chances of any half dozen bully-boys Milo might send against them. But what of that? If half a dozen did not prevail, Milo could send a dozen, if a dozen did not suffice, two dozen. No: Mala was right, it was better for all concerned that we should make ourselves scarce, as soon as we had rested from our voyage.

'But you will not go,' insisted Valgius, 'until my wife and I have demonstrated the hospitality for which the people of Rhegium are famous.'

Far from being the formidable woman Valgius's banter had suggested when he was in Rome*, his wife was a quiet, retiring, young-middle-aged Roman lady of the old school, by no means prim and proper, yet always mindful of propriety, and not given to wearing her heart on her sleeve - which made the warmth and friendship she extended to us the more moving and valued.

Nor was Valgius's boast about Rhegium hospitality an idle one, and for three days we could not have been better looked after had we been the emperor himself; but the time came at last when Mala felt it would be prudent to depart.

'I have always wanted,' he said, 'to see Ephesus again; I feel sure it will look rather different from when I last was there.'

It was a pleasant voyage, the captain and crew friendly, the sea for most of the time calm as a mill-pond, ruffled only by a mild breeze, just enough to take edge off what would otherwise have been excessive heat, as the sun shone down from an azure sky, day after uneventful day.

---

* See *Quintus Propertius and the estate of the Placid Praetorian*

We experienced that strange feeling, inseparable from a long sea voyage, of being cut off from the outside world, cocooned in our own little universe of creaking deck and splashing oars, of wine-dark sea and cloudless sky, of shoals of silver fish, white soaring gulls, the muffled thud of the hortator's drum, the delicious aroma from the cook's galley as meal-times approached, the balmy evenings as we sat on deck and sipped our wine and chatted inconsequentially.

Occasionally, we encountered other vessels, and all waved in friendly fashion as the ships passed, and banks of oars were raised in formal greeting. For a short time the breeze died down, and we came across a little sailing vessel, utterly becalmed – 'as idle as a painted ship, upon a painted ocean,' said Mala – and doomed apparently to stay there forever and a day if the wind did not spring up again and catch its sails; the three fishermen aboard seeming nonetheless quite unperturbed.

But it was a long voyage, and despite its pleasures – nothing to do but eat and drink and laze about all day: by Jupiter, it's tough - we were all relieved when the ship finally docked, and we made our way into the thriving, bustling, self-important city of Ephesus.

If you've seen one tourist trap, you've seen 'em all. You get the lines of grotty little wine-shops, with not an amphora of half-way drinkable stuff between them; hot-food stalls, selling pasties and pies that back home they might feed to the slaves in the quarries, if they had merited especially harsh punishment; countless purveyors of 'local arts and crafts', misshapen artefacts turned out to a pattern in some dingy sweat shop by slaves working twenty hours a day, going for a song at five denarii, when a couple of sesterces would have been daylight robbery; the lines of litter-bearers, jostling for the privilege of taking you to the place you name, by the most roundabout possible route, for a fare that would have been extortionate for a circumnavigation of Rome; scruffy young children of all hues and sizes, selling sweetmeats, fruit, their sisters, all with an engaging grin as they hold out their palms for your coins…

Mala laughed out loud when one little urchin, carrying a basket of oranges almost as big as himself, rushed up and tried to get him to buy.

'Plus ça change, plus c'est la même chose,' he said, and Julia Carolina smiled. I, of course, had no idea what he was talking about, until he translated for me later, and so I addressed myself to the task of finding somewhere to stay.

'The last time I was here, I spent my first couple of nights in an inn, not a bad place as they go. It's a bit close, though, to one of those ubiquitous establishments, that employ a bevy of beauties who are no better than they should be. We could stay at the inn to begin with, if it is still there, while we are looking for somewhere to rent.'

Had this been Italy, the proposal would have been vetoed on the spot, since, as we all know, most inns there are barely fit for human habitation; this, however, was Ephesus, where they order things differently, and it was agreed; and so we hired litters, and made our way to the place I named, the litter-bearers guffawing and making crude remarks as they passed the sign, set in its marble slab, pointing to the finishing-school for young ladies I had mentioned.

The inn was basic, but clean – a rare boon, that – and the proprietor, an avuncular character who had gone up in the world and now owned several such establishments dotted throughout the city, was keen to share his sense of good fortune with his guests, and welcome them all as long-lost brothers. His bonhomie became a little trying after a time, but he meant well, the wine he served was quite potable, and the slave who prepared the meals knew his job. What more could one ask?

We had, again, changed our identities a little. I did not hide, but did not flaunt, the marks of my rank, and thought it safe to use my own name. Mala posed as a friend who had come to Ephesus to research the turbulent history of the ancient city, with Julia Carolina, of course, as his wife – which in truth she now was, according to the arcane ceremony they had insisted on when still in Rome, though not in Roman law while she remained the property of Carilius Milo.

Next morning, we did what any sensible visitor to Ephesus does, and went sightseeing. I had seen it before, but despite what I have said about tourist traps, was still impressed. Mala and Julia were even more so, as excited and awestruck as any country bumpkin on his first visit to Rome. They gawped at the Temple of Artemis, gazed for a long while, lost in admiration, at the vast expanse of the amphitheatre, and seemed impressed even by the marble-tiled streets and paths we were walking on.

All the time, in their strange tongue, the two commented incessantly, and it almost seemed that they were comparing the city with some other.

At one point, turning away from a small building of no especial merit, Mala even observed: 'What a good place this would be for a big public library. And some day, Marcus, take it from me, one will be built.'

Time passed all too rapidly for Mala and Julia Carolina that morning, and for me also for different reasons: I felt the familiar rumblings. I was delighted therefore when Mala paused, and uttered magic words.

'We have been exploring all morning. May I conjecture – it is only a conjecture, mind – that my friend Marcus could force himself to partake of a little wine and food - only a little, of course?'

Now he was talking my language.

It's a big empire, and although Roman law is ubiquitous, in other respects locals are allowed to get on with their lives much as they have always done. Ephesian customs, as I had discovered on my previous visit, were very different from those I was used to at home, and it did not take us long to find a little food shop – 'More like a restaurant,' Mala commented, whatever that meant – where men and women alike were happily eating and drinking and chatting together, as they never could have been in a public place in Rome.

We found a table for three, and I went to the marble-topped bar to order wine, but as I turned to go back to our table, I saw, sitting by himself, a dark, greasy-haired, sullen-looking man, staring intently at Mala and Julia Carolina. I recognised him at once. It was the Spaniard we had met at Milo's villa weeks before, the man in charge of African operations.

'He has twigged who we are, there is no doubt,' said Mala. 'I wonder what he is doing here, so far from his supposed patch. Luckily it will take time for any message he might send to reach Milo, and by that time I hope events in Rome will have moved on, to the distress of quite a number of villains. We are into September now, and Nerva will soon…'

He broke off, and I never did discover what he was going to say about Nerva, though I wondered what that aging senator, long past his prime, could have to do with anything very much.

The reason Mala had broken off was all too plain: into the tavern, flanked by two nasty-looking goons, was the other man we had met at Milo's, the egregious little banker, accountant, or whatever he was. He took in the scene, saw us sitting there, raised his eye-brows in surprise, and then went to join the Spaniard.

'Curioser and curioser,' said Mala. 'Who next: Milo himself?'

That was not to be: yet.

The next day was spent house-hunting. We looked at a number of unprepossessing little villas on the outskirts of the city, and one enormous town-house only a stone's-throw from the amphitheatre, that looked as though it had not been lived in for thirty years, but found nothing really suitable at a price that was remotely realistic: neither Mala nor I were short of the ready, but we saw no reason to buy rapacious absentee landlords the latest in gold-plated chariots, just for the privilege of occupying temporarily their grotty little premises.

The proprietor of the inn, when he learned of our lack of success, surprised us by offering a whole suite of rooms for less than half of the asking price of some of the dilapidated hovels we had been inspecting. It was an offer we could not refuse, and, as subsequent events were to show, it was as well that we did not.

Only a few days after we had established ourselves in our new accommodation, Julia Carolina was unwell. It was nothing serious, and the proprietor's homely wife assured us she would look after the invalid – 'like she was me own daughter, sir, you can be sure' – and so Mala and I decided to stroll down to the harbour: another wise decision, though we would never have guessed at the time.

The harbour was busy as always, host to a mixed bag of tiny fishing-smacks, unkempt coastal traders, substantial merchantmen, and one enormous naval trireme which, though as yet we had no inkling, we were destined to get to know well before our Ephesian adventure was over.

We sat at a table outside one of the less-disreputable-looking wine shops, sipping something they said was wine, presumably because it came in an amphora; but so does lamp-oil. Mala muttered that – I think I've got it right – he had sprinkled better stuff over fish and chips – *chips?* –and we agreed to try somewhere else, rather than further risk poisoning ourselves.

We moved on. The next squalid-looking establishment was a mite better. Their best – one shuddered to think what the worst might be like – was still only any-port-in-a-storm kind of stuff, but a strong-willed man could manage to force it down, faute de mieux. I began to understand why some people, like our friend Valgius, preferred to stick to beer: it does not foster illusions, you expect it to be foul and it is, but at least it's cheap.

We had not been sitting there long when our attention, like everyone else's, was caught by a sleek, white-painted masterpiece of a ship, gliding, almost swan-like, into the harbour. Its lines were as elegant as they were functional, every yard of her impressive length screamed 'class', and even the crassest landlubber could see that she had to be one of the fastest things afloat.

'A ship like that,' Mala observed, 'is a work of art as surely as a poem by Virgil, or a statue by Phidias. It lifts the spirits just to see it.'

'It doesn't lift mine,' I replied; 'superb though it is. That is the racing-galley of Carilius Milo.'

After a while, a small party came ashore: Milo himself, flanked by the usual beasts-masquerading-as-men who formed his bodyguard, assorted sycophants, and two nubile young women, who looked decidedly unhappy. We moved back into the shadows to avoid being seen, though we knew it would not be long before the Spaniard and the little accountant informed Milo we were in Ephesus.

'What I would like to know,' mused Mala, 'is whether that excrescence has come to Ephesus because he has discovered we are here, or whether he is engaged in some nefarious business or other quite unconnected with us. The latter, I would guess: we covered our tracks pretty well, and he would hardly drag his African supremo, and that other funny little man, all this way, just to help dispose of us. Something is afoot.'

We discovered what it was the very next day. One of the advantages of lodging where we did was that we could sit and watch the world go by – or, more accurately, not go by, but go in, and out of, the dubious establishment almost opposite. It probably catered, as most do, to a wide range of tastes, and certainly did to a wide range of clientèle, old and young, poor and prosperous, hurried and leisurely, blatant and shamefaced.

By mid-morning they started to arrive, but a good hour before that the two long benches on each side of the door would be filled with the poor wretches on offer – not that they all looked like poor wretches: brazen hussies, many of them – parading their charms for any passer-by to see; or for any inhabitants, like us, of our grandiloquently named inn, *The Silver Amphora*.

The morning after the arrival of Milo's galley, I found Mala staring intently at the line of women on the bench furthest from us. I was about to make some crack about telling Julia Carolina what he was up to, but the grim look on his face dissuaded me.

'Look,' he said; 'do you notice anything about the two at the end?'

The two he pointed out were, like the rest, clad in low-cut, shamelessly revealing gowns, but unlike most they were not laughing and chatting, but sitting silently, their unhappiness manifest; one, indeed, was quietly sobbing.

'I notice they look very unhappy,' I replied.

'What I notice, is that they are the same two young women who came ashore from Milo's galley yesterday.'

The 'hostesses' – I believe that is the euphemism - were being overseen by an androgynous creature of quite indescribable ugliness, wielding a vicious looking cane as though she wanted only the slightest excuse to use it. The women on the benches, even the blasé old-stagers, looked at her apprehensively, and the two we were interested in positively cowered when her gaze rested on them. But, unexpectedly, a call came from within, and she hurried inside, muttering some warning to those assembled on the benches.

It all happened in a flash. The moment her back was turned, the unhappy pair, hand-in-hand, leaped from the bench and rushed across the street to the inn; and as though on cue, Mala left his post by the open window and dashed downstairs.

He was back almost immediately, leading the two frightened women.

'None of the inn staff saw them; they should be safe here for a while – but be prepared for trouble.'

Julia Carolina had joined us, and was soon doing her best to comfort the women. The one who had not been crying before had now finally cracked, and was weeping inconsolably; the other seemed unable to comprehend that, for the time being at least, she was no longer a captive.

I saw outside a great commotion as the absence of the two was discovered. The androgynous jailer ushered the remainder inside, and then, accompanied by a hefty-looking man as ugly as herself, strode towards the inn.

In no time there came a pounding on our apartment door. Mala answered.

'Where are the two women?'

'Two women?'

'They came in here, and we want them.'

'In here? What makes you think I would harbour women from your kind of establishment – and with my wife here? Has it not occurred to you that those you are looking for might have entered this building by the front door, and gone straight out of the back? I must ask you to leave.'

The two had no way of knowing whether Mala was bluffing, lying, or genuinely incensed. They contemplated trying to force an entry, but saw the look in Mala's eye, and me behind him, and decided there were better ways of pursuing their investigation.

'If you are hiding those sluts,' said the androgynous one, 'you will regret it. Carilius Milo...'

'...is a louse,' said Mala, 'and if you happen to see him, tell him so from me.'

Having little alternative, they left, in no good grace.

'We must get these young people safely away from here. Fortunately, I know just where they can go. First, though, as soon as they are feeling up to it, we must question them.'

It took a little while for the two women to calm down sufficiently to answer Mala's questions, gently though he put them, but once they had started there was a flood of information.

They were not slaves, but free-born, and of the middling class. They had been kidnapped at Brundisium, and joined two dozen others held captive on Milo's galley – several of whom, as far as they knew, were still there. The rest had been put ashore at various ports they had called at briefly, to be sold to unscrupulous masters who cared not where their victims came from, and knew that many of their customers would pay a higher price for free-born women than for slave girls.

The racket had been going on for years, the two women had learned, and was empire-wide, though until now Asia had been a minor scene of operations, but Milo and his henchmen were in Ephesus now to expand their activities, and build up a substantial eastern network.

'So now we know what the swine is up to. Things begin to fall into place. Let us hope events in Rome do likewise. In the meantime, there is work to do, and first, we must exercise our theatrical talents once more.'

Thus it was that, later in the day, a bunch of country bumpkins, two of whom were bent and aged women, joined the throng leaving the city en route for the surrounding villages. They were joined after a mile or so by a young Greek, driving a wheeled vehicle, who took the women aboard and set off over the hills. Their three companions, now laden with farm produce, returned to Ephesus, peasants obviously bound for the market.

'That was Annaias, the Diogenes youngster,' explained Mala, as we peeled off our disguises. Diogenes, I recalled, Mala's Greek cook, had a young son twenty years old or so. 'I sent him here to prepare the ground, in case our sudden departure from Rome should become necessary – as it did.

'The question now, though, is our possible departure from Ephesus: do we stay, or do we join the two women, and Annaias, in the safe village?'

'Milo is here; he knows, or soon will, where we are lodging; he is certainly not best pleased with us, and doubtless he will invoke the law to regain custody of Julia Carolina. I think making ourselves scarce might be a good idea.'

'Except that I am awaiting news that could transform the whole situation.'

'News?'

'From Rome. I believe there will be developments. I can't go into details, but reading the signs… Trust me on this, Marcus. The question is, how long will they take, once things are set in motion.'

'At least Milo does not have his private army here, which is a relief, but no doubt he can call on a bunch of thugs of one kind or another; and there is the crew of the galley.'

'He won't use the crew far from the harbour, in case he feels the need to make a quick getaway. But what I am wondering, is whether we can get our retaliation in first.'

'Meaning?'

'Milo, in kidnapping freeborn Roman women, has gone a little too far. His previous crimes, organising robberies, receiving stolen goods, even murder, he was able to cover up, or get away with thanks to the protection of Licinius Populus. That protector is gone; we can produce victims of his kidnapping; and the authorities here are reputedly honest and committed guardians of law and order. I do not believe that they will be happy to learn that their fair city is to be the home of the sort of thing Milo is now involved in.'

'True,' I said. 'Moreover, the officer in charge of law and order in the city is a friend of my family: I have been thinking since we arrived that I should pay him a courtesy visit.'

'Now you tell me. By all means make your call, Marcus, and, if I may, I will accompany you, and whisper a word or two in the worthy's ear.'

Our meeting with Julius Gratulus, the deputy prefect, was not as satisfactory as we had hoped, though through no fault of the man himself. He remembered me, as well he should, for not only had our parents been friends, but we had served in the same legion together, though he in a more elevated rank, since he was six or seven years older, and a committed career soldier.

His greeting was cordial, but reserved, in keeping with his whole character. In many respects he was a throwback to earlier times, a modern exemplar of republican virtues, strict, stern, just, incorruptible, and with a sense duty of which Cato himself would have approved.

'I have heard of this Milo,' he told us, 'though I have never come across him personally. His name stinks throughout the empire, but he has a genius for avoiding trouble, and has enjoyed the protection of friends in high places.'

'One friend in particular,' said Mala, 'who now is dead.'

'Licinius Populus. I shed no tears when I heard of his demise.'

I don't suppose he had shed tears since he was a small child, if then, but I took his point.

'There are still those left in Rome, whom many would shed no tears over, if they were to join their ancestors,' I observed.

He looked at me disapprovingly. He knew I was referring to Domitian, and he knew that I knew that he shared my opinion of the brute, but he was a serving officer, and a dutiful one, and he would defend to the death the reigning emperor, whatever his personal feelings about the man.

'That as may be. The immediate question is how we can scotch this man Carilius Milo. Whatever his sins, he is still a free Roman citizen, and a rich and powerful one at that; I cannot move against him without evidence.'

'We have the two women,' Mala pointed out. 'I can get them to sign depositions. There may well be others in the establishment where they were being kept, and there certainly are aboard Milo's galley. If you raided both…'

'And that is the difficulty. My force – I can hardly call it a force – is very, very badly overstretched at present. More than half of them are out of the city at the moment hunting bandits, the troops we can normally fall back on are away on manoeuvres, and those that are left, who are by no means the best, are spread so thin on the ground it is all they can do to maintain something like law and order and contain the normal everyday crime. Raiding Milo's galley would take a considerable force, which I simply do not have.'

'There is a naval trireme moored quite near Milo's vessel. Surely the admiral would put men at your disposal.'

'Undoubtedly; unfortunately the ship sailed away just this morning, on a trip to Myra. It will not return for some days.'

He then turned to Mala.

'There is another matter, Quintus Propertius Mala. I am told this Milo creature has made a formal request that I arrest you, and seize a slave he maintains belongs to him.

'That is a matter I am duty bound to pursue. Fortunately,' he allowed himself the suspicion of a smile, 'I had to inform Milo, as I have informed you, that with the men at my disposal it will be two or three days before I can attend to things. Nevertheless, if you decided to join the two women you rescued in what you say is a safe hideout, it might not be a bad idea. It goes without saying that officially I will not have slightest inkling of where you might be: but you might like to leave a sealed note with my clerk, so that I can find you in case of emergencies.

'Meanwhile, you can be sure I will keep an eye on Carilius Milo and his doings as best I can, and I will make a move as soon as I have the resources to do so.'

It was less than we had hoped for, but as much as could be expected in the circumstances. We collected Julia Carolina from the lobby where she had been guarded by a pair of Julius Gratulus's best.

'And now?'

'We make preparations for leaving Ephesus. First, though – if you do not mind terribly, Marcus – food and drink. Let us try the place we went to first. Our friends might or might not be there, but it will not hurt to precipitate matters, and see just what they have in mind. Bring your sword-stick, though – just in case.'

We went straight to the eating-house – which this time Mala called a 'bistro', which meant no more to me than the other word he had used - and saw, the moment we entered, Milo, with the Spaniard and the little accountant, seated at one table, and two of the ubiquitous thugs at another.

As we sat, Milo at once came over. He looked insolently at Mala and me, and then let his gaze rest on Julia Carolina.

'My property, I believe.'

'Lay one finger on that lady,' said Mala very quietly, as he and I rose to our feet, 'and you will wish you had never been born.'

Milo's reply was to sneer, and then turn to one of his thugs.

'Take her,' he instructed.

Give the man his due: he did try. He strode to our table, and tried to grab Julia Carolina by the arm. He did not manage even to touch her. Instead, Mala, eschewing the 'carati' that I had seen him use so effectively in the past, unleashed a blow that would have felled an elephant. Such was the force of the uppercut that the thug's feet literally left the floor, and he flew, rather than staggered, crashing into the table where Milo's confrères were sitting, before sliding to the floor, his broken jaw sagging, and from the look of him likely to be out for days.

Milo's other guard sprang forward, but discovered, to his displeasure, that Mala was not the only one possessed of a strong right arm. Half his teeth disappeared down his throat as I hit him, and he joined his fellow on the floor, blissfully unaware of the rest of the proceedings.

Milo, deciding he no longer liked the odds, beat a strategic retreat, even though the Spaniard had now leaped up, knife in hand, looking ready to join in the fray.

Mala cast the man a glance of contempt.

'If suicide is your intent,' he said, 'go right ahead.'

With no-one to back him up but Milo and the ineffectual accountant, the Spaniard needed to examine no entrails to decide on the best course of action, and he stepped back with a curse.

The resident bouncer, meanwhile, had been observing the fracas with growing consternation. He knew it was his bounden duty to do – er – something, but he was much happier handling emetically-challenged teenagers after their first binge on the wine, or persuading little old ladies to leave the premises instead of arguing about their change, than tackling two such as Mala and me. His sigh of relief was heartfelt, as Mala helped Julia Carolina to her feet, and the three of us left the tavern briskly.

'Damnation,' I said; 'I wish we had had our food and wine before all that happened.'

'I wish it had not happened at all; but it has, and a strategic withdrawal is called for.'

We paused only to collect our belongings from the inn, and then to head for the livery stables of Fabrienus Fabrianus, the best in Ephesus. There, to my surprise, three superb horses, and a sturdy pack animal, were produced at once, and I appreciated afresh how very thorough Mala's preparations had been.

Each horse was saddled, and now I must tell you of something rather strange. From the sides of each saddle dangled two leather straps, and attached to the ends of the straps were beehive-shaped metal hoops, each big enough to hold a man's foot. I had never seen their like before.

Did I tell you I used to love horses, until I had that bad fall in Dacia? After that, I would climb aboard one of the brutes only if I had to, and pretty reluctantly at that.

But now I love them again, thanks to Mala's funny metal hoops. It is almost unbelievable, the difference they make, once one inserts one's feet into the – *stirrups*, did Mala call them?. Immediately, one feels more stable, more in control; it seems almost that there is a greater rapport with the animal itself – and, an additional bonus, how much easier is mounting and dismounting. How is it that we Romans, with all our much-vaunted ingenuity, should have failed to come up with so obvious a device?

No matter. Mala showed me how to adjust the straps until I felt thoroughly comfortable, Julia Carolina, I noted, mounted without fuss, looking far more at ease than a women atop a horse had any right to be, and we were soon cantering towards the outskirts of Ephesus, and not long afterwards galloping over the hills that bordered the city.

It was a long and roundabout journey, but eventually we came to a little village. They must have been keeping a lookout for us, for the moment we reached the village, there was Annaias, the Diogenes offspring, flanked now by a bucolic individual who would have been recognised as a farmer the world over, and by a dark-haired beauty who kept fluttering her eye-lids at the Greek, and who obviously had the bright lights of Rome squarely in her sights.

'Welcome, master. Quarters have been prepared for you. I did not know when I reserved them how many companions you might have, or whether you would be bringing any slaves, but there will be plenty of room.' He looked at Julia Carolina somewhat doubtfully.

'This,' Mala reminded him, 'is Julia Carolina, my wife. Afford her every assistance and every courtesy.'

A roomy, one-time farmhouse had been set aside for our use. There were no slaves in the village – all were now free citizens of the empire, though not of Rome – but when it was discovered we had not brought our own slaves, there was no shortage of volunteers to act as paid servants, our Greek's dark-haired paramour, Martita, in the forefront of those anxious to serve Julia Carolina.

There followed two of the most idyllic weeks of my life. For many years I have been an urban creature, a Roman of the Romans, my life bounded by the high walls, defined by the seven hills and by the myriad buildings, humble and magnificent, ugly or sublime, which together go to make up our mighty city. Nevertheless, I have always been, at heart, a countryman. Hesiod's *Works and Days*, and the eclogues of Virgil, remain my favourite reading, and I dream longingly of the time when I can buy a farm, such as the one my father had owned when I was a child, and leave the bustle, and the corruption, of the metropolis behind me. Even Rufus's Place I could learn to do without; well, maybe.

For a time, in this unsuspected corner of Asia, it was as though my dream had come true. The villagers were sterling people, Diogenes' son, Annaias, was a tower of strength, and as for the two young women we had rescued in Ephesus, it was a joy to see them gradually blossoming after their ordeal.

I knew in my heart, though, that it could not last. Nor did it. Stepping outside the farmhouse one morning, I saw, just at the outskirts of the village, a bunch of a dozen horsemen. All were ugly of face and ugly of intent, and all armed with swords which they looked as though they knew how to use. They saw me at once, and dismounted. I rushed inside to get my sword, and warn Mala of the danger; he waited only to bundle Julia Carolina and the girl Martita out of the back door, and then joined me to face our would-be killers.

There were nine of them, two having stayed back to guard Carilius Milo, whose band, of course, they were. That worthy, who had probably been responsible for more killings than any other man in Rome, true to his type had no stomach himself for bloodshed.

The nine advanced confidently towards the two of us.

They did not know what hit them. From nowhere, it seemed, twenty or more of our stout new friends from the village suddenly appeared, armed with the tools of their trade. Now, the sword is a weapon developed over centuries and used in a thousand battles, and in trained hands it is deadly. It is amazing, nonetheless, how effective against it can be simple agricultural implements - a scythe, a sickle, even a hoe, let alone a blacksmith's hammer - when wielded by a sturdy countryman defending his patch against an intruder – especially if the swordsmen are taken by surprise, and outnumbered more than two to one The thugs simply melted under the onslaught, and in less time than it takes to tell, Milo and his two bodyguards were the only three of the intruders left standing.

They had tried to mount their horses, but Mala and I were having none of that. The fight with the bodyguards was fierce but brief – 'Two against two,' I remarked afterwards; 'it hardly seems fair,' - and with Mala's point at his throat the terrified Carilius Milo fell to his knees and pleaded for mercy, with all the fortitude of a sick child.

'Get up,' ordered Mala. 'Get up, and give me a good reason to run you through. As I told another villain once, I do not kill men in cold blood, but, by Jupiter, I pray that you give me some excuse.'

But then an idea came to him.

'Marcus,' he said, 'you can write. Would you care to produce a document for me?'

He told me what he wanted, and I grinned. 'Your scribe is at your service,' I assured him, and went indoors to find stylus and papyrus. The job did not take me long, and when I gave Mala the sheet he at once showed it to Milo.

'This, as you will see, is a bill of sale. It names a fair price for the slave Julia Carolina, and here,' he reached into the leather bag he was never without, and threw a large handful of coins at Milo's feet, 'is that price. You will sign the receipt and the deal is done.'

If Milo had even contemplated refusing, Mala's sword would have given him to think again, and if Mala's had not, mine would. He grabbed the stylus I offered him, and scribbled his name – not forgetting to pick up the coins. But then he regained a little of his courage.

'You will never get away with this,' he snarled.

'Even if you do not live?'

'So it was cant when you said you did not kill in cold blood; I am not surprised – you filthy foreigner.'

'I would not kill you,' said Mala, 'but my friend Marcus here, I am sure, has no such scruples; and he is a true-born Roman. He, too, does not kill without good cause, but I do not think he would baulk at ridding the world of such a louse as you.'

'Not for a second,' I said, lifting my sword as though I was ready to do the job there and then - which I was.

'That would indeed be foolish of you,' said Milo, and to our surprise there was now an unpleasant smile on his face, 'for you would have to explain your action to these friends of mine.'

We heard and saw them at the same moment: they were some way away but galloping rapidly towards us, a full band of cavalry, proudly displaying the fact that they were the personal troops of the prefect himself.

There was a centurion in charge, an officer of the household guard, of commanding presence and fully aware of his power and his status – and of the thirty men at his back. Milo smirked as he rode towards us.

The centurion dismounted, and seeing my garb, came straight up to me.

'Marcus Vectorius, knight?'

I assented.

'I am commanded to give you this letter from my superior, Julius Gratulus. I am further commanded to find one Carilius Milo.'

Milo, though now a little puzzled, made himself known to the centurion.

'Carilius Milo, on the direct orders of the emperor Nerva, I place you under arrest.'

He was a fool to break and run: troops such as these are paid to act first, and think afterwards. The three javelins hit him simultaneously, and that was that.

The letter the centurion delivered to me expanded on the centurion's reference to 'the emperor Nerva'. Domitian had been assassinated only a few weeks previously – the emperor's own wife was implicated, it was said - but the news from Rome had only recently reached Ephesus.

'It goes on to say that the Senate confirmed Nerva as emperor, and that among his first acts had been to order a thorough crackdown on organised crime, which he has said for far too long has been getting out of hand.' I told Mala.

'From that moment, then,' said he, 'Milo's goose was cooked. Nerva's agents will have trawled through the late Chief Investigator's records, and have got on to him in no time. Presumably Milo knew nothing of this: doubtless he had left Rome shortly before the change of regime, to organise his Asian racket.'

'Exactly. Moreover, Julius Gratulus tells me Milo and his bunch had been out of Ephesus – looking for us – when the news became public there. Hence his unpleasant surprise when the troops he thought were going to rescue him did no such thing.'

The rest was routine. The centurion, whom we got to know quite well, entered with relish into the job of winding up Milo's empire. The Spaniard, and the little accountant, were arrested, and the former resisted, which was the last thing he ever did. The establishment opposite our inn was closed down – temporarily – and several of those in charge, including the androgynous overseer, were offered a career change they could not refuse. Milo's galley was raided, his followers rounded up, and the women aboard freed.

'Milo's followers,' the centurion told us, 'talked; the little accountant was especially forthcoming. As a result, various unsavoury characters, as far apart as Pergamum and Myra, have found their life-styles precipitately altered for the worse – much worse. It was a clean sweep, and for my part I find the air in Ephesus, and the whole region, altogether sweeter.'

'Amen,' said Mala.

And so, after a few days more, we said farewell to our centurion friend, and again boarded ship, this time, by special dispensation, the huge trireme of the Imperial Navy. The voyage was not so pleasant as the outward trip, for military ships have their own ways, and are set in them, though we were looked after well, and the captain was agreeable enough when his duties allowed, as were his officers. We also had the company of the two women we had rescued and several of their erstwhile companions, all embarrassingly grateful towards us for their deliverance.

It was a relief, nevertheless, to disembark at last at Ostia, there to hire a wheeled vehicle to take the three of us, and our considerably swollen luggage (for what visitor comes back from Ephesus unladen?) to Rome.

There remained, in my mind, only one mystery.

'Mala,' I said, 'in Ephesus just before the fracas, you made some reference to Nerva. Surely you were not privy to the plot to kill Domitian, which sounds like purely a palace affair; and even if you had been, how could you know Nerva would be his successor? You kept referring, too, to "events" you were expecting to happen back in Rome. You often seem to know things you cannot possibly know. There are times when I would suspect you had second-sight, except that I don't believe in second-sight.'

'Marcus, Julia Carolina and I told you just a little about our background when we returned from Milo's villa, but there was much we did not say, not least because we were afraid you would not understand, or believe even if you did. We did not want you to think us liars, or charlatans..'

'That, never,' I replied. 'As for understanding and believing: try me.'

'We will indeed, as soon as we return to Rome, and not merely tell you, but show you, things that will amaze you. Marcus, I will a tale unfold whose lightest word will harrow up thy soul…'

And (though still with reservations) he did. That, however, is another story – and such a story! But it is one I must set down elsewhere, when I think that you, dear reader, are in turn ready to understand, and to believe

Quintus Propertius and the Treasure of the Dumnonii

Rufus's Place is not what it was. For a start, it is no longer Rufus's. That estimable man, after much deliberation – and a word or two in his ear from his wife and family – at last decided to sell-up, and take his ease in the country: he had bought a small farm, and a good overseer and a small bunch of slaves to run it, and departed to enjoy a placid and well-earned retirement. His successor, though affable enough, was —well, you know how it is: not the same.

Our group was dwindling, too. Ventidius Silo, as you might recall*, was the first to go, in rather unpleasant circumstances. Servius Javolenius was now far away, with his legion, and had already seen some sharp action. (Those Dacians are going to need a good sorting out, one of these days.) The aged Aspiades, his former tutor, had at last gone to the great Academy in the sky, and though a slave, was sincerely mourned by all of us. Gaius Cornelius, and a bunch of his staff from the Treasury, had been seconded to Brundisium, to introduce a little financial discipline and probity to so-called servants of the empire there, who had long regarded such concepts with uncouth mirth and now were about to learn to laugh on the other side of their faces.

Mala himself, thoroughly married in proper Roman fashion to the newly-freed Julia Carolina, and therefore master in his house like any

---

* See *Quintus Propertius and the affairs of Ventidius Silo*

Roman, unaccountably found himself just a little bit less free than he had been to come and go and drink wine with his friends, until whatever hour the thought crossed his mind that perhaps he should go home.

As for me, I was in the same boat. After the disaster of my first marriage, I had determined to keep women (not *all* women, of course – if you know what I mean) at arm's length for the foreseeable future, but Servius Javolenius's sister, whom I had known for years as a gangling teenager, suddenly to my amazement transmogrified into a beautiful young woman, and I was lost.

'A second marriage,' said Mala cynically, 'is the triumph of hope over experience.'

'And your hope has been most fully realised; I believe mine will be also.'

And so it has been; and yet… But I've said that Rufus's Place is not what it was, so perhaps it does not signify.

Mala was less at Rufus's Place for other reasons than his marriage, or the change in the ambience of the place. He seemed, constantly, inordinately busy, and keeping some of Rome's best tradesmen inordinately busy also: glassmakers, metalworkers, carpenters, tanners, you name it. He himself had had an extension built to his house, which he called his 'lab', whatever that meant, and he spent long hours in there, as, from time to time, did Julia Carolina, doing Jupiter knows what.

'Wait and see, Marcus,' was the answer he gave me, whenever I asked him, and I had to curb my curiosity.

Still, we did get to Rufus's from time to time, though it was as well that Mala and I had not been there that morning: it does not do to visit the emperor when under the affluence of incohol. We had been 'invited' to visit the Palace at short notice and with no explanation, and when Caesar calls, even a relatively benign old stick like Nerva, you go.

'Whatever the emperor wants,' I observed, 'it should be a pleasanter visit to the Palace than some we've taken.'

Nerva was not quite as I had remembered him. I had met him only socially, a couple of times, before his elevation to the purple, and he had seemed then a bit of an old dodderer. Now, however, though clearly not in robust health, he had real presence, a presence compounded in part of the aura of his rank, and partly of natural dignity, and owing nothing to the kind of terror-inspiring presence one associated with the late unlamented Domitian.

He was, indeed, positively affable as he greeted us.

'Two of my most valued subjects!' he exclaimed. 'Welcome. Be seated. Not too early for wine? I think we can find something half-way drinkable.'

'If you can't,' I thought, 'who can?'

He could. Nor was he sparing in dispensing it. He smiled as he pressed another cup on me.

'You're probably thinking I want something from you,' he said. 'You would be right, though I must stress that I issue not a command, but a request. Unwilling servants do not perform well; strange, how few rulers seem to know that.'

We wondered what was coming.

'You two have gained something of a reputation as investigators. Indeed, the post of Chief Investigator is still vacant: perhaps I should offer it to one of you?'

Mala responded at once.

'If you did, Caesar, I would beg to be allowed to decline. I am strictly an amateur: the day-to-day routine of the professional would soon dull my edge. I fear I would be a great disappointment to you.'

'And you, Marcus Vectorius? Much was expected of you when you finished your military service – yet I am told you perform your present duties with no good grace.'

He held up his hand as I started to protest.

'Do not deny it; and I do not blame you in the least. Some of the piddling tasks my so-called helpers dream up would be resented by any man of spirit.

'But you will have need of your spirit, and your strength and courage, and you too, Quintus Propertius Mala, if you accept my commission. I want you to perform an important service for me - in Britain.'

2.

'We have three days to make up our minds,' Mala explained. The four of us, as often nowadays, were gathered together at Mala's, and relaxing after a gourmet meal.

'If we go,' I said anxiously, 'you will take Diogenes?'

Diogenes was Mala's Greek cook, and in my view the very best in the empire.

'*If* we go,' said Mala, 'and if we go *en famille*: that is what this gathering is about. Do the ladies want to leave Rome for that barbaric land? Nerva thinks it would be a good idea, to provide cover. The two of us alone would be just a bit too conspicuous, whereas, paradoxically, two well-off families, with their retainers, ostensibly making a tour of the northern empire, would be far less likely to attract the wrong kind of attention. But the choice is ours. For my part, I would be unwilling to leave Julia Carolina alone in Rome, and if she does not want to come, I will not accept Nerva's commission.'

'If you did go, might you not be recognised?' asked Livinia Javolenia. 'I understand you lived among these Britons - the Dumnonii, is it? – when you were young.'

'They are a scattered tribe,' replied Mala quickly. 'We would be going to the capital, Isca. I lived some way to the east, in a small community on the coast.'

I saw Julia Carolina suppress a smile, and tried to control my own. Though I do not like keeping secrets from my wife, we had agreed that Livinia was not yet ready – if she would ever be ready – to be told our friends' amazing stories.

'Isca Dumnoniorum,' mused Julia Carolina, 'but what will it be like now…?'

We kicked around the pros and cons for some time. The women, Julia Carolina especially as might be expected, were quite fascinated by the idea of going to such an exotic destination. Livinia found the prospect exciting, but also daunting. She had not been more than a few score miles from Rome in her life, except for a brief voyage to Massala, which she had hated. Though intellectually she knew better, in her imagination she was not sure the Britons were not one-eyed monsters like Cyclops, or fearsome cannibals with four arms and dragon's teeth. She had read, too, of the appalling massacres at Verulanium and Londinium by the rebels under Boudicca during Nero's reign, and had shuddered, as every good Roman does.

'They were the Iceni,' I assured her, 'and they live miles away from where we would be going. They would pose no threat, even if they had not learnt their lesson – which most assuredly they have.'

This reassured her a little, and before the evening was over, it was agreed. We informed Nerva the next morning.

I had not been looking forward to yet another protracted sea-voyage, especially around Spain and the west coast of Gaul, notorious for storms and for the many ships that had gone down there. Fortunately the emperor had other ideas.

'You will travel overland,' he said, 'with three of my trouble-shooting teams from the Treasury - and an escort.'

We knew Nerva had been keeping a sharp eye on financial goings-on, not because, like Vespasian, he was parsimonious, but because on the contrary he had been throwing money around like water, and was rather keen to know where all of it was going. What we did not know, until the very day of our departure, was that among the Treasury operatives who were to accompany us would be Gaius Cornelius, fresh back from his labours in Brundisium.

'One mustn't ask for too much,' he said, somewhat grumpily. 'We have had two whole days leave since returning from parts south. Now we can look forward to the joys of Gaul and Britain. Still,' he went on, 'Nerva is a generous soul, and there are tidy bonuses for us all, so I must not complain. It's good that you will be coming along with us. It is even better – begging your pardon, Marcus – that we will be accompanied by a body of troops from one of the best legions in the army.'

'You must mean XIII Gemina,' I said; that was my old legion.

'You're right: they are going north to relieve part of a garrison, and the emperor thinks it a good idea for us to tag along with them. I am all for it - and guess who will be with them.'

'I would like to think it would be Servius Javolenius, but I don't suppose it will be. The last I heard, he was having a spot of bother with a bunch of Dacians, and got an arrow in his arm for his pains. He's O.K., though.'

'More than O.K.,' said a familiar voice.

'Servius!'

'Servius at your service,' he punned. 'I was told I had to escort a bunch of civilians, but I wasn't told it would include a couple of wine-guzzlers from Rufus's.'

'Three,' said Mala, who had just joined us; 'and two ladies.'

'And a dozen slaves,' I added, 'including one who is the best cook in the world. Gentlemen, if Mala is as hospitable as I know him to be, you don't know your luck.'

'You must dine with us whenever your duties allow,' said Mala. 'I will instruct Diogenes to prepare something special for a wounded war-hero.'

'Wounded? I don't know what story you've been hearing, but the arrow scarcely grazed my shoulder. And as for war hero: fiddlesticks.'

That was not what the official citation had said, and I suspected our friend of being over-modest.

'You extricated your troop from a very nasty ambush, and – I quote – "showed outstanding courage and leadership qualities in getting them to safely, though wounded early in the action".'

Servius looked embarrassed.

'It was nothing – certainly not compared with your exploits four years ago, Marcus..'

It was my turn to be embarrassed, but I was saved further discomfiture by the arrival of a large, covered carriage, drawn by two horses, which swayed somewhat on its axles.

'Now you must meet the two ladies,' said Mala, 'Marcus's wife, and mine.'

Julia Carolina was the first to alight, and Mala introduced them. Servius Javolenius showed the reserve, and the impeccable manners to be expected of the aristocrat that he was, but there was no such reserve when my wife Livinia emerged from the carriage.

'Livinia! Marcus, you old dog, why did you not tell me?'

'I did, immediately the deed was done, and so did your father: our letters must have reached Dacia just after you left.'

'No matter. I am delighted for you both. I have not even had time to pay my respects to my father, or he would have told me the news. In fact I must see to that duty right now, though I fear it will be the very briefest of greetings. If it had not been for that storm near Rhodes, I would have been in Rome two days ago: I had been looking forward to a brief rest at home.'

'The best laid plans of mice and men…' said Mala. *Mice?* Do mice make plans?

'It is lovely to have Servius with us,' said Livinia, as her brother rode away, 'but I do not quite see why we need such a large escort. Gaul is pretty peaceful nowadays, isn't it?'

'Apart from bandits, there as nearer home, it is a pretty peaceful province at last,' I agreed, 'except near the German border. Unfortunately we will be going near the German border: one of the Treasury teams has work to do there.'

'But I thought the Germans were peaceful nowadays.'

'Ha! They have been given some short, sharp shocks from time to time, but there are always hot-heads among them ready to have a go, usually raiding isolated settlements. Occasionally their raiding parties number a hundred or more, so Servius's men will be very welcome if we happen across a bunch like that.'

'Would they dare attack the Roman army? Isolated settlements are one thing, but surely they would be deterred by well-armed troops?'

'Maybe yes, maybe no: it depends on numbers. If they think they have sufficient advantage, they might risk it.'

Livinia shuddered.

'I thought it was Britons I would have to worry about; now it seems it is Germans as well.'

'Three cheers for the Pax Romana,' I said, 'but in some places we could do with a bit more Pax.'

'Nevertheless,' observed Mala, 'I do believe we are entering a period in the history of the world, during which the condition of the human race, or at least those fortunate enough to live within the Roman Empire, will be at its most happy and prosperous.'

'In contrast,' added Julia Carolina, 'to what they more usually have to endure: the crimes, follies and misfortunes of mankind.'

3

The journey was onerous, though less so than I had feared. It was good to have friends with us, and Gaius Cornelius's Treasury colleagues – there were three teams of three - far from being the dry-as-dust accountants I had feared, were thoroughly good fellows like Gaius himself, and fitted well into our company.

The soldiers were – well, soldiers: grousing half the time, swearing all the time, questioning the parentage of their decurians whenever those worthies' backs were turned, and generally behaving as squaddies the world over traditionally have, when finding themselves on a long march, instead of the soft billet of a big camp miles behind the lines, full of complaisant – well, Mala called them *hors de combat,* and said something about a pun; I wouldn't know…

But they were good and experienced legionaries for all that - some fifty of them rather than a full century, an unusual number - and I noted with approval the way my young brother-in-law handled them, and the respect he already had from his veteran centurion.

For the most part, in Italy and on into Gaul, we civilians stayed in inns, though on a couple of occasions our military friends erected quite excellent tented accommodation for us within their camp, with that speed and efficiency which has made the Roman army the envy of he world. Diogenes then cooked for all, to the great approval of the soldiery.

The inns varied, as could be expected, from the so-so to the horrid, even though each day two of the Treasury men – ostentatiously accompanied by a decurian and half a dozen guards – went on ahead to find the best they could and to warn the proprietor that important visitors were on their way.

Our third night in Gaul, however, was a revelation. The village was too tiny to be on any but the most large-scale maps, but the inn would have graced any habitat in the world. The proprietor had been to Rome in his youth, has been duly impressed by everything except the accommodation he had been incarcerated in, and returned determined to shame anything Rome, or all Italy, had to offer. His establishment was small, comfortable, clean, welcoming, and stocked with array of local wines that were as cheap as plonk and as good you would find at most pretentious establishments in Rome.

Two of our escorts' horses had gone a little lame, and we were only too pleased to stay an extra night at this remarkable establishment, and when eventually we left, it was with great regret all round. Mala remarked that since the Romanised Gaul who was the proprietor had shown what an inn *could* be like, it was time the atrocious establishments nearer home were brought into line.

'Someone needs to introduce a rating system,' he said, 'and to provide an incentive for the inn-keepers to meet certain minimum standards. Perhaps, when we return, I will see what can be done.'

'Here comes the Michelin Guide,' said Julia Carolina, but none of us knew what she meant.

There was one incident, though, before we took our leave, that was a little less pleasant. A big, unkempt, long-haired man barged his way into the room where meals and wine alike were served, and demanded, loudly and with no good grace, beer. He sat at a nearby table, and stared insolently at our party, very audibly muttering something about 'bloody Romans', which was hardly wise of him, since he was considerably outnumbered.

We had been joined by Servius Javolenius's centurion, and he at once identified the intruder as a Briton. He, we knew, had seen service in Britain, and his father indeed had been killed in Verulanium by Boudica's savages, and so he was not best disposed towards the race, though he knew that there were many different tribes, by no means all of whom regarded Rome as an enemy.

'If that man does not shut up, sir,' he said to Servius Javolenius, 'I will be pleased, with your permission, to teach him some good Roman manners.'

'And I,' said Mala, 'some good British ones: most of the Britons I have known would disown a lout like that as soon as look at him.'

'And I,' added one of our Treasury friends, 'would be only too pleased to dock his pay!'

We laughed, and the tension was relieved a little, though the man continued to eye us with dislike, and one misplaced remark would undoubtedly have led to a fracas. He probably surmised, rightly, that we would not have attacked him en masse, and felt that he could handle any one of us individually. In Mala's case at least he would have received a terrible surprise, and I myself would have liked a go at him; as for the centurion, no-one in his right mind, however big and tough, would have thought him a pushover. Moreover, though doubtless the Briton had a knife concealed somewhere about his person, we all had very much more than that: Servius and the centurion were in full uniform, armour and all, Mala and I had the *sabres*, as he had called them, which he had had made especially for us, and even the Treasury men sported unaccustomed short-swords.

Perhaps it was this that persuaded the barbarian to have second thoughts, for eventually, with one last sneering glance, he downed his last cup of beer, and left the inn.

4

'So that's a Briton,' said Livinia. 'I can't say I liked the look of him.'

'At least he didn't have horns; didn't that make you feel better?'

'Do not joke about serious matters, Marcus. He looked the kind of person who would murder you in your bed, given half a chance.'

'And Nero looked as though butter would not melt in his mouth, and he *did* murder people in their beds, and out of them, including his own mother. Do not judge by appearances.'

'Sound advice,' interjected Mala, 'but there are exceptions. Livinia, you are right: he did look a most unsavoury character to me.'

'And did you notice the way he stared at you? Can you be sure he did not recognise you from your time in Britain?'

'Quite sure. Britain is a big place, and he did not look at all like any of the Britons I knew.'

'Nor I,' said Julia Carolina, with a mischievous look in her eye I had come to know well, 'and some of my best friends are Britons.'

Livinia looked at her in amazement.

'Friends?'

'But why not? You must know some Greeks who are estimable people, and Spaniards, even Egyptians. Why not Britons? It is what people are in themselves, not what race they belong to, that really matters.'

Livinia, Roman through and through, daughter of a senator, and always conscious of her rank, took some time to get her head round that one.

'Remember Aspiades,' I reminded her. 'He was a Greek, and a slave to boot, but your whole family liked and admired him – as did many of us.'

'But that's different; he was almost like family himself. He was offered his freedom several times, but refused it, and no-one ever thought of him as a slave – not even my father.'

'Yet he was a Greek,' I reminded her.

'Greeks are not like other foreigners. They had a long civilisation behind them when we conquered them. Some even say their culture was superior to our own: I have heard you yourself allege, Marcus, that Plato and Aristotle are the greatest philosophers who ever lived, and that their dramatists are head and shoulders above any Roman. The Britons have no-one of that stature – that I have heard of.'

'Perhaps they once had,' said Mala, 'and perhaps they will again. You have mentioned, Livinia, that you dote on the love poetry of Catullus. Listen.'

He recited, first in his own language - one of them - and then, straight off the cuff, in Latin. Even in the original, of which we could not of course understand a word, it sounded strangely captivating; translated - and Julia Carolina told me afterwards it was a brilliant translation - it suffered not a whit in comparison with Catullus; Ovid himself would have been proud of it.

An similem aestivae pingam te, care, diei...?

'That poem,' said Mala, 'was by a *British* writer. Do you consider it the work of a barbarian?'

'Of course not: it is beautiful. But surely it was not written by a modern Briton?'

'No; and the Britons you will meet in Isca Dumnoniorum, let alone that lout who just left us, are sorry fellows compared to the man who wrote those lines, and to his contemporaries. But some would say that most modern Greeks are sorry fellows compared with their ancestors - even Aspiades was no Plato, and certainly my cook Diogenes, excellent though he is, is not.'

A thought struck me.

'Mala,' I said, 'what of the Gauls?'

He smiled.

'You have heard a snatch of this before,' he said, and again recited in the original, and then translated into Latin. It was clearly a different language from the first, but again we were impressed by its rhythms, so different from our accented Latin verses, by its sonorities, and, when Mala translated, by its imagery:

Le ciel est par-dessus le toit...

From the translation, I recognised some of the lines he had uttered in the Forum, when we had been investigating the disappearance of Ventidius Silo:

The sky above the roof-tops,
So blue, so calm...

'And now I am really confused,' said Livinia. 'First the Britons, now the Gauls: was *everyone* civilised at some time – civilised enough to write fine poetry, at least?'

'Civilisation,' replied Mala, 'is not so easy to define as you might think, and certainly you would be lucky to find Britons or Gauls to-day who are aware of their one-time glories. At present Rome stands supreme, as once did Greece, and before her Egypt. Perhaps only to the east, far beyond the Indies, is there a civilisation in any way comparable – though,' he added hastily, 'as to that, we have little to go on but hearsay.'

'I have even heard,' Julia Carolina put in, 'that there are men in the world who have learned to fly in the air, like birds, though using not wings, but great machines to assist them.'

'Impossible; these are children's tales. No machine could make a man fly.'

'No? Think of a bow, or still more, a trebuchet: what are they, if not machines that give flight – to arrows, and to stones? Is it so far-fetched to conceive of a machine that might do the same for a man - maybe not so violently, more controllably, but no less surely? Rome has great engineers; might not one of them, some day, devise such a machine?'

As I lay in bed that night, I thought long and hard about what Mala, and Julia Carolina, had said, about the poetry of Britain and of Gaul, about history and civilisation, about the different races of the world, about the supposed great country beyond the Indies – and about men flying.

They had told me much about their background before we left Rome, but there was much, I knew, that they had still not revealed – for first, they had said, they would have to instruct me in some of the esoteric lore and learning of their homeland, without which I would not understand what they had to impart. I could not begin to imagine what they meant.

I knew they had come from a great land beyond the western ocean, though both had been born, and had lived the earlier part of their lives, elsewhere – just where, they did not enlighten me, though I felt sure that Britain was involved somewhere along the line.

I had long ceased to be amazed at the existence of so great a republic as theirs, unknown to Rome, and at so great a distance beyond the Pillars of Hercules, for Mala had explained to me something of the true size of the earth, and that it was, incredibly, a sphere. Now came this revelation that there was another great land far to the east, that also could vie with Rome in extent, and in achievement.

My old certainties were beginning to crumble. I had known – or had thought I knew - as surely as I knew that the sun rose in the east, that I was a citizen of the greatest empire that the world had ever seen. Now...

It was not the only serious discussion we had, and indeed I began to look forward to the evenings, when our travelling was done, and we could gather together, during or after our evening meal, and discuss this and that and anything and nothing – much as we used to do at Rufus's in its hey-day.

Often the talk turned to politics, and none us felt inhibited about expressing our views now, as we had during Domitian's rule, when a chance remark out of place might reach the wrong ears, and prove one's last.

Mala had been in an expansive, some would say rather outrageous mood.

'But,' I said heatedly, 'what you are advocating is *democracy* – democracy more extreme even than the Greeks' '

'Indeed,' replied Mala.

I was appalled. Here was the man I respected, almost revered, above all others, giving support to a system of government that, prima facie at least, was bound to result in the worst of all possible worlds.

'But this implies mob rule,' I exclaimed, 'the predominance of the lowest common denominator. Even slaves would have their say, and...' I was about to say 'women', but I caught Livinia's glance, and beyond her Julia Carolina looking at me with raised eye-brow, as though she had divined what I was thinking.

'All this,' agreed Mala. 'The stupid, the apathetic, the malicious, the ignorant, the mendacious – all have their say, under this system of government I tell you of, this democracy. That is why, following a certain wise man, I can raise only two cheers for democracy – if that: more truly, one only; but for any other alternative I have ever heard of, I cannot raise even half a cheer.'

'Though my father would disown me for saying so,' put in Servius, 'I would think the best system of government is that proposed by Plato: an oligarchy of the great and the good.'

'And then?' rejoined Mala; 'quis custodiet ipsos custodes? Rome had something of the kind for many years, and where is the Republic now?'

'Then you accept the inevitability of Julius Caesar and Augustus and their successors – including Caligula, and Nero, and Domitian? Would not your democracy be equally bound to develop into some similar, autocratic system?'

'Not necessarily,' replied Mala. 'Safeguards against just such development can be built in.'

Gaius Cornelius had been listening with a frown on his face.

'What you are saying, Quintus Propertius, sounds uncomfortably like treason.'

'Not so. Do not confuse the theoretical with the actual. I am describing a theoretical ideal, the best – or, more accurately, the least bad – system of government that I have ever heard mooted. I am not suggesting that to-day's Rome either could, or should, adopt such a system: in the world of the here and now and for the foreseeable future, a strong, and with good fortune benevolent Caesar is to be preferred; indeed, is a necessity.

'However, as you know from recent history, the emperor might be neither strong nor benevolent. In that case, to whom does Rome turn?'

'The army,' said Servius without hesitation. 'The army has made and unmade emperors, and perhaps will do so again: the army, or even the Praetorians.'

'And when some general of the army deposes the emperor and become Caesar himself – forgive me for repeating the question: quis custodiet...?'

'Would your ideal democratic state have no army? How would it defend itself?'

'It would of course have an army, but the power of the generals would be carefully delimited, and their troops' ultimate oath of allegiance would be to the state: dare I mention SPQR?

'I do not pose the question *quis custodiet* lightly,' he went on. 'The Platonic oligarchy has much to be said for it – except that the evidence of history does not support it. However idealistic and altruistic the oligarchs, the Guardians, may be to begin with, they end up, inevitably, looking after not the interests of the state they are there to serve, but their own.

'It is in the nature of human beings, and in the nature of power: power tends to corrupt, and absolute power corrupts absolutely. I would add a corollary: power tends to attract precisely those with the greatest propensity towards corruption, and therefore least fitted to wield it. '

5

Our discussions became less frequent as we penetrated further into Gaul, heading north and east, and drawing ever nearer to the German border.

'This,' Servius warned us, 'is the most dangerous part of the journey. The border is porous, the forts are too far apart, and the tribes on the other side are the most troublesome of all.. Most of them would love a re-run of the Teutoburg Forest if they thought they had half a chance of arranging it.

'Luckily, unless they really do have a full-scale invasion in mind, they are not likely to come over in really large numbers: a score or two, maybe a hundred if there is something really special afoot; I would not expect more. A hundred, we can cope with.'

'Unless we fall into an ambush,' said one of the Treasury men, anxiously. They were nice enough fellows, these civil servants, but martial ardour was not their most distinguishing feature.

Servius smiled.

'We had thought of that, believe it or not. Scouts have been out ever since we came near these border regions.'

We made our way slowly through the rather arid countryside, avoiding the few wooded areas, and with scouts constantly deployed. Once we came across evidence that our German friends had indeed been around: an isolated farmhouse, burnt to the ground, with a dozen bodies – or what was left of them – men, women and children, indiscriminately slaughtered, some of them unspeakably mutilated.

'They have been dead at least a week,' decided Bilbus, the centurion. 'I doubt if any of the perpetrators will be anywhere near here by now.' But just to make sure, he detailed half a dozen further scouts to comb the surrounding countryside.

They were experienced men, and did a good job, and we were relieved when the third day came after we have left the farmhouse, and none of them reported any sign of the Germans.

'They must have done their dirty work, grabbed their booty, and scampered back to their hovels,' said Bilbus.

'And then perhaps come back for more' I said. 'Look.'

The dust cloud was unmistakable, even at such a distance, and it could only have been made by a body of men – a sizable body at that. They must have been just over the brow of the furthest of a small range of hills we could see in the distance, and the question that at once exercised our minds was whether they were coming in our direction.

We observed the dust-cloud for some minutes, and concluded that, for the time being at least, they were getting no nearer, but seemed to be on a course more or less parallel with our own, and perhaps a mile and a half away. However, the hills which hid them from us, and us from them, continued for a little way, but then gradually sloped down to a broad plain, dotted with the occasional small copse, and bisected by a narrow stream, and our paths would be bound to converge.

'They will see us when they get down there,' said Servius. 'I wish I knew how many they were. I would send scouts, but there is little cover, and they would almost certainly be spotted, and I would rather not advertise our presence until the last possible moment.'

'We could observe them from there,' said Mala, pointing to a distant ridge. 'There's more cover.'

We looked at him in surprise. Mala was no fool, and surely he could see that the ridge was too far away for an observer to see more than an undifferentiated mass of our potential foe. Mala anticipated our objections.

'I have here,' he said, reaching into his ever-present leather bag, 'a little gadget that might be of use.'

He took out a long tube, in which we could see, set in one end, a circular piece of glass – a lens, such as the one he had used to solve the Marius murder*. At the other end, fitted into a narrower tube that he showed us could slide back and forth inside the other, was another, smaller lens.

---

* See *Quintus Propertius and the Misfortune of Marius the Glassmaker*

I remembered what he had told me, months before, about what he had called 'the science of optics', and about a 'telescope'. Could this be what the object was?

He held the small lens to his eye, pointed the contraption at a clump of trees almost on the horizon, and slid the small tube backwards and forwards. He then handed the instrument to Servius Javolenius.

'Close one eye,' he instructed, 'and look through this with the other. Slide the small tube until everything is clear.'

Puzzled, Servius did so, and after a few seconds almost dropped the thing in astonishment.

'The trees,' he exclaimed, 'they seem to come closer - far closer…'

'And so would anything else,' said Mala. 'Now would you like me to climb that ridge and see what I can see?'

Servius, still looking in amazement at the 'telescope', agreed at once, and Mala rode away.

When he returned, his face was grim as he reported to Servius.

'It is a much larger party than you had expected. The best part of a hundred men. They are armed to the teeth, and clearly bent on mischief.'

'All on foot?'

'As far as I could tell. They were dragging a wheeled contraption of some kind, but no heavy weapons.'

Servius Javolenius surveyed his force. There were fifty soldiers in all, ten of whom, plus Servius himself and the centurion, were mounted, as were Mala and I, and the nine Treasury men. The rest of the party consisted of Livinia and Julia Carolina, in their coach, and some dozen slaves, half of them women.

Servius consulted his centurion.

'A pre-emptive strike?' he mooted. 'A quick foray by the cavalry could do useful damage, and just might deter the enemy if they think there is a larger force behind them.'

'You are right about inflicting useful damage, sir, but they will soon enough know our true numbers, and discover they outnumber us two to one or more. Those are odds we should be able to handle, if they fight in their usual ill-disciplined manner, but it will be tough.'

'And we have civilians and women to take care of,' observed our friend. 'Fortunately Gaius Cornelius's men, and Quintus and Marcus here, are all mounted, and Julia Carolina and my sister both know how to ride and can use the carriage horses if necessary. They should easily be able to make their escape, since the Germans have no cavalry, and leave us to concentrate on the fighting. The slave women must crowd into the carriage also – they will be in the way here.'

He said nothing of what the slave women could do if we were attacked: there were only two carriage horses... The male slaves would join in the fight, though a fat lot of use they would be, except perhaps Diogenes, who grasped a great meat cleaver and looked suitably fierce.

'Imagine you are defending your kitchen against unwanted intruders,' I instructed him with a grin. That should do it, I thought; Horatio won't be in it. I was less than happy, though, at Servius's suggestion that Mala and I should go with the women.

'Our place is here with you,' I said. 'Gaius Cornelius's people have no military experience, but Mala and I are fighting men, and you will need every man you can get.'

Mala nodded in agreement.

'Indeed I will, and there are no two other men in Rome I would sooner have at my side; but it is precisely because you are fighting men that you must go. There might be more of them, and indeed there are other dangers besides Germans in these parts; would you have your wives protected only by our pen-pushing friends?'

There was no arguing with that – fortunately, as it turned out, and so Julia and Livinia and their slaves piled into the carriage, but the horses were saddled, and we gave strict instructions that they should be unhitched in quick time at the slightest hint of trouble. We were to make for the nearest fort, a sizable establishment about twenty miles to the north-east.

As we readied ourselves, the centurion, and the ten mounted auxiliaries, made ready for their surprise attack on the Germans from the rear. The rest of the force, meanwhile, set off at the double towards the plain, where Servius had decided on the best ground for the inevitable battle. He had spied out the land with Mala's telescope, which had fascinated him greatly.

'I can think of half a dozen ways in which this will be useful in war,' he said. 'You must have as many as possible made, to equip the legions.'

'That had been my intention,' said Mala, 'and I have left orders in Rome for a further batch of lenses to be ground. The instrument, though, has other uses than the military, which I will be pleased to show you when this little business is over.'

6

It was afternoon when we left Servius and his men, and since we would not make the fort until the following day, and there were no intervening villages, after a time we kept our eyes peeled for a spot to make camp, and in a few hours came to what seemed like a suitable place. Though we did not have the manpower to construct more than the most primitive defences, I insisted we do what we could, and we set guards as a matter of course, though in truth we were not expecting trouble at that distance from the body of Germans, nor indeed, did we suppose that any survivors of the impending clash with Servius's force, assuming our friends defeated them as we prayed they would, would head in our direction, rather than back across the border as quickly as they could.

We were wrong. They came on us shortly before sunset, and the first we knew of it was when there came a terrible scream from the woods a few yards from the camp, and then another, more piercing still. I had given orders that no-one was to leave the confines of the camp, but one of the Treasury men, unused to military ways, did not know that in circumstances like these an order was an order, to be obeyed implicitly. Livinia's personal attendant, a pretty little dark-skinned girl of no more than sixteen or seventeen, had gone with the would-be Lothario as soon as her duties were done, as readily as though for a stroll in the park. We came across their bodies next day, and… but I will say no more of that.

There came another cry, and another, and one of our sentries pitched forward with a great broad-bladed spear in his back, and his companion was cut to pieces before he could so much as lift his sword.

There were ten of them, tall, blond-haired savages, and they split into two as soon as they saw us, three of them coming on to where we stood, the others making for the carriage where the women were.

'Get over to the carriage,' ordered Mala, 'at the double. I will take care of this bunch, and then join you.'

Three of them? I knew Mala was good, but this sounded like quixotism. Such was his tone, however, that of the born commander, that we obeyed, Gaius Cornelius and I, without a second's demur. As I glanced backwards, I saw Mala reaching into the leather bag he always had with him.

The next few minutes were too full and fraught for me to take any notice of what Mala was up to. One of the accountants succumbed immediately to a great brute wielding an axe, and the others were hard-pressed in no time.

There came a loud noise, like – I cannot really describe it: like the crack of a whip, magnified twenty-fold, is the nearest I can get – and then two more; next moment Mala was with us, sabre in hand, turning to help the inexperienced accountants. I managed to put paid to one German, and Gaius Cornelius, though no military man, rather fancied himself as a swordsman, and was a regular at the gym; now he had a chance to try it for real, and to my approval was holding his own and more against a brute twice his size, whom at last he skewered with as neat a little one-two as you could imagine. Mala took care of another, and the four pen-pushers between them managed somehow to account for one of the remainder. The three still left, not liking the odds, cut and ran.

'I will get them,' said Mala, leaping after them. 'I do not want them linking up with any others who may be around and coming back for another go.'

The Germans disappeared from view, as did Mala, and Gaius Cornelius ran after them to help. He had not taken a dozen strides, however, when there came three more of those whip-like cracks, and Mala reappeared.

'I had hoped,' he said grimly, 'never to have to use that; but needs must: thank Jupiter I had it with me. We could not have handled all of those swine otherwise.'

I did know what he was talking about, and filed it away, as I had so often in the past, for future reference. Gaius Cornelius and his men looked in awe at the Germans Mala had despatched before he joined us at the carriage, lying there stone dead, two of them with great holes in the chest, the other with a neater hole in the forehead, and the back of his head blown clear away.

Mala had told me once before that he possessed a weapon deadlier by far even than his sword; obviously he had used it, but what it could be, none of us could imagine. Only Julia Carolina looked unsurprised.

One of the surviving Treasury men, still visibly trembling after the unaccustomed bloodshed, muttered something about 'the gods among us,' and seemed almost more frightened of Mala than he had been of the Germans.

Mala cut him short.

'Listen,' he commanded, 'and learn, and believe. I am no god; I have used no magic. What destroyed the Germans was an artefact, built by clever engineers, just as catapults and trebuchets are artefacts built by clever engineers. This was an especially clever one, but given time, I could explain to you how it works, and as an intelligent man, you would understand. Say no more of gods, or of magic.

'And if it makes you any happier, you can share the first watch with me.'

None of us slept well that night, least of all Mala, but there were no more alarms, and after administering the last rites to our dead next morning, we set off again for the fort, now less than three hours away even at the speed the carriage could manage.

7

The fort was a large one, almost a village in itself, and adjacent to a genuine village that had grown up in its shadow. Within the fort as well as just without, were to be found eating-places, shops, taverns, storehouses, workshops, and of course the inevitable premises of ill-repute where the off-duty soldiery flocked to rejuvenate themselves in preparation for the next day's exertions.

In the village, there were little huts where Gauls of the most menial class, scarcely better than slaves, had their being, but there were more substantial dwellings also for the many better-off: traders, merchants, bankers even, who made hay while the sun shone, as it did most brightly for the surrounding population when a camp of this size was deposited in their midst.

There were men and women of other races, also, Spaniards, Greeks, swarthy Africans – and even, as Mala and I discovered on entering one of the taverns after our women-folk were safely stowed away for the night, Britons: for there, now with a bunch of his compatriots as evil-looking as himself, was the unsavoury character we had encountered a week or so before.

I am sure he recognised us, for he looked hard in our direction as we entered, but he made no sign, turning instead to talk ostentatiously loudly to his companions, and downing great mouthfuls of whatever foul concoction was in the large tankard in front of him.

There was no anti-Roman muttering this time, which was wise, because in addition to the polyglot collection of individuals who sat at the various tables drinking the poison of their choice, there were numerous off-duty squaddies, who would have taken very unkindly indeed to the sort of disparaging comments the fellow had risked at our earlier meeting.

One in particular would have taken to them most unkindly, for it was Servius's centurion, Bilbus, who had promised to teach the gentleman some manners when he had been so forthcoming previously: he entered just as we had found a table, saw the Briton, raised an eye-brow, and then came over to join us in reply to our welcoming call.

'Nice company we have;' he jerked his head in the direction of the Britons.

'Charming,' agreed Mala. 'What I would like to know is whether it is coincidence, or something else, that Ugly Puss has crossed our path again. But never mind that creature: what of you? You are back safe and well. How went the battle? How is the tribune?'

'He too is alive and well, and he has a victory to be proud of under his belt – but it was a hard-fought engagement. You were right, Quintus Propertius, there were more than a hundred of them. The cavalry cut down quite a bunch, but they still, outnumbered us two-to-one when they charged.

'Charged! Will they never learn that a wild charge against disciplined troops requires far more than a two-to-one advantage to have a hope of succeeding? Our javelins took out plenty of them before they even reached our line – funny how they lose their enthusiasm, with a pilum in the gut - and the line held. After that, it was standard tactics: no picnic, but the outcome was inevitable. The cavalry attacked again from the flank, and within half an hour it was all over, and such few of the Germans as survived were running as fast as their legs could carry them. The cavalry cleaned up a fair number of those; only a dozen or so escaped.'

'But it must have been a pretty tough half hour while it lasted,' I said. 'How many men did you lose?'

'Ten, and another half dozen or so hurt, some badly, but we counted well over sixty German bodies when it was over, and many more wounded; we despatched those, of course. I suppose those who escaped headed back home pretty damn quick.'

'Not all,' I said. 'We had a little dust-up with ten of them. They killed four of Gaius Cornelius's men, and my wife's slave-girl..'

The centurion whistled.

'I wish we had sent a unit after you, but we never suspected they would head anywhere but home.'

'No matter: we took care of them, or at least Mala did: he accounted for seven of them, to be precise.'

The centurion looked at Mala with unusual respect.

'I had heard you were good, sir; but *seven*...'

'It was no big deal: I was rather well-armed; any man could have done the same.'

The centurion looked at him quizzically, but Mala said no more, and so we sipped our wine, and amused ourselves by looking around the tavern.

It consisted of one long room, but could as well have been divided into two. In one area were the squaddies, a miscellaneous collection of the local peasantry, the Briton and his entourage, and the usual bevy of over-painted and under-dressed young ladies, some of whom might once have aspired to be vestals, but now were manifestly no longer qualified for the role.

The second, smaller area was where we were seated, and its clientèle included a centurion from the camp garrison and a couple of his decurians, a handful of the more prosperous-looking Gauls, and even, to my surprise, a narrow-striper, a greying-haired, young-old man, who made plain that he had seen it all before, and was destined to see it all again before he passed on to happier climes.

After a time his sole companion left, and he came over, none too steadily, to our table.

'May I join you? It is not often we see new faces here, except the riff-raff below the salt there. My name is Publius Cotta, and I am supposed to look after the finances of this benighted post. Why is it that military men have so little grasp of financial reality? – begging your pardon centurion.'

Our companion grinned.

'Because our money comes from the public purse, citizen, and we all know the public purse is a bottomless pit – except when it comes to our pay, of course.'

'You jest,' said our new friend, 'I hope; but all too many of your confrères think that what you say is literal truth. There are supposed to be three men from the Treasury in Rome coming to help me sort things out, since the local oicks who are supposed to be my assistants will never manage it. I've seen nothing of them as yet; you wouldn't happen to know anything of them?'

'I fear we do,' I told him, 'and only one of the team that was supposed to drop off here will be able to lend you a hand: the other two were killed by a bunch of Germans we fell in with, as were two other Treasury men.'

'Damn,' said the equestrian. 'I wait six ruddy months for help, and two thirds of it has to go mixing it with frigging Germans before they even get here.'

'I'm sure they would sooner have been here,' I told him. 'One got a spear in the back before he even knew there were Germans in the vicinity, and the other was chopped to mincemeat seconds later – as we all nearly were.'

'They have caused a bit of trouble here and hereabouts,' said Publius Cotta. 'Nothing big – isolated hit-and-run raiding parties – but a nuisance.'

'Especially to their victims,' agreed Bilbus, our centurion; 'we came across some of them. But we also came across a party that *was* big: over a hundred of them. It was stragglers who escaped after we had dealt with the main party that my friends here met up with.'

'A hundred: that's bad.. Still, even that many won't feel emboldened to attack the fort.'

'Most of that particular hundred won't be attacking anything any more. I killed at least eight of them myself, and we all had our share;' and then, turning to Mala, 'and thanks to you, sir, I did it more efficiently than I would have believed possible. Those "Stirrups" are worth their weight in gold. Servius Javolenius tells me there is a chance they will be made standard throughout the army, and I can't wait for the day. It will change the whole nature of mounted warfare.'

'Perhaps not quite that, but they should certainly help. I am glad you found them useful.'

'As did my men. One or two were a bit sceptical at first, but they were soon converted, after they had tried them in action.'

''Stirrups', did you call them? Explain, please.' The equestrian was intrigued.

Mala gave a brief description.

'Ingenious, and yet so simple – but apparently very effective. From your description, too,' he added approvingly, 'they should not be too expensive to manufacture.'

Mala assured him, with a slight smile, that it should be possible to turn out thousands, without denting the imperial coffers too badly..

'And,' he added, 'I will see to it that you personally have a pair before we leave. I brought several spares along with me, and it should not be beyond the metal-workers at the fort to copy them, if the commander is interested.'

'He will be; he's a progressive man.'

8

We stayed at the fort longer than originally planned, not least because Servius's men needed time to recover, but also because Gaius Cornelius, and the equestrian Cotta, were indulging in a good deal of head-scratching as to how best to use the severely depleted teams from the imperial treasury. Cotta was forthcoming as ever about the deficiencies of his assistants.

'Do you know what the standard excuse of those oafs is?' he demanded. '"Abacus error"; *abacus* error! Do the ruddy machines have minds of their own?'

'They will have,' I heard Mala mutter, and filed the remark away for future enlightenment.

It was decided eventually that two men would stay to help Cotta, and that Cornelius himself and the two others would pay a flying visit to the smaller settlement in Belgica that needed investigating, but would then go on to Londinium. Cotta was not pleased to have only two men instead of three, but he accepted the inevitable with good grace, and we departed on amicable terms, especially he was delighted with the stirrups Mala made sure he received before we left.

Servius's battered forces, now ten short and with half a dozen more in no great shape, had been due to split at this point, most of the men to replace a contingent from the fort who were due back in Rome, the others to continue with us, but in the event a mere half dozen could be spared as our escort, supplemented by a dozen auxiliaries recruited from the local populace, wild-looking men who, Livinia admitted, frightened her almost as much as the Germans had done.

'Next time we travel,' I suggested, 'we should go to Egypt. The Egyptians are quite different from these northern savages, and would be quite unlikely to attack you with sword or axes like these fellows. Mind you, ' I added, 'there are quite a few who would cheerfully drop you in the Nile for the crocodiles to feast on, if they thought they could get away with it.'

Livinia was not amused.

The rest of our journey, however, was uneventful, Gaius Cornelius and his two colleagues leaving us temporarily when we reached Belgica, and the Gallic auxiliaries making their way back as soon as we reached the little port from which we were to embark.

I will say nothing of our crossing of the narrow strip of water that separated Gaul from Britain, except that so foul was the weather, so rough the sea, so decrepit the flat-bottomed scow we travelled in, and so unkempt, incompetent and uncaring the so-called skipper and his motley crew, that those score or two miles added up to the most unpleasant journey, by far, that I have ever taken in my life – including those weeks spent scrambling across mountains in full kit, in the depths of winter, encountering the well-know Dacian hospitality most of the way.

But we endured it, because we had to, and eventually our purgatory was over.

Next stop, Londinium, though it proved less a stop, more a pause for breath, since another ship, about ten thousand times better than the first, was waiting to take us the length of the south British coast to the territory of the Dumnonii.

We had no time to explore the delights, such as they might be, of Londinium, but we did admire some of the impressive new buildings that were going up, and noticed too how many of the natives we saw had become thoroughly Romanised, even to the extent of wearing togas – an amazing development, when one considered that less than forty years before, every Roman in sight had been slaughtered with the utmost savagery, and the city itself practically razed to the ground, by Boudicca and her barbarians, some of them perhaps the fathers or grandfathers of these very people,

One or two of these 'new Romans' even addressed us in what they imagined was Latin; we pretended to understand.

But one did not address us at all, in any language. We saw him as we emerged from our temporary lodging to make our way to the riverside mooring – Ugly Puss, as Mala had dubbed him, the Briton we had already encountered twice on our journey, along with nine or ten of his companions. They were mounted now, and all stared long and hard at us as we climbed into the open carriages that had been provided for us and our belongings. Servius ordered his men at the ready, but Ugly Puss made no attempt to approach, merely waiting until we were under way before wheeling his horse round and riding in the opposite direction.

'Well, well,' said Mala, 'the proverbial bad penny. My belief in coincidence does not extend quite this far.'

'Nor mine. Why is he dogging our footsteps? What does he know of our mission?'

'Nothing, surely. What do we know of it ourselves?'

We had been given sealed orders by Nerva, to be opened only when we reached Isca Dumnoniorum, where the local Roman authorities, he told us, would fill us in on any details we needed to know, and had been instructed to co-operate with us fully.

But. though the man's repeated appearance on the scene was worrying, nothing could be done about it now.

'Doubtless,' said Mala, 'all will be revealed in due course; I only hope it will not be not an unpleasant experience.'

Our sea voyage this time, along the coast, was pleasantly different from what we had endured from Gaul, but we fretted to reach our destination, and when at last our ship entered the wide estuary that led to Isca Dumnoniorum – or Caer-Wisc as the natives call it - and finally tied up at the quayside, we were more than relieved to disembark.

Word had been sent ahead of our imminent arrival, and we were met by a Roman official of some kind – we could not quite determine his status – and by two Britons who clearly were his subordinates. They greeted us cordially, though looking a little askance at Servius and his armed and armoured men, and at our retinue of slaves, and escorted us into their 'city'.

It was not an impressive place, at first sight. Most of its buildings seemed to be made of wood, or of a kind of painted clay, topped with a roof of straw, though here and there a few more substantial structures, obviously Roman, towered over the rest. We had been told there was a fine basilica, and a bath-house, in the centre of the town, but could not see them as we made our way from the dockside to the quarters that had been arranged for us.

These proved very acceptable indeed, better than we could have expected in such a place, and we settled in readily, happy to relax at last - and yet wondering, not without apprehension, what lay in store for us in this wild, western part of the empire.

9

Publius Tasgetius was one of those people you take to at once. Of late, I have become suspicious of such people, distrusting my own judgement after my encounter with Aurelius Dabrix, the Gaul, who had pulled the wool over all our eyes, except, eventually, Mala's.

Tasgetius, too, was a Gaul, and I wondered again at the way the empire was developing. There had been a Tasgetius in great Julius's time, a minor chieftain, amicably disposed towards Rome – and murdered by his subjects for so being. Now here was this man, a member of the same tribe, a full Roman citizen, and holding high office – a deputy to the governor, no less, and, in effect, top man in the entire territory.

'Welcome to this sunny heaven,' he said expansively.

'Where it rains six days out of seven,' muttered Mala, looking out at the downpour that was descending from leaden skies. This was the Britain I had heard of, drab, dull, cold, wet – even in midsummer.

Tasgetius saw my reaction and was amused – he seemed constantly to be amused, at one thing or another, though underneath, I knew, he could be a hard man: a very hard man indeed.

'Cheer up, Marcus Vectorius. Imagine you have to stay in these parts for a year at a time! I'm sure you would love it, up on the moors in mid-December, in a howling gale, the snow a yard deep, and no shelter for miles around… And when it's not snowing, rain: the natives like to tell us it's the rain that makes the grass so green, to which the obvious reply is: so bloody what? But you are a countryman, I understand; perhaps really you delight in all this?'

'I like lush green grass as well as the next man,' I replied, 'but not at this price.'

'With respect,' said Mala, 'perhaps, in view of our mission, we should put aside talk of the weather, and open our sealed orders.'

'I wish I could put it aside: these Britons when they are making polite conversation seem to talk of nothing else.'

'A national failing, no doubt,' smiled Mala. 'But now, may we, in your presence as instructed, open our sealed orders? After coming all this way, we are still in the dark as to just why we are here, and would very ,much like to know what our task is to be."

'I, too, have sealed orders, to be opened only on your arrival. Let us break our seals together, and see what joys our emperor has lined up for us.'

The two men read their respective parchments, Mala then passing his over to me, and I in turn to Servius.

'It seems straightforward enough,' I commented. 'We are to escort the treasure of the Dumnonii back to Rome, ensuring its safety - guarding it with our lives, if necessary.'

'What is this treasure?' asked Mala. 'Is it a large hoard, gold, jewels, or perhaps something small of special significance, a crown, a sword, some insignia?'

'None of those things,' said Tasgetius, suddenly more sombre and serious. 'We are talking not of gold or jewels or some other precious object, but of a person: Covorilla, rightful heir to the throne of the Dumnonii. She is a little girl of nine or ten, a wonderful creature who captures all hearts: it is she who is known as the treasure of the Dumnonii.'

He shook his head morosely as he spoke.

'And…?'

'And your task will be less straightforward than you think – perhaps impossible. She has disappeared, along with her nursemaid. We have been searching frantically for her these last three days. She may well be dead.'

'How did she disappear? Where? When? Has she been kidnapped? Why do you think she might be dead? Do you have any theories – or suspicions?'

'To answer your last question first: indeed I have my suspicions, but can prove nothing. Burro would like to take them in and sweat them, but of course that is impossible, in view of the political situation here; they are powerful men – and intent on becoming more powerful still.'

'Burro?'

'The Briton in charge of security here. Since the legion's departure back in 75, the tribe has been allowed a small force, chiefly for internal security, though occasionally they do have the odd skirmish with their fellow-tribesmen further down the peninsula. Their other function is to guard their king and his family: you can think of them as a kind of cross between the Praetorians and the vigiles – though they do not fight fires. 'Burro is in charge of the search for Covorilla, though of course he reports to me – reluctantly.'

'I would like to meet this man.'

Mala was now in his element: a mystery to investigate, a missing person to find, villains – presumably – to chastise.

'You had better meet him first, before you say 'like';' Tasgetius was now smiling again, though ambiguously. 'He is an… interesting man. I will send for him at once.'

He came promptly, this Burro. He was a big man, and an impressive one, clad in some gold-bedecked local uniform. He was manifestly of some status, long-haired like all these Dumnonii, but well-groomed, proud, assured – not in the least put out by the presence of a group of high-ranking Romans.

'These gentlemen are on a mission from the Roman emperor.'

'I know. My men are not blind and deaf.'

He had taken the initiative at once.

'You are Romans, and I don't like you. I don't like any of you. You came into this land uninvited, you imposed your rule by force of arms, and you maintain it the same way. I wish you would all go back where you came from, and stay there.

'But I am a realist; I know you won't. Therefore I make the best of a bad job. You have introduced a semblance of law and order, I admit that, where often there was not much, and law and order is vital. That is why I am prepared to do the job I do, even under a Roman: I am helping not Rome, but my own people; but I would help them far more happily if my only superior were my own king, rather than an alien official.'

He look hard at Tasgetius as he spoke; that worthy smiled at him.

'There's one thing about you, Burro, you do not dissemble. I do not think you would make a very good politician.'

'Politicians!' The Briton spat. 'What need of politicians, if you have a good king?'

'If he is a *good* king,' said Mala. 'My friends and I have had this discussion, not long ago. We have emperors rather than kings in Rome, and at present we do have a good one; but have you not heard of Caligula, of Nero, of Domitian, of Commo…' he broke off. 'Those three?'

Commo?

'We Dumnonii have no such monsters; our kings have sometimes been strict, even harsh, but always just.'

'Long may that continue.'

'If it does not, we know what to do. We respect our kings, but they rule only with the consent of the governed.'

'The sina qua non of a free society.'

'Which brings us to the matter in hand,' said Tasgetius. 'Burro will tell you of his investigations, but first you must understand something of the political situation here. It is true that Britain is ruled ultimately from Rome, but much power is delegated to the locals, and just which among them it is delegated to depends on many factors – as I am sure you know.'

We nodded.

'At present, despite what Burro has said, the Dumnonii have no king. The old king died a year ago; his son, the father of Covorilla, was killed in a riding accident only a few months after coming to power. Her mother had died at her birth. She is the rightful heir, but cannot come to the throne until she is of age, which is sixteen years; until that time, we have a Regent, and an advisory Council.'

'May they rot in hell,' said Burro.

'There have been, I believe,' said Mala, 'good regents: somewhere, at some time, once or twice, perhaps even two or three times in the whole history of the human race; for the most part, though, trust regents as far as you can throw them.'

'A good principle,' said Burro. 'I am beginning to like you, Quintus Propertius, even though you are a Roman.'

'A Roman by adoption,' replied Mala, 'though also by conviction. Despite what you said earlier, Burro – and we all know that Rome has come to its present position by conquest, and that at times it has been heavy-handed and worse - it stands to-day as the one great civilising influences in the world. O*n balance* - and these things always must be judged on balance – it should command the support of every fair-thinking and right-thinking man.'

'Let us not get into politics,' said Tasgetius, 'or we will be here all night; except politics of the Dumnonian variety. Let me fill you in on the salient details.

'The Regent is one Arruntius Manissus; to make matters more tricky, he is half-Roman, and a son of the old king, though born on the wrong side of the sheets - which of course, under Dumnonian law, excludes him from ever taking the throne himself.

'He has a candidate for the job, though, a young half-witted rake called Marrabo, only son of one of the old king's brothers, now dead. There is a surviving brother, Pallabrium, who, many think, should have been Regent himself, but the law states that a son of the king, even though illegitimate and debarred from the throne himself, must have precedence. But for that, we might have been saved a great deal of trouble. Pallabrium is a member of the Council, though outnumbered by Arruntius Manissus's cronies; he is also the legal guardian of the rightful heir, the little Covorilla.'

'Pallabrium is one of the great men of our time,' said Burro. 'He would be Regent automatically, if Arruntius met with an unfortunate accident. And don't think I haven't thought about it, but I will not lift a hand against a son of the old king, even one such as he, unless he gives just cause.'

'I would have no such scruples,' said Servius Javolenius. 'If this man is an enemy of Rome, I would be prepared to cut him down without hesitation.'

'With the immense force at your command?' sneered Burro. 'Six men, is it? The legion II Augusta left these parts long ago, and good riddance.'

'But there are other legions in Britain,' replied Servius; 'and if there were a threat to Rome, they would be here soon enough.'

'No doubt,' returned Burro, 'stamping on their subjects as usual.'

'And if the positions were reversed, you would ignore those plotting against you? You do not strike me as a man to turn the other cheek.'

'Gentlemen, gentlemen, let us not get heated. I was outlining the politics of the Dumnonii; let me continue.

'Most of the tribe are fiercely loyal to their rightful king or queen, like Burro here, but a minority, small but powerful, are unhappy with the notion of a woman ruling them. They would prefer even the popinjay Marrabo. The Regent, though he cannot proclaim as much openly, is their leader. His right-hand man, Calthron, a thug of the first water, would take on Burro's job – if we allowed it. We have the final say, of course, but it would be difficult not to agree with the nomination if Marrabo came legally to the throne – as he would if Covorilla were to die. That is why the disappearance of Covorilla is so serious, and why I recommended some time ago that she be removed to Rome for safe keeping. Hence your presence here.'

'Then we must find her; but you said you fear she might already be dead?'

'Unlikely, but not impossible.'

'They would not dare kill her out of hand,' said Burro. 'They would lose support even among their own followers. They could, of course, arrange an "accident", but it would need to be very, very convincing, and if any connection with them were to be established they would be sunk. That is why I am convinced she is still alive, and why I will leave no stone unturned to find her.'

'Then let us work together,' said Mala. 'Put aside your animosity towards Rome. You will not change your views, nor should you, but if I am any judge, you are not a man to let personal feelings prevent you from doing your duty.'

'That I am not; I will work with you – and be pleased to bid you farewell when this business is over.'

'Fair enough. Now tell me the precise circumstances of Covorilla's disappearance.'

'She was riding, as she often did, near the old fortifications our ancestors built long ago, about eight miles from here. Her uncle has a lodge there, and she often stays days on end: she loves the open heath land.'

'Guards?'

'Three of my best men were detailed to look after her, and one rode with her wherever she went. But you know how children are: she delighted in riding off as fast as she could, daring her nursemaid and the guard to try to catch her. But on this occasion, Dalgio, my man, was thrown from his horse, and when he picked himself up, found it had cast a shoe, and gone lame. And don't tell me that was an accident.'

'You trust the man?'

'With my life. He is devoted to the little princess, and to her cause; he is shattered at what has happened. He ran after her – *ran* – but of course could not keep up with the horses. He then ran back to the lodge, to get a fresh horse, and all three of the guards rode as hard as they could in the direction Covorilla had gone. They did not find her, nor her nursemaid.

'I blame myself for that nursemaid,' he went on; 'I should have insisted that she be replaced as soon as I heard that she had become friendly – very friendly – with one of Calthron's men. Covorilla was fond of her, and she seemed fond of the little girl, but I should not have let that deter me.'

'Assuming Covorilla was abducted, with or without the connivance of the nursemaid, was there anywhere close by where she could have been hidden?'

'Nowhere: it is an area quite bereft of habitation, apart from Pallabrium's lodge. Covorilla must have been taken right out of the area, though in which direction, we have no means of knowing.'

'It is going to be a question of *cherchez la femme*,' said Mala. 'If we find the nursemaid, whether she betrayed her trust or not, we will find Covorilla; and the best way to find the nursemaid is probably through her beau. You know him, this man of Calthron's?'

'Intimately,' said Burro, grimly. 'He is the son of my late wife by her first marriage.'

'It is the classic case of son not getting on with stepfather,' Tasgetius told us afterwards. 'The boy was ten when his widowed mother married Burro, remembered his real father well, and resented Burro as a usurper. The funny thing is that even though not blood-related, they are very alike, and not only physically: each is proud, haughty, blunt, and rather pig-headed. I suppose it was almost inevitable that as Burro allied himself with Pallabrium's party, Felgio would gravitate towards Manissus and Calthron, to assert his independence, though in truth he has little in common with those villains. I hope that one day he will come to his senses, and see througthem for what they are. Otherwise he might come to serious harm.'

'Talking of this man Manissus and his confrères, when can we meet them?'

'This very evening. I have arranged a dinner for you and your ladies, as honoured guests, and a dozen local dignitaries and their wives.'

10

Arruntius Manissus was an important man, and knew it, but he did not throw his weight around at Tasgetius's dinner, preferring instead to exercise his considerable charm – all smiles and no substance, as Mala said afterwards – and to treat us as welcome visitors bringing a breath of civilization to this backward outpost.

It was the Roman side of his background that he chose to emphasise, even though his status rested on his being the bastard son of the former king of the Dumnonii. He wore a toga – as did several of the others – and could have been mistaken for a high-class Roman, by any but a high-class Roman. His small-talk was easy and fluent, he displayed a ready if somewhat off-beat sense of humour, and he was especially attentive to Livinia and Julia Carolina, entertaining them with anecdotes to illustrate Dumnonian life and customs, recommending little local delicacies that appeared on the tables, and in all making himself as agreeable as possible.

Marrabo, the man who would be king, was as different again. Where Manissus was suave, he was gauche, where Manissus was subtle, he was crass, where Manissus was at times genuinely witty, Marrabo's attempts at humour were embarrassingly crude – and where Manissus drank his wine sparingly, Marrabo downed cup after cup, until soon his speech was slurred, his movements unsteady, his eyes glazed. After a time he ceased to converse except in meaningless grunts, turning his attention solely to his wine and food, downing vast quantities of both in the most uncouth fashion imaginable.

His uncle, Pallabrium, eyed him with ill-concealed disgust. This was a man no-one could ignore. A barbarian, a member of this obscure, backward tribe, he nevertheless would have stood out in any company in the empire: in the Senate, he would have spoken, and they would have listened; in the Forum, the mob would have flocked to hear him, and in this heterogeneous company of Romans and Dumnonii, he seemed equally at ease with both, switching smoothly from the guttural local tongue to impeccable Latin, and showing an impressive familiarity with our culture, and that of the Greeks. (Like Manissus, we learned afterwards, he had spent some years of his youth in Rome, and clearly had absorbed much that it had to offer.)

'I do not believe,' said Mala afterwards, 'that Pallabrium is his nephew's greatest fan, and that is the nephew's loss. Pallabrium is a man of substance.'

Mala was putting into words what all of us felt. What we felt about Manissus was something else again. To Livinia – sweet, innocent and trusting Livinia – he was a man of charm, not least because he was half Roman. To Julia Carolina, he was a smoothie, but no worse than others she had met. To Servius, he was a barbarian, his veneer of Roman sophistication just that – a veneer. To Mala and me, also, his sophistication was but a veneer, and what it concealed we had both divined, and it was not a pretty sight: not a pretty sight at all.

All of these reactions, however, we revealed after the event. What happened at Tasgetius's dinner before that overshadowed, in all our eyes, any impressions Manissus, boss man or not, had managed to make, and even the impact of the upright and estimable Pallabrium.

This was the noisy arrival, the best part of an hour late, and far too uncouth and under the influence to apologise even to our host and his complaisant wife, of Calthron, Manissus's enforcer.

He was a big man, as big as Burro, raw-boned, long-limbed, innately powerful. Though clad in some Dumnonian finery that, apparently, betokened his rank, and though groomed as he had not been on his previous appearances, he was every inch a barbarian, an ill-bred creature but little removed from primeval savagery. He was the kind of man you would have hoped to see sent to the arena, so that his fellow primitives there might teach him just a little of half-way civilised conduct, before they cast him into well-deserved oblivion.

We recognised him at once, of course: he was the Briton we had met, at the inn in southern Gaul, at the fort, and again in Londinium, and he was still the manifestation and the epitome of the alien, barbarian enemy.

He strode in, as though he owned the place, with not even a nod to Tasgetius, his host, and settled himself next to Marrabo, where that worthy had been just conscious enough to keep a seat for him throughout the evening.

It was Servius Javolenius who precipitated matters. Seated as he was at the couch right next to where the barbarian had thrown himself, he rose ostentatiously, looked full in the face of the intruder, and moved to a seat as far away as he could get.

Everyone had noticed, and there was silence; no-one was in any doubt as to what Servius's move had been meant to signify.

The barbarian himself was in less doubt that any. He sprang to his feet, his hand on the jewelled hilt of the dagger that hung from his belt.

'Is my company not good enough for you, Roman?' he demanded.

Servius pointedly ignored him. The man became more incensed, his accent more guttural.

'You, you filthy jumped-up Roman piece of dirt: I was talking to you.'

Servius was an aristocrat through and through. He eyed the man up and down as he might some wretch in chains in the slave market, and this time as he turned away made a gesture of contempt.

It could have got very ugly at that point. Calthron had half-drawn his dagger, Mala had sprung to his feet ready to intervene, and two others of Manissus's party had looked as though they were only too ready to do likewise. Tasgetius, however, had already gestured to his guards, Romans all, part of the small force that were still stationed in the area, and two of them unceremoniously grabbed the Briton, while a third kept his spear at the ready as he faced the man. Tasgetius nodded, and they bundled him out of the room forthwith, and then out of the house.

'I say,' protested Marrabo, 'that was my friend.'

'Then you should choose you friends more carefully,' Pallabrium told him curtly, pointedly glancing at Manissus as he did so. The Regent did not miss the point, and was clearly furious, not only with what Pallabrium had said, but with the whole incident. He controlled himself with an effort and spoke to Servius.

'I must apologise, Servius Javolenius, for the behaviour of my countryman, and to you, Publius Tasgetius, and to your guests, for this inexcusable abuse of your hospitality.

Tasgetius waved dismissal.

'A little too much of your local fermented apple-juice,' he said; 'these things happen. No doubt,' he added mildly, but the look in his eye as he addressed Manissus was anything but mild, 'your retainer will wait on me to-morrow and apologise.'

The slight emphasis on 'your retainer' spoke volumes.

'I will see to it.'

'Then let us have more wine, and a bowl of fine local strawberries and the thick cream your womenfolk make - a local speciality,' he said to us, as the servants answered his summons.

The rest of the evening passed without further incident, though the party broke up earlier than might otherwise have been expected.

11

'Nasty business, and very nearly nastier.' I said.

'Nasty man,' Livinia insisted.

'More to the point than his nastiness, is what he has been doing, dogging our footsteps all these weeks.' Mala said.

'Can anyone at court be in cahoots with these people?'

'Most unlikely. Nerva stressed the need for secrecy throughout, and so far as I know confided to no-one. We made it as plain as we could, in Rome and en route, that we were simply ordinary citizens embarking on a kind of Grand Tour.'

'Hardly ordinary, with an escort of soldiers.'

'That was readily explained: they were there to guard Gaius Cornelius and his Treasury friends; as far as we were concerned their presence was fortuitous, and we were merely hangers-on. Moreover, it meant we took a somewhat roundabout route here, which was less suspicious than making a bee-line for Britain by the shortest route through Gaul.'

'But meeting that lout Calthron again and again cannot have been fortuitous.'

'Of course not, which further suggests that any leak must have been at this end. We know that Tasgetius wrote to the emperor suggesting that Covorilla be removed. We were to arrive, still in the guise of tourists, and spirit her away before Manissus and his faction had any inkling of what was going on. Only Tasgetius, Burro, and Pallabrium knew of the plan. Manissus must have seen Tasgetius's letter, and sent Calthron to find out what he could. Our meeting in the inn might have been just a stroke of luck for him, but at that point he put two and two together and happened to come up with the right answer. He backed his hunch and followed us. If it had not been for our escort, he might well have tried to put paid to us. Indeed, I wonder if our encounter with the Germans was entirely a chance encounter.'

'I am surprised Manissus did not send someone with a little more nous, and a little more manners,' said Servius.

'But if it had been a smooth, Romanised, thoroughly civilised Briton crossing our path, would not we in turn have been more suspicious? However, that is water under the bridge. More important is to discover just how much he, and his master, really know, and to try to find out who leaked the contents of Tasgetius's letter; and more important than either is to find what has happened to little Covorilla. That, as I have suggested, might best be achieved by finding the nursemaid, via Burro's stepson.

'Tomorrow is going to be a busy day.'

Early next morning, we again found ourselves in conclave with Publius Tasgetius, and this time the mood was sombre indeed: no small talk about the weather (which, as it happened, was sunny enough for Italy), no half-amused smile on the deputy-governor's lips, nothing but earnest concentration on the business in hand.

Burro was there, and he looked the grimmest of all.

'We have just fished a body out of the river,' he told us.

Tasgetius took up the story.

'It was the clerk who wrote my letter to the emperor suggesting that Covorilla be removed to Rome. He had been tortured. We found a note in his desk confessing to telling the Regent: he thought it was his duty. Somehow, whoever killed him gleaned that he was no longer to be trusted and that he was on the verge of telling us what he had done.'

"*Whoever* killed him'?' snorted Burro. 'The murder had Calthron's signature all over it. He was probably attending to it when we were being polite Roman-fashion to Manissus and his traitorous cronies, and stuffing our faces. Doubtless that is why Calthron was late.'

'Very likely, and it further explains Calthron's trip to Gaul. He and his hangers-on were sent to find out what they could about any unusual *prominentes* heading apparently for Britain. Our cover was effectively blown not long after we left Rome,' said Mala.

'And Manissus knows everything – which is why he decided to move, and snatch Covorilla before you even arrived here. If Calthron had not got to that scribe first, I wish I could have got my hands on him; he would have wished he had never been born.'

'Meanwhile, we have to find Covorilla, and that brings us to your errant stepson.'

'I could find him, and take him, though that might mean a battle against Calthron's thugs – not that I would mind that. It might not do a lot of good, though: I have brought Felgio up to be tough, and he will not break easily.'

There was some pain in his eyes as he spoke.

He really is fond of the boy, I thought, and yet he would do what he conceives to be his duty, and torture him if he thought it would lead to Covorilla.

'I do not think it need come to trying to break him,' said Mala. 'Subtler methods would be more effective. Felgio must be found, and tailed – night and day. Sooner or later, probably sooner, he will make contact with the nursemaid. Have you men capable of such tracking, without being recognised, or even seen?'

'I have such.'

'You will need at least three different men, and they must relieve each other every two or three hours. At each new stint of duty, they must change their garb, into something as different as they can find from what they have worn before. They must be as invisible as possible, yet as keen-eyed as hawks.'

'Do not teach me my job, Quintus Propertius.'

'So be it.'

And so it was. It took only two days before one of Burro's men sent a message back to say that Felgio had been seen heading for the high moors, as fast as his horse could carry him. Unable to follow, the tail had taken himself to a nearby tavern favoured by Calthron's men, and kept his ears open.

It was not long before he heard some banter about one of their absent colleagues, and a young woman with whom he was besotted, and then a reference to 'Jebthro's farm'.

'I know it,' said Burro. 'It is just on the edge of the moor; it has been semi-deserted for a year or more. Jebthro was well-off once, but the poor fool is reputed to be heavily in debt to Manissus; he now makes his living dealing in corn and animal-feed, and lives in the city. They must have leant on him pretty heavily to get him to agree to imprison his own princess, though: he is weak, but I had not thought wicked.'

'If indeed she is there,' I said. 'Perhaps there is only the nursemaid, and perhaps she truly is in league with Manissus and his mob.'

'Maybe so, and maybe no, but it is the only lead we have, and I propose to pay a visit to Jebthro's farm without delay.'

'In force?'

'No; a large body of men leaving the city would be conspicuous, and would probably lead to word being sent ahead, and the immediate spiriting away of Covorilla. I will go myself, instructing a very few of my men to leave town separately. We will rendezvous near the farm, and then descend as quickly as we can to prevent anyone getting away. It is a small place; there can't be too many guards.'

'I would like to join you.'

'And I.'

'You two, if you like, but only you two. Above all,' turning to Servius, 'you and your soldiers must keep away: you would give the game away in no time.'

It seemed strange, this relatively minor provincial official, a barbarian, giving orders to a military tribune of the empire, but Servius was no fool and saw the force of Burro's argument, and acquiesced readily.

'You can go with my man Dembro,' Burro said to Mala and me; 'he knows the place to rendezvous: it overlooks the farm. When we have seen what the situation is, we pray to the gods - and go in.'

Mala and I, and the man Dembro, rode eastwards out of the city, ostensibly in the direction of the area where Covorilla had disappeared, but a wide circle soon saw us heading due west. We rode in silence: Dembro might or might not have been a conversationalist, but the fact that he knew no Latin would hardly have helped; Mala and I were both wrapped up in our own thoughts, well aware that we might be heading into considerable danger.

Burro and two others were waiting when we reached the rendezvous, and within minutes of his showing us the lie of the land, the six of us were galloping at full speed towards the somewhat dilapidated farmhouse.

It was easier than it should have been. Remarkably, no-one was keeping watch, and we reached the farmyard to find only two rather scruffy-looking farmhands tending a handful of equally scruffy-looking animals, and two guards, obviously part of Calthron's private army, who were busily engaged in a game of dice and were taken completely by surprise as we galloped in. Not surprisingly, they showed no stomach for a fight with six armed horsemen. Burro's snort told us what would have happened to any of his own force who took their duties so lightly, but none of us complained; instead we herded them all into a barn, left two of Burro's men on guard, and entered the substantial farmhouse.

Dilapidated the outside may have been, but the inside, even though the building was no longer regularly occupied, was remarkably well-appointed for the dwelling of a barbarian: further evidence, I thought, of the way the influence of Rome was spreading, even to these remote parts. But we did not stop to admire the furnishings.

'May the gods be praised!'

Burro's reaction was shared by us all, as a little, golden-haired girl rushed towards him, with that childish, uninhibited joy that sends a warm glow through the sentimental – and many others among us. She bubbled; effervesced; her words of delight came pouring out a hundred to the dozen, as she clung to Burro, on whom, obviously, she doted.

That stern and formidable man in turn was transformed – 'Just a big softie, at heart,' said Mala – as he bent to answer and comfort the child.

'Princess, we have come to take you home.'

No less delighted than the little girl, we noted with interest, was the young woman who was her nursemaid.

'We thought you would never come,' she cried. 'Felgio insisted we had been taken for our own protection, to save us being kidnapped by the Romans,' - she looked doubtfully at Mala and me – 'and would not believe me when I told him it was Manissus who wished us harm.'

'And how did you know?'

'I had overheard that brute Calthron talking with his officers about an accident that would befall little Covorilla, and debating whether my attachment to Felgio meant it would be safe to spare me. Calthron said he was for getting rid of me at the same time as Covorilla, and if Felgio didn't like it, he could do the other – or suffer the same fate.

'Felgio said I was imagining things, and that Manissus was an honourable man whose only thought was for the welfare of Covorilla, and of our people. He is so obstinate – and yet I cannot help loving him with all my heart.'

Her distress was real, and it was deep; even Burro's doubts were stilled, the more so when she went on:

'Sir, you are his father; can you not convince him how wrong he is?'

'I? He would as lief listen to me as to the demon of the moors. Yet I fear that if my words will not convince him, my sword will have to. I know my duty.'

Spoken like a Roman, I thought. To put one's country above parental love – that is the true mark of a noble citizen, and our history abounds with stories of those who have done so.

'But now we must hurry,' Burro went on. 'We have horses: two of my men must make their way back on foot. I want to be away from here before Calthron's thugs turn up.'

What was Mala's phrase? *–the best laid plans...*

12

There were at twenty of them or more, and how they managed to reach the farm without our hearing them, and without Dembro, who had been placed on guard, giving the alarm, I will never know. They burst into the room., each wielding a wicked-looking spear, and none of us had time even to put hand to hilt of sword. I saw Mala reach for the leather bag at his waist, and then think better of it, as two men rushed towards him and held spears at his throat. Burro and I were similarly cornered, and then the leader of the band, who was Calthron himself, strode into the room.

'So – a lovely haul: the mighty Burro, and two filthy Romans as well. What a pity we were not here when you arrived, for then we would have fought, and I could have cut you down on the spot.'

'Do it, then, 'said Burro; 'murder is your speciality.'

'And of course your faithful son would avenge you,' sneered Calthron. 'Perhaps, when the time comes, I will have the young man put paid to you himself; I have no doubt he would enjoy that.'

But for the two spears, Burro, we knew, would have sprung on Calthron and strangled him with his bare hands. Calthron knew so too, and revelled in the other's frustration, but after goading Burro to fury, he turned to us.

'You, Roman pigs, I would cut you down with no less pleasure. Unfortunately my orders are that you should not be harmed – yet. But when the time is right…'

He laughed.

'Such treacherous parts, these,' he said. 'Boulders have been known to fall and crush a man; trees likewise; others have been torn to pieces by the wolves; the Great Mire has claimed still more. I fear there will be a spate of such 'accidents' before long. But not yet, alas, for so Manissus has ordered. You are safe now; but to-morrow is another day.

'And then, great Burro, you will be no more. and your exalted post will be vacant; and King Marrabo will know just the man to take your place.'

He laughed again, and barked orders. We were deftly disarmed, bundled out of the room past the bodies of Dembro and Burro's other men, all of whom had been speared before they had chance to raise the alarm. We were thrust into the barn where Calthron's two guards had been held so briefly, and then trussed up with rough ropes, hand and foot, and thrown to the floor. Calthron came to make sure we were helpless, and kicked Burro viciously in the ribs.

'Have a good day,' he leered, and left, laughing his evil laugh.

We struggled with our ropes, but soon enough knew it was futile: the men who had bound us knew a thing or two about knots, and none of us could make any impression. Burro whispered that he had a concealed knife, but there was no way either he, or we, could reach it. Nor was there anything within reach in the barn we could use to try to fray our bonds – no sharp stone, no grindstone, no agricultural tools, even of the primitive kind these people used.

'We are finished,' said Burro, bitterly, 'and again it is my fault. I should have left a message as to where we were heading, except that I did not word to get to Manissus, or to Calthron. Little use it was: Calthron found us anyway.'

'It was a perfectly sound precaution, and you must not blame yourself. Calthron was probably heading here as a matter of course. But will your men not mount a search, as soon as you do not return?'

'Undoubtedly; but this is a big area, with many scattered farms. It would not occur to anyone to look here first. I would not have thought of it myself as a likely hiding-place, had not my man heard what he did in the tavern. Just looking at random, it might be days before anyone stumbles on this place. By then, it will be too late: Calthron will certainly press Manissus to get rid of us as soon as possible – and Covorilla also.'

What he said was so obviously true that we could not argue, and we lay there on the hard floor in silence, each wrapped up in his own thoughts.

At length the sun went down, and what little light had filtered into the barn was gone. In the pitch darkness, I nodded at first, then dozed, and eventually fell into a troubled sleep. My dreams were vivid. Calthron figured prominently in them, and I kept seeing his leering, gloating face as he told me in ghastly, spine-chilling detail of what was about to befall me. At one point, I thought he was going to finish me there and then, as he grasped my shoulders, and began to shake me, as a dog shakes a bone, or a lion its victim in the arena. I cried out...

A hand was clasped over my mouth.

'Silence; they must not hear us. Still, while I cut your bonds.' The Latin was uncertain, but the meaning clear enough. As the ropes fell from my arms, I sat up, and saw that dawn had come, and in the half-light could make out two figures, the one who had freed me now bending over Mala, the other, more distant, setting Burro free.

Burro started to say something, but the man cut him short.

'Be quiet,' he whispered, 'and for once in your life stop giving orders. Listen, and do as I say.'

Burro swallowed hard and nodded.

'There were ten of Calthron's men here. The two who were guarding the barn will trouble us no more, but that still leaves eight. Here are swords – but still we are but five.

'Two of my former comrades, moreover,' he spat, 'are in the main farmhouse with Covorilla and Sylvana, with orders to kill them instantly if they hear any attackers. We must get to them without the others hearing, though how we are to cover the length of that long room before they do their worst, I do not know. We have no long bow, or javelins.'

The heavy spears the Dumnonii used were for stabbing only; what we needed was a pilum or two.

'You must leave the two guards to me,' whispered Mala. 'I have the means to kill them before they move against their prisoners. You must be ready to handle the others: four against six, and the advantage of surprise: you should be able to hold them until I join you.'

Burro looked doubtful.

'Trust me on this.'

He turned towards the door of the barn, but at that moment it was kicked open, and three of Calthron's men came rushing towards us with drawn swords. Burro clove one almost in two, the young man who had spoken to him so peremptorily engaged with another, and the third turned to run, shouting as he did so.

Mala sprinted as fast as he could towards the farmhouse, as the man who had run away turned back, joined now by his three remaining companions.

'Four against four,' I said to myself, 'this is more like it.'

One thing I learned that morning: these Dumnonii are no mean fighters. Burro and his two countrymen were by no means having things their own way, and I was having to learn to cope pretty damn quick with a whole new method of fighting.

I was just about holding my own, when one of the young men who had freed us took an almighty blow in the ribs that felled him, but instead of finishing him off – which wasn't necessary: he would do no more fighting for many a day – his adversary turned, and joined the savage who was pressing me.

It would have gone ill, I fear, but there came suddenly from the farmhouse, two of those loud bangs such as I had heard when the Germans attacked us in Gaul – whiplash-like cracks, magnified many fold.

We were all of us startled, and, involuntarily, paused, but it was Burro who recovered by far the quickest, and he had despatched his man before that worthy had even begun to regain his composure.

He at once sprang to engage the second of my attackers, while I, with a lucky thrust, put paid to the first. I ran Burro's opponent through the back, and we both prepared to help the second of our young rescuers, but he, too, took care of his man before we were needed, and so there we were, with four very dead villains, and one badly-bleeding young tribesman who was all too clearly in need of attention.

We carried him into the farmhouse, there to find Mala comforting the little Covorilla, the nursemaid staring at him in astonishment, and the two guards stretched out on the floor, one quite dead with a gaping hole in his chest, the other on the floor, groaning, quite out of action with a smashed and splintered shoulder. Burro strode straight up to him and ran him through.

'So perish those who would murder women and little children,' he said with satisfaction. 'Roman,' - he turned to Mala – 'you have done well. I salute you.'

Mala acknowledged the compliment with a little nod. The nursemaid, meanwhile, had rushed up to the young man who had freed us, and threw herself into his arms.

'So that is Felgio,' I said; 'I suspected as much.'

'And he has come back to the fold,' replied Burro; 'not before time. But let us look to this other young man, for we owe our lives to him as well as to my son.'

'More,' said Felgio. 'Branthro was with Calthron's band who surprised you. Like me, he had been foolishly taken in by Manissus, until he, like Sylvana earlier, heard Calthron's talk of 'King Marrabo', and of 'accidents' happening. As soon as he reached town he sought me out and told me; we rode here at once – and the rest you know. I beg your forgiveness for my stupidity.'

'Talk no more of it.'

We turned to the injured Branthro.

It was a nasty gash, not life-threatening given proper care, but the man was weak from loss of blood, and obviously in no condition to be moved. Covorilla and the nursemaid, Sylvana, were also very distressed, and in need of rest and calm. And yet, we did not want to stay at the farmstead for a moment longer than necessary, in case Calthron and more of his men returned.

Burro was decisive.

'We need more men here, and quickly. I do not care who sees them leaving Caer-Wisc now. Felgio, you must go. You are still suspect among my followers, but this note, with my seal, should convince them. Go straight to my camp, but see that word of what is happening reaches Tasgetius also.'

'And Servius Javolenius,' I put in. 'He has only six men, but they are battle-hardened, and we may need every man we can get. If Calthron comes, we do not know how many fighters he will bring with him.'

Burro nodded: 'See to it.'

Felgio left at once, and we were left to survey our defences, such as they were.

'We cannot defend the whole farm,' said Burro, 'but this farmhouse is a different matter, even with only three of us. The door is stout, and can be further reinforced; the windows are small; and, thank the gods, the building is made of our local granite, not of wood: at least they will not burn us out.'

'Perhaps they will not come,' said Sylvana, timidly.

'They are bound to, some at least, to relieve the men who were on guard. The question is whether Calthron will come himself, and whether he will bring a large force. I believe he will; too much is at stake, and he will want to leave nothing to chance.'

The farmhouse, so-called, consisted chiefly of one long room, with a few very small, windowless rooms off, for sleeping, cooking, and washing. The main room itself had three windows, set high; no glass, of course, but stout shutters that could be fastened with long hooked poles. It was well-furnished, and included two heavy cupboards, which we dragged against the door.

'A good battering ram would break it down,' said Burro, 'but nothing less.'

Eventually Mala, who had been keeping watch, called down to us.

'I can see a bunch of horsemen on the brow of the hill where we made our rendezvous. I would say there are at least thirty. Unfortunately I left my telescope behind, and it is too far for me to make out whether they are Calthron's men or yours.'

'They will not be mine; there has not been time. Even if they set out immediately Felgio delivered my orders, we are going to have to hold off this lot for half an hour to an hour – if we can.'

All too soon, the clatter of hooves announced the arrival of our visitors. One of them dismounted, went straight up to the door, and cursed as he found it barred against him.

'You, in there,' he said. 'You are promised safe conduct if you deliver up Covorilla to my protection.'

He spoke in Latin, but Burro replied in the local tongue, and what he said sounded less than polite. The result was immediate.

'As I hoped: you have signed your death warrants.'

Soon there came the crash of an axe against the door, which stopped after a few blows. The immensely thick oak door was heavily studded with iron, to discourage just such an assault, and did its job well.

'They will soon improvise a battering-ram, even if they did not bring one with them,' predicted Burro. 'Then we will have problems.'

It took them some time, during which our peace was disturbed only by the occasional arrow whistling through the narrow window and clattering safely to the floor behind us. Eventually, however, we heard raised voices outside, the rush of feet, and the door shuddered as the tree-trunk or whatever they were using crashed into it.

Whoever built that door, built it well. Charge after charge it withstood, before, at last, it succumbed. The timber shattered, the cupboards we had wedged behind it were sent flying out of the way, and half a dozen of Calthron's men, swords drawn, clambered over the wreckage.

They barely crossed the threshold. Burro's great sword put paid to two before they had entered the room, Mala's flickering blade accounted for two more, and when one broke free into the room, it was to find me waiting. I engaged him briefly, and then Burro turned and finished him off before we had exchanged half a dozen blows. The sixth man suddenly remembered something urgent outside he had forgotten to take care of, and scrambled back over the wreckage of the door.

It was only a temporary respite, and others were soon bunching up to attack, urged on in the foulest language (as Burro later told us) by Calthron himself. We knew that Calthron's men numbered more than a score, and that we were bound to be overwhelmed in all too brief a time. Each of us resolved to sell his life dearly, and awaited the onslaught, though Mala, I noticed, had taken from his ubiquitous pouch a heavy-looking metal object, which he was eying with some interest.

'Only four rounds left, alas,' he said, 'and my spare ammo is back in Isca.'

Ammo?

It was Mala's sharp ears which caught the sound first.

'Ha!' he cried. 'The Seventh Cavalry – just in time as usual.!'

Seventh Cavalry?

It was Servius and his men who reached us first, cutting down those bunched round the door with merciless efficiency. Three had entered the room, but were never to leave it. Two were disposed of immediately, and the third turned to escape, only find his way barred by two resplendently uniformed figures with swords at the ready. It was Servius Javolenius, and his centurion, Bilbus.

The latter's eyes lit up.

'It is the gentleman who needs a lesson in manners! Your permission,. sir?'

A good officer, Servius: he knows when to delegate authority. He would have loved to take care of Calthron – for it was he – himself, but denied himself the pleasure. Burro, too, had wanted the privilege, but both watched as Bilbus carefully advanced on his man, his heart at this moment very much in his duty. We would each of us, Servius, Burro, Mala, and I - it goes without saying - have leaped forward in an instant if the centurion looked like being bested – this sort of fight is no time for chivalry: what fights are? – but our man was not a veteran of a score of hard-fought battles for nothing. Calthron fought well, but Bilbus forced him back inexorably before, finally – very finally - unleashing a cut that removed Calthron's sword from the fray – and most of the arm holding it. A slash to the neck followed, and Calthron was no more.

'And he did not even say *touché*,' muttered Mala.

Burro looked at the centurion with respect.

'You have cheated me of my satisfaction, Roman,' he said; 'but you have done the job well. I doubt I could have bettered it.'

It was as near a compliment as Burro was likely to pay to a Roman, and Bilbus accepted it with a little flourish of his gladius.

'One down, one to go,' said Mala. 'Now for the Regent.'

13

'It will not be simple,' said Burro, back in Isca Dumnoniorum, where we had been joined by Tasgetius and Pallabrium. 'Manissus still has considerable support, and I do not know that we can pin anything on him personally.'

'But Calthron was his creature; everyone knows that.'

'And everyone know Calthron was a vicious, headstrong animal, quite capable of taking things into his own hands for his own purposes, in defiance of Manissus's orders, which of course is what the Regent will say at once. He will tell all who will listen – and many will – that he abducted Covorilla only to save her from a Roman plot; and the very presence here of Quintus Propertius and his companions will reinforce his story.'

'And after all, in a way it is true,' acknowledged Mala. 'We were indeed going to spirit Covorilla away – but genuinely for her own safety, and with your agreement and connivance, and that of Pallabrium also.'

'Which gives Manissus further ammunition: Pallabrium and I are – traitors; collaborationists: or so Manissus will say. I, a collaborationist with the Romans!' He laughed bitterly.

'You are both patriots, devoted to your rightful ruler, and recognised that Rome, too, had her interests at heart.'

'Rome had its own interests at heart; if it had been to her advantage to back Manissus and dispose of Covorilla, that is what she would have done.'

Servius Javolenius looked shocked; but not Mala.

'True; and if the positions had been reversed, the Dumnonii would have done the same. We like to think we are honourable men, and so do many of our leaders, but honourable or not, where the well-being of the country is concerned, it is surprising how even honourable men will put that first.

Some call in *Realpolitik*, and it is as well that grown men learn as soon as possible that that is the way the world is.'

'To act dishonourably would seem to me next door to treason.'

'Treason? What is treason? Treason never prospers, for if it prospers, none dare call it treason."

'You are a cynic.'

'No; I am observer of the world, and of the way it truly is. It is often not a pretty sight.'

'That is so true, Quintus Propertius, though hardly an original observation: I see you have read widely, as well as observed deeply.' It was Pallabrium who spoke.

'This philosophical stuff is all very well,' interrupted Burro, 'but we have a problem on our hands. How do we get Manissus, and prevent him turning what should have been a disaster for him into a disaster for us?'

'I thought you would have had a way,' smiled Mala; 'I have seen that that sword at your side is not for decoration.'

'Give me half a chance, and knowing what I now know I will send him to his ancestors with delight, son of the old king or not.'

'No!'

Tasgetius and Pallabrium spoke as one.

'Quintus Propertius jests,' went on Pallabrium. 'Such a move against the rightful Regent would precipitate civil war, no less. That no-one wants.'

'Least of all Rome,' added Tasgetius.

'What Rome wants is to me immaterial,' replied Burro, and I saw Servius Javolenius's look of disapproval. He is a fine fellow, Servius, but diplomacy is not his strong suit, and his ideas of propriety, including political propriety, are a mite old-fashioned. In particular he tends to regard lesser breeds without the law essentially *de haute en bas*. He had respect for Burro's integrity, and his courage – but still, the man was a bloody barbarian for all that.

'And yet,' I thought, 'he respects Pallabrium as much as any of us; that man's stature would impress anyone, much as the Briton Caractacus is said to have impressed the emperor Claudius those many years ago.'

'I was indeed speaking in jest,' Mala told Burro. 'I know your methods, and in the right circumstances they are admirable. In those circumstances, there are few men if any I would sooner have at my side; but these are not those circumstances. What is called for now is diplomacy, subtlety, and perhaps a little low cunning. I have an idea…'

He turned to Pallabrium.

'Your brother, the old king, what was he like? I mean, physically: tall, short, dark, fair, blue-eyed…? Tell me.'

'He was a fine figure of a man, every inch a Dumnonian king: tall, strongly-built, raven-haired when young, handsome, grey-eyed – why do you ask?'

Mala ignored the question.

'And his other son, the young king, Covorilla's father?'

'A chip off the old block: the spitting image of his father when young. But again: why do you ask?'

'Because Manissus is quite different: short, stocky, red-haired, blue-eyed, and rather ugly.'

'The mother's influence,' replied Pallabrium, but I noted that he looked a little uncomfortable.

'But the mother was Roman. Was she not dark-haired, like most Roman women? And tall, perhaps, sinuous – as such women often are?'

'She was a whore; a respectable whore, if you admit such a concept, staidly married to some minor Roman official, widowed young: there are plenty such creatures in Rome, though they are not known, here among the Dumnonii. As for her being dark: there was, she said, red hair among her ancestors. I can see what you are getting at, Quintus Propertius, but you will get nowhere. My brother accepted the child who became Manissus as his own, and there was an end to the matter – whatever others might have thought. It would have been more than a man's life was worth to question it; even mine.'

'But the old king is gone, and we may question it now,' said Mala. 'She is still alive, this woman, I am told?'

'Yes, living in comfort where my brother installed her, gossiping, spreading rumours, even playing politics when she dares – a despicable creature now, in her dotage, as she was in a different way when young.'

'I think I would like to meet her.'

'I can see you might *want* to, Quintus Propertius; but *like* -no.'

'Point taken,' said Mala. 'Nevertheless, I must swallow my dislike. I think this woman might have things to tell me…Where can I find her? Manissus will soon be trying to wrong-foot us, and he will not be gentle about it. If I can get our retaliation in first, so much the better.'

'Retaliation in first?'

'If 't were done, when 'tis done,' he replied, "t were well it were done quickly.'

He strode out, Pallabrium by his side talking earnestly.

Mala told me of his interview with the woman immediately afterwards.

'She actually tried to vamp me,' he said, 'at her age. Some women are still handsome and striking when so old, but this creature…

'When she realised she was barking up a gum-tree, she became suspicious; she clammed up. Who did I think I was, questioning her about her private life? She, too, was a Roman – a Roman lady. I had no right to interrogate her. She had been a favourite of the old king, a woman of importance, and her son was a great man among the Dumnonii, Regent, no less. He would not permit any jumped-up Roman fly-by-night to harass *her*.

"Fly-by-night I might be',' I told her, 'but I have a commission from the emperor himself. Do you think the mere Regent of a savage tribe on the outskirts of empire has any clout against *that*? You will do well to co-operate. Old women are not immune from the emperor's wrath, and the arena is large enough for all, especially those misguided enough to dabble in dynastic matters. So tell me everything, and be truthful, as you value your life.'

I had seen Mala in this mood, and well knew that he had overawed far stronger characters than this aging courtesan. I also well knew that there was no way in the world that Mala would send an old woman, or anyone else, to the arena. (He had once confided in me that he regarded the arena as the worst blot there was on Roman civilization, which I thought was going a bit far, though I am no enthusiast for the Games myself.) I knew he would not condemn the woman thus, but she did not. To reinforce his point, he showed her the emperor's seal on his commission, which would impress anyone.

'I thoroughly terrified her,' he said. 'It was bullying tactics, and I do not like frightening women, but it was necessary and justified and I would do it again.'

He would, too, I thought. Mala was a strangely gentle man in some respects, but when necessary he could be ruthless. This woman had evidently had the wit to divine as much.

'I asked her first about her relationship with the late king,' he went on. 'It had been, she admitted, a one-night stand – which I already knew, from what Pallabrium had told me. He also told me the old king immediately regretted it.'

'And yet when the child was born, he adopted it without demur.'

'He thought it was his duty. The whoreson must be acknowledged, and I suppose there was great sport at his making.'

'Did he have no suspicion that the child might not be his? That's what you're getting at, isn't it?'

'Of course it is. But it was the old story: middle-aged man on his last fling; sob-story when child was born; no suspicion on the king's part that she had been no better than she should be, long before she met him, and was long after, for that matter.'

'And the child's obvious lack of resemblance to him?'

'He might have wondered at the blue eyes, but the auburn hair, the stocky frame, the less-than-handsome face – these came later. They would not have been noticeable in a baby.'

'Did you tackle the mother about these wayward features?'

'It was one of the chief points of my visit. She blustered at first, as she had to Pallabrium and others who had dared raise the issue long ago, about auburn hair and blue eyes being in her family, and coming out in one child or another every generation.'

'And how did you take that story.'

'I informed her, very authoritatively, of some elementary genetics – as I must explain to you some day, Marcus; it is a fascinating study. She was awed. She thought it was magical lore, instead of basic science, and it softened her up completely. She felt there was nothing she could hide from me, or dare.

'To make assurance doubly sure, I reminded her again of how the emperor would react if I told him she had been withholding information, and then asked her directly how many of her former lovers were still alive. It was a slim chance, but I had to take it.'

'And?'

'She said there were three, so far as she knew. One – keep this to yourself – was none other than Tasgetius's father: bed-ridden now, I understand, but still in the land of the living. The second, she insisted, was a nobody: a servant in her husband's household she had fancied one day. He, too, is retired from active work, living in obscurity in some hovel in a village a dozen miles away. I gleaned that he had tried to blackmail her once, when younger, until a bunch of thugs the lady could call on in the old days caught him in town late one evening, and took him behind the bath-house and beat the daylights out of him.'

'Nice lady,' I commented. 'Not that I mind what happens to blackmailers, whoever their victims might be; they deserve all they get.'

'This one was certainly discouraged. But it was the third man the woman mentioned – her name is Livinia, by the bye, but don't tell your wife – who really interested me. He had been very young when she seduced him, scarcely more than a boy – she was in her thirties – another servant in her husband's household. He too, like the Regent supposedly, had a mixed Roman-Dumnoniorum ancestry. His father was a sailor, from one of those trading-ships that visited these parts even before Claudius's conquest. He had had a fling with one of the local lasses during his run ashore, and then sailed away, leaving her to nurse the consequences.

'This boy is now a man, old, but by no means in his dotage. He still plies his trade as a fisherman, operating from a tiny village at the very mouth of the river.'

'And just when did this boy enjoy the lady's favours?'

'That, of course, is the crux, and I pressed her very hard and at last managed to get it out of her. It was the very day, the very afternoon, in the evening of which she took herself off to the old king's bed.'

I whistled.

'This is incredible. If it means what it seems to mean, Manissus is finished, holed below the water-line, up the Tiber without a paddle. If he is not the king's son, he cannot be Regent, and if he is not Regent all his plans fall apart.'

'Not quite,' said Mala, 'but perhaps near enough for present requirements. We cannot prove it, of course, but absolute proof should not be necessary. I have taken the precaution of getting a written deposition from this less charming of the Livinias, confirming all I have told you. Now, we must find this aged fisherman, and help him summon up remembrance of things past. Coming?'

14

We opted to ride rather than take a boat down the estuary, making our way first to the little village a few miles to the south where the road Claudius's legions had built started arrow-like to distant Lindum. Our route then took us over the wild moor where Covorilla had been abducted, past the earthwork fortifications Burro told us his ancestors had built, Jupiter knew how many eons before, and finally to the tiny, primitive settlement, occupying the corner of land where river met sea, and where, we hoped, we would find our once-youthful Lothario.

It did not take us long. Half a dozen cheerful-looking fishermen were clustered on the beach, some mending nets, some tending to sails, and one, older than the others and perhaps because of that excused such labours, sitting on an upturned coracle. He had a small knife in his hand, and the bone of some large fish, and was busy carving it, with practised touch, into some elaborate shape or other.

'That,' remarked Mala, 'must be the earliest piece of scrimshaw I have ever seen.'

Scrimshaw?

It was not the carving, however, which took our eye, but the man himself. Though seemingly not far short of sixty, he was still sturdy, and broad-shouldered. Though the plentiful hair on his head was largely grey, it was flecked with dark gold, and the hair on his naked chest likewise. Though big-boned, and with powerful legs, when he stood as we approached, we could see he was not tall. Though is face had character, he was not a handsome man, but his blue eyes were steady as he looked us up and down.

'Romans, by the gods,' he said, suspiciously. 'What brings the likes of you to our poor hamlet?'

'You,' replied Mala, 'if you are the man I take you to be.'

He looked surprised, and then perturbed.

'I hope you are not from that crone Livinia.'

'Yes, and no,' said Mala. 'We are not in any sense her men, if that is what you mean, but it is because of what she has told us that we have sought you out.'

His reaction took us by surprise. His eyes blazed.

'Will I never be able to forget that youthful folly? Will that she-devil never leave me alone?'

'Whatever that she-devil has done in the past, or may wish to do in the future, you need fear her no longer. I am quite sure she will be leaving these parts, and sooner rather than later; she might even be going to Rome.'

The fisherman's whole attitude changed.

'Leaving? Perhaps even to Rome? The gods be praised.'

'And meanwhile, she is powerless.'

'Is that what you have come to tell me?'

'That, and to ask for your help and co-operation. We would like you to come with us back to Isca.

'You need not worry,' he added; 'you will be amply compensated for missing your catch – more than amply.'

'We need to return at once,' I added; 'do you have a horse?'

I realised the foolishness of the question as soon as I had asked it. The fisherman laughed.

'A horse? Do I live in a palace like that of Corigdunum? Does the sun rise in the west? Both are as likely as my owning a horse – or anyone else in this place. But you ride back, and I will be there almost as soon as you. It will take only a short time to get my boat ready, the tide is favourable, and there is a fair breeze. One needs no horse to get from here to Caer-Wisc.'

He was as good as his word, and we met him at the quayside in Isca, and hurried him in a covered, wheeled conveyance that Tasgetius had provided to the governor's headquarters. We entered the assembly-room at once, where Pallabrium, with half a dozen of his countrymen, as well as Burro and Tasgetius himself, were in conclave.

'This is Marco,' Mala told them, indicating our catch; 'the father of you-know-who.'

Several of the Britons looked uncomfortable, though eye-brows were raised as they took in the fisherman's appearance: if proving paternity depended on looks alone, the job was done.

'I am going to ask Marco to tell you in his own words the story of his youthful activities,' Mala went on. 'He will readily answer any questions you might have.'

'It was back in 61,' Marco began, but was at once interrupted.

'How can you be so sure?' one of the Dumnonii demanded. 'It is a long time ago. Is your memory so very good?'

'I remember the year because we had just received the news of the defeat of Boudicca and her followers; my mistress ordered a donative to all of her servants, in celebration.'

'And a very special donative to you,' remarked Burro.

The fisherman flushed angrily, but thought better of any retort. This, after all, was what he was here to talk about. I had the impression, indeed, that he was glad to get it off his chest at last: he had bottled it up for so long, living in fear both of Livinia's threats, and of the vague, unspecified menace of Manissus himself in the background.

('He is lucky to be alive,' said Mala afterwards. 'Only the uncertainty of what might come out, if he died suddenly, protected him.')

When the narrative was finished, the sceptical Councillor who had interrupted him first, looked at him in some disgust.

'You are asking us to believe,' he said, 'that this Roman lady, twice your age and a woman of some status in the community, who could have had many more suitable men, and who indeed ensnared our own king, would bother with a mere boy of – what, sixteen, seventeen summers?'

'In those days,' Burro interrupted, 'she would bother with anyone. She collected men as some of these Roman women collect jewellery, and like them, she could never have enough.'

'I know what I know,' went on Marco, stubbornly. 'Yes, I was surprised when she summoned me. But what young man lets surprise deter him, in such a situation? Besides,' he permitted himself a wry smile, 'I was her servant, and bound to obey.'

The Dumnonii expect,' whispered Mala to me, 'that every man this day will do his duty.'

Tasgetius had laughed out loud at the fisherman's remark, and some of the councillors, men of the world, looked equally amused. Burro was not.

'You have heard his story,' he said impatiently, 'and it corroborates in every detail what the woman herself has just told you.'

He turned to one of the guards.

'Bring her in.'

The man left the room instantly, and returned moments later with an ancient, ugly, but jewel-bedecked crone, who, when she saw Marco there, cast him a glance of naked hatred – which he returned, with interest.

Mala in turn stared at her meaningfully, rather ostentatiously playing with the scroll that contained his orders from Nerva, with the emperor's seal on it prominently displayed. He addressed the woman and the man both.

'We have heard both your stories, and they agree,' he told them. 'Do you now, in each other's presence, and before this assembly, swear to the truth of what you have said?'

Though for the woman it was obviously like pulling teeth, they assented.

Two of Tasgetius's staff had been sitting at a table, scribbling furiously. At Mala's gesture, one of them rose, four scrolls in his arms.

'Here are transcripts of what you have each said, in Latin and in Dumnonioran. You can both read, and both know something of each language. Read the version of your choice, and if you agree it is correct, please confirm as much in writing'

Livinia Clodia read the Latin version cursorily – I think she was past caring – and scribbled rapidly in a crabbed hand. Marco, to our surprise, went carefully through both, and then added his piece to each with a flourish. Mala gathered up the scrolls and presented them to Pallabrium.

'These,' Pallabrium announced, 'will be presented to a meeting of the full Council, and in accordance with my authority as deputy-leader thereof, I convene such a meeting now. Messengers will be sent to all Councillors, and to the Regent – so-called. The meeting,' he added significantly, 'will take place not here, but in the basilica.'

Though Pallabrium had their depositions, he wanted both Livinia and Marco, but especially the latter, to be there in person when the Council heard their evidence, and gave orders accordingly.

He was to be disappointed. As we stepped outside to make our way to the basilica, Livinia Clodia, now more composed, pushed her way to the front. Unwise. Two javelins came hurtling towards our party.

Bilbus's reaction, as always, honed by long training and experience, was almost instantaneous. He moved his great shield like a featherweight, and the spear that would have pinned Marco to the door fell to the ground with a clatter.

Livinia, out in front, had no such protection. She did not even cry out as the heavy iron shaft took her full in the chest, and she fell dead at our feet, her bangles and bracelets incongruously clattering.

Servius's men in turn hurled their javelins at the two men who were running away as fast as their legs could carry them. One was brought down, though whether by the pilum in his back, or the one in his neck, we could not say. The other man disappeared around a corner, Burro and two of his men in pursuit.

Well, they caught him, and questioned him, and he stoutly refused to talk – for just a little while. Like our friend Molo back in Rome, Burro had brought the art of *persuasion* to a fine pitch.

15

Subdued by what had happened, we made our way to the basilica in the centre of the town, pausing only to admire the magnificent bath-house nearby, built for the legion that had once occupied the territory.

'II Augusta certainly knew how to look after themselves,' I said somewhat enviously. XIII Gemina had never managed anything quite like that, though our fighting record was just as distinguished. But they always were pampered darlings, right from Augustus's time.'

The meeting was brief, subdued, focussed, and decisive. Marco sat impassively, looking with no vestige of parental love at the son he had involuntarily spawned.

Manissus himself, composed at first, more and more lost his cool as the proceeding went on. His die-hard supporters, characters as unsavoury as himself, looked equally discomfited. Others, who had allied themselves with him only because of their misgivings about a woman ruler, and were basically honourable men who had had no inkling of the lengths to which he was prepared to go, looked grimmer and grimmer as Pallabrium, who, among his other many qualities, commanded the brain and the skilled rhetoric of a lawyer, built up a case that could not be answered.

'And not only,' he finished with a flourish, 'is this man a usurper, no son of the king my brother; not only has he plotted to take the life of our rightful ruler, Covorilla; not only has he committed matricide – for here is the man who murdered the Roman lady Livinia Clodia, and will testify that it was on Manissus's direct orders; also he is guilty of that most heinous of crimes, *patricide*.'

There was a gasp. The Dumnonii, I had gleaned, like us Romans, regarded patricide with particular horror, the worst of all acts of violence.

'Manissus, I tell you again, ordered not only the death of his own mother, but also, as his man will tell you, of this,' – he gestured towards Marco – 'his rightful father. Only the swift action of the Roman centurion who was guarding him saved his life.'

That Marco's paternity had by no means been proven beyond reasonable doubt was conveniently overlooked by everyone. They were, almost to a man, outraged, quite as much as by the planned act of regicide.

After that, it was formality. Manissus, as a half – indeed, three-quarters – Roman, had the right to appeal to Tasgetius; Tasgetius was not interested. Again, because of his Roman blood, they gave him the option of falling on his own sword, and to his credit, he did so, we were told, bravely.

After the verdict, and before the meeting dissolved, one of Pallabrium's supporters rose to his feet.

'Our tribe cannot be without a lawful ruler. A Regent is still needed until Covorilla is old enough to rule. By all the laws of succession, that Regent must be Pallabrium, and it is our duty to endorse his appointment. I so move.'

Tasgetius called us all together next morning.

'There remain two questions,' he said. 'The first is what to do with that oaf, Marrabo. He is implicated in Manissus's conspiracy, but only peripherally. Though he would willingly have become king if Covorilla had died, and would not have enquired too closely into the manner of her death, we cannot prove he was actually involved in the plot to murder her.'

'Exile?'

'Ideally, yes, but I fear it might not be practicable. Pallabrium himself is in two minds. We must remember that although Manissus and his enforcer are gone and discredited, there is still opposition – what might be called 'respectable opposition' – to the idea of a queen. 'Look what Boudicca did for the Iceni,' they say. 'Look at the queen of the Brigantes, who betrayed the hero Caractacus.'

'They are a minority who mutter thus, but the feeling runs deep, and many are influential men.'

'And so,' said Mala, 'on the one hand to exile Marrabo would cause much ill-feeling, when the main task now is to heal the divisions among the Dumnonii; on the other, if he stays, he is bound to become the focus of any resentment against the rule of Covorilla and of Pallabrium; and though he is a fool, he is not beyond stirring up trouble if he can.'

'I knew your brother,' said Burro then, to Pallabrium. 'How could so fine a man have sired so worthless a son?'

Pallabrium smiled wryly.

'It is a question many men have asked throughout the ages,' he replied.

'And will again,' interjected Mala. 'Such misfortunes are not confined to one people: Rome had Vespasian, and his son Titus; but Vespasian also begat Domitian.'

Finally, after more discussion, it was agreed that Marrabo would stay.

'But I will talk to him,' said Pallabrium, 'and I shall not mince words. I will try to knock some sense into that empty skull.'

'And I,' said Burro, 'will keep a very, very close eye on him, and on those with whom he associates.'

So that was settled.

'There remains the other question,' said Tasgetius, 'though on that I believe we are all agreed – even Burro; and whether we are agreed or not hardly matters, since we have a direct order from the emperor.'

'He might well rescind it,' said Mala, 'if we wrote to him and told him the situation has changed. But we are agreed, as you say, Tasgetius, that it has not changed totally. Covorilla might still be in some danger, even with Manissus and Calthron out of the way. We are all agreed, too, that some time in Rome, during her formative years, would be of inestimable value, both to Covorilla personally, and to the Dumnonii.'

'True,' said Burro. 'It would not be so in an ideal world, but this is not an ideal world.'

'And what a boring place you would find it if it were,' smiled Mala. 'No enemies to smite; no suspects to – help you with your enquiries; no Romans to curse…'

Burro gave a deep laugh.

'A palpable hit, Quintus Propertius!'

And so that, too, was decided.

Burro and Mala had formed a close bond through the troubles they had seen together, and I, too, had come to get on well with the big man. As for Bilbus, after the way the decurion had dealt with Calthron, and then had saved Marco's life, they became bosom pals, two brave and experienced fighting-men, finding they had much in common, each with a tough, hard exterior – and quite soft underneath.

Mala was invited to attend meetings of the Regent's Council, and returned each time more impressed.

'That man Pallabrium,' he said, 'is positively Churchillian.'

Churchillian? Julia Carolina evidently knew what he meant, and nodded.

As for little Covorilla, her excitement at the impending transformation in her life, even though it would mean leaving behind her guardian and her beloved Burro, was palpable. She took especially to Julia Carolina, who patiently helped her improve her Latin – already remarkably good for one so young. The child was happy, too, with Livinia – *my* Livinia – all of whose racial prejudices, never in truth more than skin-deep, had been stripped away by our experiences in Isca Dumnoniorum. She delighted in instructing the little girl in how an aristocratic young lady would be expected to behave in polite Roman society, and how important was a keen sense of decorum.

The nursemaid, Sylvana, was, naturally, to accompany her charge, and so, almost as naturally, was Felgio.

He, too, had taken both to Mala, and to me, and we both in turn came to like and respect him. He was a keen swordsman – as were most of these Dumnonii – and I showed him our sabres, so different from the broad-bladed Roman gladius, and from the long handled weapons he was used to. I coached him a little in their use, and he proved an apt pupil.

He was an apt pupil with Mala, too. It was not Mala's swordsmanship that excited him most, however – though he watched in awe as Mala demonstrated his incomparable skill – so much as his 'telescope', and the explanation Mala gave him of how it worked.

'He is very quick,' Mala told us; 'an exceptionally intelligent young man. I will have much to teach him when we reach Rome, and he will learn fast.'

'Burro will be sad he is going,' said Julia Carolina, 'so soon after they have become reconciled, even though he is to swallow his feelings and visit Rome next year. He is clearly very fond and very proud of his stepson.'

'Son,' said Mala.

We all looked surprised.

'Had you not guessed? Burro's late wife had been forced first into an arranged marriage; Burro was her choice all along. Before the betrothal... The boy knows now, and has come to terms with it.'

'These Dumnonii,' remarked Livinia, 'seem to have a very *flexible* view of matrimony.' She giggled, and I looked at her sternly.

'That is irrelevant,' Mala went on. 'We will watch Felgio go far, I am quite sure. He will be the prototype of a very illustrious line: we have plucked from obscurity what would have been a mute, inglorious Nuton. I believe he is destined to become the first British scientist.'

Quintus Propertius and the Felgio Hypothesis

'And then,' said Felgio, 'the damn thing blew up in my face. 'Stable in low concentrations', that man told me,' he pointed an accusing finger at Mala, but smiled as he did so. 'Admittedly, you did not tell me how low.'

'I said very low,' replied Mala, 'and obviously you have just learned something about experimental verification: you have discovered 'very low' means lower than the concentration you used.'

'And what was the concentration?' asked Julia Carolina. Though a woman, she seemed well-versed in this esoteric lore. (To Livinia Javolenia and me, of course, it was so much gibberish. 'Blew up.' What did that mean?)

Felgio answered the question: more gibberish.

'Then you are a very silly boy.' ('Boy'! He was over six feet tall and built like a house.) 'You knew that much might be dangerous. Do you want to lose a hand, or an eye – or your life?'

Felgio smiled again.

'I reckoned I had done my 99% perspiration for the day; I was trying the 1% inspiration.'

Julia Carolina suppressed her own smile.

'Don't be arrogant. That definition we quoted to you was by a genius. What makes you think you are a genius? Go and get yourself cleaned up. Dinner is almost ready.'

The youngster departed obediently.

'He is, though,' said Mala.

'Is?'

'A genius. He is more, far more, than merely very intelligent. I said back in Isca Dumnoniorum that he was destined to become the first British scientist; I now say he is destined to become the first great British scientist. Nuton, look to your laurels.'

'Who is Nuton?' asked Livinia, innocently.

'He is probably the greatest scientist who ever lived,' replied Julia Carolina.

'You are a bit sloppy with your tenses,' observed Mala.

'What does that mean?' asked Livinia, now even more puzzled.

'Merely that he likes correcting my grammar.'

'But what was wrong with saying that this man Nuton, whoever he is, is the greatest something or other? Your grammar sounded O.K. to me.'

'Tense,' said Julia Carolina.

'Tense?'

"Is' was wrong; I should have said 'was', or even 'will be' – I think. You see, Nuton is dead, but he has not yet been born.'

I had got used to these obscure, seemingly outrageous remarks that Mala and Julia Carolina came out with from time to time – she, especially, being less guarded than Mala, sometimes to his disapproval. Livinia, although she had known them now for some time and very much looked up to her somewhat older friend, was frequently nonplussed; besides, she did not know what I knew of their background – though that itself, I was aware, was far less than there was to tell.

Felgio, supposed barbarian though he was, seemed to have no such trouble accepting this unusual pair and their cryptic remarks. Many things in Rome were strange to him, and it seemed that Mala (who was now in effect his guardian), and his wife, merely provided an added touch of the outré.

I had feared that, as a young aristocrat – for such he was, his father, Burro, being a great man in the kingdom of the Dumnonii – he might be bowled over by the multi-faceted attractions of the great city, and become, as so many have and so many doubtless will, idle and dissolute. Mala likewise had been concerned.

'The attractions of Rome have undone many a man more mature than a nineteen-year-old from a backward tribe at the outskirts of empire,' he said. 'We must watch young Felgio carefully.'

We need not have worried. What indeed had bowled the young man over, even before we left Britain, was the strange knowledge Mala was instructing him in: 'science', he called it, explaining that it had various different forms, any of which a man might devote a lifetime to studying.

'I am no scientist myself,' Mala told me, 'except in an interested-layman kind of way, though I have a smattering of knowledge in various fields, and access to more. Julia Carolina had completed much of her training as a physician before she was – taken to Rome, and knows far more. I was, though, a keen amateur of astronomy, and ipso facto to some extent of optics, as you have seen from my magnifying lenses, and my telescopes.'

I had indeed seen: the pock-marked surface of the moon, with its craters, seas and mountains; the myriad stars, far, far more than could be guessed from observations with the naked eye; Jupiter, a vast world, floating in a dark sky accompanied by its four satellites – or Saturn, majestic, surrounded by its awe-inspiring rings.

These wonders Mala had revealed to us, via the great 'telescope' – 'a decent-sized one at last', he told us, 'and no light-pollution,' – which he had installed on the roof of his Aventine villa.

All this, so mind-boggling to me, and to Livinia, young Felgio took in his stride.

He was learning, too, something of the strange language Mala and Julia Carolina often conversed in. I had picked up a few words and phrases myself, and was a little chagrined that this young man seemed to absorb in a matter of days what it took me weeks of effort to master.

'His Latin, too, is already far better than when he left Britain,' Mala observed. 'He has almost as much facility as a linguist, as he has as a scientist. No doubt before long he will know Greek better than Diogenes.'

Felgio was musical, too. Julia Carolina had a sweet singing voice, and would sometimes entertain us with strange songs in her own language – strange to our ears, but captivating nonetheless, even entrancing; and Mala himself would sometimes join in. Felgio listened intently and with obvious delight, and soon showed how well he had picked up the various melodies, and even the words, singing them enthusiastically in what Mala called a 'rich tenor' voice.

We were a little disconcerted at first, especially my conventional wife, by the spectacle of high-class Romans, and even a high-class Briton, making music like common entertainers, but they assured us that in some countries, and some ages – where? when? – it was considered a positive advantage, indeed almost a requisite, for those in the upper echelons of society to command such skills. After that, Julia Carolina even coaxed Livinia herself into trying a simple tune or two, and she, to my surprise, admitted – a little shamefacedly – that she had thoroughly enjoyed it. (What her father, the senator, or even her somewhat traditionalist brother, would have thought of it, I did not dare to ask: they have apoplexy at the merest mention of Nero and his 'performances'. Still, I suppose I could point out to them that the emperor Titus was said to sing well, and he was no Nero, but they would probably reply that even so great an emperor had human weaknesses. You can't win.)

Little Covorilla enjoyed the music too, clapping her hands delightedly whenever she was allowed to listen, and begging Julia Carolina to teach her also how to sing.

'Very well,' said Julia Carolina, 'music will be added to your curriculum. You are going to be a very busy little lady.'

2

When we had reached Rome after our eventful trip to Britain, the emperor Nerva had at first been undecided as to where the ten-year-old Covorilla, heir to the throne of the Dumnonii, was to live. He had thought at first of an establishment of her own, with a suitable retinue of slaves, tutors, guides, and counsellors, to look after her and to instruct her in the ways of Roman high society – and of what was expected of the dutiful ruler of a subject kingdom.

The girl wanted none of it. She had formed a close bond with Julia Carolina – as, to a lesser extent, with my wife Livinia Javolenia – and, though somewhat in awe of Mala himself, begged to be allowed to live with them, if they would have her.

There was never any doubt about that. Mala's residence – which he had long maintained was far too large for the two of them and their handful of slaves (though I did not see what that had to do with it: as a wealthy Roman, he had a position to keep up) – easily accommodated the little princess, her maid Sylvana, the latter's suitor Felgio, and assorted bodyguards, litter-bearers, tutors and parasites Nerva insisted should accompany her.

Despite the tutors, it was Julia Carolina and Livinia who were most prominent in the little princess's education, both of them helping with her Latin, Julia with history, geography, music, and the arts, Livinia with some of these, but taking it on herself especially to instil the social graces.

Mala joined in occasionally, though Covorilla still regarded him with a mixture of awe and apprehension. I gleaned that this must have had something to do with the way he saved her life, and that of her nursemaid, back in Britain, by some means even I had never been able to understand –

for he had burst into a long, long room where they were held, the guards were close by the princess and her companion, weapons to hand, with orders to kill them instantly if any attempt was made at rescue, and yet in a trice, they were disposed of, one dead, the other with the bones of his sword-arm shattered, before they could inflict so much as a scratch on their captives. I had long understood that Mala had at his command some secret weapon of great power, but as yet he had not divulged its nature.

Sylvana, too, had been amazed and shocked at what happened, but when she divulged her secret to Felgio, he himself was more excited, intellectually excited, than awed.

'So that's where this stuff leads,' he exclaimed. 'The expanding gases must be somehow confined...'

I had no idea what he was on about, as usual. I had come across them just as Sylvana had finished her tale, and could see that Felgio was torn between wanting to stay with his betrothed, as she now was, and getting back to the 'lab' to quiz Mala on what he had been told, and had surmised.

I was heading for Mala's hideaway myself, with a message from none other than the emperor, to whom I had been summoned unexpectedly that morning, and so the two of us made our way there together, Felgio excitedly talking about 'compression' and 'explosive power' and other esoterica, while I pretended to comprehend, but didn't.

Mala was bent over a workbench, seemingly putting little pieces of metal into a kind of wooden frame. With him, little to my surprise, watching intently, was our new friend, Trebonius, a high-ranking imperial freedman who had had much to do with seeing Covorilla safely established with Mala and Julia Carolina, and with appointing the small staff Nerva had decided was suitable to her age and station.

Trebonius was a middle-aged, avuncular man, conscientious to a degree, utterly devoted to Nerva, to whose household he had once belonged, and a somewhat unexpected convert to the new learning, the 'science' Mala was now increasingly busy pursuing, and propagating. He had even, at his own expense, had a smaller copy made of Mala's 'telescope', and as his wife told us with mock reproach, spent far more time observing the heavens than in discharging his duties as paterfamilias of a large household.

In truth Trebonius discharged his duties most diligently, for that was his nature, but he did indeed spend much of such free time as he had in observing the heavens, or in visiting Mala in his 'lab' and keenly interesting himself in whatever my great friend was doing.

'Look here,' he said as we entered, 'what do you make of this?'

He picked up a sheet of parchment from a pile on the bench, and handed it to me; and yet it was not parchment, nor yet papyrus, but something much thinner, lighter and whiter. It was covered in writing, in what I gleaned was Mala's own language – one of them – but with lettering of quite amazing regularity.

I handed it to Felgio, but he put it down on the bench with scarcely a glance.

'I have seen this substance before,' he said. 'I helped Mala develop and produce it. Paper, he calls it. As for the writing – ' he turned to Mala – 'you have managed it at last, then. Very impressive. You were expecting it to take longer.'

'And so it would have done,' replied Mala, 'if Julia Carolina had not had a brainwave. I did what she suggested, and the ink is now just the right consistency – and furthermore, it will be easy and cheap to produce.'

'And the paper is spot-on, too,' said Felgio, a trifle smugly I thought.

'Don't worry, your contribution will be duly acknowledged. I am not one of those who milk the work of their assistants, and then put their own name on the bottom of their scholarly article.'

'This is all very interesting,' I put in, 'but I come with a rather important message: we are summoned to an audience with the emperor.'

'I hope it does not mean another trip to Britain, much though I would like to meet up again with Burro and Pallabrium.'

'I don't think so. Nerva hinted it might have something to do with politics.'

'That is the worst news I have had to-day.'

Mala did not know it, but he was soon to have worse – much worse.

3.

The palace was bustling when we arrived, not only with the normal admixture of petitioners, officials, scribes, senators, foreign dignitaries and slaves, but also with soldiery: Praetorians, of course, but, standing apart, a group of high-ranking officers from the army in Upper Germany – between whom and the Praetorians, there was clearly no love lost.

'Something's afoot,' I said.

'And I think I know what it might be,' said Mala. 'The emperor is to make an important announcement this afternoon, and I will have a little wager with you he will name his successor: though keep that speculation to yourself.'

I knew Mala kept his ear pretty close to the ground, and often seemed to have information that I could not see how he had come by, but this was surprising indeed.

'I suppose you are going to tell me who it will be?'

'I could hazard a guess. Just look at these fine fellows from Upper Germany, and use your little grey cells.'

I had no time to follow his advice, for a flunky appeared from nowhere, and addressed us, in what seemed an unnecessary loud voice.

' The assistant comptroller is ready to see you now. '

I evinced no surprise, for I had been told this would be the ploy. In fact, as soon as we had left the main concourse, we went nowhere near the haunts of the assistant comptroller, but instead were ushered along familiar passages, and into the presence of Nerva himself.

'Good, ' he said, as soon as we entered, 'now we are all here.'

His appearance shocked me. Although we had seen him several times since our return from Britain, most recently only a few weeks ago, he seemed to have aged years. His face was haggard, his skin parched, and there was a pained look in his eyes that he made no attempt to conceal. Nevertheless, his voice was firm as he introduced us to the three others in the room.

The first was Gaius Corbus, the new Chief Investigator, a hard man, we had heard, and ruthless in the service of his emperor, but just and honest also – a million leagues from his hated predecessor.[1]

The second man I recognised as one of the up-and-coming young senators Nerva had appointed shortly after becoming emperor a year or so before. I was not aware that our paths had crossed, but he recognised me, and nodded in greeting.

The third man was something else again. He was plainly, unostentatiously dressed, almost in disguise one would have said, but there was no hiding his military bearing, his air of command, his aura of authority, young though he was. We were told his name, but I did not recognise it. Mala took the introduction in his stride, but looked at the man with interest.

The emperor wasted no time in getting down to business.

'You know I am to make an announcement to-day; some may have guessed what about. I apologise now to the Senate ' - he nodded in the direction of the young senator – 'for revealing here, and later in the Forum, what should be first for that august body, but needs must.

'I am about to announce my successor.'

I saw Mala suppress a little smile.

'I know well, ' Nerva continued, 'that I have none too much longer to live, and it is essential for the stability of the realm that I choose without further delay who is to be the new emperor. You, Aulius Hadrianus, are to convey the news personally when you travel to Upper Germany, for I have chosen the one whose loyal protégé you are: the present governor, the distinguished and esteemed Marcus Ulfius Trajanus. I know you will all serve him as faithfully as you have served me.'

We gave our assent as one.

'Nevertheless, I must tell you that the succession is not cut and dried. The Senate will endorse it, of that I have no doubt; so will the legions – most of them. But the Senate has no troops, and the legions are all far

---

[1] See especially *Quintus Propertius and the case of the Placid Praetorian.*

away. The Praetorian Guard, on the other hand, number nine thousand men – and they are here in Rome.'

He paused` and looked at each of us in turn.

'You are all intelligent and sophisticated men, and not unaware of the political situation.

'You, Aulius Hadrianus, though you have been out of the city for some time, will doubtless have been kept well informed.

'You, Caecilius Galienus, have been unstinting in your support in the Senate, and it is thanks to you and your close associates that things are not even more difficult than they are.

'You, Gaius Corbus, know better than any the specific details of the troubles I have had and have still to face.

'And you, Marcus Vectorius and Quintus Propertius, though you have not been intimately involved in the great affairs of State, are astute and observant men and cannot be unaware of the way the world is; moreover, you have done me great service, and soon I am going to call on you for more service still.'

I saw Mala frown slightly. He was, I knew, reluctant to let anything distract him from the 'research and development', as he called it, that he was pursuing with the Briton, Felgio, with Trebonius, and with his unusual wife, and the thought of another commission from the emperor, which of course would have to take precedence over all else, was not likely to please him.

'I have said that you are all aware of recent goings-on in Rome, and of the implications. I do not need to tell you that the recent execution of Petronius Secundus and his associates is the most serious; nor, I am sure, do I have to tell you that those executions were carried out utterly against my wishes, despite what I was forced to say afterwards.

'I am Caesar; I am all-powerful; and yet I was held prisoner in my own palace and forced to commit a most heinous crime, which I will regret for the rest of my life. Hail Caesar!'

He was, and looked, bitter.

'It was one of the few mistakes the great Augustus made,' Nerva continued, ' to establish the Praetorians in the city as he did, though any student of the politics of the time can understand why. It was one of the mistakes Tiberius made, not to challenge them head-on, after he had disposed of Sejanus, except that by that time it was perhaps too late. Nero compounded the situation, with the power he gave to the loathsome Tigellinus.'

('Why the history lesson?' I wondered, as the emperor continued.)

'Vespasian, a great general, and Titus likewise, had earned the support of the army, and my predecessor, Domitian, bought that support with bribery and favouritism. To them the Praetorians posed no threat, but Domitian bought them as well, just to make sure.

'Not surprisingly, the Praetorians were among the few in Rome who grieved when Domitian was assassinated. I, as his unwelcome successor, have no such support, which leaves those Praetorians holding the real reins of power. So long as Petronius Secundus, as co-commander, was with me and had the backing of some of his troops, I could rule as an emperor should; once that backing was gone, and Casperius Aelianus was de facto sole master of the Guard, the situation inevitably deteriorated. Aelianus has nine thousand men, and I have –' he looked around, and smiled, 'a few friends.'

'You have the support of the great majority in the Senate, Caesar,' said Caecilius Galienus.

'For which I am grateful,' replied Nerva; 'but as we agreed at the outset – the Senate has no troops.'

'It is true that many in the army also were sorry to see the end of Domitian, for he treated them well and they were not interested in politics,' said the young soldier, 'but I do not believe, Caesar, that they would join the Praetorians in any real further challenge to your authority. The Petronius Secundus affair was a different matter: a one-off.'

'I hope you are right,' said Nerva, 'but the army is not in Rome. Nor do I believe Aelianus and his followers would again attempt to storm the Palace, though the possibility cannot be ruled out. Nevertheless, they have already seriously undermined my authority, and will do so further if they can. Indeed. they have been doing so, persistently: more subtly than in the Petronius affair, but no less assiduously. It is to try to neutralise them that I am announcing my successor, and have called you all here to-day.

'But let Gaius Corbus tell you more.'

The Chief Investigator was only too willing, and some story it was. We were all solemn and more than a little shaken by the time he had finished.

'And so, gentlemen,' Nerva took over again, 'what we are faced with is a combination of Casperius Aelianus and an unscrupulous hard-core of his officers; a few disgruntled politicians still loyal to the memory of

Domitian; two or three very rich and powerful businessmen, who want to be richer and more powerful still; and supporting them and doing their bidding, some of the worst and most vicious criminal elements in Rome. An unholy alliance, and though I do not believe the Praetorians are likely to march in force to my Palace, these people might be able to do almost as much damage as though they were.

'The question we are faced with, therefore, quite obviously and urgently, is: what is to be done?'

4.

'So that's the game,' said Mala, as we left the Palace – by that same door, as it chanced, that we had used before on far less happy occasions: not that our interview with Nerva had us exactly singing with joy. 'We again have to discommode the ungodly – without, at the same time, treading too hard on the toes of the Praetorians.'

'It will, perhaps, be a little easier, now that we have an official position,' I suggested. 'Special Advisors to the Chief Investigator: an august title indeed, considering that the Chief Investigator himself does not even, officially, exist. With Molo we will still request, rather than command, but with some of the upstarts from the other cohorts it will be pleasant to make them jump to it a little.'

'As a matter of fact, I was going to propose that our first call should be on Molo; he is a canny old bird and might well come up with some useful ideas – which would be a good thing, because, frankly, at the moment I haven't a clue where to start.'

'We could start,' I suggested hopefully, 'at Rufus's Place: we can send a message to Molo asking him to meet us there.'

'If Rufus were still in charge,' replied Mala, 'I would like nothing better, but, frankly, the more I see of him, the less I like the new incumbent. He was nice as pie when first he took over, and he is still civil – but there is something shifty about him. The clientèle is changing, too: Gaius Cornelius is hardly ever there these days, and as for young Suetonius, I have not seen him for weeks.'

'He knows we are well in with the emperor,' I replied. 'Nerva has never exactly been his flavour of the month.'

'True,' said Mala. 'He implies... But I won't go into that. Some of the new habitués, though, do not exactly fill me with a spirit of bonhomie.'

'Perhaps for that very reason, we should go there, and keep our ears open.'

'You have a point. At some later date, we will do as you suggest. In the meantime, though, it is as well we call on Molo, and his merry men, chez eux.'

Molo, former senior decurion with XIII Gemina, and in my opinion unfairly passed over for still higher rank, and now in charge of the smartest bunch of vigiles in Rome, was busy, when we found him, talking rather sternly to a scruffy, weasel-faced little man, who looked as though he would be only too happy if the ground opened up and swallowed him on the spot. In truth, I must admit, Molo was talking to him not rather, but *very* sternly; very sternly indeed. I had seen him talk thus to seasoned legionaries, tough-as-leather veterans who had been through a score of campaigns; and they had blenched. This abject creature was by no means as tough as leather, and the only campaigns he had seen had been conducted in the nether regions of the Subura, or elsewhere in Rome's murky underworld.

'And so,' Molo concluded, 'I am going to let you go – this time. But there had better not be another time, or I will hand you over to a little session with Marcellus here, and he is not half such a kind and gentle fellow as I am.'

I knew Marcellus, Molo's second-in-command, a great hairy ape of a fellow, almost as broad as he was tall – and he was very tall. I also knew him to be a most friendly and affable man, a bit of a humorist in fact – off duty. On duty, his looks did not belie him, as scores of the ungodly over the years had found to their dismay.

The little man looked apprehensively at Marcellus, and back to Molo, and then scurried away with palpable relief before the latter could change his mind.

'One of the usual suspects?' asked Mala.

'A persistent offender. He is the lightest-fingered villain in Rome, but we can hardly ever catch him with the goods on his person. We've frightened the daylights out of him a few times, but he keeps popping up again, like a bad penny.

'Still,' he went on, ' he is far from the worst of our worries. Macrobius Pulcher is back in town.'

Mala whistled. Our run-in with Macrobius Pulcher, towards the end of Domitian's reign[2], had been brief, and, so far as it went, we had come out on top, but it had not been a pleasant encounter. The thought that he, and his gang of thugs, were again running around loose in Rome did not exactly fill us with joy.

'There are even rumours,' Molo continued, 'that he has some sort of tie-in with Casperius Aelianus, and if that is so, include me out. I know my duty, and I would love to nail the bastard, but I don't tangle with the Praetorians – not, like, ever.'

He was a brave man, Gaius Molo, and a conscientious one, but quixotic, he was not. Nor, for that matter, am I, and so I was a little disconcerted when Mala seemed interested, and even pleased, at what any sane man would have regarded as most unwelcome news.

'Don't you see, Marcus,' he explained, 'this could be just what we are looking for: a possible connection between the criminal underworld, and the gentlemen the emperor is interested in scotching.'

There was nothing wrong with Mala's logic; it was the implications that bothered me.

'Whatever, we cannot make any move against Casperius Aelianus and nine-thousand Praetorians, or against anyone who enjoys their protection.'

'Amen,' said Molo.

'Do not be so sure,' replied Mala, 'and do not be so sure it is nine thousand Praetorians. Aelianus enjoys the loyalty of the majority, of that there is no doubt – for the time being. But his forcing Nerva to execute Petronius Secundus by no means had unanimous approval: Petronius was, after all, co-commander, and certainly popular in some quarters. Furthermore, the Praetorians may be, many of them, a nasty bunch, and too big for their boots, but their officers are not fools. They can read the runes.'

'Meaning?'

'Nerva's naming Trajan as his successor has gone some way to spiking Aelianus's guns.'

---

2 See *Quintus Propertius and the Demise of Marius the Glassmaker.*

(*Spiking his guns*?)

'The Praetorians may be the bees' knees here in Rome, and when they moved against Petronius they knew there were many in the legions who agreed with them, but they must know they would not have a prayer of gaining their support against a general of Trajan's standing. Nor is Trajan likely to look kindly on Aelianus: would any emperor who was sure of his power tolerate a Praetorian Prefect who had forced his predecessor to execute a loyal follower against his will? Take it from me, Marcus, and I am very, very sure of this, Trajan will attend to Casperius Aelianus in due course and in no uncertain fashion. He may be able to cause more trouble while Nerva still lives, but the skids are under him. The Praetorians, at least those with a bit of savvy, will suspect as much, and if they were not too personally implicated in the Petronius affair, will be careful about where they let their commander lead them from now on.'

'Then you mean he's a busted flush?'

'Not at all; merely weaker than he was, thanks to Nerva's cleverness in naming Trajan to succeed him. He is still a dangerous man, and he can still cause a lot of trouble; it is just that he will have to be much more subtle about it.'

'Which brings us back to Macrobius Pulcher. What is he up to, and how does he fit into Aelianus's little schemes?'

'That is precisely what we have to try and find out.'

Molo had been listening patiently, and with some interest, and now he broke in.

'I might be able to help you. We have been keeping a close watch on Macrobius Pulcher and his merry men, and hoping the Praetorian connection was only a false rumour. We picked up one of his mob only this morning, on a charge of G.B.H.: he made the mistake of beating-up a stallholder, just as three of my men came along. He is here now, and not feeling too happy.'

I could imagine why.

'Would you like to talk to him? I have no doubt Macrobius Pulcher will be along soon enough with some tame lawyer, but up till then we might be able to persuade the gentleman to answer a question or two.'

I saw Marcellus, Molo's side-kick, look suddenly interested, and surmised that, yes, the gentleman might be 'persuaded' to answer a question or two.

Unfortunately he did not have the chance. There was a commotion outside, raised voices, and suddenly the door was kicked open, and four men barged in.

Two of them, though out of uniform, could have been recognised anywhere as Praetorians. The third was a tall, thin, slightly cadaverous character from whom, instinctively, one would have been reluctant to buy a used chariot.

The fourth man we recognised at once, and it was mutual.

'So: you two – gentlemen.'

'We two,' agreed Mala, 'and no more inclined to join your fan-club than we were last time.'

'It matters not; I can deal with you when I'm ready, and I will. I am here to demand the vigiles release my man, Sextus Vulso, into the custody of the Praetorian Guard.'

'I have the necessary authorisation here,' said the thin man, who, we had rightly surmised, was the tame lawyer. 'We will take Sextus Vulso at once.'

Molo looked doubtful. He had good cause to detest Macrobius, and he wanted to refuse, but feared he was out-gunned – legally, if not for the moment physically, for he had a dozen men or more he could call on if it came to a fracas.

It was Mala who now took charge.

'I am afraid that will be impossible,' he said firmly.

'And who do you think you are?' sneered Macrobius Pulcher. 'We came to release my man from the vigiles, and it is the watch commander we are here to talk to.' And turning to Molo. 'Release him; these documents are in order.'

'I said that was not possible,' said Mala again. 'As to who I am: my companion and I are on the personal staff of the emperor, and outrank the commander of the vigiles, the excellent Gaius Molo here.' He produced the authority he had received from the emperor only that morning, and I mine, and I do not know who was the more surprised, our friend Molo, or Macrobius Pulcher himself. It was the latter who recovered swiftly.

'Our precious emperor,' he said, 'is well known to consider himself to be as bound by Roman law as the meanest of his subjects. These documents are legally valid; release the prisoner.'

'Again I say it is impossible – legally impossible. The prisoner cannot be released into the custody of the Praetorians, when there are no Praetorians here.'

The two stalwarts Macrobius had brought with him bridled, and he pointed to them triumphantly.

'These men are Praetorians.'

'You say. Where are their uniforms, their insignia, their badges of rank? For all I know these could be just two of your own unsavoury thugs, or a couple of layabouts you picked up in the street.'

One of the putative Praetorians snarled, and took a step towards Mala, who did not flinch. The man paused, decided he did not like the look in Mala's eye, and stepped back.

'Real Praetorians,' went on Mala, deliberately provocative, 'are reputed to be brave fellows – but look at the way this one has just backed down. I suggest you take these two out-of-work actors, or whatever they are, and tell them to stop impersonating their betters, and wasting our time.'

Macrobius Pulcher looked furious, but he was beaten, for the time being at least, and he knew it.

'We will be back,' he hissed, 'and then Jupiter help you.'

As soon as they had gone, Mala turned to the vigiles.

'They will be back, I have no doubt of that. By then, though, the bird will have flown. I want to take this Sextus Vulso character away with me, as quickly as possible. Can you lend me a couple of men, and get me a litter? You, Marcus, could act as a decoy. Here is my plan…'

It worked like a charm, though I cannot deny I was a little apprehensive about tangling with the Praetorians, when they returned, as it were, officially.

First, Mala and two of the vigiles departed post-haste, Mala in the litter with the thoroughly-cowed (and gagged) Sextus Vulso, the vigiles giving every impression they were escorting a prominent citizen. Then three other vigiles, and I, left in the opposite direction, but not until a look-out had warned us of the approach of Macrobius Pulcher, accompanied now not only by his lawyer and two different Praetorians, in full uniform, but by a third, a centurion no less.

We made sure they caught a glimpse of us as we rounded the corner of a building, and then scurried away as fast as our legs could carry us. We made good speed, though not as fast as we might, had two of the vigiles not been carrying the third on a rough stretcher. (You may take it as a coincidence, but the third man was clad in a tunic of very similar cut and colour to that worn by the departed Sextus Vulso; you could almost have thought it was the same garment…)

The Praetorians caught up with us at last, planted themselves in front of the stretcher, and ordered the bearers to stop. Macrobius Pulcher came up, panting, and looked at us triumphantly.

'So: trying to spirit him away, are we, in defiance of a legal warrant? Centurion, this is my man, whom you are to take as ordered.'

He turned to the stretcher, and his mouth fell open.

'What do you mean, "your man"?' I demanded. 'This is one of Gaius Molo's men; the poor fellow has broken his leg and is in great pain, and his comrades are carrying him to a physician as fast as they can.'

The man in the litter was indeed groaning with pain, the improvised splint on his left leg only too plain to be seen.

'I kept my fingers crossed,' I told Mala afterwards, 'in case they insisted on accompanying us to a doctor, where they would soon find out that the man had not broken his leg, or anything else. As it was, however, the centurion seemed far more annoyed with the despicable Macrobius and his lawyer than he was interested in us. He had clearly not relished in the first place taking orders from a civilian, especially such a civilian as Macrobius, and he said something angrily about 'wild-goose chase', and stormed off, leaving the two villains looking utter fools.'

'Which they are,' agreed Mala, 'and much more - as I hope to demonstrate to them, and to the world, in the fulness of time.'

The next day, Mala and I questioned the hapless Sextus Vulso, in the safe house the Chief Investigator had provided. So, no less thoroughly and a good deal less gently, did that worthy himself.

We all drew a blank. The man was the most minor of minor operatives, one of the strong-arm men Macrobius kept as his personal bodyguard – hence his eagerness to have the fellow back – and in no sense privy to any plans or schemes his boss might have been cooking-up.

'I do not need to let him go,' said Gaius Corbus. 'He is still facing a charge of G.B.H., and a few days in my cells would doubtless be good for his soul. He'll get away with it, of course: they will lean on his victim, who will be too terrified to press charges, and he will walk away from court with a smirk on his face. Unless, of course,' – he looked thoughtful – 'he happened to meet with a little accident before he could even come to trial. Dreadful places, you know, the cells where we keep these people: damp, dark, stone steps, slippery…'

I shuddered a little. Corbus was known not to be the kind of ruthless psychopath his predecessor had been, but he had not advanced this far in the service of his emperor because of his taste in kid gloves, and if he genuinely thought the interest of Nerva and of the empire required that his prisoner meet with an 'accident', an accident the man would have.

'It might be better to let him go quite shortly,' suggested Mala, 'with the assault charge still hanging over his head. Find the man he beat up; spirit him away, and keep him safe; let Vulso know he can be dragged back here at any time – as soon as his accuser can be found – and that, as you say, "accidents" do happen in the cells. Have him tailed constantly, though, so that he does not simply "disappear". I will have a word in his ear as to how generous the emperor can be to those who have the wit to give him unstinting service.'

'Is he worth the trouble?' I asked. 'We have established that he is small-fry, and knows nothing.'

'He has not been looking for anything. From now on, he will be.'

'Can he be trusted?'

'Not at all. Enlightened self-interest is the name of the game; we convince the lout of which side his bread is buttered, and hope he has the sense to take it in. I might also mention to him, of course, how very angry Nerva gets at people who try the double-double-cross: something about the Tarpeian Rock, perhaps...'

And so it was decided.

'We cannot do much more, at the moment, than wait,' Mala said as we walked back towards the Aventine. 'We must give Comrade Vulso a little time, and Molo and his men time also. Meanwhile, I will use my telescope regularly – but in the daytime, and it will not be pointed towards the planets.'

5.

The next few days were uneventful, for me at least. Livinia and I had been invited – almost commanded, on security grounds – to stay at Mala's villa, but he himself appeared but rarely, except for meals, preferring to spend his time either on his roof, where his telescope was situated, and from which much of Rome could be seen, or in his 'lab', with or without – though mostly with – Felgio, and occasionally Trebonius.

We were thrown more than usual into the company of Sylvana, Covorilla's maid and Felgio's betrothed. Her position in the household was, to us, a little anomalous. She was certainly no slave, nor yet a freedwoman since she had never been a slave, and yet she was a servant. To compound matters, she was to marry into the family of one of the great men of the Dumnonii, after which her own status would be elevated indeed. The young princess treated her almost as an equal, and clearly expected everyone else to do so.

Mala and Julia Carolina seemed to have no problem with this; Livinia and I gradually came round to accepting the situation, and found there was much more to Sylvana than met the eye. Once her own awe, indeed fear, of Romans was overcome, she talked as freely with us as her halting, but improving, Latin allowed, telling us something of her background.

'I am not of the Dumnonii,' she told us, to our surprise, 'but was born into the Regni, of which my father was a minor chieftain. I was sent to the Dumnonii court as a gesture of goodwill and friendship, and while I was there, the old retainer who had been looking after Covorilla died. By this time the little girl needed a tutor as well as a nursemaid, and Covorilla's father asked me if I would like to undertake the task for a short time. When he in turn died, Pallabrium asked me if I would care to stay on indefinitely. My father agreed: and here I am. I must say i never expected to see Rome, or to meet such wonderful people here.'

'And yet I suspect it is not a Roman you regard as the most wonderful of all, nor was it only the pleasure of looking after Covorilla that persuaded you to stay with the Dumnonii,' smiled Livinia.

'It is true that I love Felgio above all men,' said the girl simply, 'but my wonder is reserved for the Romans I have met: I have even been in the same room as the emperor himself. Most wonderful of all, though, is our host, your friend Quintus Propertius Mala, and indeed his remarkable wife also. Never have I met such beings; they seem almost like demi-gods – beings from another world.'

'But they are not,' I told her; 'they are as human as you or I. And yet, although not from some other plane of existence, they are indeed from another world – a land far, far away across the ocean. They have told me a little of it, though not as much as I would like: they tell me there are marvels I would not believe, because I could not understand: not because I am too stupid to understand, but because to do so would require understanding of other things, and those understanding of other things still, and those of others…'

'And Felgio is beginning that understanding,' said Sylvana, proudly. 'Julia Carolina says he grasps things more quickly than anyone she has ever known, and I have even heard Quintus Propertius say much the same.'

We knew that to be true. Mala himself was probably the cleverest man I had ever met – and I had met a few – but even he seemed almost in awe of the young Briton.

'I had planned to construct,' he told me, 'a very clever instrument known in my own country, a kind of super magnifier, but much, much more powerful than the simple lenses you have seen: think of it as a kind of super-telescope for close-up use. I mentioned casually to Felgio how the thing worked, but only in the sketchiest outline. He worked out the detail for himself, by sheer reasoning power, set the lens makers and others to work, experimented a little with the results – and now the lab has a fully functioning, powerful microscope. You have no idea just what a feat that was, Marcus, but take it from me – it was mighty, mighty impressive. Julia Carolina, especially, is quite delighted with the instrument.'

'Julia Carolina?'

'I have told you she is trained in medicine, and she is shortly to pass on some of her knowledge to a gathering of Rome's leading physicians, and to demonstrate Felgio's microscope at the same time.'

'A woman trained in medicine,' I observed, 'is going to encounter some prejudice.'

'No doubt; but since she knows far more, about the functioning of the human body and about curing the ills to which it is subject, than any of them has ever imagined, the prejudice will be overcome. Any still harbouring such prejudice will be a damn fool, and will soon learn that he is. Julia Carolina is writing a book, that will revolutionise Roman medical practice.'

'Is there anything,' I asked, 'that in time you are not going to revolutionise?'

'Not much,' replied Mala briefly, 'but things have to fructify: fructify, young Marcus,' and with that I had to be satisfied for the nonce.

6.

Though it seemed like weeks, it was in fact only a few days before we heard from the miserable Sextus Vulso. A nervous looking character, clearly no more than a messenger, knocked hesitantly at the portal of Mala's villa, thrust a tablet into the hands of the doorman as soon as he answered, and scurried away without so much as a word.

Mala did not need to guess whom the tablet had come from. He read it carefully a couple of times, and pronounced it genuine.

'It is from comrade Vulso: it contains a couple of coded phrases I told him to use – but whether he is genuine in what he says, or is attempting a double-cross, or perhaps even was writing under duress, we cannot know.'

'What does he say?'

'He wants us to meet him near the Campus Martius, a little before sundown, when he says he will be off duty and able to get away for a time without anyone taking much notice. He says he has learned something he daren't commit to writing, but thinks it important. He says you and I should come alone, because his meeting more than a couple of men, if noticed, would look suspicious.'

'If he is seen with us it will look suspicious anyway: we are not exactly unknown in Rome, especially to Macrobius Pulcher and his villains.'

'My thought exactly. Nevertheless, I think we should go, because it just might be the break we are looking for. We will take our sword-sticks, of course, and I will have something else that should see us through, unless we are attacked by a small army.'

'Marcus Vectorius,' I asked myself, 'why do you let yourself be talked into these situations?' But I tagged along nonetheless.

We thought it best to acquaint the Chief Investigator of what we were planning and where we were going, and he counselled extreme caution. He would have provided us with a bodyguard, but Mala persuaded him that even if they kept a discreet distance behind us, they might still be spotted, and spoil the whole enterprise. Reluctantly, our nominal superior agreed.

We made our way very slowly towards the Campus Martius, at first through throngs of citizens, artisans returning home from their labours, shopkeepers who had shut up their premises for the night, slaves bearing last-minute purchases, ladies of you-know-what-kind, preparing for their nocturnal labours, and occasional bunches of young men-about-town, looking for fun, or trouble, or for the aforementioned ladies of the night.

The crowds thinned out, however, as we drew nearer to our destination, and soon the streets were almost, and then quite, deserted.

They came at us from three directions, four suddenly appearing in front, four more from a side alley, and a further bunch cutting off our retreat. They were all armed, with stout sticks, clubs, daggers, and in one case a nasty-looking home-made spear. They advanced slowly and deliberately, and I clutched my sword-stick, and prayed to the gods I didn't believe in.

Despite the odds, Mala looked not in the least perturbed; a faint smile, even, was playing around the corners of his mouth, though I could not imagine why. He drew from his ubiquitous leather bag a strange-looking metallic object, its polished black sides gleaming in the setting sun.

'This is going to be noisy,' he said. 'Don't be too surprised at what happens.'

But then he hefted the device, looked at it with sudden consternation, and let out an almighty curse.

'How could I have been so stupid! I was showing it to Felgio when the message arrived from Vulso; the clip must still be on the bench in the lab.'

'Clip?'

'Marcus, I fear I have brought you to your death. We can take a few of these thugs with us, but we cannot handle a dozen or more, even with our swords. If only…'

He said no more, for they were almost on us.

It is funny how there is always one, braver, or more stupid, than the rest, who rushes ahead of his fellows with death or glory in his mind.

It was death. The fellow aimed a blow with his massive club that would have crushed his intended victim's head like an egg-shell, which Mala avoided with ease; next moment that wicked point that I had seen at work so often was buried in the man's gut. The spearman, who was only a little behind the other, tackled me with confidence, secure in the six-foot length of his weapon, but unfortunately for him, he had very little idea of how to use it: in the arena he would not have lasted ten seconds; it took me very little longer to put paid to him.

So far so good, but the others were more canny: they came at us together, from two directions, and we were only too aware that those behind were almost on us also. We might with luck dispose of two or three more, but it would not be long before a blow from one cudgel or another caught us a full-blooded crack, and we would be done for. I prayed again to the Jupiter I hoped I was wrong about, and waited for the end.

Jupiter answered, with his fabled thunderclap. There came from nowhere a bang like nothing I had heard before, and one of those facing us dropped like a log, a gaping hole in his chest. Another bang, and one of those to our side lost his enthusiasm in an instant, along with part of his head. The rest stopped, as astonished as I was, and then there burst through those in our rear a big, wild-looking figure, holding a long club-like weapon of wood and metal; he rushed up to Mala, and thrust something into his hand.

'This is what you want,' he said briefly, and Mala at once took from his bag the metal object I had seen earlier, and pressed the thing into a cavity in its handle. Felgio - for it was he - did something or other to the contraption he was carrying, pointed it at the nearest bunch, and again there came that almighty crash; a man screamed and fell, his arm and half his shoulder shattered. The rest wanted no more of it, and turned and ran. One man, however, a burly fellow clad in a black tunic, was too slow: Mala caught him with a flying tackle, and the man came down like a log.

'That's the way to deal with the All Blacks,' remarked Mala with satisfaction.

All Blacks?

He pulled the fellow to his feet.

'So: it is our double-crossing friend.' He put the point of his sword to the man's throat. 'Do you want to die now - or will you talk this time?' The man looked terrified.

'We have a little trick back home,' said Felgio, 'that involves tying a length of rope around a man's temple, just loose enough to insert a stick, which we proceed to twist. The rope tightens, and we twist it again. Very few twists loosen even the most stubborn tongue.'

'It sounds an interesting idea,' said Mala callously, and Vulso looked more terrified still. 'When he sings, however - and sing he will, this time - I want it to be in the presence of the Chief Investigator.'

'A good idea,' I put in, 'and it would be a good idea to make ourselves scarce; we are rather too close for comfort to the Campus Martius, and we don't want those fellows to return with a cohort of Praetorians.'

'Let 'em come,' said Felgio, and looked at his thunder-producing contraption with interest.

'Marcus is right,' said Mala. 'Even with that, and my own little toy, a cohort would be too many to cope with. Let us go then, you and I.'

We walked though certain quite deserted streets, dragging our prisoner with us, until we got him at last to the haunts of Gaius Corbus and his public-spirited assistants. They proceeded at once to question – I think that is the term – the unfortunate man.

Although, as Mala had predicted, he talked - as who would not have? – what he had to say amounted to little enough. He confirmed – though it had to be literally dragged out of him, and was – that he had betrayed us at once to Macrobius Pulcher, that that worthy himself had set up the trap, hoping it would be the end of us, and that something big, he knew not what, was in the offing. That was all, and if anyone might think the creature had more to tell but was determined to conceal it, he does not know Gaius Corbus's interrogators when they really set their minds to the task.

Gaius Corbus had been looking on impassively as his men did their work. When they had finished, he eyed Vulso, what was left of him, with disgust.

'So: the double-double-cross after all. Not wise. The arena? The Tarpeian Rock? Too public, both of them. But there is a ship leaving Ostia to-morrow for parts African. The captain is a good friend of mine, and as for the senior hortator – he used to be in my employ: a jolly fellow. I am sure they will look after you well, and teach you the finer points of oarsmanship into the bargain. You'll end up an expert –if you survive – for you've the rest of your life to practice.'

And that, to all intents and purposes, was the end of the treacherous Sextus Vulso.

'Which is all very well,' remarked Mala, as we left the Palace, 'but it gets us no further forward.'

'It does, a little,' Felgio said. 'I recognised one of friend Volvo's confrères before he scarpered, and I know where he drinks. It is a wine-shop just off the Subura. It is run by a man called Laberius, though it is called, for some reason, Rufus's Place.'

7.

Some days elapsed before we were able to make our way, with less than the old enthusiasm, to Rufus's Place. In times past our visits there had been among the highlights of our existence: the ambience of the place, the good companions, the friendly banter and earnest discussions, the inexpensive but excellent wine – all these had combined to make our visits something eagerly to look forward to.

Now, it was different. Our genial host, the eponymous Rufus, had been replaced by the oily Laberius; one after another our companions of old had abandoned their regular visits; even the wine – which, we had been assured, came from Rufus's regular suppliers – had lost something of its savour. As for the clientèle in general, as Mala rather quaintly put it, the whole tone of the establishment had gone down.

Laberius was cordial, as usual, and remembered our habitual tipple.

'The usual, gentlemen? Haven't seen you for a while…'

'Business,' replied Mala; 'the emperor's business. I'm afraid that takes precedence even over the pleasures of the grape.'

Laberius nodded. He was looking a little uncertainly at Felgio, who, though dressed like an upper-class Roman, quite clearly was not.

An unkempt individual at an adjacent table had divined as much. He looked contemptuously at Felgio, and then, in a loud and clearly wine-fuelled voice, spat rather than spoke his piece.

'I didn't know we allowed barbarians in here!'

Felgio half-rose, but Mala restrained him. Looking straight at the man, he spat out his piece in turn.

'Clearly, they do: uncouth guttersnipes who in Rufus's day would not have got over the threshold.'

The man pushed back his stool, and Mala stood to meet him.

'More 'carati',' I said to myself, and waited with interest for the man's comprehensive come-uppance. It came, but not as I had expected. Instead of aiming a blow, or producing a knife, the creature suddenly looked hard at Mala, and then at Felgio, and in turn at me, and turned pale. With a curse he dived for the door.

Mala was too quick for him. In an instant he had twisted the man's arm behind his back, and dragged him over to our table.

Laberius looked concerned. He knew we were customers of old, he knew we had some status – I, a long-standing, if relatively insignificant narrow-striper, Mala also, since our return from Britain, a member of the equestrian order. On the other hand, loud-mouth was evidently one of his cronies, whom he was expected, perhaps required, to help.

'Really, sir,' he said to Mala, torn between respect for his rank and fury at what had happened, 'I cannot have my customers treated in this way. I must ask you to release this man.'

'And I must ask you not to interfere when I am going about the emperor's business. Marcus Vectorius and I are on Nerva's personal staff, and we have good reason to believe this worm is up to no good. We are taking him in for questioning, and anyone who tries to stop us will wish he had never been born.'

Laberius, now more furious still and controlling himself with difficulty, was nevertheless no fool. Even if he had thought he could call on enough assistance to handle Mala, Felgio and me – a pretty big job of handling, as he had the sense to know – Mala's reference to the emperor had carried conviction.

'Very well then, sir, perhaps you will leave my premises, and take your – victim with you.'

To my surprise, Mala laughed.

'Come on, *victim*,' he ordered. 'No doubt you had a deprived childhood, and your parents never understood you. One of society's hard-done-by innocents, I can see that's what you are. Laberius there almost had me in tears. Victim - ha!'

Once outside, Felgio looked at our prisoner with interest.

'You recognised him at once, I see, as he did you,' he said; 'I needed to see him in the light.'

I was puzzled, and showed it.

'You would not have noticed,' Mala explained. 'You were mostly facing those who attacked us from the front. This louse was behind us, but he was definitely with the bunch who had a go at us when we went to meet Vulso - though he is not the man Felgio told us about.'

'A further visit to Gaius Corbus, then?' I suggested. 'I suspect we might have another one here who is destined for a nautical career.'

It was not pretty, but, as with Vulso, it was very thorough, and the man talked – and talked, and talked, as though his life depended on it, which as a matter of fact it did. Unfortunately, as with Vulso, what he said, gushingly and earnestly though he came out with it, did not, except in one particular, amount to much. Like Vulso and his other comrades – comrades! – he was pretty small beer, and not privy to any schemes and dreams his boss Macrobius Pulcher might have harboured. Indeed, Macrobius was very much a one-man band, his unsavoury helpers, numerous though they were, no more than that: helpers, hired thugs, who welcomed the rich pickings he led them to, but did not bother their heads too much, and were discouraged from bothering their heads too much, about more then the basic nuts-and-bolts of their little enterprises. Theirs was not to reason why…

One nugget of information the wretch did come out with, though, that was of some significance. Macrobius Pulcher was dead. Unusually for him, he had been amongst the foremost of those who had tried to kill us, thinking no doubt that he was in no danger, and had received the full blast from the device – musket, did Mala call it? – that Felgio had used to discourage them.

'I had wondered if it was he,' remarked Mala, 'but with half his face gone, it was difficult to be sure.'

It was thus not entirely surprising to be told that Macrobius's gang was no more. Gaius Corbus confirmed as much: reports had been coming in for some days, both from his own agents, and from the vigiles, that left no doubt.

'Your friend Gaius Molo is of the opinion that some of them will continue to be a nuisance in greater or lesser degree, but as an organised menace, they are no more. Indeed, some have already left Rome, for what they hope will be less inhospitable climes; we must endeavour to see their hopes are dashed. Some will undoubtedly find their new enterprises inconvenienced by our sterling vigiles, and still others, like this wretch here, can look forward to the joys of a life on the ocean waves. Unless, of course,' he turned to the deflated thug, 'they would prefer to spend the rest of their days in the quarries. Not that their preferences and predilections will really come into it.'

It was Scylla and Charybdis, and the man knew it: sweating in the bowels of a galley, chained to a massive oar, or sweating in the quarries, chained to his fellow sufferers – and in either case encouraged, liberally encouraged, by the lash, whenever his enthusiasm for his new career seemed in the slightest to wane.

In all, it was, for us if not for him, a satisfying, yet ultimately unsatisfactory, end to an unpleasant episode.

'That the Macrobius mob, and the eponymous Pulcher himself, are no more, can only be a cause for rejoicing,' Mala observed; 'Gaius Molo is positively over the moon; so are the tenants of Macrobius's filthy apartment buildings, whom he exploited and terrorized in equal measure. So, I suspect, are you, and so am I.

'But where has it got us? We still do not know what tie-up the villain had with Casperius Aelianus. We do not know what they were planning, nor do we have the slightest inkling of their time-table. We do not know who else is involved, either denizens of the underworld, or the rich backers Nerva mentioned. In short, friend Marcus, we, the supposedly incomparable investigators, are as pig-ignorant as when we left the Palace those days and weeks ago.'

8.

More days passed before Mala had cause to feel happier. Livinia and I were back home now, but I called on Mala each morning, to review 'progress'; and of course we were in constant touch with the Chief Investigator, and with Gaius Molo and the other vigiles throughout the city.

Things were simmering, we felt sure, and others felt it too. I do not know how one measures these things, but the whole atmosphere in the city, the general mood, had been subtly changing, and not for the better. There was almost an air of unreality to it, and of uncertainty.

'It reminds me of '69,' old Publius Corfax, still a Senator though he had seen eighty summers, confided in me, 'and I can do without another year like that.' He had got through the notorious Year of the Four Emperors unscathed, but by the skin of his teeth, and I could well understand his concern.

It had all started, of course, many weeks before. The execution of Petronius Secundus and his fellows had been the catalyst. Prior to that there had been an air of optimism, almost of light-heartedness. Domitian had gone, his excesses now but a memory; Nerva in his short reign had proved a wise and moderate ruler, a respecter of the law, a stranger to the wanton use and abuse of arbitrary power; men felt they could go about their business without the fear, the hitherto ever-present fear, that the Chief Investigator's minions, or the Praetorians themselves, would suddenly descend on them, and put an abrupt end to their happiness, their plans and aspirations, and probably their very lives as well.

Yet there were those, even apart from the cronies of the late emperor, and not a few of them far from insignificant citizens, who were suspicious from the outset. There had been other emperors, from long before Nerva until recent times, who had started well - Domitian himself, Nero, even Caligula – but who had changed as time went on into monsters, living embodiments of Mala's dictum that absolute power corrupts absolutely. Might not Nerva – old and infirm and seemingly civilised though he was – prove the same? Or if not he, some as-yet-unknown younger and more ruthless successor?

It was partly to dispel such doubts, as well as potentially to clip the wings of Casperius and his Praetorians, that Nerva had named the esteemed general Trajan as his successor, but the ploy had worked only up to a point. There's many a slip... and Trajan and his legions were far away. Might not Casperius Aelianus, who with his cohorts was on the spot, attempt one last despairing throw of the dice, even if he knew it was doomed? Might there not ensue a Reign of Terror, before the rightful emperor could come to the rescue – if he ever did?

'And if they know what I – er, suspect, that Trajan will not come straight to Rome even after he becomes emperor, but will spend many weeks touring the provinces before he even sets foot in the city, they would be more apprehensive still. I am a little apprehensive myself, Marcus, despite what I have, er, surmised about events to come: the future is not immutable, as we know, but nor is the past, as my very presence here testifies...

'But enough of that: we have work to do - pleasant work, to begin with, as it happens. Caecilius Galienus has invited us to dinner: there are some people he wants us to meet.'

It was a fairly large gathering, and there were a number there of fairly exalted status. We were surprised therefore to be seated on couches right next to Caecilius Galienus, and facing two men of most unusual appearance – unusual even for so cosmopolitan a city as Rome had now become. Though clad conventionally, if expensively, in tunic and toga, and though evidently, almost ostentatiously, at ease in Roman high society, there was no doubt that they came from pretty far afield. Their hair was jet-black, and swept back over high foreheads; their cheek-bones were prominent, and their eyes narrow, and their mouths also; their skin was dry, and light brown in colour, though with almost a yellowish tinge to it.

Their hands were long, delicate, and perfectly manicured. They sat a little apart from the rest, and joined in the general conversation only the barest minimum that common courtesy demanded, but occasionally were seen talking animatedly to each other in what was presumably their own language – and, it seemed to me, at one point they were possibly quarrelling.

Common courtesy demanded of us, in turn, that we not spend too long in observing them, for our fellow-guests were a convivial and talkative bunch. Besides, the lavish feast our host had provided itself required plenty of attention.

'By goodness, Mala,' I said, 'your estimable Diogenes himself would be hard-put to beat this.'

'Doubtless if I gave him his head, he could produce something to match it, but even though I could afford it, I am reluctant to spend as much on one meal as would feed a normal family for six months. But well-off though I am, Caecilius Galienus could probably buy me several times over, and I suppose he has to do something with his money.'

Our host did indeed, and it extended to providing entertainment no less lavish than the food. I will not even attempt to list all the attractions, but there was a troupe of African dancing-girls, from somewhere beyond even the southern border of Egypt itself, who especially took my eye – though when I tried to describe them afterwards to Livinia, she seemed singularly uninterested. Funny creatures, wives.

It all ended eventually, however, the guests one by one, steadily or otherwise, pouring themselves into their litters, and trotting away accompanied by the small army of stalwarts Galienus had provided as escorts. The high-cheek-boned pair had been among the first to go, taking leave of their host with funny little bows, and of the rest of us with the barest inclination of their heads.

'They went their separate ways,' our host told us afterwards. 'I invited them together because they are obviously fellow-countrymen, wherever their country might be, but I am told they are no longer close associates, and indeed not especially friendly.'

He had asked us to stay behind, precisely because he wanted to discuss the two.

'What did you think of them?'

'They were hardly sparkling conversationalists,' said Mala. 'The taller, younger one seemed as though he might be an interesting fellow, but every time he really got stuck into a conversation, whether with us or anyone else, his companion rather rudely interrupted, and started yakking away in their own language.'

'So I observed,' agreed Caecilius Galienus; we had divined he was the sort of man who doesn't miss much. 'Did you notice the jewels on the older one's hands – his name, by the bye, is Marco Chen - quite small, very understated, but if I'm any judge, worth a fortune?'

'Very much the style of both of them,' I suggested. 'Clearly they are Somebody, and keen to leave no-one in any doubt of the fact, and yet conversely they do not want to be seen to thrust it under people's noses.'

'Granted that they are filthy-rich,' said Mala, 'where do their riches come from? The older one I surmise is a business-man, but the other looked as though he would not soil his hands with anything so sordid as commerce.'

'Then he would make a Roman patrician,' smiled Galienus, 'though in strict truth their status, money apart, is nothing. Chen has been in Rome for three or four years, and Domitian granted him citizenship just before he died. There has never been any suspicion that he would rise higher in the social order. The other is a more recent arrival.'

'Then you were doing them a distinct favour, inviting them this evening, among such a distinguished company.'

'They get around a good deal; money talks, rank or no rank.'

'But you still have not told us where the money comes from.'

As to the younger one, Lucius T'yang, I do not know. Chen dabbles in property, does a little silk-trading, and he owns a chain of laundries that are said to be popular with the plebs.'

'That figures,' said Mala, smiling, but he did not explain.

'But you did not ask us to stay behind merely to discuss their commercial activities,' I said to Caecilius Galienus. 'What more is there about them that interests you?'

'Only this: that one of them is thought to have some tie-up with Casperius Aelianus.'

'The business connection at last!' exclaimed Mala, now all ears. 'Nerva mentioned rich businessmen, but did not know just who was involved.'

'Nor do we. There are several candidates, apart from our exotic friends of this evening, and we are keeping a close eye on them; at least, The Chief Investigator is: did he not tell you?'

Instead of answering, Mala reverted to the question of the unusual pair.

'You say one of them might be involved with Casperius, and presumably with his little plots. Which one?'

'That is the difficulty: we do not know. Prima facie, I would suspect Chen: if there is money involved, he is bound to be interested, and he is said not to be over-scrupulous as to where it comes from. On the other hand, there are some indications that his companion might be the one, despite his disdain for commerce. He is clearly very intelligent, and may not be above a little intrigue – or a lot. But he plays his cards pretty close to his chest, and is a hard man to fathom.'

'Inscrutable?' said Mala. 'Surprise, surprise.'

'All too much so; and the other one too, in lesser degree. However, the only hard information we have refers only to "an exotic man from the Aventine", but they both live on the Aventine.'

'And hence are my neighbours,' remarked Mala. 'I suppose I should be neighbourly and visit them.'

'That is just what I would like you to do,' said Galienus, 'if it does not interfere with any other plans you might have. Visit them; cultivate them even; and use your – what do you call them: little green cells?'

'Grey,' said Mala, 'such as they are.'

Next morning found Mala up at the crack of dawn. When I called on him, he and Felgio had been hard at work in the 'lab' for several hours.

'I have to keep an eye on him,' explained Mala, 'otherwise he might bring the whole place down about our ears. He is getting delusions of grandeur: he is already thinking far beyond his 'musket', and has talked of something a lot bigger and more potent. I think he wants to ask Nerva to inaugurate a whole new legion – a kind of Royal Horse Artillery.'

'Artillery? Every legion has artillery – catapults, ballistae, trebuchets: but they have nothing to do with horses.'

'When I have time, I will explain to you about guns and gun-carriages; but not right now.'

Again I had to be content, and I put the remark down in my little black book, along with all the others. It is a purely mental little black book, of course, like the one my first wife used to have, to record the names of my drinking companions. 'I would have been home earlier, dear, but I met up with...so-and-so' and down in her little black book would go so-and-so's name. After a time, though, she cottoned on, and the only name she took to putting in the black book was 'Marcus'.

Mala paused for a moment and the looked at me closely.

'But you look bothered about something: what is it?'

'When Caecilius Galienus was telling us about possible suspects, he talked of Corbus keeping an eye on some of them, as though we should have known that; but we didn't. Is Corbus deliberately keeping us in the dark? And if so, why? Surely he can trust us with the information?'

'Not necessarily. I must acquaint you with the concept of 'need to know'. In any operation of this kind, it is best that all involved, however trustworthy, know only as much as they need to in order to carry out their assignments. I know I am trustworthy, I know you are trustworthy, and I feel sure Corbus regards us as such: but suppose, just suppose, that we weren't. Suppose that Casperius got to us, and offered us untold riches and power if we threw in our lot with him, while continuing ostensibly to serve the emperor. The less we knew, the less we could harm Nerva's cause – as Corbus is well aware.'

'But that is preposterous; I would sooner die, than betray the emperor, and I am sure you would too.'

'True – and were I to die, I would prefer to die quickly. But supposing, loyal as we are, we were nevertheless captured by evil men and put to torture: even strong men break, and the less we knew about activities we were not immediately involved in, then, again, the less we could harm Nerva's cause. 'Need to know' is a sound principle in these matters, and it is no slur on our loyalty and integrity that we have not been made privy to all that Corbus and the others in our camp are up to.'

I saw the logic in what he was saying, but still did not like it, and said so.

'We are not here either to like or to dislike, Marcus; we are here to do a job.'

'And the job, I suppose, involves calling on your neighbours as soon as possible?'

'Of course. I am sending a message to Marco Chen explaining that I have only just discovered that we are near neighbours, and asking if I might visit him this afternoon; I mentioned that my close friend Marcus Vectorius was also hoping also to get to know him better: I take it that's O.K. by you?'

'Very much so. Quite apart from our investigations, I am curious to know just where he and his companion hail from.'

'As to that, I think I have a pretty good idea. I won't say so now, but I'll write it down, and afterwards you can see if I am right.'

He produced a sheet of the *paper* Trebonius had shown me the day we had had the audience with Nerva, and proceeded to write on it with something that looked like a stylus, but wasn't. He folded it and put it in his leather pouch.

9.

I had been in rich men's houses before – I mean really rich, not rich in the sense that Mala and I and even Caecilius Galienus are rich, which we most certainly are compared with the mass of the populace, but thoroughly, disgustingly, filthy filthy rich: like the late unlamented Carilius Milo, or the much more respectable Lucinius Cotillion, who used to be my father's patron. They both had villas covering acres, stuffed to the gunnels with art and artefacts from the far corners of the empire, all of it notable not so much for its intrinsic merit, as for the fact that it was horribly, hideously expensive.

Marco Chen's pad was not quite like that. Though sizable, it was not as big as some, and though there were plenty of doubtless expensive artefacts around, they did not shout at you in quite the same way as others I had seen. Nevertheless, the sheer opulence was unmistakable.

Above all, though, it was different – exotically different. For a start, the atrium, not big enough to hold a chariot race in like Milo's, but far from small at that, was like no atrium I had ever seen before, far stranger even than Mala's, which was certainly not conventional. There was none of the heavy and imposing statuary one would have expected to encounter, no trace of household gods, no murals, no mosaics – and no vistas, not even a glimpse of any inner courtyard with the expected fountains and flora, the seating and statuary, and all the elaborate aids to gracious living one would normally have taken for granted in such an up-market shack.

Instead, the atrium was completely enclosed, only two small doors leading off to the remaining areas of the villa. The floor was covered with thick, lusciously thick carpets, their pile under foot as soft as moss. On the walls, all the walls, every inch of them, there were tapestries, and hangings of silk – silk galore, shimmering and almost scintillating in the mid-day sun that streamed through the one high-set window.

There were furnishings, too: couches more appropriate to a dining-area, but of unusual, and exquisite design, and slender chairs and stools to match; there were little, beautifully-carved tables, which at first glance one m might have thought were Egyptian, but which one soon realised could not be.

I have said there was an absence of statuary, but I meant of statuary in the conventional sense. There was no shortage of statuettes, little figurines of ivory, of silver, of glass, even of elaborately carved and polished wood. Many of them were of strange, semi-abstract shape, that hinted at birds, at beasts, at human beings even, without quite representing them in recognisable, realistic detail.

And there was the smell, an odour faint yet all-pervasive, slightly sweet, slightly pungent, reminiscent of a temple ceremony but subtly different, pleasant and yet – somehow not wholesome.

Marco Chen was polite enough in his greeting, yet far from fulsome: I had the impression that he was not really pleased to see us and had responded to Mala's note proposing a visit only because he knew it was the thing to do.

Yet even if only skin deep, the politeness was there: he knew what was expected of him, did Marco Chen, if he was to flourish in high society, and he applied what he had learned diligently. His manners were impeccable, his conversation easy, and his wine of the best – and liberally bestowed, perhaps too liberally for the time of day.

But the talk was small talk, amiable but inconsequential. Chen was surprisingly fluent in Latin, considering that he had only been in Rome a few years - though his accent you could have cut with a knife - and the skilful way he steered the conversation away from any topic he did not wish to pursue showed that he was nimble-minded, too: nimble-minded, and fully aware of what he was about.

Which was stalling. Mala himself, skilful in the extreme, was probing as far as he could without being blatantly obvious about it, but Chen would not be drawn, either on the great issues of politics that were exercising everyone's mind, or the trivia of social chit-chat some find of even greater interest: the unprecedented run of the Greens, with their new Lusitanian star; the scandal of Junius Plessus's wife and the three gladiators; the unseasonably warm weather that had accompanied the Saturnalia –

whatever subject was broached, he commented on it but briefly, and then moved on.

Only when Mala mentioned his origins did he show concern, at one point bordering on agitation, but his response took the form of clamming up even further.

'You came originally from a long way away, Marco Chen, or so we surmise.'

'Yes.'

'Far to the east?'

'Yes.'

'They say there is a great land beyond even the Indies, about which Rome knows little.'

'It is said.'

'A land vast and rich and powerful; perhaps even greater than Rome.'

'As to that, I could not say.'

'But clearly,' said Mala, abandoning his questioning, 'its sons include men of talent, who have the ability to prosper even in foreign climes. Your name, Marco Chen, is one to conjure with, here in Rome.'

Chen acknowledged the compliment with a deprecating wave of the hand, but I could see he was pleased.

There followed more small talk, more wine was offered, and refused, and then the visit was over.

'And a fat lot of good it did us,' said Mala. 'He is a villain, of that I have no doubt. He took what I said about his name being one to conjure with as a compliment, but I know that in some circles it is said to smell as strongly as those joss-sticks he was burning, but far less fragrantly.'

'Joss sticks?'

He explained.

'But how can you know this, Mala? Does your country have contact, then, with this mysterious land to the east, as Rome does not?'

'We hear stories,' replied Mala, 'just as we hear stories of Rome. It is thought that some intrepid travellers have visited the land, and a few are said to have returned, bearing strange tales.'

'Including reports of these joss-sticks?'

'Indeed.'

I had a brain-wave.

'Mala,' I said, 'you have told me that your land lies far, far to the west, across the great ocean, and that it is bounded on the other side by another ocean, even greater in extent. You have also told me, what seems so hard to believe, that the earth is round. Could you then, by going further west, across this other great ocean, come eventually to this mysterious realm we are talking about, which from here we can only get to by going east? Indeed – I know this sounds fantastic, but it is a logical corollary – could you not, by going on and on, return to where you started from?'

'Good thinking, Marcus: you are using your undoubted intelligence to good effect at last. What you say is, theoretically, true, but the distances are vast. When Julia Carolina has finished constructing the great globe she and Felgio are working on, you will see just how vast, and get a clearer idea of Rome's place in the scheme of things. Be warned, though, that it might make you feel humble – very 'umble, sir, very 'umble.'

Humble? What could he mean? I am a Roman, and ipso facto proud; being humble never comes into it. I knew Mala well enough, however, not to dismiss anything he said: if he told me I would feel humble, I probably would.

·

Our visit to Lucius T'yang, on the morrow, could not have been more different from our tête-à-tête with Chen – and it was far more fruitful.

That was just as well. I could see that Mala was fretting at our lack of progress, at the complete dearth of hard evidence, or even of useful clues.

'So far, Marcus, we have been getting nowhere, fast,' he remarked as we walked towards T'yang's secluded villa, further up the Aventine by some distance either than his own, or Chen's. 'Surely we are due for a bit of luck by now?'

T'yang's place was nothing like his countryman's. At first sight, it was utterly conventional, and could have been mistaken for that of any Roman of reasonable means and unostentatious good taste. A young girl, of perhaps sixteen or seventeen summers, was standing by the side of the foreigner, but he waved her away as we entered.

'My niece,' he explained, 'but this conversation is not for her, and she knows her place.'

Mala remarked almost at once on the difference between T'yang's villa and Chen's.

'I believe,' said T'yang, 'that when in Rome, one should do as Rome does. It is only good manners. Good manners, however, are not Marco

Chen's strong point: he is low-born. Do not call him my countryman, however. He comes from the same empire, but is no more strictly my countryman than, say, a Mauritanian is yours. Call him simply a fellow-subject of my emperor.'

'You have an emperor?' I showed my surprise.

'Yes; the latest in a distinguished line.'

'The Han dynasty?' asked Mala. T'yang looked at him narrowly.

'Yes, indeed; but how could you know?'

'I must have heard it somewhere,' said Mala; 'I am a collector of miscellaneous information, ill-considered trifles and matters of significance alike: you could almost call me a magpie. It is interesting, though, that this snippet of information proves to be correct. There is much, Lucius T'yang, that I would like to learn from you about your great country, which fascinates me more, the more I hear of it. Marco Chen was not very forthcoming.'

'Nor could he have been: he is an ignoramus as well as a boor.'

I was right then, I told myself, in surmising that there was no love lost between these two.

'But you did not come here to learn of my country,' our host went on, 'though I perceive that your interest is genuine. You did not even call as a matter of courtesy. Unless I am very mistaken, you are here because you want to learn more of Marco Chen, and you want to do so because you suspect him of criminal activities; and if you do so suspect, you are almost certainly right, for the leopard does not change his spots, and Chen has long been a villain of the first order. I have chased him half-way across the world, on a mandate I have from his imperial majesty himself.'

This was information indeed. Mala made a decision.

'Then, Lucius T'yang, we are three of a kind, for Marcus Vectorius and I are also, for the time being, on a commission from our own emperor.'

The foreigner raised his eyebrows, but said nothing.

'I am going to trust you, Lucius T'yang, for if I am any judge, you are a trustworthy man. We are indeed interested in Marco Chen, but it is not because of criminality in the narrow sense. I am not free to go into detail, but I can tell you that high politics are involved – and possible treason.'

'You interest me greatly. I said that the leopard does not change his spots, and Chen dabbled in politics – of the murkier kind – back home also. That is one reason why my emperor is especially keen to have him back, though if he falls foul of Roman law and you dispose of him, that will be almost as satisfactory.'

'We suspect him,' said Mala, 'of having some tie-in with important people, including one very important person indeed, whose name I am not at liberty to divulge at this juncture.'

'Casperius Aelianus?'

'I did not say so.'

'Nor did you need to. I have followed political affairs very closely since I have been in Rome – it is part of my brief, and I will be reporting back to my emperor – and it is not rocket science to deduce the reverberations of the Petronius Secundus affair have not yet died down.

'It is not simply deduction, though. I do know for a fact that Chen has some sort of association with Aelianus, though I cannot yet say what it is. However, I can tell you that I have an agent in Chen's household. He is a good man, and I am confident that he will come up with something before long. When he does, I will, of course, inform you.'

'That will be greatly appreciated,' said Mala, 'and in turn, anything we discover that is not actually classified, we will pass on to you.'

'My gratitude will be of the highest.'

We left shortly afterwards. As we walked a way, I had a thought.

'Mala, before we went to see Marco Chen, you wrote something down, an that paper stuff you use. May I now know what it was?'

He handed the sheet to me, and I read.

> *I believe our exotic friends come from the great land far to the east I once told you about. They are ruled by an emperor: the latest of an illustrious line, the great Han dynasty.*

10.

'Progress at last, Marcus,' Mala enthused, and we have recruited no mean ally into the bargain. I was looking forward to reporting what we have found at this afternoon's meeting with Nerva, but I wonder why he has summoned us to the Palace ahead of time, and why the messenger said it was so urgent? Has Corbus also made a breakthrough of some kind, or has there been some less welcome development?'

When we reached the Palace, we were ushered at once into the emperor's sanctum sanctorum, there to find a state of near turmoil. Nerva was dictating at top speed to a clerk, others were rushing in and out, and a high-ranking officer, whom I recognised as one of those from the Army of the Rhine we had seen when first we visited the Palace to hear of Nerva's concerns, was issuing orders to two subordinates in an urgent tone, and when he had finished they saluted and scurried away as fast as their legs could carry them.

Nerva finished his dictating, the clerk in turn rushed from the room, and we advanced to where the emperor was sitting.

'Thank Jupiter you are here!'

'Is there trouble, Caesar?'

'Trouble? Only this: Gaius Corbus and Caecilius Galienus have both been assassinated.'

This was appalling news. Galienus, we knew, had been a tower of strength, and as for Corbus, he was all but irreplaceable.

'I grieve for Galienus's young wife,' said Mala, 'and their child – only a few weeks old.'

'As will I,' said Nerva, 'when I have the leisure to do so, but as of now my mind is on more pressing matters. If only I had the troops at my command, I would find those responsible, and deal with them summarily; and their commander as well.'

'Praetorians?'

'Undoubtedly. Galienus and Corbus left the Palace together last night; we had been discussing the latest developments, and Corbus was to have briefed you this afternoon.'

'Did they not have bodyguards?'

'Of course: who would venture out late at night without? Corbus had four of his own men, and you know what they are like; Galienus had three former gladiators. Yet they were cut down to a man, along with their masters. That is why we are sure it must have been Praetorians: the guards would have been a match for any number of ordinary street thugs. I dare say they put paid to a number of their attackers, but the rest carted the bodies away. There must have been a sizable band of them.'

'There would have been, no doubt.' The officer spoke for the first time. 'You don't catch our precious Praetorians risking a fair fight against equal numbers.'

He spoke with the characteristic disdain of the campaigning soldier for the home-based, supposedly elite unit.

'Yet they are supposed to be good,' said Mala.

'They are trained to the eye-brows, no doubt about that,' replied the officer, 'but they are soft nevertheless. Not one of them has seen real combat for years, some of them never. I look forward to having the chance, one day, of dealing with them. If they get stroppy, my lads from Upper Germany will know how to sort them out – and enjoy doing so.'

'I'll wager XIII Gemina wouldn't mind having a go, as well,' I put in.

'A good bunch,' agreed the officer. 'I understand you once served with them, and with distinction.'

'But neither the Army of the Rhine, nor XIII Gemina, is here in Rome,' pointed out Nerva. 'We are back to our original problem: nine thousand armed thugs are here on the spot.'

'There will not risk open rebellion, Caesar. When you made my general in effect co-emperor, he was well aware of the danger, and of Aelianus's delusions of grandeur. That is why I am here: I did not have chance to tell you, following the terrible news of the murders. Trajan has sent me specifically to warn Aelianus against any rebellious move. I will be going straight from the Palace to the Campus Martius to deliver the message.'

'You are a brave man. What if Casperius has you killed on the spot; he is clearly no respecter of persons, and he may feel that now he has gone this far, he has nothing to lose in going further.'

'I almost wish he would,' said the officer, 'for then indeed he would be signing his death-warrant. I am the personal representative of Marcus Ulfius Trajanus, and my general knows how to look after his own. If Aelianus touched one hair of my head, vengeance would be certain, and it would be terrible. Caesar, with your permission, I will go now.'

'He may be right,' said Mala, as the soldier left, 'but he is still a very brave man.'

'And I look for another, a brave man and an able one. I need, and I need urgently, a replacement for Gaius Corbus. Quintus Propertius Mala, you are the new Chief Investigator. I suggested the post to you once before, and you turned it down with alacrity, but this time I issue an order, and I will brook no denial; and you, Marcus Vectorius, are to be his Deputy. That, too, is an order.'

'Naturally, I will do as I am commanded,' said Mala.

'Naturally,' replied Nerva, drily.

'But is this wise, Caesar? In the first place, though I am a Roman citizen, and thanks to your generosity and munificence, an equestrian, I am not Roman born, and there will be those who will be unhappy that such as I should hold such an important post.'

'As to that,' replied Nerva, 'let them be unhappy. But you forget that this is not an official post in the usual sense: it is in the gift of the emperor, and you are on the personal staff of the emperor, rather than simply a servant of the state. So your reservation does not signify. But you have other concerns?'

'Only this, Caesar, and it is the more important consideration: being in charge of the substantial department that Gaius Corbus ran so efficiently will take time and effort that could be better used, better used in your interest: field-work, detective-work, leg-work, call it what you will: being out there, actually looking for the villains who wish you ill.'

'Then,' said Nerva, unsympathetically, 'you will have to do as your emperors have been doing, for the good of Rome, since the time of

Augustus onwards, and burn the candle at both ends. It is not beyond human capability to do two jobs at once.'

Mala saw there was no way Nerva was going to change his mind, but he had one more shot in his locker.

'Of course I will serve you to the very utmost of my ability, Caesar. I am right, though, am I not, in assuming that this is a temporary appointment while the present emergency lasts, and that you will appoint someone more suitable when it is over?'

'That is my intention,' replied the emperor; and then his old sense of humour returned briefly. 'But cheer up, Quintus Propertius, and you too, Marcus Vectorius: the pay is good. Not that either of you need it,' he added with a chuckle.

That was true enough: it had been true even before we left for Britain, and when we returned, successful in our mission, we had both received substantial donatives from the imperial coffers.

'Then we had better earn it, Caesar,' said Mala, catching the mood, 'and we went some way towards doing so this morning.' And he succinctly told the emperor of our encounters with the exotic duo, Chen and T'yang.

'You think this man – how is he called? Lucius T'yang – is to be trusted. You say he, too, is in the personal employ of his emperor, whoever that worthy might be; his first loyalty, then, will be to that emperor. Do not forget that, Quintus Propertius, however much you might be impressed by his character and his supposed integrity.'

Mala took the point (it is well to take the point, when the point is made by Caesar) but then, looking very solemn, reverted to the news we had been given when first we reached the Palace.

'These dreadful murders, Caesar: where did they take place?'

'Not a hundred yards from the Palace,' replied Nerva. 'That is almost as dreadful as the murders themselves. It is a deliberate affront to my authority.'

'Deliberate indeed. But who is responsible? "Praetorians" is too broad a term. Which Praetorians? On whose orders? Is Casperius Aelianus himself the one who planned the murder, or was it one of his underlings? He has surrounded himself with some pretty unsavoury characters; maybe one of them took it on himself to rid Rome of this – to the Aelianus camp – troublesome pair. If so, we might be able to find out who, and if we do, it could be in interesting indication of how the balance of power stands, as to whether Aelianus tries to protect them.'

'But surely he would?' I interjected. I had not even considered any other possibility.

'Not necessarily. Power is slowly but surely slipping away from Casperius Aelianus, and he knows it. He is still extremely dangerous; he still has some scheme in mind, we don't yet know what, aimed at discomfiting you, Caesar, and at perhaps pulling his own chestnuts out of the fire at the same time; but he is far from the near-omnipotent thorn in your side who brought about the execution of Petronius Secundus.'

'True; and it will be interesting also to see how he reacts to the message sent by Trajan.'

'Very interesting, and the brave Orcus should be back very soon to tell us.'

'If he is coming back,' said Nerva, morosely. 'He might be stretched on the ground at the Campus Martius at this moment, with his throat cut.'

'I think not,' replied Mala, 'for all the reasons he gave before he left.'

We did not have very long to find out. A flunky appeared and whispered in Nerva'a ear; he nodded impatiently, and the man left post-haste; almost immediately, in strode Publius Orcus, accompanied by two other officers, all three resplendent in gleaming armour and the full insignia of their rank, each positively exuding military authority. I looked at them enviously. I, too, had wielded authority in my time, and I, too, had looked the part.

'I have delivered my general's message, Caesar, and I did not mince words. I told Casperius Aelianus to his face that if ever again he exceeded his authority, ever again set himself against you, his rightful emperor, Trajan's wrath would be dreadful to behold, as well as very final. And if any of those he commanded were misguided enough to follow him in such enterprises Trajan's legions would come to Rome, and then... I made sure that such of the Praetorians who were there, officers and men, heard the message precisely.'

'And what was the reaction to such blunt words?'

'Casperius Aelianus tried to bluster a little, and to remind me where I was and that he had nine thousand men at his back. I told him that Trajan had the armies of the Rhine at *his* back, but that I was not there to discuss, to argue, to negotiate, or even to listen.

'I have delivered the message from my general,' I told him, 'and I would advise you to take heed. But he instructed me to add one thing: though his wrath can be terrible, to those who serve him loyally and well, he can be generous in the extreme. I bid you farewell.'

'Well,' said Mala, admiringly, 'you certainly know how to make your meaning clear; and it was a masterpiece to mention Trajan's generosity. In an ideal world, or even a half-way sane one, that would be the end of it, and to all intents and purposes the end of Casperius Aelianus. But we do not live in an ideal world, nor yet a half-way sane one. Casperius Aelianus is a wounded animal; wounded animals are dangerous.'

'If only we had some clue as to what he has been planning,' I said. 'We can surely rule out any attempt at a military coup now, but what else can he do? A campaign of assassination, Corbus and Galienus only the first? Your leading supporters in the Senate, Caesar: will they be the next to go?'

'Such a campaign,' said Orcus, 'would be construed as open rebellion by my general as surely as though Aelianus again attacked the Palace in force, and he has the sense to know it. Whatever else may be in his mind, you can rule out a campaign of assassination.'

'And yet we have had two assassinations already, of men very close to the emperor.'

'The more I look at the circumstances of that,' said Mala, 'the more I think my early conjecture was correct, that it was not Aelianus himself, but some hot-heads among his followers, who devised and carried out the attack. I shall make it one of my prime objects to find out just who they are, and to bring them to justice.'

'That might have to await the arrival of Trajan and his troops,' said Nerva, 'though perhaps that is not so very far in the future. I feel the chill of January in my bones as never before, and fear that Nature will do Casperius Aelianus's work for him, at least as far as I am concerned. That does not worry me: all men must die. The question is, how much damage will be done to the realm, perhaps even to Trajan's succession itself, before I go – or before Aelianus can be brought to book. Redouble your efforts, Quintus Propertius; we must find precisely the nature of this danger, for danger I am convinced there still is, and scotch it for good – if we can.'

'And with your permission, Caesar, I will repair now to Gaius Corbus's domain, to get on with trying to do just that.'

'He has not long to live,' said Mala, as we walked towards Corbus's offices, 'a few weeks, perhaps only days, and the interregnum, which is what to some extent it will be with the new emperor still out of the country, will be the most dangerous period. I know well how this should end,

Marcus, and if it does I will predict that the accession of Trajan will usher in a long period of unparalleled prosperity for Rome and its empire, under a succession of great rulers. But I know, as I have said before, that neither the future nor the past is immutable. Things may not turn out as I foresee.'

The past not immutable? What could he possibly mean by that? And what had the past to do with it? We live in the present, as I told him.

'You do,' said Mala briefly, and I was more puzzled still.

I was puzzled, too, that night, racking my brain to think just what could Casperius Aelianus do to upset the apple-cart. Surely his wings had been clipped by the blunt message from Trajan, who would soon be emperor: Nerva was clearly a dying man. The skids were probably under his alien ally, Marco Chen, if the combined efforts of Mala and of Lucius T'yang were as effective as we hoped. The gangster Macrobius Pulcher was no more. The Praetorians themselves would be wondering which way the wind was blowing: Casperius Aelianus might boast of the nine thousand men at his back, but for that very reason he might have to guard his back.

No: he surely now was a busted flush, a wounded animal, with his strength ebbing away.

'Here's to Trajan,' I said, and raised an imaginary glass in tribute, and despite the outrage of the two murders, I went to sleep that night in better frame of mind than I had been for some time.

What a fool I was: for there was one thing of which I was ignorant, and three I had forgotten.

The one of which I was ignorant, Mala informed me the very next day. And the three I had forgotten?

First, was what Mala had so truly pointed out: that a wounded animal can be dangerous: very dangerous.

The second was that, at our very first briefing, Nerva had talked of rich and powerful *men* – plural – being involved in plotting against him.

And the third? It is inexcusable. I am an educated man; I have studied history, and politics; I take a keen note of what is going on in the society I live in. Yet I had forgotten, as others had before me, and to their cost, the one eternal, ever-present, over-arching fact of Roman life.

I had forgotten the Roman mob.

11.

It was not a meeting I had been looking forward to. Mala, engaged night and day as Nerva had suggested he should be with his new responsibilities, had asked me to convey his sincere apologies that he could not yet be there in person, and to pass on his deepest sympathy along with my own.

Galienus's widow was scarcely more than a girl, and yet, as befitted a daughter of one of the oldest families in Rome, and the bereft wife of one of the closest associates of the emperor himself, she remained utterly in control of herself throughout our interview; but she could not hide the pain in her eyes. It had been a love-match, we knew – rare enough in Rome these days – and her grief went far beyond the conventional protestations.

And yet, she could be practical. She had been, she told me, in her husband's confidence, privy to the details of his investigations and of his suspicions, and knew of our involvement in the attempt to discover, and to counteract, whatever was being plotted. She knew, too, that it must have been Galienus's activities in that direction that had led to his murder; it made her the more determined to be of help.

'It was only as he was going out to see the emperor that he told me of his latest notion. He said it was still so tenuous that he was not even as yet going to mention the matter to Nerva and to Corbus. I think, though, that it is right that you and Quintus Propertius should know at once.'

'Anything,' I said; 'anything you can tell us that might help, in however slight a degree, to foil those who are plotting again the emperor, and to catch those responsible for the foul murder of one of the finest men in Rome. No matter that Galienus might have had only suspicions, rather than proof: it might give us a lead, and all leads are valuable.'

By way of reply she went to a small table set against a wall, and opened a large casket. From it she took out a scroll, which she handed to me.

'It is not exactly proof, but rather more than suspicion,' she said; 'Galienus was convinced there was more to this than meets the eye. He had one of his best agents pursuing the matter, but had been wondering whether it was yet time to bring in you and Quintus Propertius: he did not want to trouble you with what might prove to be a red herring, when you were so busy with your own investigations. I suggest you read this, Marcus Vectorius, and make of it what you will, and then contact the agent, the freedman, Prastus, who will tell you all he knows, as I have instructed him. I have told him also that he must from now on work for you, as he did for my husband, faithfully and diligently.'

'I thank you, as will Quintus Propertius; I will read this most diligently, and will contact the man Prastus without delay.'

'I thank you in turn, Marcus Vectorius. I am but a woman - though my husband said I was more like a partner – but may I ask that you keep me informed of what is going on? I am not stupid, I have some ideas of my own, and I might recall scraps of information that Caecilius passed on to me that could be relevant; if I can be of use, I do so wish to be.'

And she was – but I go before my horse to water: I will tell you of that anon.

The document Calpurnia Pulchra had taken from the casket at first sight did not seem especially interesting. It was in two parts, the first no more than a bill of sale, for grain: a substantial quantity of grain, recently shipped, apparently, from Egypt. The second part of the scroll was a simple message:

This, and a few more like it, should do the trick.

It was apparently from one Festianus, and it was addressed to a person of some substance; a person of some considerable substance indeed: his name was Casperius Aelianus.

Prastus was not hard to find; by trade he was a metalworker, one of the best in Rome, according to Mala, who produced everything from fine swords (he had made the sabres Mala and I now proudly sported whenever we were outside the confines of the city itself), through bespoke breastplates and helmets for the exalted of the army, to sturdy gates, fences, miscellaneous iron parts for siege weapons, and, of late, a plethora of strange objects, large and small, to Mala's own commission and design.

I should not have been surprised, therefore, though I was, a little, to see with him in the shop that fronted onto his large and noisy foundry a broad-shouldered customer I recognised at once. It was the Briton, Felgio, who was urgently engaged in showing the man a sheaf of drawings, of whatever new-fangled contraption – I assumed – either he or Mala had come up with and wanted making perfectly to their specifications: preferably by yesterday.

'Greetings, Marcus,' the young man said as I entered the shop; 'what brings you to the hearth of this estimable workman?'

'Not metalwork,' I answered, turning to Prastus, 'though I know I would find none better anywhere in Rome. I come from the widow of Galienus, your late patron, with a request that you tell me what you can about this.'

I handed him the scroll.

'Only that it took me a devil of a job to get it, that I hope the person whose office I liberated it from doesn't discover it has gone, or there will be hell to pay, and that I hope, further, one day to hear that said person has been invited to take a bathe in the Tiber, wearing concrete boots. I will not be leading the mourners.'

'Not a nice man?'

'Not a nice man,' agreed Prastus, 'and he does not keep nice company. But I will tell you about that shortly. You must be Marcus Vectorius: Calpurnia Pulchra said I should expect you.'

'I am indeed. Now, what can you tell me about this bill of sale, and its attached note?'

'That is for wiser heads than mine, Marcus Vectorius: my late patron's, or now yours, perhaps? I know only that Festianus is a grain merchant, among many other things; that the bill of sale is a duplicate; and that the original is probably now in the hands of someone I had sooner not tangle with.'

'Casperius Aelianus, clearly.'

'Or one of his minions. He sent a centurion, no less, to collect it; it was while the big lout was talking to Festianus that I removed the copy from a desk drawer: I thought it might interest Galienus, who had asked me to find out what I could about this – businessman, I think he calls himself, though I have already found out enough to suggest a few alternative appellations.'

'And just what you have found out, I would like you now to tell me.'

The metalworker looked a little doubtfully at Felgio.

'You may speak freely in front of this young man: he is a friend, and confident, and the protégé of Quintus Propertius Mala. In fact, he saved our lives just recently, and with one of the artefacts you made for him at that.'

'That funny wood and iron club? I don't know how he did it, then – the thing was not even weighted properly, and why he asked for the iron bits to be hollowed, and very precisely at that, I cannot imagine. Had he wanted it, I could have produced a club that Hercules himself would have been proud to own; but that... Some club.'

Club! Felgio and I exchanged glances. We did not enlighten the man, but, reassured, he launched into his story.

It did not add up to as much as I had hoped, though we soon came to understand why Prastus regarded the term 'businessman' as very much a euphemism. One nugget of information, however, did greatly interest me.

'He has a partner in a number of his enterprises, a character as shady as himself. Funny-looking character: foreigner, from somewhere out Parthia way, or beyond – if there is any beyond. Name of Chan, Chin, or something of the sort.'

'Marco Chen?'

'That's the man: another I wouldn't trust to sell me a used chariot.'

I doubted if Prastus had ever been in, let alone owned, a chariot in his life, but the expression was becoming a common one, and I nodded.

'Nor I,' I agreed. 'Prastus, you have done well. Continue to keep your eyes and ears open, and "liberate" any other document you safely can that you think might be of interest. Report either to me, or to Quintus Propertius. Meanwhile, I must go and tell Quintus Propertius himself what I have learned to-day.'

'I will tag along, if I may,' said Felgio. 'I, too, have something to tell him.

I did not dissuade him, though I doubted that Mala, despite his deep commitment to the 'research and development' he and the Briton had been working on so assiduously, would be very interested in anything along those lines at this juncture: our more mundane but more pressing investigations were now taking every iota of his energy, his time, and his reasoning power; and rightly so.

We were ushered into his private office – formerly Corbus's, and before that the haunt of his unspeakable predecessor – and he looked up at us with a somewhat haggard expression.

'I told Nerva before we left for Britain that I was not the man for this job,' he said. 'I wish he had listened. Administration is simply not my forte.'

I knew Mala well enough to be sure that if he really put his mind to anything – anything – he would make a good fist of it, but to be suddenly pitched into the job of Chief Investigator, at a moment's notice and with no previous experience of the large department Corbus had built up, no familiarity with staff or procedures, was certainly asking a ,lot of him.

'I've had a bit of trouble already with some of my so-called helpers,' he told us. 'They were very much Corbus's men –most of them – or if not his, their own. They have been doing vital work, and risking their lives, day in and day out, in the service of the emperor, under the command and firm guidance of Gaius Corbus, who was an exceptional man. It is not surprising that they do not see why a complete stranger, and an upper-class twit at that and not even Roman-born, should suddenly appear and start dishing out the orders.

'I have had to read the riot act to two or three of them already, and I think they at least have got the message, but others are still a bit sullen.'

'They are a hard bunch,' I said, 'and I don't envy you.'

'They are fundamentally sound,' replied Mala, 'most of them. There are one or two who in essence are not very different from some of the villains we have encountered: that they find themselves on the right side of the law is as much a matter of chance, as of choice. Even they, though, I am pretty sure, are loyal enough. As for the rest, they are good men, and will continue to do good work, once I have gained their confidence.'

'Which you will soon do, I am sure.'

'Your faith is touching. But never mind that; I have much to tell you. Corbus kept his cards close to his chest – too close, you might think, for if we had known from the start what I now know, we might have been saved a deal of trouble.'

"Need to know',' I asked; 'is it really such a good idea?'

'Touché; but now we do know, and a few more things are falling into place. For instance, I am now almost sure that Marcus Chen is in cahoots with a villain as nasty as himself, and a home-grown Roman one at that.'

'Yclept Festianus?' I asked smugly.

'My, my; you have been busy. Tell me more.'

I rapidly sketched in the results of my morning's activities: the interview with Calpurnia Pulchra, the bill of sale and its attached note, the revelations of Prastus the metalworker.

'This ties in with what Corbus had divined, but goes further. Grain: what is the significance of that?'

'Ask the mob, if they don't get their bread and circuses.'

How I wish we had pursued that line. Even a little thought might have provided the clue we lacked, but Mala's normally sharp mind was tired from absorbing the mass of information he had inherited from Gaius Corbus, I was intrigued by the Festianus-Chen connection and anxious to follow it up, and neither he nor I was sufficiently receptive to put three and two together when he imparted his next piece of information, which is a pity because it would have put us firmly on the road to cracking the whole case.

'You remember,' said Mala, 'that Nerva spoke of Aelianus having cronies among rich businessmen, among criminals, and among disgruntled politicians? We have dealt with at least one of the criminals gangs, we know something of the business angle; but now, what of the politicians?'

'That is where Galienus should have been able to help, but alas, he can help no more. But perhaps,' I had a sudden thought, 'his widow can. I hate calling on her again at this time, but fear I am going to have to.'

'Yes; and ask her if Galienus had anything on this man, the esteemed, the one-and-only, the latter-day self-appointed tribune of the people, Publius Volusius Stolo.'

'That worm!' I exclaimed; 'that rabble-rouser? He thinks he is in the line of Gracchus, or even Clodius, but he has neither the political nous of the one nor the drive and conviction of the other. He appeals to the lowest instincts of the lowest members of society. Fortunately he hasn't the wit to cause real trouble, even though he can be a damned nuisance from time to time. I am surprised the emperor has not him neutralised long ago, but of course the man does have some powerful friends, and we know how circumscribed Nerva is in what he can do.'

'Precisely. As for Volusius not having the wit to exploit his undoubted mob appeal: perhaps he hasn't, but there are others in Rome who have. As yet we do not know of any connection between this tuppeny-ha'penny demagogue and the other villains we are interested in, but Corbus obviously thought there might be. That is one of the lines we must follow up.'

'All of which,' interrupted Felgio, 'reminds me of what I came here to tell you: there was a riot in the Forum earlier this morning.'

'A riot?'

'Not a really full-scale one, but big enough. Molo was there with every man, and most of those from two other districts as well. They were just enough to contain things: they broke a few skulls, and the rest hesitated about taking them on, but finally thought better of it. It was a close call, though.'

'And what was the riot about?'

'I don't know for sure; something to do with bread, I believe.'

And still the penny did not drop.

'Was Volusius involved?'

'Not at the time, but Molo thinks he might have been behind it.'

'Mala,' I said, 'you are now Chief Investigator; you have men at your command; cannot you arrest this loathsome creature, and damn the consequences?'

'I am very tempted to do so. On balance, though, when I weigh up all the implications and ramifications, I think perhaps I had better not – yet. But I will certainly put it to the emperor, and if he thinks I should move, I will.'

But the emperor did not think so; in which the emperor was wrong.

I have always thought that if you have an unpleasant task to perform, the best thing is to get it over with as quickly as you can. I did not like intruding again on Calpurnia Pulchra's grief, especially so soon after my first visit, even though she had said she wanted to help, but I knew it had to be done, and so I headed straight there as soon as I had left the Palace.

'Publius Volusius? Yes, of course I know of him. Galienus would speak of him from time to time, and always with the utmost contempt.'

'As a man if principle, he could scarcely do otherwise. What I want to know, Calpurnia Pulchra, is whether his contempt was more than that; whether he thought Volusius might be implicated in any way in the conspiracy we are concerned with.'

'He certainly thought it was possible, but he did not tell me anything concrete; unless,' she thought for a moment, 'unless there is anything significant in the fact that Volusius has been exchanging visits with that strange eastern man…'

'Marco Chen?'

'No, not he; the other one.'

Great Jupiter! I thanked Calpurnia Pulchra for what she had told me, and rushed back to the Palace. There, I burst into Mala's office without ceremony.

'Mala,' I said, 'I have something really important to tell you.' And I dropped the bombshell about Lucius T'yang.

'This is news indeed. If Lucius T'yang is not what he seems, if he is indeed hand-in-glove with a worm like Volusius, can we believe a word he has said? Might he not be, after all, just as close to his unsavoury compatriot as that worthy was to others we wot of? As I observed at Galienus's dinner party, Marcus, there is something inscrutable about these Orientals; might they have been pulling the wool over our eyes, most comprehensively, all along? This indeed is something we will have to look into.

'But later, for I have news for you, of even greater moment: Nerva died, not half an hour ago.'

12.

'And so the de facto interregnum is here,' Mala went on. Trajan is far away, Casperius Aelianus is here on the spot, licking his wounds and ready to lash out - and we, we are in the middle., minding the shop, holding the fort - call it what you will.'

'If you are looking for metaphors,' I replied, 'I call it a tough row to hoe, not least because still, after all this time, we do not have the slightest idea what is being planned, and until we do, how can we take steps to counteract it?'

'By hard work, by perseverance, and if we were superstitious men, Marcus, by prayer: prayer for a little good luck.'

He paused, as one of his men, a surprisingly cheerful-looking young man to find in such a place, came in and handed Mala a note.

'The messenger said this was urgent.'

Mala read the scroll with a slight frown on his face.

'This could be the luck we need,' he said, 'or it could be just leading us up the garden path. What do you make of it?'

He handed me the message. It was from Lucius T'yang, asking us to call on him urgently.

'I have something to tell you,' the message went on, 'that I cannot but think might be of great importance.'

'You will have to go,' said Mala. 'I am going to be kept mighty busy here for Jupiter knows how long. Quite apart from the little troubles we wot of, it is going to be a while before things settle down. I have already sent a message post-haste to Trajan, but it will take time for his reply to reach Rome: I hope he will appoint a deputy to rule in his place until he has finished his perambulations. The Senate are hurriedly convening, but they will not do much more than talk. Meanwhile, the office of Chief Investigator might be an unofficial one, but a helluvalot of stuff seems to landing on my desk calling for decisions. I'm beginning to feel like a ruddy proconsul.'

'And a good one you would make,' I thought - but I left the thought unsaid: Mala was not in the mood for flattery, indeed never was, however sincere the flatterer.

My feelings were mixed as I ascended the Aventine towards T'yang's substantial residence. On the one hand, the man had been impressive when Mala and I interviewed him, and in Mala's judgement, which I respected, was sound, a man who could be trusted, and who was on our side. On the other hand, Calpurnia Pulchra's revelation that he been seeing the notorious Volusius, apparently on quite a regular basis, raised all kinds of questions.

I was a little cool, therefore, when I entered T'yang's well-stocked study, and refused - really! - the cup of Falernian he offered.

'You look solemn, Marcus Vectorius.'

'I have cause to be, and if I had not reason enough to be solemn beforehand, I have now, for I have just heard that the emperor is dead.'

'And I, too, have been so informed: the messenger I sent to the Palace brought back the news. He says our friend Quintus Propertius is busy in the extreme, which is doubtless why you are here alone.'

Our friend?

'Your note sounded urgent, Lucius T'yang. Did it have anything to do with Publius Volusius Stolo?'

He was not disconcerted, only mildly surprised.

'You certainly are on the ball, Marcus Vectorius. It does indeed concern that oily demagogue. I have been seeing quite a bit of him of late, and pumping him all I could. He is a stupid man, though not without low cunning, and I felt sure he would reveal something eventually.'

'About?' I was still a little suspicious, but T'yang's explanation had been quite open, and eminently plausible.

'About my dear countryman, among other things. He revealed, willy-nilly, that there is some sort of tie-up between himself, that charming man Chen, and Chen's equally charming business associate, Festianus. Moreover, they have some joint enterprise that is close to fruition, the exact nature of which, alas, he did not reveal. I thought you should know of that at once. It is an intriguing tie-up, do you not think: the demagogue, and the two shady entrepreneurs?'

'It is, especially since they are all probably in league with Casperius Aelianus.'

'And yet if I have read the situation aright,' said T'yang, 'Aelianus must be a rather worried man right now. Is our new emperor likely to forgive him for what he did to Petronius Secundus, and to Nerva himself? He might, of course: Casperius Aelianus is an unscrupulous man, but emperors, especially new ones, like to have unscrupulous men at their beck and call. That is true in Rome, as it is in my country.'

'And you, Lucius T'yang, who are at the beck and call of your emperor: are you an unscrupulous man?'

'Not totally, but sufficiently to do my job, Marcus Vectorius. Make no mistake about this: were I convinced that the interests of my emperor and of his empire were diametrically opposed to yours, I would not scruple to do you down in any way I could, and that notwithstanding the fact that I like you, and your impressive friend Quintus Propertius also. It is called patriotism, Marcus Vectorius, and I judge that is something you are no stranger to.'

'Well, that it honest enough. Go on.'

'And so in other circumstances we could be enemies, and that would be a pity. But it could happen. But judge for yourself how likely it is to happen. These are not those circumstances; the interests of my emperor and yours are not opposed; on the contrary, insofar as curtailing the activities, and ideally the life, of Marcus Chen are concerned, they are identical. He has done mischief, great mischief, at home; he is plotting mischief here. I cannot deal with him unaided, and you in turn can benefit from my assistance. What, then, is the problem?'

'It lies only in the company you have been keeping. Publius Volusius is one decent men avoid, for they do not like the stench in their nostrils.'

'Nor do I. It does not take any man in possession of his faculties to sum up such a one as he, even if his reputation has not preceded him. But I have told you: I have cultivated him as a way of getting at my countryman, and to an extent I have succeeded. Having discovered something I thought you should know, I have immediately communicated with you, as I said I would. We are on the same side in this business, Marcus Vectorius, and I am playing my part.'

It was all so obviously true that I was won over again.

Well, we all make mistakes.

'I need a drink,' I said to myself, not for the first time in my life. There was no way I was going to Rufus's Place, after our last little episode there, but fortunately there are other wine-shops in Rome, some of them not too bad, not too bad at all. I settled for one about three blocks from Rufus's, a little up-market for my taste, and ipso facto rather lacking in atmosphere, but, by Jupiter the wine is good - and expensive.

'Treat yourself, Marcus, my lad,' I said, twisting my own arm unmercifully, 'you're a hard-working servant of the empire, and deserve the best.'

It was a big place, and the tables in the centre were a bit exposed, but around the walls there were some nice little niches where a man could sit and relax in relative peace and quiet and commune with his thoughts, if he so chose.

I did so choose, but: what was it Mala had remarked, about the best-laid plans of mice and men? My plans went awry the moment I heard the familiar voice.

'Marcus! Come and join us.'

'Felgio: I thought you would be in the lab playing with your toys at this time of day. And Gaius Cornelius: what brings you here?'

I had not known they were acquainted, but it seems Mala had introduced them at some function or other, and although one would have thought they had little if anything in common, they got on surprisingly well.

'I was explaining to our young friend,' said Gaius Cornelius, 'something of the difficulty of keeping track of empire-wide expenditure, and he was explaining to me some new numbering system Mala has taught him, that looks quite interesting. It involves a concept called 'zero', and it is amazing how…'

I let him ramble on. To be honest, I could not care less about numbering systems, new, old or middle-aged, but it was a relief nonetheless to drag my thoughts away from plots and conspiracies, double-dealing and deception, and villains of all kinds, sizes, shapes and nationalities. There was something almost infectious about Cornelius's enthusiasm, as of Felgio's. Cornelius was a man who loved his work and, metaphorically speaking, carried it around with him, and was only too ready to talk of it at the drop of a hat.

'And so,' I said to Felgio, when Cornelius had paused briefly for breath, 'your funny numbers and symbols are going to do wonders for the Imperial Treasury, and the poor saps like Cornelius who are on the treadmill there?'

'That, but much, much more. This "mathematical reasoning" Mala and Julia Carolina have introduced me to is, if anything, even more exciting than their "science". There is something pure about it, Marcus, something untainted by the world.'

'If it is untainted by the world,' I said, 'it won't go far in the Treasury.'

'Don't be facetious: I am deadly serious. This is Big Stuff. It is untainted by the world in its essence, but its applications to the world are limitless. Take differential calculus...'

'You take it. It's bad enough listening to Cornelius taking about accountancy as though it the poetry of Virgil; it is even worse when you come out with this esoteric stuff and pretend it gives you a direct line to the gods.'

'In a way, that is just what it does.'

'Very well; ask the gods if they will send down a little more of their nectar: I'm right in the mood for it.'

The gods obliged; and again; and again; and, come to think of it, several times more as well. We made it home, which was something of a feat. If Cornelius felt the way I did next morning - and he must have done, for he had as much as any of us - he must have wondered when he got to work whether he was using his trusty abacus, or some badly-broken, out-of-tune lyre.

I said we made it home, but in fact I didn't. Discretion - and Felgio's helping hand - took me to Mala's rather than to my own abode, which was a little further away. I sent a message to Livinia explaining that I was rather unwell - 'must have been something I ate, dear' - and, almost before I could take off my tunic, collapsed into the cot Mala's steward led me to.

Next morning was - well, you know what it's like: the blacksmith practising his trade on the back of your skull; the taste in your mouth that has nothing to with wine, but a great deal with errant parrots, not yet house-trained; the nasty swell, or is it a Force 8 gale, that causes the deck of the ship you are standing on - and why did they substitute the deck of a ship for what used to be a nice firm floor? - to move up and down and left and right and inside out, all at the same time... Don't deny it: you know what it's like, and serves you right.

'A little wine with your breakfast figs, Marcus?' asked Julia Carolina sweetly. She was not censorious, merely amused, and I am not sure Livinia's cold aloofness - and it would have been cold, no doubt of that, and very aloof - would not have been preferable.

Felgio was harder still to bear. He had been in the wine-shop with Gaius Cornelius before I even arrived, he had kept up and more than keep up with everything I downed, and he was only nineteen, for Jupiter's sake, and had not had my years of conditioning, conditioning that should have allowed me to commiserate with him: 'I know how it is, my boy: you must learn to pace yourself...'

No: I suffered, and he bounced.

'Just taken a run to the top of the hill; air lovely and bracing; nothing like early morning exercise...'

Expletive deleted.

And yet it passed off, as it does, and, as I have noticed before, as soon as it did my mind was crystal clear once more, and I was able to get the previous day's events into some sort of focus. I ticked off in my mind those I had talked to or talked of.

'Calpurnia Pulchra: young, sweet, hurting like hell, but so helpful, and so determined to be.

'Festianus: a nasty piece of work if ever there was one, not a mobster like Macrobius Pulcher, but a louse from the same mould.

'Marcus Chen: into something, no doubt of that, and something disreputable, involving also the most disreputable of companions.

'Publius Volusius: the kind of populist hole-in-the-air that surfaces from time to time throughout history, unwholesome, amoral, but with a superficial charisma which the gullible - which is to say the majority - fall for every time. Also up to something: but what?

'Lucius T'yang: a strange man, but a sound one. Honest about his ultimate loyalty, but on our side in this business, and already very helpful.'

I paused as I mentally jotted down their names, and then, with a grin, added three others.

'Prastus the metalworker: a freedman, a nobody, but a sterling character nevertheless; a man you could rely on.

'Gaius Cornelius: salt of the earth. A bit limited in imagination, a bit one-track in his enthusiasm, a bit of a nerd in fact; but good to have around.

'Young Felgio: a sheep in wolf's clothing. A barbarian warrior, son of a barbarian warrior, but a late-blossoming man of astounding intellect; yet modest withal.'

'And,' I added ruefully, 'he can hold his liquor!'

I went back again over the names of the ungodly, and for good measure added that of Casperius Aelianus. Just how were they all connected? Just what could they be plotting together? Just when would their plans ripen into action? Just where would we find the clue that would enable us to forestall them?

'And just who is going to do the forestalling?' asked Mala. 'I, for one, do not feel up to forestalling a stampede of sea-urchins.'

He had just come in from the Palace, and I had told him what I had been going over in my mind. I would guess that he had no sleep at all since I last saw him, or at best a quick catnap between bouts of frenetic activity.

'I am all in. I am going to get a little much-needed shut-eye, and let no-one disturb me, on pain of death. After that, and a good meal, I might be ready to tackle things again.

'And talking of a meal, I reckon we need a council of war. Ask Livinia to join us, and Gaius Molo and his wife also; and Felgio and Sylvana; I would ask Calpurnia Pulchra also, but it is too soon, much too soon.'

'Yet I believe she would want to come,' I said on impulse. 'She is a remarkable women, and she will yield to no-one in her determination to see the scum who murdered her husband brought to justice.'

'Then invite her, Marcus, if you feel you can. Certainly the more heads the better: we need all the ideas we can get, and a fresh approach might throw light where we can see only fog and murk.'

Thus it was that, early that evening, the nine of us were reclining on our couches, after a meal simple by Diogenes' standards but superb nevertheless, waiting for Mala to initiate the proceedings.

13.

To our surprise, it was Felgio who took centre stage.

'May I say a word or two, Quintus Propertius? I have been thinking hard about the case, and my thoughts might be of some slight value.'

'You have the floor.'

'Well, please understand, what I am putting forward is only a tentative hypothesis, but I hope you will agree that it is at least a tenable one. I have tried to be as parsimonious in my assumptions as possible, as rigorous in my analysis as my understanding of logic allows, and careful to put forward only such conclusions as I am confident the facts will bear. I fear I might not have succeeded: doubtless you will tell me I have not been parsimonious enough, not rigorous enough, not careful enough. Nevertheless, for what they are worth, I would like to put forward my suggestions.'

'My goodness,' whispered Julia Carolina, 'we'll make a professor of him yet.'

What followed was masterly. I will not bore you with the details, though in fact none us found them boring in the least: fascinating, rather.

Felgio marshalled his facts, his deductions, his conclusions, in a manner that held us spellbound. He moved from one set of facts to another, from one postulate to the next, from event to event, from revelation to revelation, from antecedent to consequence, easily, fluently, and utterly convincingly.

'You realise, of course,' he concluded, 'that we have far fewer facts than we would like, and that in my analysis I have had to make a little go a long way. Nevertheless, as I said at the outset, I have tried not to go beyond what the evidence will support.'

'This boy,' I thought to myself again, 'less than a year ago was but an unlettered tribesman, and a love-sick young fool to boot. Now he could be Plato in his Academy.'

'I will sum up, then, if I may, after which, no doubt, you will shoot me down in flames.' He smiled at Mala and Julia Carolina as he spoke, but I am sure he knew that not even they either would or could do any such thing.

'First, there are the businessmen, the merchants: Chen dabbles in laundries, in property, in silk, and in grain.

'Festianus is also into property, but as well as that he is into wine, into jewellery, and, again – grain. He also owns a small fleet of ships, which plies between Ostia and Egypt.

The common factor there is grain, and, in Festianus's case, the ships to carry it in.

'And then there is the odious Publius Volusius, demagogue, rabble-rouser, all-round pain in the neck. Common factor? Again, grain: if you want to see the rabble roused, deny them their bread and circuses.'

'Give us this day our daily bread',' said Mala, 'and 'give' is the operative word.'

'Precisely. And the Praetorians, under the charming Casperius Aelianus? Supposing you have just had your wings clipped by Nerva's announcement that Trajan is to be his successor. Supposing that you still hope to salvage something from the wreckage, perhaps even to turn the tables. What about interfering with the grain supply, with the aid of those who actually carry the grain, and get it into the warehouses, in Ostia and in Rome? The grain belongs to the emperor, we know, but it is the merchants he pays to transport and to store it, the Chens and the Festianuses of this world, who have the actual, physical control. Of course in the normal world that control is only nominal, for if they tried to deny it to the emperor and his hungry subjects, he would send his Praetorians to seize it, and they would wish they had had more sense. But if the Praetorians are not his, will not do the emperor's bidding, and have an agenda of their own...?

'Suppose, further, that you have a tame demagogue in your pocket, and having seized control of the grain, you lay the blame for its non-distribution at the maladministration of the new emperor, and get the mob to behave as the mob is always only too ready to do. And suppose you have a word in the ear of certain generals, in Egypt where the grain actually comes from and others nearer to home, remembering that not all of them are enthusiastic supporters of Trajan, and that there is still plenty of resentment in the army at what happened to Domitian. We have a potent brew there, have we not?'

'Whoever controls the grain,' said Mala, 'controls the mob; and whoever controls the mob, controls Rome.'

'Not quite,' I said. 'However numerous, the mob would be no match for well-armed troops in sufficient strength.'

'But well-armed troops in sufficient strength opposing other well-armed troops would sooner have the mob with them than against them. What if, instead of finding a peaceful and welcoming Rome, Trajan found a city in turmoil, the mob on the streets, and nine thousand Praetorians as well as the armies of Egypt and elsewhere opposing him? And the food the people are clamouring for in the hands of his enemies?'

'Civil war,' I said; 'the year 69 all over again, and the outcome by no means certain.'

'It would be a very long shot,' said Gaius Molo, 'on Aelianus's part. Maybe Chen and Festianus do have physical control over the grain, and maybe they will go along with his plan, but he cannot be sure the mob will jump to it when required, however persuasive Volusius may be; he cannot be sure ambitious generals, in Egypt or elsewhere, will set themselves against Trajan; and he cannot even be sure that all of his own men would go along with him when they really thought about the possible consequences.

Moreover, what of the aedile? He is the man actually in charge of the grain, and he carries plenty of clout.'

'Bought,' replied Mala, 'or maybe just frightened. After all, the clout his high office gives him depends, ultimately on physical force, and for the physical force he has to rely on the Praetorians.

'All you say is true, Molo, but if, and if, and if... I prefer to think that if Felgio's hypothesis is correct and that is indeed what is being planned, we had better do something pretty damned quick to nip it in the bud.'

'But what? Felgio's analyses is masterly, and I am gob-smacked by it like all of us, but it does not put troops on the streets, and troops on the streets are what we greatly need.'

'Not necessarily,' replied Mala. 'Troops ultimately might be needed, but even then, troops in the background might suffice: Trajan's troops. In the meantime, since we cannot even now countenance open confrontation with the Praetorians, we must try the old, old tactic: divide and rule. In other words, we pick our enemies off one by one.'

'And how do we do that?'

'By striking at the weakest link first. We know that the initial shipment of grain must be already here, some in Rome, but more in Ostia. My guess is that it might just be stored away in one of Chen's warehouses, either hidden, or disguised as something else. We must find it, we must remove it, and we in turn must stash it away where it is safe from prying eyes.'

'I suppose I must go to Ostia, and see what I can see?'

'Yes – but be extremely careful: these people play for keeps.'

'I would like to come along too,' said Felgio.

'I am not sure I can sanction that,' replied Mala. 'There might be considerable danger, and if anything happened to you, Burro would have my guts for garters.'

'I have been taught to look after myself, and it was Burro, my estimable father, who did the teaching. If he knew I had let myself be talked out of something just because of a little danger, he would have *my* guts for garters.'

Mala yielded, and I was not sorry. Felgio was very much the sort of person you would choose to have at your back in an enterprise such as this, and besides, he was taking along his 'club' – thunder-stick, musket, whatever –and I well knew how useful that could be in a tight spot.

'We will set off first thing to-morrow morning. Felgio, you had better stay at my place to-night, and on the way I would like to let T'yang know what we are up to.'

The evening was bitterly cold, and we pulled our cloaks about us as we entered T'yang's spacious premises. Hospitably, he offered us hot wine, which we downed gratefully.

'You are making progress at last,' he said. 'I wish I could come with you to Ostia, but to-morrow I have to demonstrate that I have become truly one of you: I have to call on my patron!'

'And the best of Roman luck!' I smiled.

'And to you.'

As we walked away, I noticed that Felgio had something of a puzzled frown on his face.

'What is worrying you?'

'Nothing I can quite put my finger on, but it is niggling at the back of my mind. Doubtless it will come to me if I stop trying too hard to think of it.'

The next day was bracing, cold but sunny, and although the road to Ostia was not a particularly pleasant one, nor the journey as short as it might have been, I thoroughly enjoyed the ride, thanks not least to the stirrups Mala had introduced me to, and which were now becoming all the rage in Rome. Nevertheless, it was well into the day when we reached the busy port, and the sun on the horizon was beginning its descent towards the sea, and we were glad enough to find the little inn where we had decided to lodge for the night.

The accommodation was far better than it would have been only months before. Immediately on his return to Rome, Mala had initiated the rating system for such establishments he had talked about at the delectable little inn we had found in Gaul.[3] More accurately, his former steward, Statilius, now a freedman, had done so, acting on Mala's instructions, and already the system was beginning to bite, for which we were more than grateful.

We were not there, however, to admire our trim little room, nor even the wine, decent though it was, that the innkeeper pressed on us (though of course we drank it). It wanted scarcely an hour to dusk, and we were anxious to find Chen's warehouse as soon as possible.

It turned out to be a big, featureless building not a stone's throw from the harbour.

By now the area was almost deserted, and we were unseen as we made a careful reconnaissance of the building, eventually finding a side-door that was not locked. We slipped inside, and looked about us.

The interior was gloomy, little of the fading light penetrating through the few high-set windows. Perhaps that is why we did not see them. Why we did not hear them is a testimony to their cat-like stealth, and, doubtless, to the fact that we were expected, for one moment we were alone, not for a

---

3 See *Quintus Propertius and the Treasure of the Dumnonii*

moment suspecting that there was anyone else in the building at all, the next, there were three of them, two holding spears at our throats, the third deftly removing my sabre from its scabbard, and relieving Felgio of his 'club', which he looked at with some disdain. It was as complete a surprise as could be imagined, and I wondered who could have betrayed us: Mala's new steward, perhaps, who could have overheard our plans after Felgio had given his analysis; one or other of the litter slaves Calpurnia Pulchra had brought with her, who of course were an unknown quantity?

There was little time to speculate, for our captors, ex-gladiators all, and all too obviously eager to ply their trade of letting blood if we gave them half a chance, were prodding us towards the far end of the warehouse, and through a door and into a large office-like room. They threw down our weapons, and prodded us still further until we were face-to-face with their master.

He looked at us sardonically.

'An enterprising man, no doubt of that, are you not, Marcus Vectorius? And you have brought this barbarian with you for company. How thoughtful, for you are going to have little enough company for many hours to come, except for the rats that make their home here; and one other, who awaits you, though I do not believe you will find him much of a conversationalist.'

He laughed unpleasantly.

'Listen carefully: you are dead men, if my plans mature as they should. Dead men: but just in case - just in case, for I am a prudent man - I am letting you live for a while, for in extremity, if the unlikely happens and things do go wrong, you might be useful as bargaining counters. That is the only reason I do not have you eliminated on the spot.

'Do not bank on it, however. I see little that can go wrong now. So commune with your souls, or whatever you Romans do when you know you are to depart this life; and if there is time, I will introduce you to a little procedure that is popular where I come from. We call it the death by a thousand cuts.'

The eyes of the Oriental, for of course it was he, were cold and cruel as he spoke; cold and cruel and gloating, were the eyes of Lucius T'yang.

They trussed us up expertly and far from gently, and took us back into the warehouse, where they threw us to the ground in an alcove behind a stack of packing-cases. They sneered as they left, and made it clear, as though it was not clear already from the very nature of the men, that any or all of them would be only too happy to carry out T'yang's death threat, when and if, as seemed only too likely, the time came.

We heard a groan, and looking around as best we could in the gloom, observed in an adjoining alcove what seemed like a large bundle rather than a human being. As T'yang had observed, he was no conversationalist: he was clearly in considerable pain, and only the occasional groan betrayed his presence. He did not, or could not, respond when we called out to him.

'And now what?' I asked. 'I have been a blind fool. I should have known that swine was lying through his teeth when he said he was on our side. He was too plausible, too plausible by far. I should have asked myself whether it was likely he would make common cause with us, against one of his own countrymen, and how likely it was that he was pumping Volusius about Chen, rather than being hand-in-glove with him in his little schemes.'

'Yes, and no,' replied Felgio.

'No?'

'Undoubtedly T'yang is involved in the little schemes, as you call them, or we would be lying here trussed up like this. Whether he is hand-in-glove with Chen is another matter. We take Chen's guilt for granted, but quite another explanation is possible: that was what was bothering me before we left Rome; but I will tell you of that later. As of now, we must free ourselves, and as quickly as possible.'

'And how do we do that? The last time I was bound and helpless like this, I was freed by a deus ex machina by the name of Felgio. I do not think he is going to come to the rescue at this juncture.'

'O ye of little faith,' he said to my surprise. 'He will not free you immediately, for first you must free him.'

'What on earth do you mean?'

'Only that Mala mentioned the idea quite casually one day, and as with everything Mala says, I took good note. More to the point, I took action.'

I wondered what was coming.

'You have noticed, have you, that I am wearing heavy riding-boots of the kind favoured by Mala?'

I could hardly have missed them. They were unlike any I was used to, but Mala swore by them, and had tried, unsuccessfully, to get me to have a pair made for myself. They were great, calf-length things, with pointed toes and thick, deep heels, altogether too heavy for my taste. Felgio, on the other hand, had taken to them readily.

'Well, Marcus, these are not only good for riding horses. Now, this is going to be difficult, bound as you are, but if you can manoeuvre yourself so as to be able to get your fingers on my heel - either heel...'

He was right: it was difficult in the extreme. It was equally difficult to locate the little catch, just under the instep, which he instructed me to slide firmly to one side. It was the devil's own work to turn the heel of the boot as he instructed me, and unscrew it round and round until it came right off. No easier was it to insert my fingers in the little hollow that was thus revealed, and extract the tiny knife, its blade scarcely an inch and a half long, that nestled in the cavity.

As for holding the tiny knife firmly, and twisting myself around so that I could get at the ropes binding Felgio's wrists, and then actually to begin sawing them - well, although the little blade was sharp as a razor, it proved almost beyond me.

But not quite; and after what seemed like hours of straining and sweating and cursing, and hearing Felgio curse too as I nicked his wrist time and again, the job was done, and his arms were free.

'I am glad you did not sever an artery and leave me to bleed to death,' he remarked; 'but thanks indeed,' and after rubbing himself vigorously to restore the circulation, he tackled the ropes around his ankles. Even with his hands free, it took time, and more time still before my ropes in turn were severed, and we were afraid that at any moment our captors would see fit to return, and we would be sunk.

Thank Jupiter - I'll turn into a believer yet, if I'm not careful - our luck held out, and after a few moments of hard rubbing to restore my own circulation, we turned to the bundle that was our unfortunate fellow-prisoner.

He groaned again as we approached him, and we could see that in addition to being in bad and battered shape, he had a nasty gash in his leg, that had bled profusely, and could only have been inflicted by a sword. Only pretty severe beating could have produced the bruises on his face, and there was blood also, caked on his cheeks and under his eyes.

Nevertheless, and even in the fading light, we recognised him at once. I was surprised, but Felgio less so, to see that it was Marco Chen.

'So the villains have been falling out,' I whispered to Felgio. 'No bad thing, if we are aiming to divide and rule.'

'Do not jump to conclusions, Marco. Admittedly we all thought of this fellow as a villain, but the emergence of T'yang as the prime blackguard puts a different complexion on things. If Chen is indeed an accomplice, I hazard a guess that he has been an unwilling one.'

'I don't know how you figure that one out, but we'll let it pass. More to the point is what we do now. Do we free Chen? And whether we do or not, do we tackle those louts in there, or do we make our escape, and come back in force - if we can find the force in time? I'm all for making ourselves scarce, but taking Chen along with us; if he can walk.'

The Oriental groaned as though on cue, and opened his eyes.

'Please free me, but first listen. I heard what you were saying. If you go from here, we are lost: T'yang's plans are near to fruition, and if they leave here and get back to Rome, nothing can stop them. Yet if you tackle them, I fear you are lost also. Alas, I am no fighting man, even when fit, and at present I can hardly stand.'

'We can handle them,' said Felgio confidently.

'There speaks the folly of youth,' I said. 'You and I both know how to look after ourselves, but they are four to two, and three of them are trained killers.'

'And T'yang is a deadly swordsman,' added Chen.

'You forget my little toy,' replied Felgio. 'If it is where they threw it, and I can get to it in time, the odds will be very different. It is a long shot, I know, but what alternative do we have? If we try to get away, the door we came in by is almost certainly locked by now, and if we tried to break it down, they would hear us and be on us before we could get out, or even if we did manage to, Chen is in no condition to run.'

'Then we risk all on the one throw of the dice. We burst in, hope our weapons are where they were, and that T'yang and his thugs are all at the further end of the room.'

It was a desperate gamble, and we both knew it, but we were desperate men, and there was little to be gained by contemplation once we had made up our minds, and so we silently made our way to the office, took a deep breath, and kicked open the door.

It was, thank all the gods at once, exactly as we had hoped. We reached our weapons almost before they realised we were there, and I had my sabre in my hand, and Felgio his 'club', before any of them could move.

But then, they were quick. The three gladiators drew their weapons, and rushed towards us with the speed born of long training, and T'yang was only marginally slower. They had only to cover a few yards, but it was enough for Felgio: came that ear-splitting bang, and another, and two of the killers would kill no more.

The third, however, had not hesitated an instant, despite his amazement at what had happened to his companions. He aimed a blow at Felgio with his sword that would have finished the matter there and then, but the Briton stepped back and, using his weapon now indeed like a club, gave the man such a crack on the arm that he dropped his gladius with a yelp. Even that did not stop him, and he had grappled with the Briton before he could raise his weapon for another blow. They fell to the ground, arms and legs flailing.

I do not know what the gladiator's preferred weapon was in the arena, but doubtless with it he was a match for most men, or he would not have survived so long. Wrestling, however, was not a skill he commanded, and although he was as big and strong as Felgio, it was soon clear what the outcome was going to be.

Not that I had time to watch, for T'yang was coming forward, wielding a nasty-looking, slim-bladed, slightly-curved sword, of a design I had not seen before, and he soon demonstrated that he knew how to use it. Mala would have sorted him out, though even he would have had to be careful; for a mere mortal like me, the man was a handful and a half. Three times in the first couple of minutes, only a desperate last-minute parry prevented my being sliced like a side of bacon, and my counter-attacks met empty air as T'yang leaped back with amazing athleticism.

Mala had taught me well, however, and over the months I had come to prefer the sabre to my more accustomed gladius, and practised assiduously and enthusiastically almost every day of my life. Gradually I began to get the hang of the foreigner's style of fighting, gradually I found it easier to keep out of trouble, and gradually I found I was able to mount my own attacks, and disconcert my opponent as earlier he had disconcerted me.

I cannot describe just how I terminated matters, unless you are familiar with my weapon and its techniques; suffice to say that it involved a double-feint, a rapid beat attack that was also a feint, and a final lunge in the low line. My blade was at a sharp upward angle as it entered T'yang's body just above the groin, and it emerged half-way up his spine. His interest in the contest ceased abruptly.

So, almost at the same time, did that of Felgio's opponent, for the young Briton had at last get the hold he wanted, and he snapped the gladiator's back like a rotten twig.

Chen hobbled into the room at that point, amazement and satisfaction mingling as he surveyed the four bodies.

'It is well, but it is not over. Festianus still lives, and so does Publius Volusius, and even without T'yang they can get on with the mischief; so far you have but delayed them.'

'And the mischief is…?'

'I thought you had fathomed that, else why are you here? The grain supply: that is the key.'

I confess I had had some doubts about that, even when Felgio produced his brilliants analysis.

'Even if the grain here in Ostia is still prevented from reaching Rome, which is now unlikely, it is but a small proportion of what is already there, safe in the imperial granary. It is that which the authorities can distribute when the time comes, unless the Praetorians throw a guard round the place, which I am sure we agree is unlikely, else how can they pose as its saviours? So what else is planned?'

'Fire,' said Chen and Felgio, almost as one.

'Fire?'

'Is it not obvious? First, the grain in reserve here is denied the authorities; then, the imperial granary is set ablaze; the mob, egged on by Volusius, run amok; the Praetorians then…'

'Okay, okay: you do not have to draw a diagram.'

'The whole thing is being co-ordinated from T'yang's residence. Festianus and Volusius are there, awaiting word from here. So, alas, is my daughter.'

'Your daughter?'

'You probably know her as T'yang's niece, for so he took to introducing her after he had kidnapped her. It is that that has forced me to go along with his plans. The businesses, the legitimate ones I built up and the shady ones he has introduced, are all in my name, but they all belong to him: I am but the front man. All the calumny that has been heaped on my head - and I know there has been much - rightly should have been heaped on his, and of course on Festianus's. I was helpless while they held the power of life and death over my daughter.'

'And she is still at T'yang's home?'

'Undoubtedly.'

'That puts a different complexion on things. Felgio, I do not like riding at night, but we must get word to Mala without delay. Chen, we will first accompany you to the lodgings where we were to have stayed the night; the good landlord will see that your wounds have attention, and provide you with food and a bed. To-morrow, Mala will send an escort for you, and if you are fit, a carriage to take you to Rome. By the time you reach there, let us pray your daughter is safe, and the remaining villains are in custody, or in Hades.'

'And the Praetorians still in the Campus Martius,' added Felgio.

'Amen.'

14.

The ride to Ostia had been pleasant; the ride back, along the dark and deserted road, was not. Several times we were nearly lost; twice, we heard the murmur of voices in the distance and made out the glimmer of torches, and wondered if we were to fall prey to bandits - 'the remnants of Macrobius Pulcher's mob,' I thought; 'that would be an irony.'

To our relief it was not to be, and we at last found ourselves outside Mala's door, just as the sun was rising.

Mala appeared at once.

'You come most carefully upon your hour,' he exclaimed; 'but you look sick at heart, for it is bitter chill. Come, you must eat.'

As we ate the simple - simple! - breakfast that Diogenes rustled up for us, we rapidly filled Mala in on the events of the previous day.

When we had finished, he looked at us with some relief.

'You have done well, but you are lucky to alive.'

'Piece of cake,' said Felgio, grinning, but Mala was not amused. 'And it is water under the bridge. How do we tackle the remaining pair - leaving aside Casperius Aelianus - preferably whilst ensuring no harm comes to Chen's daughter?'

'That is the question. They do not yet know that the Ostia end of things has gone awry for them, which might give us the advantage of surprise, but I do not see how we can force an entrance to T'yang's residence and be sure of saving the girl, and none of us can exactly go up to his door and ask to come in just to pass the time of day: we are too well known, and if T'yang told the others before he left for Ostia what he knew of our plans, they will be aware that we are on to them.'

'They know you,' said Julia Carolina, who had now joined us, 'but do they know me, or Livinia? I think not.'

'What of it? If you think I would sanction you or Livinia going into that den of wolves, you are crazy; and even if I would, Marcus would certainly veto Livinia's involvement.'

I nodded furiously.

'Why not let Livinia speak for herself, when you have heard my plan. Listen…'

It was plausible, it was clever, it offered the best hope anyone had come up with of accomplishing what we wanted - and Mala and I opposed it to the hilt.

'Very well, then,' said Julia Carolina, 'what is the alternative? And how do you propose to save the life of that innocent girl?'

At last we gave in, and we sent a litter for Livinia, who arrived none too pleased at being dragged out of bed at such an hour. Julia Carolina explained to her what she had in mind, and I was hoping Livinia, who after all is a timid girl, would beg to be excused.

Not a bit of it.

'You are right, Julia Carolina, we cannot use our own names, but since they do not know what we look like, that does not matter. I will pretend to be --- ----,' she named the wife of a prominent senator, 'and you her country cousin. I am sure they would agree if they knew what this is about, but since they don't, and both happen to be out of town, who cares?'

She giggled.

'This is no giggling matter,' I told her bluntly. 'If they suspect who you really are, they will have no mercy; and I will never forgive myself.'

'Nor I,' added Mala. 'You must be careful in the extreme.'

'Of course,' said Julia Carolina sweetly. 'I must do as my husband says: not as he does. I will not get myself into fights with champion gladiators, be tied up by Dumnonian rebels, allow myself to be ambushed by thugs, taken into custody by the Chief Investigator…

'Especially,' she smiled sweetly again, 'now I think of it, I will not risk the wrath of the Chief Investigator!'

It was not exactly normal etiquette, but that did not deter Julia Carolina and my giggling wife: they took a litter to T'yang's villa, instructed their escort to hammer on the door, and then explained innocently that they were calling on Lucius T'yang's niece, of whom they had heard so much, with a view to getting to know her and of introducing her to polite society. Had

Lucius T'yang himself been there, he might have known how to cope, which could well have been by stalling and telling them his 'niece' was indisposed or not there; neither Festianus nor Volusius were quick-witted enough, and besides, they were both a little in awe of such supposedly aristocratic women and felt, at least until their plans materialised, that they must treat such people with kid gloves.

Chen's daughter, who boasted the thoroughly Roman name of Livia Fortuna, was duly brought out, but both Festianus and Volusius hovered in the background, ready to intervene if they felt that anything out of line was being said or proposed. Julia Carolina and Livinia Javolenia, however, knew better than that; the talk was all small talk; invitations were issued to the young girl to visit them before long, at which Volusius intervened to say she said she must talk to her 'uncle' about it; and then they rose to leave.

'You have your own litter, of course?' asked Livinia.

'Well, no: I go out very rarely.'

'My dear! You must get your uncle to get you one at once - a young lady of your station. Come, I will show you mine.'

She ushered the girl towards the door, which Julia Carolina peremptorily ordered the doorman to open. He was not himself one of the thugs, but a well-trained house-slave who was accustomed to obeying orders that came from on high without a second thought. He released the door just as Festianus cried 'No!', and our ladies ushered the girl out, as we rushed in.

'We' were Felgio, Mala, and I, and three of Mala's stalwarts from the Investigator's department; we barged in without ceremony, and confronted Festianus and Volusius.

'In my capacity of Chief Investigator,' said Mala, 'I am placing you gentlemen under arrest.'

Festianus cursed, draw a heavy dagger, and called for help. Three tough-looking louts appeared from nowhere, one of them armed with nothing less than a standard-issue pilum. He made to throw it, as Festianus rushed forward towards Felgio. This was unwise on both their parts; came the well-known loud bangs, and the two heroes next moment were flat on their backs, great red patches staining the fronts of their tunics. The other two, who were not gladiators but merely hired thugs, stood with their mouths open looking at the dead men and back to Felgio, while Mala's operatives grabbed them and bound them in no time with practiced hands.

As for Volusius, he cringed, and babbled like a frightened child, and begged for mercy.

'Mercy?' said Mala. 'I don't know the meaning of the word.'

Volusius whimpered.

'Shut up, you miserable little worm,' I said impatiently; 'this man does not kill in cold blood.'

He looked relieved, so I added: 'Except after due process.'

Mala ordered the third of his helpers to brings the creature along, and soon we were heading for one of the safe houses the Chief Investigator had at his disposal dotted throughout the city; one with a little suite of good, strong cells. When Volusius and the two thugs had been safely accommodated, Mala sent his minions to collect the bodies of Festianus and his misguided javelin-thrower, and to instruct T'yang's slaves to say nothing, but nothing, of what had happened, to anyone whatsoever.

He then had Volusius dragged from his cell, and deposited in the room I remembered from the time of Sextus Vulso, the room that was dedicated to the gentle art of interrogation. I saw one of Mala's men prepare to get involved, but Mala waved him back.

'I do not think you skills will be needed for this excrescence,' he said. 'By the time I have finished with him, he will be co-operating with the very greatest enthusiasm.'

Volusius shuddered.

'Now, you unparalleled -----,' Mala used a word in his own language I had never heard before; it needed no imagination to guess its meaning; 'listen, and listen very carefully: for let me tell you, your life depends on it.'

'First, your little plot is busted. You know Festianus is dead; so is Lucius T'yang, killed with his own hands by Marcus Vectorius here. The fire you were planning will not take place: my men, and the vigiles, are even now rounding up those who were going to do the dirty work for you.

'I have documentary evidence, loads of it, which T'yang thoughtfully took to Ostia with him, detailing precisely what you were planning, who was involved, and your own specific part in the whole filthy business. There is enough here to send you to the arena a dozen times over.'

By this time Volusius was almost gibbering with fear.

'And this is a Roman,' I thought to myself contemptuously. 'He hasn't the guts of a new-born kitten.'

'Your hoped-for allies in Egypt and elsewhere,' Mala went on, 'will soon know that your scheme has failed, and if push comes to shove they will deny any knowledge of so heinous a plot: so look not for succour there.

'With no interference with the grain supply, no fire, no riot, your friends at the Campus Martius will have no excuse to interfere, and realising that Trajan's position as emperor is secure, they will not dare to do so without such excuse, and even with that excuse, they might well have been having second thoughts.'

I would say that Volusius looked even more dejected, but he could not have looked more dejected than he did before Mala even started his spiel. Perhaps he was trembling more, though that would have been difficult too.

'But what if the mob do riot? You would like that, would you not, and would like to be there to egg them on?'

Volusius looked interested for the first time.

'Well,' went on Mala, 'You will have your chance. Even now, I am told, the mob are gathering in the Forum, thanks to the false rumours you have been spreading. They are waiting only for their beloved Publius Volusius to stir them up. They would be disappointed if you did not put in an appearance, and it doesn't do to disappoint the mob.'

I wondered what he had in mind. The idea of letting Volusius address the great unwashed after all did not seem a very good idea to me.

'Do you see this young man?' Mala gestured towards Felgio. 'Do you see the little toy he has in his hand? Do you remember what happened to Festianus and his goon? My friend Felgio will be there with you in the Forum; he will be pointing this toy in your direction; he will listen carefully to what you say, as will others of my operatives nearby - who will be armed with bows and spears.

'One word: one solitary, ill-advised word, one syllable, even, out of place, and your head will be blasted from your shoulders, and your body will be a pin-cushion, before you can as much as draw a further breath.

'So think carefully. It is still just possible - no more than possible: I make no promises - that if you do exactly as you are told, I can persuade the emperor to spare your miserable life. If you do not, that life is over. This is what you have to say…'

The Forum was, as usual, an unnerving place with a huge crowd gathered. Most of them no doubt were respectable citizens, though gullible, and getting more and more worked up about the rumours they had heard; a sprinkling were agents provocateurs, planted by Festianus, though many of those had by now been rounded up; some were of the professional trouble-maker persuasion, happy to join in any antisocial activity wherever they could find it; there were even some young men-about-town, and young women too, along for what they hoped might be a cheap thrill. They would have been sorely disillusioned had things really got out of hand.

And there was Volusius. It was amazing, the transformation in the man, with an audience to play on. No longer was he the diffident, terrified little weasel of a creature we had in custody at the safe house; no longer did he seem small and weak and insignificant; no longer did he look as though he would not say boo to a goose, or that boo said to him would make him jump out of his skin.

Instead, as I have said, he played on the crowd, as a skilled musician plays on a lyre, or as, we are told, Cicero would play on his audience when he addressed the court. It was masterly; it was frightening; it was also rather disgusting, to see the way otherwise rational beings were swayed by the rhetoric and the humbug and the twisted logic he came out with. He warmed to his task more and more as the minutes passed, and as he perceived his audience was lapping it up, groaning or yelling or even laughing as he decided they would, putty in his hands, but sentient, seething putty, infinitely malleable and still infinitely dangerous. He had a story to tell, and he told it, and they hung on his every word.

But it was our story, Mala's rather, and he did not deviate from it. He told them of the plan to interfere with the grain; to set fire to the imperial granary; to starve the good people of Rome and leave them prey to evil forces. (He did not specify which evil forces, and very carefully did not mention the Praetorians.) He named Festianus and T'yang as the chief plotters, proclaimed loudly that it was the other Oriental, Chen, who had helped uncover the plot, and that I - 'this brave young equestrian who accompanies me, Marcus Vectorius' - who had rescued Chen after his capture, and killed the villain T'yang in single combat.

He did a good job, all right, and he would have done just as good a job, been just as persuasive, left the mob just as convinced, had he been putting the diametrically opposite case and fingering us, and others who served the new emperor, as the real culprits.

'And so,' he concluded, 'be gone; get to your houses; fall upon your knees; pray to the gods for the wellbeing of these servants of the empire who have thus saved the people of Rome from famine; and pray, too, to Jupiter Best and Greatest to keep guard over our great new Caesar, the all-powerful, the incomparable, the emperor Marcus Ulfius Trajanus.'

'You would hardly have guessed,' remarked Mala afterwards, 'that this same creature was up to his eyebrows in a conspiracy that would have seen the same incomparable Trajan out on his neck, and his brave servants, us, hurtled from the Tarpeian Rock.'

'It was all an illusion,' said Felgio; 'a magician's trick. That was no more the man we took from T'yang's dwelling this morning, than I am a reincarnation of Vercingetorix the Gaul!'

'The sickening thing,' I added, 'is that when it was all over, he came up to me like a mongrel with its tail wagging, looking for praise and a fresh bone as reward for his efforts. I told him to do as he had instructed the crowd to do, and fall on his knees, and pray: pray that the mighty emperor he had praised so fulsomely would not have him chopped as soon as he reached Rome.'

"But I did as you asked!' he cried out - wept, almost.

'You did as you had to,' I replied, 'and now you go back to your kennel, where you belong.'

There was one coda to this episode. For several days, and indeed nights, Trebonius, and his son, were closeted in Mala's 'lab', evidently working hard on some project or other; Mala and Felgio joined them from time to time, but for the most part left them to their own devices.

At last Trebonius appeared, tired-looking but triumphant.

'Done! Sufficient copies to keep half Rome amused.'

'Not quite,' said Mala, 'but you have done a great job. Let us have a look.'

We all piled into the lab, to find, stacked on benches, tables, the floor, everywhere, bundle after bundle after bundle of the paper Trebonius had first shown me, what seemed like aeons ago. Each, like that first sheet, was covered in writing, all of it amazingly even and regular. Moreover, each sheet was covered in the same writing: each was, in every respect, identical. But what scribe, or whole scriptorium of them, could have produced such identical copies? It was impossible; and yet there they were.

Each had at the top, in very large lettering, the words TEMPUS ROMA. Underneath, in equally large but subtly different lettering: GRAIN PLOT FOILED! And underneath that, clearly and succinctly written, was an account of what T'yang et al had been up to, and of our nipping their plans in the bud. It was a reiteration of what Volusius had said when he addressed the crowd, shorn of the rhetorical flourishes, and it left the reader in no doubt of what had been going on. There were even little portraits of the main players in the drama, woodcuts Mala called them, T'yang himself, Festianus, Chen, Mala, Felgio, and even your scribe.

'The first Roman newspaper,' exclaimed Mala; 'an historic document indeed; the first example of printing from movable type, probably the most important, as well as the simplest, of all the technologies I am going to introduce to Rome. These copies, thousands of them, are going to be distributed free to all and sundry; those who can read, will read them to those who can't; all who can talk, will spread the news. Information, the one thing tyrants and other villains hate the people to have, from now on in Rome available to all. If I do nothing more, this alone justifies my existence here.'

15.

'And so we should be able to draw a line under this whole business,' said Mala, as we relaxed over a flask of his best, 'but for one thing: in a very important sense, we are back where we were when things began. Casperius Aelianus and his Praetorians are still at the Campus Martius, and despite what I said so confidently to Volusius, we still do not know which way they will jump.'

We all looked concerned. He had spoken with such certainty when briefing Volusius, that none of us had doubted for a moment that he was right; but now…

He regarded us for a few seconds, and then looked very serious.

'I regard the next few weeks as the most dangerous of all. On the face of it, we have won: the major villains are disposed of, Volusius is in custody wondering if he has many more weeks to live, the grain supply is secured, the mob are content - insofar as they are ever content.

'But I have just had this message from Casperius Aelianus; listen.'

From Casperius Aelianus, Prefect of the Praetorian Guard, to Quintus Propertius Mala, Chief Investigator: greetings.

It has come to my notice that you have foiled a criminal plot of the most heinous kind. Every patriotic Roman must congratulate you. Rest assured that the Praetorian Guard in turn stand ever ready to intervene when needed,, and will never be backward in doing their duty as they see it.

Hail Caesar!

'That sounds to me,' I said, 'like a thinly-veiled threat.'

'We are back to the wounded animal,' replied Mala. 'He must know in his heart of hearts that Trajan is now secure, and that therefore his own fate lies wholly in the emperor's hands. He may still hope that he can convince Trajan that he has acted always in the best interests of Rome, and therefore can still be a useful servant; or he may decide that he has shot his bolt, and decide to take down with him as many as he can.'

'Meaning: us?'

'Among others: there are many in the Senate, friends and allies of Galienus, whom he would love to get even with.'

'What is to be done?'

'Nothing, except wait. I have written to Trajan setting out in detail all that has happened; I have suggested a possible line of action, which I suspect he might go along with. Until his messenger reaches Rome, however, we can do nothing.'

'Then let us praise the divine Augustus,' I said, 'for the postal service he inaugurated. Before that, it would have taken aeons for messages to go back and forth. Now, we need wait only a week or two at most; but it is going to be a very long-seeming week or two.'

I was right: the time did indeed drag, as we tried to go about our business, wondering as each day dawned if it would be our last. Again Livinia and I had moved into Mala's villa, which now felt more like a fortress than a private residence.

'We cannot stop nine thousand Praetorians,' said Mala, 'nor even nine hundred. Nevertheless, if they try anything, we can discourage them pretty severely. Felgio has had three more of his little toys constructed, and enough ammunition to do considerable damage: he will instruct you how to use it, Marcus, and Trebonius also, and that young son of Trebonius's: a promising lad.

'For my part, I have my own little toy, which the ungodly might be less than pleased to be introduced to.'

He took out the small metal object that he had produced when Macrobius Pulcher's thugs ambushed us.

'I presume,' I said, 'that that is the weapon you used against the men who were guarding Covorilla back in Britain: a kind of miniature version of Felgio's weapon, smaller and not so powerful, but still capable of inflicting damage.'

'Smaller, certainly, but as for less powerful: this is far, far more potent a weapon than Felgio's. His is a wonderful artefact to have produced from scratch, but it is only a pale imitation of the real thing. This is the real thing, and small though it is, I could kill half a dozen while Felgio was still taking aim, and I could do so at a distance that Felgio's weapon could not begin to match.'

'And these weapons are common where you came from? Your legions are equipped with them?'

'No: our soldiers are equipped with weapons far more deadly still.'

'Then if your country and Rome ever went to war, Rome would have no chance?'

'Rome is my country, for better or worse. Moreover, the country I came from is so far away, so very, very far, that conflict with Rome is quite impossible. My travelling here from there, and Julia Carolina's also, is a kind of miracle.'

'And yet, on the "globe" your wife has just had constructed, your country, though an immense distance across the seas, is not so far that some day, our ships, or yours, might not cross that distance. The country of Chen and T'yang is further away still, and yet they are here. Is their presence also a miracle?'

Mala smiled, and shook his head.

'Then what is this miracle, that brings you, and Julia Carolina, to Rome?'

'Two separate miracles,' replied Mala, 'fifty years apart.'

'Fifty years?'

'Yes; and I will perhaps explain to you, some day, how Julia Carolina might have been my grandmother.'

'What nonsense is this? Julia Carolina is a woman in her late twenties; you yourself are little older. Grandmother!'

'All very true,' agreed Mala, and would say no more.

I have known Mala now for some years, and we have been through much together; we are firm friends; he has told me a little of his background, and amazing enough it is; and yet there are times, like this, when I feel I scarcely know him at all.

The same applies to Julia Carolina. She is friendly and approachable, indeed at ease in the company of men in a way that is almost un-Roman (and influencing my wife to be likewise, in a way that I do not always approve of), and yet there is something about her that is - strange. I do not mean only her esoteric knowledge, her training as a physician, her exotic music, her fluency in the strange language Mala commands, and indeed to a lesser extent in the second outlandish tongue he sometimes lapses into.

No: it is deeper than that. Sometimes, as I have observed her, I have seen her lost in reverie, her thoughts no doubt leagues away in her home country, from which, I had gleaned, she had been plucked most precipitately, and deposited in Rome - there to become a slave, until rescued, so fortuitously, by Mala.

Once, we visited the estimable Rufus, on the farm to which he had retired, and I observed again what a fine horsewoman she was, almost as at home atop her animal as she was walking on her own two feet.

I remarked as much to Mala.

'She could ride almost before she could walk; pure county set, my wife, doncha know.'

I did not know, and he know I didn't, but he likes his little enigmatic joke, does Mala. *County set*: what is that supposed to mean?

Mystery was piled further upon mystery when Chen and his daughter came to visit us. The Oriental was slowly recovering from his ordeal, not least because of the skilled attention he received from Julia Carolina. He had blossomed into a quite different person from the somewhat surly individual we had first encountered - 'just like my dear old uncle,' remarked Livinia - and his young daughter, freed from her captivity, had blossomed likewise.

With Chen we had many discussions on matters of serious moment, for though he was woefully ignorant of our culture, and about the Greeks knew nothing at all, he was an intelligent man, and in his fashion an educated one, well familiar with philosophical and ethical concepts we had thought were the province only of Plato and Aristotle and their successors. He kept quoting a home-grown philosopher - 'Con-' something: I never quite caught the name - who sounded a man of high intellect indeed, and to both his and my astonishment, Mala displayed some familiarity with the man and his thought. The two would discuss these arcane matters animatedly, just as, in the old days, Mala and the Greek philosopher-slave Aspiades had done over a flask of Rufus's best.

'How on earth could Mala know all this?' I marvelled. 'This is not the 'magpie' picking-up of trifles he mentioned once to T'yang.'

Though their discussions ranged widely, and they were often in agreement, when they came to talk of democracy, even the Greek variety, let alone the extreme form we had heard Mala propound, Chen would have none of it.

'It would not work: men need a strong ruler, and a hierarchical society. Giving every Tom, Dick and Harry the right to participate in government is a recipe for anarchy. I repeat: it would not work.'

'But it does work: not as perfectly or in as trouble-free fashion as we would like, because men and women are not perfect, but work it does, and it maximises the freedom and well-being of the populace as no other system can.'

'And where is this, Quintus Propertius Mala?'

'In my country, and others.'

'The great land across the western ocean you have told us of, or some never-never land that is but a figment of your imagination, and your idealism: your admirable idealism, may I say?'

'What I tell you is neither idealism, for the democracy I describe falls far short of the ideal, nor the product of my imagination. It exists: it is the form of government of the country I lived in before I came to Rome, and indeed of the country I was born into, and that other in which I spent the latter part of my childhood and youth.'

'Among the Dumnonii?' I smiled. 'I do not recall our friend Burro as any kind of democrat, still less his countrymen.'

'I have told you,' said Mala, a little impatiently, 'that my story of living among the Dumnonii was a little fiction I conjured up on the spur of the moment out of necessity, on that day long ago at Rufus's Place.'

'And yet,' interrupted Julia Carolina, 'it is true, as he has also told you, that my husband did once live in the area now populated by the Dumnonii; as, for a short time, did I.'

Felgio looked suddenly very interested.

'But how is that? Assuredly you are not as ancient as the stone circles, and the ruins of huts, that we find on the moors, and yet the Dumnonii have been in the land they now occupy almost as long as those mysterious structures themselves. How, then, can you have lived there?'

He stopped suddenly.

'By all the gods! Those equations of - who is it? Orckin? - you found for me, that neither you nor I fully understand; the concepts that are implied by them, which you have tried to explain to me; these suggest something utterly fantastic.'

'And what is that?'

'They tell me that Time, which we all believe we understand, is not what we might think; that in a strange way, the Past, and, incredibly, the Future, might co-exist. Causation is turned on its head... There are paradoxes, I can see that, but are they not resolved by the idea of parallel universes?'

The rest of us had no idea what he was talking about, but Mala and Julia Carolina looked suddenly alert.

'Our cover is blown,' said Mala to his wife, 'thanks to this tame genius here.' But he said it in his own language, which I just managed to get the sense of.

'Not blown,' said Felgio, in the same tongue, 'for I would not let this speculation of mine go any further; and at present, speculation is all it is. But if it is true...' He looked at the two, and his expression was one of awe and wonder. 'Tell me it could be true.'

'It could be true.'

What more would have been said, I do not know, nor do I suppose the rest of us would have begun to comprehend, but at that moment Mala's incomparable cook, Diogenes, appeared, to let us know his latest masterpiece was ready for our delectation, and at the same moment the head steward, almost trembling with apprehension, announced a visitor.

'Casperius Aelianus, Prefect of Praetorians.'

I saw Julia Carolina go pale, and Felgio, without a word, crossed the room to where his club-that-was-not-a-club was leaning against a wall. Mala, who now was never without the little metal version of the same weapon, drew it and held it at the ready.

The Praetorian strode into the room. He was in full armour, but alone apart from a single trooper, who kept diffidently in the background.

'Be seated,' invited Mala, indicating a vacant couch.

'I have no time,' replied the Praetorian. 'I come to inform you that I have been summoned to attend the emperor, along with my most senior officers, and I have reason to believe,' he smirked, 'that when I return, my position will be even more exalted than that of Prefect of the Praetorian Guard.'

He looked around the room, surprise in his gaze as it rested on Marcus Chen, contempt as he took in Felgio - 'If only he had guessed,' said the Briton afterwards, 'how close he was to having his head blown off!' - and, for me and even more for Mala, hatred.

'I have come to tell you of this, Chief Investigator, and you, Marcus Vectorius; and to tell you this also - that I have a long memory.'

And with that, he turned and strode out.

'Can the emperor really be thinking of promoting him?' asked Livinia. 'Surely he knows of what the man has been plotting?'

'He knows,' replied Mala, 'for I have told him, in great detail; but Aelianus does not know he knows. The hint of promotion is but a ruse, to lure Aelianus away from his power base. I have been waiting, and hoping for this to happen.'

'What, then, can the emperor have in mind?'

'Not promotion, certainly; but I do feel sure that he will make Casperius Aelianus an offer he cannot refuse.'

16.

Julia Carolina and Livinia Javolenia were in the 'school room', as Mala called it, with Sylvana and their charge, the little Dumnonian princess Covorilla, and they had been joined by Marco Chen's daughter. A history lesson was in progress, and they were, I was amused to discover, discussing Caesar's campaigns in Gaul: shades of my first meeting with Quintus Propertius Mala!

'In the room,' said Mala, 'the women come and go /

Quoting De Bello Gallico.'

'They will have to stop pronto,' I told him. 'Chen is due any moment, and then: good-bye to our oriental friends.'

'And with regret.'

Chen arrived, wine was drunk, protestations of friendship were exchanged, and then something that had been worrying me came to my mind.

'Chen,' I said, 'you will forgive me for saying that, though you command of Latin is excellent, your accent leaves much to be desired.'

Chen smiled.

'It is hardly something I could deny, for the denial itself would reveal the truth.'

'Your late unlamented countryman, however, Julius T'yang, spoke Latin almost like a native: his diction was a bit archaic, perhaps, but that was the only blemish. How could that be?'

'Because he learned it, from his youth, among native Latin speakers.'

'Then he had been to Rome before?'

'Never.'

'Marco Chen, my friend, you are being enigmatic again. Explain, please.'

'I think perhaps I can explain,' interrupted Mala. 'I had long wondered if the story could be true, and now, it seems, it must be.'

'Story?'

'One I have heard, from time to time. Think back to the days of Crassus, and his disastrous defeat at the hands of the Parthians more than a century and a half ago. Have you not heard the story that some of his men survived the massacre, and were imprisoned by the Parthians?'

'I have heard it alleged, but no-one can know.'

'Perhaps you do not know that it is also alleged that they were released, on the promise to fight for the Parthians on their eastern frontier; that they were captured again, by adversaries hailing from further east still; that there were more battles, and more still, but, at last, they settled down in their new country, even established a city there, a Roman city, and flourished. Their new country was - Marco Chen's homeland. All this I had heard, but of proof, none: until to-day.'

'It is as you say,' confirmed Chen. 'I lived far away from that city, and never visited it; but T'yang came from much closer, and told me he spent much of his youth there.'

'So that is another mystery solved. But now, alas, you are to leave us, and we are the poorer for it.'

Chen acknowledged the compliment gravely, his daughter wept a little, and - they were gone.

'We will never see them again,' cried Livinia.

'Do not be so sure,' Mala told her; 'assuming they survive the journey, which is a long and arduous one. We have much still to do in Rome, many young Romans to educate, much to introduce that will make the empire a better, and a stronger place. It will take years. Nevertheless,' he turned to Julia Carolina, 'I cannot help feeling that you and I, at least, some day, must find ourselves on a slow boat to China.'

Roy R Johnson was educated, aeons ago, both at a minor, but ancient, public school, and a large grammar school, and has degrees from English and Scottish universities. He has taught at all levels from preparatory school (unqualified) to post-graduate, most notably professing English in American, Canadian and British seats of highish learning, but he also had a spell in the real world, working in industry and commerce.

Dr Johnson's passions include classical music, cricket as it used to be, and real ale. He holds strong non-party political views, and is especially hard on those who espouse the doctrines he himself, with such youthful certainty, was once wont to put forward.

Notwithstanding his deep involvement with 'serious' English literature, he has developed in recent years a penchant for Roman whoddunits, and, although once assured by a tutor that he had 'no creative talent whatever', has now attempted a foray into the genre himself.

Roy Johnson is married, to a one-time biologist; they have five children, and inumerable grandchildren. They live in Devon

Printed in the United Kingdom
by Lightning Source UK Ltd.
108012UKS00001B/79-135